Rita Bradshaw was born in Northamptonshire, where she still lives today with her husband (whom she met when she was sixteen) and their family.

When she was approaching forty she decided to fulfil two long-cherished ambitions – to write a novel and learn to drive. She says, 'The former was pure joy and the latter pure misery,' but the novel was accepted for publication and she passed her driving test. She has gone on to write many successful novels under a pseudonym.

As a committed Christian and fervent animal lover, Rita has a full and busy life, but she relishes her writing – a job that is all pleasure – and loves to read, walk her dogs, eat out and visit the cinema in any precious spare moments.

Rita Bradshaw's new novel REACH FOR TOMORROW, another warm-hearted saga of northern life, will be published by Headline in July 1999.

Alone Beneath
The Heaven

Rita Bradshaw

HEADLINE

First published in 1998
by HEADLINE BOOK PUBLISHING

First published in paperback in 1998
by HEADLINE BOOK PUBLISHING

20 19 18 17 16 15 14 13 12

ISBN 0 7472 5804 X

Typeset by Avon Dataset Ltd, Bidford-on-Avon, Warks

Printed and bound in Great Britain by
Clays Ltd, St Ives plc

HEADLINE BOOK PUBLISHING
A division of Hodder Headline PLC
338 Euston Road
London NW1 3BH

To my own dear family: my lovely husband, Clive,
our beautiful children, Cara, Faye and Ben,
my precious mum and late beloved dad,
and my big sister, Tonia, and her family.
I love you all

True love's the gift which God has given
To man alone beneath the heaven . . .
It is the secret sympathy,
The silver link, the silken tie,
Which heart to heart, and mind to mind,
In body and in soul can bind.

— Sir Walter Scott

Prologue – 1927

'Mam, don't do it, please don't do it. You'll get wrong, Mam—'

'Shut up, you, an' keep your blasted voice down. You know 'er next door 'as got lugholes like an elephant.'

'But you can't, you can't, Mam—'

'*Shut up!*' The thin, puny-looking boy took the force of his mother's hand full across the face, and as he reeled from the impact, clutching hold of the back of a wooden settle to steady himself, she hissed at him, 'I've no choice, no choice, do you 'ear me? You know your da, you know what 'e'd do if 'e come back an' found it 'ere, there'd be murder done. You want 'im up afore the Justice, is that it? An' stop your blubberin', that don't help no one.'

'But it's alive—'

'No it's not, it's dead. Get that into your 'ead, Jack, it's dead. An' if you keep your trap shut no one'll be any the wiser. Your da's boat don't dock for weeks yet, an' nothin'll be any the different when 'e walks through that door, you 'ear me? Now, I'm goin' out a while' – as the powerful forearm swung his way again the boy winced, expecting another blow, but his mother merely lifted her grubby shawl from the back of the settle – 'an' when I come back I'll bring you three pennyworth of chitterlings, 'ow's that?'

Her son made no response to the obvious attempt at

1

bribery beyond staring at her with great accusing eyes, and after a moment's hesitation she turned from him, wrapping the shawl round her squat shape before walking into the stone-floored scullery that made up the downstairs of the two-up, two-down terraced house. She said not a word as she passed him a moment or two later, neither did she look his way, and as the front door banged shut behind her he started to cry, great gulping sobs that shook his undernourished frame.

Outside in the dark grimy street the woman paused for a moment, glancing to her left and right before walking as briskly as her bulk would allow towards the main part of the town. If it had been daylight the mounds of filth and rubbish that littered this back street of Sunderland would have been visible; as it was the stench was enough to knock you backwards, unless you were used to it that was, and Minnie McHaffie had lived in such surroundings through all her thirty-two years of life.

'Minnie? You goin' to the Rose and Crown for a bevy, lass?'

The big, thickset woman who hailed her from a small group of women standing on one street corner would have crossed the road but Minnie increased her pace, calling over her shoulder as she went, 'I might later, but I'm goin' round to me sister's first, she's bin taken bad.'

'Which one? Her that lives in Blackhorn Street?'

She didn't answer, disappearing round the opposite corner and hurrying down the uneven pavement strewn with excrement and broken bottles without turning her head.

'Nosy so-an'-so . . .' She was muttering to herself as she went. 'Big Bertha, that's all I need, as if I've not got enough problems—' A faint mewing cry from beneath the shawl cut her voice dead, bringing her head swinging round as she looked to left and right again.

2

Damn it all, she wasn't going to make it to the docks if it started bawling, there were too many as knew her round there. The docks would have made sure of things too, there was enough floating in the filthy rat-infested water for it not to be noticed till morning, and she wouldn't be the first to take care of her problem in that way, not by a long chalk. By, the tales she could tell if she'd a mind to . . .

A louder wah of a cry settled the matter. She'd have to dump it somewhere else. But it couldn't last long wherever she left it, the October night was freezing, on top of which it was a good few weeks early. That medicine of Granny White's usually settled things in advance, but old Granny had slipped up this time. Or perhaps this one was just stronger than most? The thought brought her eyes narrowing in a face that, although appearing a good deal older than her thirty-two years, was still attractive, in a full-blown, coarse sort of way.

Oh, what did it matter anyway? As long as they couldn't trace it back to her, that was the main thing. If, by some fluke, it lived, then that was God's will and as such had to be accepted. It didn't occur to Minnie McHaffie that to talk of murder and God's will in the same breath was anathema to the Deity, and she would have been surprised if someone had suggested the concept to her. You did what you needed to do first, went to confession later, and then the slate was wiped clean for the next set of transgressions you would un-doubtedly commit. Man was weak, God knew that, why else had He provided priests and the Catholic church to ease your way through a bit?

The streets were brighter as she approached the area leading to the docks, and although it was only seven o'clock on a Monday evening the countless bars, gin shops, and stalls selling everything from faggots and peas to pigs' trotters were already beginning the evening's trade.

She was holding the mound under the shawl pressed close

3

against her stomach, but although movement was feeble it was still there. So . . . the water was out, she wasn't going to risk going down the line for this or anything else, not if she could help it. A back alleyway somewhere? Another weak cry brought hot panic into her chest at the same time as she reached the narrow stone steps leading down to the ladies' toilets. She went down them swiftly, without conscious thought, and into the nearest of the dank cubicles that smelt sourly of bleach and stale urine, shutting the battered door behind her and sliding the bolt across as she sank down onto the lavatory seat.

The cessation of movement caused more vigorous stirring under the shawl, and as she yanked the folds apart a pair of tiny arms and legs flailed wildly in the dim light from the solitary gas lamp on the wall outside, and a newborn infant, still with the smears of birth on its naked limbs, was revealed, wrapped loosely in a torn piece of rough sacking. It was a girl child, very small and weak, but as the woman looked at the tiny exposed scrap of humanity her eyes were dispassionate, the only emotion on her face being irritation.

Minnie listened for a moment, and after ascertaining she was alone in the cellar-like building she bent down and placed the child on the dirty cracked tiles to one side of the lavatory seat, the sudden shock causing it to cry again as tiny hands searched the air.

It wouldn't last long, it would be dead within minutes, you could see your own breath down here. That was the only thought in Minnie McHaffie's head as she opened the door and peered furtively across the outer area housing a row of grimy washbasins, the taps of which had long since been broken and rusted as the crust of brown on the basins bore evidence to. And then the matter would be done with. Their Jack would keep quiet; he knew what was good for him, he did, and if he didn't the back of her hand would soon remind him.

She was even smiling when she climbed the steps and stole back into the street, crossing the narrow cobbled road quickly and walking back the way she had come without once looking back at the subterranean tomb.

Part One

The Child: 1937

Chapter One

'I hate that Mary Owen, she's a pig, she is, and a liar, I hate her.'

'So do I.'

'And she smells. Even Jane says she smells and she's her sister. I don't like Jane either.'

'Nor do I.'

'I'm going to tell Matron it wasn't me who broke that plate, I am you know.' Sarah Brown widened her eyes at her best friend and confidante, who took the hint and gave a suitably awe-filled response.

'You're not, Sarah, I wouldn't dare. She won't believe you, you know Mary's her favourite and the sun shines out of her bum. You'll just get into more trouble.'

'I don't care.'

The two little girls, each in the sombre uniform of faded blue dress and starched white pinafore the institution demanded, were in the middle of a crocodile of identically attired children being marched round the stone-slabbed quadrangle by a grim faced 'Mother'. Sarah liked some of the Mothers: home-helpers who were as much prisoners of the Home as the children were, if the truth be known; but the one leading them that morning she hated with a vengeance, an emotion which was fully reciprocated by the woman in question. Florence Shawe was ugly; not just plain – ugly,

9

and her small hooded eyes, set either side of a nose that was little more than a beak, could hardly bear to focus on the beautiful little elfin child who had been a thorn in the thin spinster's side from the day Sarah had come into the main house from the foundling nursery four years before.

'Don't care was made to care.' Rebecca imparted this piece of wisdom with one eye on the silent figure leading the procession. Mother Shawe had it in for Sarah this morning and she'd try and catch them talking if she could, and then that would mean standing in a corner of the big hall with their backs to the others all lunchtime, and no dinner. And it wasn't fair – Mother Shawe was always picking on Sarah and getting her into trouble.

'Huh.'

The careless shrug of the shoulders and defiant tilt to Sarah's blond head didn't fool Rebecca. Sarah was just as scared of Matron as the rest of them but she wouldn't admit it. Rebecca decided it was safer to try and pour oil on troubled waters; as Sarah's best friend she had learned any trouble had a way of working back down to her eventually. But it was worth it to be Sarah's friend, Rebecca thought now, covertly eyeing Sarah's angry face. She didn't know what she'd do without Sarah. She put out a hand and gripped Sarah's fingers as she said, 'Let's forget about them all now, eh?' She tried a placatory smile. 'We can get Mary back later, but with Mother Shawe on her side Matron won't believe you didn't do it, and you've had your five strokes.' Which had been applied with relish on the back of Sarah's bare legs by Florence Shawe wielding the long thin cane kept for punishing unruly or disobedient children.

'I hate her.' Whether her friend was referring to Mary or Mother Shawe Rebecca didn't enquire. They had completed their ten circles of the quadrangle, which passed as morning exercise, and were now filing into the building for morning

10

lessons, bringing them fully under the eagle-eyed scrutiny of Florence as she stood with sergeant-major stiffness in the doorway.

Sarah had found, in her short life, that once a day started badly it got worse, and this day was no exception. First Mary Owen had knocked her breakfast plate off the refectory table on purpose and then said it was her, just because she'd done better at sewing the day before and finished her sampler. And Mother Shawe had taken Mary's side, although she *knew* the Mother had seen what had really happened. She hadn't even eaten her slice of bread and jam either. A low growl from her stomach pressed home the unfairness of life as she tramped up the wooden stairs to the large classroom on the first floor, and the smarting from the raised weals on the backs of her legs seemed to increase a hundredfold.

And now it was arithmetic all morning and she *hated* arithmetic, and Mother McLevy was ill and so they had to have Mother Shawe all day . . . She wished it was a Saturday so she could work outside in the vegetable garden; she never minded getting her hands dirty like some of the girls did, and she liked talking to the boys too. It was silly that they had to be in a different building to the boys, she'd found boys were much more interesting than girls. They never moaned about getting tired or having dirt in their nails, and they didn't go all loolah if a wasp flew by or they dug a worm up. Not like Mary Owen . . . The thought returned her mind to her old enemy.

Perhaps it was better it wasn't a Saturday after all. Mary was always worse on a Saturday when her mam visited, crowing over Sarah just because she'd got a mam and aunties and things. Well, she wouldn't want a mam who looked like Mary's – all fat and dirty and with bright orange hair. The thought was without conviction. The sick empty feeling that always accompanied reminders of her own lack of parentage rose as bile in her throat.

Her mam and da had been rich anyway, and they'd all lived in a big house with servants and everyone for miles around had looked for her when she'd been stolen out of her perambulator by the gypsies. She could remember her perambulator, it had been big and all pink and soft, and she'd had a solid silver rattle hanging from a ribbon attached to the satin-lined hood. She nodded to herself. She had told herself the story so often it was now unshakeable fact in her mind. And her mam and da were still looking for her, every day they looked for her and her mam would cry buckets, and one day they would drive up to the Home in a great big car, shiny with gleaming brass lamps on the front, and they would walk into the refectory when they were all eating and her mam would shout, 'That's my child', and they'd all go home. And everyone who'd ever been nasty to her would wish they hadn't when they saw how rich she was, and she'd have her friends for tea . . .

The story always went one of two ways here, depending on her mood. Sometimes she'd have Mary Owen and Mother Shawe and the Matron and everyone to her house for a party, just so they could see how lovely it all was and how kind and nice she was, and other times she would drive away with Rebecca beside her and leave them pea-green with envy, or even running beside the car pleading with her for forgiveness as she sorrowfully shook her head—

'*Sarah Brown.*'

She was brought sharply from the satisfying vision of watching Mother Shawe galloping by the side of the car, tears of remorse streaming down her shaking jowls, and into the stark reality of the classroom where, she now realized, all eyes were trained on her.

'Everyone else has their book open and ready to start the

lesson as I have requested, pray tell why you are different? Is there something about you we don't know, something that makes you special perhaps?'

The sarcasm was heavy and biting, and out of all proportion to the offence, but as Florence Shawe glared at the goldenhaired girl in front of her she wasn't seeing a ten-year-old child, but the epitome of youth and beauty and bright tomorrows; everything, in fact, that had been denied her. Not that she had ever rationalized her resentment of Sarah in so many words, even in her mind, and if someone had told her the real reason for her persecution of this child she wouldn't have accepted it, but it was true none the less. And Sarah wasn't frightened of her, that was another thing that she found almost impossible to accept. She had used the formidable weapon of fear to cover her own insecurity and inadequacies with the children all her life, and to great effect, but with this particular child it was useless. And it wasn't to be borne.

'Well? I'm waiting for an answer, miss.'

The class had relaxed as Sarah had whipped open her book and found the appropriate place with Rebecca's prompting, but now, as the Mother's tone made it clear she wasn't going to let the matter drop, the atmosphere tightened again, most of the faces expressing anticipation. Not that any of her classmates had anything against Sarah personally, apart from Mary Owen that was, but any delay in starting the dreaded arithmetic was a bonus.

'I didn't hear you.'

The light, bell-like voice was another acute irritation. How, Florence had asked herself countless times, could a child born in the gutter, as this one undoubtedly had been, possess such a voice? Admittedly she had been under the influence of Matron and the Mothers for the whole of her life, unlike some of their children who came in at a later stage of their development when they had picked up the dialect of the northern streets, but that still didn't explain the – her mind balked at the word pure, and substituted clear – tone of that voice.

'I didn't hear you, *what?*'

'I didn't hear you, Mother Shawe.'

'Everyone else heard me perfectly well as far as I am aware. Cissie, did you hear me?' A small mousy girl nodded quickly. 'And Kate, how about you?' Another bobbing head. 'So why not you, miss? I repeat, what makes you different?'

'Nothing.'

'Nothing, *what?*'

'Nothing, Mother Shawe.'

'Well for once I agree with you, Sarah Brown. It was your good fortune to come under the care of Matron Riley at an early age, and for that you ought to be down on your knees thanking God every night, because left to your own devices you would soon go astray, do you hear me? You are nothing, girl, worthless – you always have been and you always will be. You came from the gutter and to the gutter you'll return—'

'I didn't.' A voice in her head was telling Sarah to keep quiet and let the tirade pass, but she ignored it.

'You didn't?' There was a note of vicious scorn in Florence's voice as she baited the angry child facing her with blazing eyes. 'Oh well, this is news indeed.' She paused, her gaze flicking over the sea of small faces watching them with rapt attention, before she said, 'Perhaps you'd care to enlighten us all as to your beginnings then, miss?'

'I . . . I—'

'Oh come, come, don't be shy.' The venom emanating from the scrawny body was tangible and had caused an electric silence no one dare break. 'You obviously know more about it than me. Maybe you come from the gentry? Is that it, Lady Sarah?'

14

Perhaps if the story she had told herself so often hadn't been at the forefront of her mind, or if Florence Shawe hadn't hit a nerve that seemed to confirm the dream, or if the day had started better – possibly then she might have kept quiet. But before she could stop herself Sarah was speaking out loud the words that opened Pandora's box and changed her world for ever, destroying the innocence of childhood and revealing the world in all its ugliness.

'My mam and da wanted me, they did, but I was stolen away.' Her chin was up and she was facing the woman who loathed her, thrusting away Rebecca's hands as they tried to pull her back down in her seat. 'But they'll come to get me one day and then you'll see. They live in a big house, a great big house, and there's white linen tablecloths and silver knives and forks, and a maid that answers the door—'

'*That's enough.*'

'It's true, it is.' Sarah appealed to the rest of the class who were sitting with open mouths, swinging her arms wide and pivoting on the heels of her coarse leather boots. 'My mam's looking for me—'

'*Your mother left you in a filthy toilet to die of exposure when you were just a few hours old.*' Florence didn't shout, she didn't have to. 'You were abandoned, do you hear me, not stolen. There is no big house, no maid – she didn't want you.'

Sarah knew she had to deny it. Mary was there, and Jane, she couldn't let them believe such lies, but there was a sickness in her that was rising up in her throat and making her ears ring, and she couldn't get the words past it.

'You were left there and you were found, and brought to the foundling nursery that same night by the constable.' Florence was growing uncomfortable now, there was something in the child's face that was frightening and she found herself wishing she had never started this. But Sarah always

15

brought out the worst in her, she told herself irritably. The child set out purposely to annoy her wherever possible. It was easy to bring the excuse to mind; she had used it often enough in the past when the little quiet voice of conscience had prevented sleep from coming.

What would Matron say when she found out one of her Mothers had revealed confidential information? This last thought had the power to make her voice flat when she said, 'So we'll have no more of this storytelling, Sarah, and I think you'd better—'

'Shut up, you.' Sarah's face was as white as a sheet, her blue eyes dilated and round. 'You're a rotten liar, that's what you are, a dirty rotten liar.'

'*Sarah.*'

'My mam's looking for me—'

'We'll talk of this later; children, page twenty please—'

'And I wasn't left in a filthy toilet, I was stolen and I had a silver rattle.'

'Sarah, sit down at once.' Florence had advanced to the child's side with the intention of pushing her down in her seat, but something in Sarah's face stayed her hand and actually caused her to retreat a step or two. 'I shall take you to Matron if we have any more of this.'

'I don't care, I'll tell her what you said and that you're a liar.'

'You're being very silly. You know that, don't you? Now, sit down and begin your work.'

The ringing in her ears was worse, cutting out all conscious thought, and Sarah was as surprised as Florence when she found herself clinging to the teacher's bony back as she tore and bit and kicked for all she was worth. She was aware of screaming, and a resultant pandemonium that was all noise and frantic movement, but even when she was hauled off the now prostrate figure beneath her flailing limbs she

16

continued to fight, until the red mist before her eyes gave way to a deep consuming blackness that took her down and down.

'Sarah? Sarah, lass, open your eyes. Come on now.'

Sarah recognized the voice as belonging to Mother McLevy, her favourite Mother, who was big and buxom and had a northern accent so thick you could cut it with a knife. Most of the other Mothers tried to adopt the pseudo-upper-class intonation Matron favoured for her staff, but Mother McLevy was a northerner born and bred, and proud of it, besides being something of a rebel to boot.

She was sitting by the side of Sarah's bed in the infirmary, and had been for nearly an hour despite the heavy cold that had confined her to bed earlier in the day, and her faded blue eyes were full of pity for the young girl lying so deathly still in the narrow iron bed. What a to-do, and all because of Florrie Shawe's evil tongue, the wicked old bitch. What on earth had possessed her to go for the bairn like that? She shook her head at herself – why ask the road you know? The mere sight of the bairn had been like a red rag to a bull from the moment Sarah had left the confines of the foundling nursery and moved into the main house. Sarah was too beautiful, that was the trouble, and Florrie couldn't stand it.

There were some, like herself, who had come in as Mothers from a life outside. A life that had been full – a darn sight too full in her case, she thought wryly, bringing her to a place where she needed food and shelter and didn't mind working all hours of the day and night for the security it represented. And then there were the other sort, like Florrie. Born and raised in the workhouse, Florrie had been institutionalized from birth, and looking like she did there'd been no man prepared to take her on. So, to Florrie and others like her, the Home was a step up from the workhouse

17

and to be grabbed at, but resentment and frustration were always there just under the surface. But this was the last time Florrie was going to vent her bitterness on this bairn, by all that was holy it was, Maggie promised herself grimly. She'd see to that.

'Mother McLevy?' Sarah's whisper brought Maggie's eyes to her face. 'I feel funny and . . . and my head hurts.'

'Aye, I know, lass.' There'd be a darn sight more than her head hurting before Matron was finished with her, Maggie thought grimly. That particular lady wouldn't let a little thing like provocation or justice interfere with her punishment at such a severe and public flouting of her rules. The reflection prompted her to say, gently, 'Whatever made you do it, lass?'

'She said . . . she said . . .'

'Aye, I know what she said, lass.'

There was silence for a full minute and then the whisper came again, 'Mother McLevy, it isn't true, is it, what – what she said?'

Now how did she answer that? Maggie took one of the limp hands lying so still either side of the small shape and thought rapidly. She was under no illusion as to why Matron had sent for her to sit with the child. The old biddy was sharp-eyed and cunning with it, she knew the little lass would accept the truth from her when she might continue to fight against it if anyone else spoke to her. Aye, she was a cunning old biddy, the Matron, but she ruled her little empire with an iron hand and it wouldn't do the lassie any good if she was to lie to her now, much as she'd like to. Matron wanted the lid placed back very firmly on this can of worms. The smooth running of the institution had been affected this morning, and order and discipline must be re-established immediately, whatever the cost to the individual.

'*Is it?*' Sarah's eyes were beseeching her to lie. 'My mam did want me, didn't she? She didn't try to do away with me

18

like Mother Shawe said, and leave me in – in . . .'

'Look, you listen here, lass.' All right, the truth had to be told, but how she did it was up to her, and a little embellishment after all the lass had gone through was only human.

'The fact is, you were found in a public place, an' that don't suggest to me that you was tried to be done away with, now then. How you got there, an' who put you there, no one knows; not Flor— Not Mother Shawe, not no one. Life was hard for a lot of folks a few years back. There was the General Strike of 1926 an' the Depression. I know whole families who were put out on the streets to starve, an' starve they did, bairns too. Perhaps your mam was tryin' to save you from that, eh? You considered that?'

Sarah shook her head, tears seeping out of her eyes as she kept her gaze fixed on the old woman by the side of the bed.

'You think it's hard here, lass, you want to see what I've seen out there.' Maggie inclined her head towards the window. 'Why do you think half the bairns in here have their mams or other kin visit 'em of a Saturday, eh? It's not that they've got no family, but their folks can't afford to have 'em.'

'I don't have no one come to see me.'

'No, I know you don't, lass.'

'Even Mary Owen's mam comes.'

Maggie thought of the big blowsy woman who worked the roughest streets of Sunderland and was notorious amongst even the foulest-mouthed sailors, and shook her head slowly. 'You don't want the likes of her visitin' you, now then.'

She did, right at this minute she did, and that humiliating self-knowledge, when added to the leaden sorrow and despair that was a burning pain in her chest, was unbearable. Her mam hadn't wanted her. Whatever Mother McLevy said, her mam hadn't *wanted* her, and she'd left her in a dirty old lavatory somewhere, where anyone could have taken her. She

19

curled up into a little ball in the narrow bed, jerking her hand from Maggie's and stuffing one fist into her mouth to stop herself screaming out loud. She wanted to die. If she prayed right now for the Lord Jesus to let her die, was that like taking your own life and a mortal sin? She didn't care anyway, she wanted to die. She should have died ten years ago, that's what Mother Shawe had said.

'Come on, hinny, don't take on so. You believe what you want to believe, about your mam an' things. No one knows for sure anyway.'

But they did. Sarah stared straight into the round fat face as she gnawed on her knuckles. Mother McLevy was being kind but she wasn't talking like she usually did, her voice was too quiet and soft, and that alone told Sarah that this old friend of hers, the only adult in her small world she had any real affection for, believed what Mother Shawe had said. It *was* the truth. A sorrow so ageless and elemental as to be unexplainable filled her mind, and she felt herself shrinking, reducing down into a tiny quivering speck, into nothing. She shut her eyes tightly but the feeling was in her head, her bones, and she couldn't escape it.

'How about if I go an' get you a sup of tea, eh? An' after you've had that, I'll come along with you to Matron an' we'll face her together?' Maggie's eyes were soft with pity but her voice was brisk now, it wouldn't do any good to let the child mope.

However, it was a full minute before Sarah opened her eyes and then her voice was small and flat when she said, 'All right, but I'm not sorry I went for Mother Shawe. I hate her, and Mary Owen and – oh, everyone.'

'No you don't, hinny, it just seems like it.'

The mild response wasn't like the Mother, and when a reassuring hand was placed lightly against her cheek for a moment before the plump figure rose creakily to her feet, the enormity of the trouble she was in hit Sarah for the first time, piercing the anguish in her soul. She was going to get wrong for this. The thought began to churn her bowels, turning them to water. She couldn't remember anyone ever going for a Mother before; what would Matron do to her? Various possibilities brought her sitting upright in the bed, her arms crossed and her hands under her armpits as she swayed back and forth in a state of animal panic.

Sarah, like every other resident of Hatfield Home, adult and child alike, with Maggie McLevy perhaps the only exception, had a deep and abiding fear of the matriarchal Matron Cox. Tall and thin, with iron-grey hair pulled tightly into a bun and almost opaque pearl-blue eyes, the lady in question had a presence about her that was undeniably threatening. In the twenty years in which she had been Matron she had changed the Home from a poorly run, flyblown hovel of a place, into three separate units that ran like clockwork. Her three Es – expediency, efficiency and enlightenment – which she drummed into her staff and their charges every Sunday morning before prayers, were the code she lived by. She was by nature a frosty, unsympathetic character, with a will of iron and an unshakeable belief in her own judgement that was awesome, added to which she didn't like children. These attributes had made her the perfect candidate for the post of matron in the eyes of the governors who had taken over the running of the Home shortly before she had been appointed. They had been horrified at the slipshod disorganization, and had asked for a tight, disciplined ship that kept the children in their place – seen and not heard – with the minimum expenditure.

Hatfield consisted of three grey-stone buildings surrounded by several acres of land and enclosed within a seven-foot wrought-iron fence, that both repelled intruders and kept the inmates securely confined within its fold.

The foundling nursery cared for the newly born infants and children up to the age of six, at which time they graduated into one of the two main houses – boys to West House and girls to East – regardless of family ties. The two sexes would rarely meet from that day on, unless it was on a Saturday afternoon between the hours of one and five, when children from both houses who had no visitors would be expected to work in the Home's extensive vegetable garden.

The interiors of all three buildings were painted throughout in dark sombre green, and each was devoid of even the smallest home comfort, the ground floor in each building being of bare stone which gave off a chill on the warmest summer day. The first and second floors, used as classrooms and dormitories, had exposed floorboards, paper window-blinds and no heating of any kind, the only relief on the dark walls being religious tracts promising dire admonishment in the hereafter to all and sundry.

The occupants of East and West Houses received a limited education for three hours every morning after breakfast and exercise, and the afternoons and evenings, until bedtime at eight, were taken up with 'home duties', a lofty phrase for the unpaid labour expected of each child.

The younger children, from six to ten years of age, toiled at scrubbing floors and paintwork, laundering clothes, cleaning the washhouses attached to each building, and scouring out the privies. The older girls prepared and cooked food in the kitchens for the two houses and the foundling nursery, attended to the physical and material needs of the infants including washing their bedding and clothes and the mountains of dirty nappies each day, and cleaned the rooms of the Mothers and the separate quarters of the Matron. The boys tended the institution's resident goats and chickens, collected milk and eggs, worked the vegetable garden and large greenhouses and kept the grounds neat and tidy.

The small army of workers were constantly reminded of how much they had to be thankful for, including the fact that they were being trained for the day they would leave the benignant confines of the Home and venture into the world outside to earn their own living. They were expected to be quiet, restrained and submissive at all times, to have no opinions of their own, and to hold the Matron and the Mothers in high regard. Any disobedience of the list of rigid rules pinned by each narrow iron bed earned immediate and severe retribution.

And now Sarah had done the unthinkable – she had not only verbally defied a Mother, she had actually had the temerity to attack her physically.

What was she going to do? What *could* she do? Mother McLevy's uncharacteristic subduedness washed over her again, increasing her terror. The Mother knew what was going to happen and it was bad. Oh, why hadn't she just kept quiet when Mother Shawe had had a go at her? There was no remnant of rebellion in Sarah now, just blind panic at what was in store. She'd ask Mother McLevy what to do when she came back; if anybody would know, she would.

Maggie knew there was nothing to be done but she couldn't bring herself to say so when Sarah tearfully flung herself at her on her return. 'There now, there, you'll be spillin' your tea, lass. Get this down you while it's hot.'

The warm weak tea was a luxury normally confined to once a day at breakfast, when it accompanied a single inch-thick slice of bread and scantily spread jam, and the sight of it increased, rather than diminished, Sarah's fear.

'She'll kill me, won't she?'

'No, she won't kill you, lass.'

'She will, she'll kill me.'

And when Mother McLevy didn't contradict her again –

23

didn't say anything, in fact, but merely looked at her, her face soft and pitying – Sarah shut her eyes tight.

Chapter Two

'I find it hard to believe the events of this morning took place, Sarah.'

Sarah had only been in the inner sanctuary of Matron's office once before, but knew from hearing the older girls talk that beyond this room was a separate sitting room and bedroom, and that both were furnished well, if not luxuriously. According to Fanny Brice, there was linoleum on the floor along with several large clippy mats, and both rooms had a fireplace in which a fire blazed most days, winter and summer.

The office leant weight to this story, its walls being a dove grey rather than the regulation duty green, and the small bookcase and large writing desk in heavy mahogany were of good quality, as were the two high-backed chairs which made up the sum total of the furniture in the small but pleasant room.

Not that Sarah was reflecting on the furnishings as she stood, white-faced and shivering, in front of the illustrious head of Hatfield Home, Mother McLevy having been dispatched before she had set foot inside the room.

'Well?' The tone was not encouraging. 'What have you to say for yourself? I trust you can offer some explanation for your shocking behaviour? You are aware Mother Shawe is in a state of collapse?'

'I . . . I beg your forgiveness, Matron.' It was the stock response to any misdemeanour and had been drilled in to each child from day one at the institution.

'Do you indeed.'

It wasn't going to work, but then Sarah hadn't expected it to. Cissie hadn't been able to sit down for a week and had had all her meals standing up, sleeping on her stomach for nights and nights after she had been sent to Matron for sneaking a piece of lardy cake from the kitchen, when she had been cleaning the big open fireplace and blackleaded hob some weeks earlier. And what was pinching a stale old piece of cake compared to what she'd done?

'You understand that such scandalous conduct must be severely dealt with, both as chastisement to you in the hope that it will persuade you from such wickedness in the future, and as a warning to others you may have corrupted?'

'I – I won't do it again, Matron.'

'Indeed you will not, child.' The words were more ominous for the quietness with which they were uttered.

'She – it wasn't my fault, not really. She said things—'

'I am aware of what Mother Shawe said to you, and also how the matter started. You were being defiant, refusing to work at the task assigned to you—'

'I wasn't!' She had committed another unforgivable sin. She had interrupted the Matron. Sarah stared aghast into the cold face, before gulping audibly and adding, 'I didn't hear her.'

'You have a hearing impediment?'

'No, Matron.'

'Then I take it you were not paying attention, and the resulting fracas was the consequence of your disobedience.'

Sarah didn't know what fracas meant but she was aware it didn't matter one way or the other, it was all her fault and she was going to be punished. Her eyelids blinked rapidly

26

and she felt the urge to go to the privy.

'I am very disappointed in you, Sarah; very, very disappointed.' The figure behind the desk rose to her feet, her movements slow and measured. 'You have been at Hatfield since you were an infant and there can be no excuse for your conduct. You are fully aware of what is expected of you, and this' – she paused just long enough for Sarah's stomach to turn over – 'this *vicious* rebelliousness is an affront to God and man and must be purged from your mind and body. Go to the cupboard and open the door.'

Sarah's eyes followed the pointing finger and she saw a cupboard built into the wall which she hadn't noticed before. When she opened it, it was quite bare apart from a line of long thin canes, each one individually secured within its own niche and standing upright, most split slightly with small fissures.

'Select one and bring it to me.'

'Please, Matron, I won't—'

'*The cane, Sarah.*'

After swallowing deeply Sarah reached inside the cupboard and lifted a cane from its position, the bamboo breached and damaged in places, and brought it over to the desk. She had ceased to think, her mind numbed by the fear that held her in a paralysing grip.

'Pull down your bloomers and bend over the chair.' There was a funny little quiver in the Matron's voice now that brought Sarah's gaze shooting to her face, and she saw the strange colourless eyes were bright with anticipation.

She wanted to do this, she *wanted* to whip her bare bum, she was looking forward to it. The thought hit Sarah like a blow, revealing as it did something not quite right, something shameful about the woman in front of her whom she had been taught to respect and fear all her life.

'Did you hear me, child?'

'I'm not taking me drawers down.' She didn't know where the strength came from when her knees were shaking so badly she could hardly stand, but she couldn't bear to expose herself to the avid gaze.

'Don't be foolish, Sarah, you are going to make matters worse for yourself.'

She didn't care, she wasn't going to take her drawers down for Matron or anyone else, it wasn't . . . nice.

'I'm waiting.'

'I'm not going to.'

'*You will do as you are told.*'

The terror was so great now it was pressing upwards in her throat, threatening to choke her, but still she didn't move.

'This is your last chance.' The tone was soft but icy cold.

Her feet seemed to move over to the chair of their own volition and she paused, glancing over at the Matron again who was now walking out from behind the desk and round to the chair, before she bent over the high wooden seat, the chair-back against her right side and the top of her head touching the floor.

'Your bloomers?'

'No.'

'You will do as I tell you, do you hear me?' Matron's voice was a hiss and as Sarah felt a hard hand yank at her clothes, she brought her left hand round to hold down her smock, only to have it smacked violently away. As her smock billowed about her head she felt strong fingers tear at her red flannel drawers, and the certain something that had surfaced earlier, and which she had not known was part of her disposition until that day, rose again, hot and fierce. She sprang up and began to fight back, using fists and feet in between piercing screams.

A ringing blow across one ear, swiftly followed by another across the other side of her head lifted her right off her feet

28

and brought her spinning round to fall across the seat of the chair, upturning it so it fell with her to the floor.

And then the Matron seemed to go completely mad, snarling like a dog as she brought the cane down with all her strength on any available piece of flesh she could reach, the wood whistling through the air with ferocious intent again and again as she vented her fury and frustration on the half-unconscious child at her feet.

That she would have killed Sarah but for Maggie's intervention was in no doubt; as it was, Maggie could barely hold the enraged woman until help, in the form of two other Mothers, came running in answer to her yells.

'*What on earth?*'

'Hold her, hold her.' As the two women took the Matron from her, Maggie bent over the whimpering little figure on the floor. 'Come on, me bairn, come on, you'll be all right.' It was a ridiculous thing to say to the blood-splattered child, and even Maggie, who had seen more of the seamier side of life than she would have liked after her husband was killed in the Great War, and she was forced to eke out a living for herself and her child working at anything she could put her hand to, was white-faced.

'What happened?' One of the Mothers came to kneel beside Maggie, the other supporting the now sagging Matron against the wall.

'What do you think?' Maggie could barely speak for the anger that was filling her body. 'You know as well as I do what she's like with 'em, she gets pleasure out of inflictin' pain. We all know it an' we're all guilty of turnin' a blind eye an' all, an' this is the result. She's near killed the bairn.'

'She's never gone this far before.'

'No, but there's plenty bin scarred for life, 'cept it's where it don't show. Well, enough's enough, I'm not lettin' this go, by all that's holy I'm not. Look at her.' Maggie had lifted

Sarah into her arms as she had been talking, the contact causing the child to cry out in pain and then turn into the ample bosom as she moaned like an animal. Sarah's smock had nearly been wripped off her small back, and she was covered all over in red and blue weals which patterned the blood-smeared skin with grotesquely raised ridges.

'The child is wilful, she needs correcting.'

At the sound of the voice behind her Maggie swung round so quickly she almost dropped Sarah. The Matron was still leaning against the wall, but other than that slight show of weakness her appearance was the same as usual, all trace of the furious rage that had consumed her a few moments before gone, and her manner imperious.

'Correctin'? You've damn near killed her.'

'A slight exaggeration I think, Mother McLevy.'

'Oh you do, do you now?' The Matron's countenance showed a vestige of unease as Maggie advanced slowly. 'Well I suggest you take a good look at your handiwork an' then say that agen if you can, you perverted swine, you.'

'Well really! How dare you—'

'Oh I dare, Matron, I dare.' There was no heat in Maggie's voice, but the flat weight of her words carried more menace than any show of anger could have done. 'An' I should have dared a good few years afore now, 'cept I needed a roof over me head an' three hot meals a day, God forgive me. But this time you've gone too far. The bairn needs a doctor, an' even Dr March can't turn a blind eye to this.'

'You are over-reacting, Mother McLevy. A hot bath and a few days in the infirmary will calm the child's agitation, there is nothing wrong with her.'

'She's havin' the doctor if I have to go an' fetch him meself.'

For a moment they stared at each other in open hostility, and then as Sarah's whimpering intensified the Matron made an obvious effort at conciliation. 'I know you are particularly attached to this child—'

'That's nothin' to do with it.'

'Nevertheless, your attachment makes you anxious about her and that is commendable of course, even if it colours your view of the present situation.'

'Oh I see, that's your tack, is it? Well how about you, Jessie? Do you think the bairn needs the doctor?' Maggie spoke directly to the woman who had knelt with her at Sarah's side. 'Are you goin' to tell it like it is, or toady to madam here so's she can whip another little 'un half to death?'

Maggie saw Jessie gulping in her throat, but she knew the woman's history; a violent father followed by a violent husband who had punched her so hard when she was expecting her first child she had miscarried the infant two months before he was due to be born. It was something Jessie had never recovered from, so she wasn't surprised when the other woman said, 'I think . . . I think she needs a doctor', although it was clear the Matron was taken aback.

'Mother Bryant—'

'You heard what she said an' so did I.' Maggie interrupted the Matron before she could say any more. She didn't bother to question the other woman in the room – Lizzie Price was a bootlicker, she wouldn't stick her neck out to save her own mother. 'The bairn needs a doctor an' she's gettin' one.'

'I am in charge of this institution, Mother McLevy, in case you have forgotten.'

'You won't be in charge of bo-diddly when I've finished – Matron.' The slight pause was insulting.

'You really think you can get the better of me?' The Matron's tone had lost its condescending note and the words were almost spat out of her mouth, a slight northern accent apparent for the first time. 'I've dealt with people like you all my life, let me tell you. You don't know your place, never have done, but I'll teach it to you, never you fear. You *dare* to threaten me—'

'An' what are you goin' to do about it, my fine mare?' Maggie had handed Sarah to Jessie Bryant as the tirade started, and now she thrust her face close to the other woman, who had drawn herself off the wall and was leaning slightly forward, like a giant bird preparing to peck. 'Whip me, like you do the little 'uns? Well I'd like to see you try. Aye, I would, because it wouldn't be me who'd bear the scars – I'd see you in hell first. You've only survived here this long 'cos to work here in the first place means we're desperate for a job, an' you know it – aye, an' use it. But not any longer. I'm tellin' you I'll bring you low.'

To say that the Matron was taken aback by this warning, spoken as it was in a low controlled voice without a hint of fear, was putting it mildly. It was clear she couldn't believe her ears, but it was only a second or two before she came back with, 'You'll regret this day, Maggie McLevy, I'll see to that. Now get out, and take that brat with you.'

'I'm goin' as far as the infirmary, an' I'm not leavin' the bairn's side either.' It was clear Maggie didn't put anything past the Matron, and this was confirmed when she added, 'An' there's more than me witness to this day's business, just you remember that. I want Dr March to the bairn afore nightfall, I'm warnin' you.'

'*You* are warning *me*?'

'Aye, that's right.' Maggie's voice was higher now, with something in its depths that made the woman in front of her take a step backwards. 'You think you're so high falutin', with your airs an' graces an' prissy way of talkin'. Well, shall I tell you what I see when I look at you? *Scum!*'

As the Matron's eyes narrowed and her jaw thrust out, Maggie pressed home what her instinctive knowledge had told her.

32

'You might fool the rest of 'em, the poor blind mares, but you can't pull the wool over my eyes. You're nothin', you came from nothin' an' you'll return to it. Gutter scum, plain an' simple.'

'*How dare you.*'

'An' one day you'll suffer for what you've done to this bairn an' others like her; God's arm is long an' He won't be mocked.'

'Get out, *get out.*'

'Aye, I'm goin', an' I want that doctor afore dark.'

The doctor arrived just before tea time and when Maggie saw him walk into the infirmary she knew God was on her side. In spite of her brave words earlier she had been sitting worrying about Dr March; she needed medical verification to take the matter further and the Home's doctor was an old ally of Matron, as well as being a nasty bit of work in his own right. But the tall young man who strode ahead of Matron didn't look the sort to be bought off.

He wasn't.

'Where's Dr March?'

Maggie had risen at the doctor's approach and now he glanced at her briefly as he said, 'Sick. Is this the young lady who has fallen? Sarah, isn't it?'

It was a cultured voice, definitely not of Sunderland origin and in strict contrast to Dr March's broad twang.

'Fallen?' Maggie's tone was high. 'Is that what she's told you?'

'Are you saying this young lady *hasn't* fallen off a wall into broken glass and brambles?'

'Doctor, please, I've told you what occurred.' Matron was at her most regal, but Maggie was pleased to note it was water off a duck's back as far as the young doctor was concerned.

'Well?' He didn't acknowledge the woman behind him

had spoken by so much as the flicker of an eyelash as he held Maggie's gaze.

'Judge for yourself, lad.' Maggie whipped back the worn, coarse cotton sheet, which was all Sarah could bear on her seared tortured flesh, to reveal the thin little body criss-crossed with lines, some blue-black and others red and stiff with dried blood. 'I've not seen a thorn bush in me life as could do that.'

'Neither have I, Mrs –?'

'McLevy, Maggie McLevy.' She had heard his sudden intake of breath when the cover was thrown back, and seen the tightening of his mouth, but now he pulled the sheet back into place and his voice was gentle when he said, 'How did this happen, Sarah? Can you tell me?'

The pain in her body had been bearable since Mother McLevy had given her half a teaspoonful of the medicine she kept for when her rheumatism was bad – the laudanum, tincture of opium, had been a heavy dose for a child – but now she found her mind was muzzy when she tried to answer the doctor. 'She . . . she beat me.'

'Who beat you, Sarah?' The voice was still gentle but when Sarah heard the Matron speak from behind the big figure bending over her, the tone was razor sharp as it said, 'Quiet, woman.'

'Quiet, woman.' He'd said 'quiet, woman' to the Matron? Sarah forced her eyes wide open now and tried to focus on the male face close to hers.

'Don't be frightened, no one is going to hurt you.' The incongruity of the statement, considering the flagellation the child had endured, and which his mind was still struggling to accept, made his voice terse when he added, 'Never again anyway. You can speak freely, Sarah, and you have my word that whoever did this will be punished.'

The word 'punished', when linked with the Matron, had

34

always had the power to make her feel sick in the past, but now she found that that particular demon had been scourged along with her flesh, and no longer had the mastery over her. 'I didn't want . . .'

'Yes?' It was soft and encouraging.

'I didn't want to take me drawers down.'

'You didn't want . . . ?'

'To take me drawers down, to be caned. It – it's not proper, but Matron said I'd got to and I didn't want to.'

Her voice was thick, the words faint but perfectly distinguishable, and as Maggie's eyes met those of the doctor over Sarah's head, he shut his for one infinitesimal moment, red-hot anger flooding his body. What the hell had been going on here? This was 1937, not the dark ages. He'd thought this sort of thing had gone out along with forcing children up chimneys to be burnt alive and other such barbaric niceties the Victorian era had perpetuated.

'No one is going to make you do anything you don't want to do again, Sarah.' Twice, during his exchange with the child, the figure behind him had begun to speak and twice he had brought his hand out in a cutting gesture behind him. 'Has she had any medication?' He spoke directly to Maggie now and she answered him without prevarication.

'Some of me laudanum, she needed it.'

'She really needs to go into hospital.'

'I don't want to.'

Both pairs of eyes returned to the mound under the sheet, and the doctor's voice was gentle again when he said, 'Hospital is the best place for you, Sarah, and you'll be well looked after.'

'I don't want to leave the Mother.'

'Now, Sarah, lass. You listen to the doctor—'

'I don't want to go, Mother McLevy.' Sarah cut across her friend's voice, her own high with apprehension. 'And you

35

said' – the deep blue eyes in the white little face fastened on the doctor now – 'you said no one was going to make me do anything I didn't want to do, didn't you?'

If the situation had been different Maggie could have laughed at the look on the young doctor's face. As it was, she put out her hand and touched his sleeve as she said, 'I can nurse her. I've had some practice in me life afore now an' I know what to do. She'll be better here, with me – less upset like.'

'And you can make sure she isn't bothered in any way?'

His meaning was clear, and Maggie nodded grimly as she said, 'Oh I can promise you that, Doctor. Indeed I can.'

'Yes, I think you probably can.' His smile was brief, but it left Maggie thinking that she bet he'd caused quite a stir among the female populace of Sunderland high society. 'I'll help you dress the wounds now. The bandages will need changing twice a day and the salve that I give you will stain the bedding but use plenty of it, it will help prevent scarring. There's a nasty lesion on her neck, watch that, and no more of the laudanum please. I'll give you a sedative which will dull the pain and keep her quiet for the next forty-eight hours, after that it won't be so painful. I'll call by tomorrow to see how things are.'

'Thank you, Doctor.'

He turned now, very deliberately, and faced the tall figure behind him over whom he towered by at least six inches. 'I shall make a full report to the governors on the state of this child, you understand that, Matron? And also to the authorities, with a recommendation that a thorough investigation is carried out.'

'What are you suggesting?' But she was frightened. This young upstart wasn't like Dr March. Dr March she could handle; they understood each other, and the considerable

36

amount of whisky he poured down his throat in her sitting room after each visit oiled any wheels that needed oiling. But this one . . .

'Suggesting? I am not *suggesting* anything, Matron, I am telling you that I intend to make a formal complaint to the governors about what I have seen here today, and also to contact the child welfare authority so that my observations do not get . . . mislaid.'

'They won't let you. The governors won't let you do that.'

'The board will have no say in the matter one way or the other, and incidentally' – there was a telling pause, and he narrowed his eyes at her before he said, 'I think you should know Dr March's illness is of a nature that will make it impossible for him to return to work in the foreseeable future. Now would you please leave. I intend to treat this child's injuries.'

'I shall need to speak with you when you have finished here.'

'I have nothing further to say to you, Matron.' His lip curled on the last word, his voice deepening and betraying the anger which he was struggling to keep under control.

'There are things I need to make clear—'

'If I have my way you will never be in charge of young lives again, is *that* clear enough for you? Now get out.'

When she made no effort to move, he took hold of one arm, manhandling her to the door where she jerked free, her face turkey red and her eyes hot as she hissed, 'Let go of me – who do you think you are? I've been Matron here for twenty years—'

'Twenty years too long.' He glared back at her, his hostility matching hers before he bundled her out of the door and slammed it shut on her furious voice. 'Now then.' Maggie watched his back straighten and his shoulders flex before he

37

turned to face the room. 'Let's make you a little more comfortable, shall we, Sarah?'

Maggie and the doctor were both sweating by the time they had finished; not with the heat, although the day was a warm one for late September and the long narrow room with its row of iron beds had little ventilation, but with the distress Sarah's pain caused them.

Rodney Mallard was glad he had sent the Matron out of his way before he had begun ministering to the girl. He would likely have strangled her with his bare hands if she had remained. How someone could do this to a child was beyond him. Maggie said much the same thing as she drew the sheet back over Sarah's body and walked across to the far side of the room, where he was washing his hands in the tin dish that served as a washbasin, a chipped enamel jug standing beside it.

'Past belief, eh, Doctor?' She gestured at the occupant of the bed. 'But I can tell you I was right glad when I saw you walk into this room. I'd have had a fight on me hands with old Dr March. He's turned a blind eye that often he'll be needin' a white stick.'

'This sort of thing is *usual*?'

'I wouldn't say usual exactly, or at least . . . not as bad as this any road, but she lays into 'em regular, an' not with her hand.'

'Not any more she won't.' He stared at her for a moment and she stared back. 'She'll be out of here within twenty-four hours, you have my word on that. You'll stay with the child until then?'

'I said, didn't I.' Maggie bristled slightly and the glimmer of a smile touched his face before he said soothingly, 'Of course, I'm sorry.'

'You can be sure I'll look after her, Doctor.' She was immediately ashamed of her testiness, but it had been a day

38

and a half and with her feeling under the weather too. 'I'll sleep with one eye open an' all.'

'That wouldn't be a bad idea, Mrs McLevy.'

They walked over to Sarah's bed together and stood looking down on the small girl, who seemed very young and very fragile to Rodney. She was fast asleep, a result of the strong sedative Rodney had given some twenty minutes earlier, her long eyelashes lying on cheeks that resembled white marble.

'She'll be all right? I mean once the pain lets up a bit?'

'Physically.' He continued looking down at the bed. 'But mentally ... What does this sort of thing do to a young mind?'

'There's worse things than a beatin', Doctor, an' they happen to girls as young as Sarah, especially ones lookin' like she does.' Maggie's voice was flat and low.

'Yes, I suppose you're right.' He turned to her now and his voice was as flat as hers as he said, 'You think me very naive, don't you?'

'Naive?' She felt embarrassed and that didn't happen often. 'Not exactly naive, Doctor, more ...' – what was the word? Maggie searched her limited vocabulary and found it – 'more idealistic. You've been brought up as a young gentleman, an' I've nothin' agen that, heaven forbid, but it's different for the likes of Sarah. I'm not sayin' there's not decent folks among the workin' class either' – her tone was suddenly defensive – 'but it's the same in every place, I suppose; it's the bairns what suffer.'

'Why is she here? Has she any family?'

'Not as I know of. She was abandoned, left as a baby.'

'I see.' He glanced round the cheerless room. 'So she has lived in the institution all her life?'

Maggie nodded slowly. 'But like I said, Doctor, there's worse places for a bairn lookin' like she does. Here she's clothed an' fed an' she has a bed to sleep in at night. When I was a bairn, it was a flea-infested flock mattress on the floor, an' that shared atween four of us, top an' tailed. Me mam worked from dawn to dusk an' still there was never enough to eat, an' me da drank his wage most weeks afore me mam could get her hands on it. When he was in work, that is.'

'But you were together, as a family.'

She looked at him pityingly. He was idealistic all right, and the poor blighter was going to have a rough time of it, because one thing was for sure, if he was working with old Dr March he was going to have his eyes opened with a vengeance. Why hadn't he got something in the better part of town, where all the nobs were? But the lad had a good heart. The thought mellowed her and her voice was quiet when she said, 'Aye, lad, that we were,' and left it at that.

Chapter Three

It was the middle of the night when Sarah awoke from her drug-induced sleep, and she was immediately aware that she hurt, everywhere; and then remembrance came, hot and sharp, causing her to cry out, 'Mother McLevy?'

'It's all right, me bairn, it's all right.'

Maggie lumbered off the next bed as quickly as her bulk, and the dose of laudanum she had taken earlier, would allow, and bent over the small girl who had raised herself slightly on her elbows. 'You settle back down, there's a good lass. I'll give you somethin' to help you sleep, eh?'

'Where . . . where is he?'

'Who, hinny?'

'The doctor with the smiley voice,' Sarah said weakly.

'Dr Mallard? You mean Dr Mallard, he's replacin' old March an' not afore time—'

'Where is he?' There was a fretful note in Sarah's voice now and Maggie's hand came to the child's brow which she found to be over-warm.

'He's gone, but don't fret yourself, he'll be back in the mornin'. Now, you have a dose of this an' it'll make you feel better.'

'I don't want it.'

'Dr Mallard said for you to have it.' Maggie was nothing if not crafty, and when Sarah took the bitter-tasting mixture without further remonstration she added, 'There's a good lassie. The doctor'll be pleased with you when he comes, now won't he, takin' all your medicine.'

'Where's . . . where's Matron?'

Maggie followed Sarah's train of thought and said, matter-of-factly and without expression, 'The doctor said for her to keep away, don't you remember? An' I'm stayin' with you till you're better, all right?' She didn't add the doctor had said he would make it his business to see Matron was dealt with. Somehow she couldn't quite believe herself he would win that particular battle.

'My mam didn't want me, did she.' It was a statement, not a question, and followed with, 'I hate her.'

'Now, now, hinny.'

'I do.' The beautiful picture she had drawn in her mind was gone, torn away with each lash of the cane, and it was this more than anything else that was causing the grinding pain inside her head. Now there was nothing except real life, and the awareness was almost too much to bear.

With a wisdom born of her roots, Maggie didn't try to shift the conversation to more comfortable ground or offer platitudes. The doctor had been right, it wasn't Sarah's physical state that was at risk, so now she said, 'You don't know your mam didn't want you, hinny, just that she couldn't keep you an' that's quite different. There were times when I was near givin' away my William after his da had died, an' that for his sake, not mine, I might add. Your mam probably thought she was doin' right by you.'

'You didn't give him away though, did you?'

'No, lass, I didn't, but he might be alive now if I had, 'stead of which the fever took him when he was barely seven years old.'

'I wish my mam had kept me and I'd died,' Sarah said dully, her tongue feeling too big for her mouth. 'I do.'

'Lass, all things pass.' Maggie sat herself down on the edge of the narrow iron bed, and carefully drew Sarah against her copious bosom, rocking her gently as they both became quiet. She continued long after she knew the child was asleep, her chin sunk into the folds of her neck and her eyes wide open.

What would become of this fierce little individual whom she loved like her own? It was a thought that had come more and more often of late, along with a sense of unease only the dulling effects of the laudanum could ease.

Sarah was too bright, too beautiful. She didn't fit into the mould the world demanded of its working class, and it was this very thing that had grated on Florrie from the moment she set eyes on the lass. The world could be unforgiving, oh aye, it could that, and not just with the likes of Sarah either. Look at the poor King, or Duke of Windsor as he was called now. All he'd wanted to do was to marry the woman he loved, and he'd lost his crown because of it. What had she read he'd said when he married his beloved Wallis Simpson in June? Oh yes, she'd got it now – 'After the trying times we have been through we now look forward to a happy and useful private life.' Well, stepping out of the mould could be got round when you were the King of England, and no doubt his life, and his wife's, would still be well oiled.

But Sarah? Maggie stared over the child's head, her face sombre. Sarah didn't have the connections or the money the twice-divorced Wallis Simpson had had. Beauty without intelligence would have been all right for the bairn – Maggie nodded silently to herself, her eyes looking inwards – the lass would have gone one of two ways then. An early marriage to one of the more determined rough types down on the docks or, likely as not, one of the madams would have snapped her up and had her working to service the never-ending supply of customers straight off the boats. Either way she would have found her niche in life. But Sarah was bright, she thought about things and felt them deeply too. Oh aye, she felt them all right, she'd never known a bairn with the capacity to feel like this one.

Maggie's mind travelled back some six years to the first time she'd felt the stirrings of a love that was soon to become fiercely maternal. She had been helping out in the foundling nursery due to some of the Mothers being down with influenza, and had come into the yard during the children's mid-morning recreation to find a little group of sturdy-legged boys surrounding two small girls, one in particular standing out as she faced her tormentors with blazing eyes.

'You're daft, you are, Sarah Brown.' One of the boys, who was verging on six and a good deal bigger than the blond-haired little girl facing him, had closed in on the small figure, who was clutching something next to her chest. 'Give it 'ere else I'll skite your lugs.'

'No, I won't.'

As the child had spoken, Maggie had noticed the other little tot – a smaller, thinner child with straight brown hair cut pudding-basin short – move closer to her friend's side, her chin rising a notch as she'd said, 'You leave her alone, Mick McBride.'

'What's going on here?'

As the group of boys had scattered, Sarah had said, 'It's the frog, Mother,' offering up her hands in which reposed a small round-eyed frog. 'They were throwing stones at it to make it jump an' they've hurt its leg, look.'

Maggie looked, and then backed a step or two as the frog made a half-hearted attempt to escape from the small hands.

'It's come from the garden and it's lost, it's looking for its mam.'

'Is it?' Maggie was not a lover of things small and green, and her voice reflected her scepticism.

'Mick McBride was going to step on it, he was.' Rebecca had chimed in indignantly at this point, her plain little face red with outrage. 'An' he kicked Sarah's legs an' all, but she still wouldn't let him have it.'

'It *is* looking for its mam.' Sarah had been quite adamant. 'She's in the pond, there's dozens of frogs in there.'

Maggie had been unable to refuse the unspoken request, and so the three of them had left the confines of the yard, and walked through to the Home's vegetable garden, depositing the small amphibian close to the large pond at the far end of the grounds before making their way back to the nursery.

The two little girls had chatted away the whole time, and at some time on the return journey Sarah's small hand had slipped into hers, and love had been born as simply and as quickly as that. Not that she didn't love Rebecca, Maggie reasoned quietly as her conscience twanged. She did, aye, she did, but it couldn't be denied that somehow Sarah had got under her skin in a way that had never happened with any other bairn except her own lad, her William.

Oh, what was she going on about? Maggie eased Sarah down on to the bed and straightened slowly, grimacing as her bones creaked. It wouldn't do her any good thinking like this and worrying. What would be, would be. The easy philosophy that had carried her through some fifty years of life didn't work so well these days. She knew in her head that it did no good to fight against the pricks, but every time she looked at the child her heart said otherwise.

Why had this child come into her life anyway? She walked across to the bed she had been lying on before Sarah had awoken, her tread heavy. When William had died she'd thought she'd go mad for a time, prayed for it, anything would have been better than seeing his poor little body stretched out on the bed in their one damp room in her mind's eye every time she shut her eyes. She hadn't slept in weeks, not really, and then someone had introduced her to the laudanum, and after that . . .

She'd made a bit of a name for herself where she'd lived. She'd heard them talk, and seen the curtains twitch more than once when she'd arrived home well-oiled and with a different bloke in tow every night. Not that she'd ever got paid for it. She shook her head at the accusing voice in her mind. But she'd needed comfort, a warm body next to hers in the long night hours when everyone else had someone. And then even that had paled, and she'd got older . . .

When she'd come to work at the Home she had never expected to feel affection for anyone again; she hadn't wanted to. Three square meals and a warm bed was all she'd asked, but she'd reckoned without Sarah. She glanced across at her, hunching her shoulders against what the child meant to her. She'd wanted a peaceful old age, a slow fading away . . .

Oh, stop your griping. That other self was scathing. She'd never been able to stand them that indulged in maudlin self-pity, and she was too long in the tooth to matter one way or the other; the little lass was all that counted. How all this would end she didn't know, but, she told herself, she'd take one day at a time. The future was too big to tackle otherwise. Perhaps the doctor would come through after all, make a stand for the little lass?

She relaxed back on the hard bed with a deep sigh, bringing her swollen legs up slowly, one after the other. But the governors wouldn't like having their charity challenged; most of them had looked the other way so often their heads were permanently fixed in that position. What was one little bairn to any of them? They came strutting round in their top hats and tails once a year, their fancy wives dressed in silk and satin with bits of lace pressed to their noses as though the place stank, and then off they went again in their fine motor cars, full of righteous satisfaction and with their social consciences appeased for another year. What did they know of real life, any of them? Her hand reached for the bottle of laudanum in her shift pocket and then stopped abruptly. No, she'd had enough the night, there was the little lass to think of and she wanted to hear her if she stirred or they had visitors.

Her faded eyes flicked towards the closed door. Not that it would do Matron any good to come back now, but you never knew with her type – the unnatural ones, because if ever a woman was unnatural, the Matron was. To get pleasure out of whipping little bairns . . . Maggie shivered, then leant back and closed her eyes. Give her Florrie Shawe any day. Spitefulness she could understand, but this other . . .

She never was sure what woke her, but when Maggie opened her eyes and saw the dim outline of Matron Cox bending over Sarah's bed, her hands pressing a pillow over the child's face, she still lay unmoving for a moment, her mind unable to accept what her eyes were seeing. And then she smelt the smoke, and saw the bed ablaze at the far end of the room, and panic propelled her upright as swiftly as her bulk would allow and with a suddenness which took the other woman completely by surprise.

'*Sarah!*'

Her shriek, when accompanied by the spring forwards that enabled her to tear the pillow out of the Matron's hands, gave her a slight advantage for a moment but almost immediately the other woman recovered, her face contorted with hate as she hit out at Maggie's face with enough force to send Maggie tottering backwards as she desperately tried to stay on her feet.

'You stupid dirty old woman.' The Matron slowly advanced on her, spitting the words through clenched teeth. 'How dare you think you can take all this away from me,

47

how dare you! I've built this place up out of nothing, nothing, do you hear me? It was a filthy, lice-ridden hovel when I took over, and I've given twenty years of my life to making it what it is today. No one – not you, not that jumped-up little doctor – will take it away from me. *It's mine.*'

'Get away from me.' There was no movement from the bed and it was that, rather than the other woman's rage and the billowing smoke, that was filling Maggie with sick dread. 'You're mad.'

'You thought you'd got the better of me, didn't you, *didn't you*? You and that fancy doctor? But it'll be my word against his when you're out of the way, and there'll be those that swear the girl fell into a thorn bush. Dr March has never had cause to doubt me in all the years he's been visiting here.'

'You bought his silence with whisky.'

'What do you know about it?' The Matron's eyes were unblinking although Maggie's were streaming in the stifling air, her lungs labouring. 'You! A fat low piece like you. You think I don't know about your little habit, your "medicine"? There is nothing that happens in this place that I don't know about, and even your dear friend Jessie Bryant will have to say you're doped most nights. Of course it'll be a mystery why you had a pack of candles alongside of you, but perhaps the child was frightened, nervous of the dark? Yes, I think that would be it—'

Sarah suddenly coughed and spluttered from the bed. It took the Matron's attention long enough for Maggie to strike out at the other woman's face with a force she didn't know she was capable of, the blow hitting the Matron straight between the eyes and felling her to the floor like a log.

She could barely see a hand in front of her now, the whole room was filled with black acrid smoke that made breathing agonizing and her eyes blind, but she reached the bed, scooped Sarah's limp body under one arm, and turned towards the door.

It seemed like an age before she felt the doorknob beneath her fingers, and at first she thought the door was locked as it remained rigid under her frantic efforts, until she remembered it opened outwards rather than inwards. She fell into the corridor outside, kicking the door shut behind her before taking great gulping pulls of clean air, her chest feeling as though it was on fire.

Sarah was stirring again, but feebly, and now Maggie crawled along the corridor, dragging the child with her, until she reached the big brass bell next to the fire bucket filled with sand, one of which was on each floor of all three houses.

The clanging of the bell sounded startlingly loud in the quiet of the early morning, but it was still some minutes before the sound of running feet told Maggie they had been found, and she could relax her aching, swimming head back against the wall where she was sitting, after telling Jessie Bryant the Matron was still in the burning infirmary.

Chapter Four

'Well, it never rains but it pours, eh?'

Sarah stared in surprise at Dr Mallard. She hadn't expected the colloquialism from him.

'Don't tell me you were trying to burn the good Mrs McLevy in her bed?'

'It wasn't me,' Sarah said indignantly, her chin jerking at him. 'Mother McLevy had kept a candle going by her bed in case I woke up and was frightened, and it tipped over and set the bedding alight.'

It was the story Maggie and the doctor had decided to tell her, fearing that the truth, on top of the events of the day before, would be too much, and Rodney was pleased at the child's easy acceptance of the fabrication. The effects of the second sedative Maggie had given Sarah so soon after the first had kept her in a drugged stupor throughout the Matron's attack, and she remembered nothing beyond darkness and not being able to breathe.

'So it's the Mother I've got to take to task is it?'

Sarah's face as she looked at him made it plain she was working out in her mind if he was serious or not, and when she grinned and said, 'She can't half be shirty when she wants to,' he assumed she'd come to the right conclusion.

'I don't doubt it.' He paused before adding, 'How do you feel today?'

'All right.' She didn't, her body ached all over from the Matron's cane and her chest was all sore from the smoke, but she didn't want to talk about that when there were more important issues at stake, issues she felt this tall, handsome, god-like person in front of her could solve. She hitched up in the bed a little, trying not to wince as her seared flesh rubbed on the cotton sheet, and glanced round Mother McLevy's room as she pondered how to put her enquiry without it sounding cheeky. But there wasn't a way. 'Dr Mallard?'

'Yes?' Rodney had prepared himself for all sorts of difficult questions relating to the night before, so it was with considerable surprise that he heard her say, 'Are . . . are you married?'

'What?'

'A wife, have you got a wife?'

'A wife?' The big blue eyes were reproachful, underlining his obtuseness, and he collected himself quickly as he said, 'No, Sarah, no. I don't have a wife.'

Sarah tried hard to keep her satisfaction from showing, but something of it came over in her voice when she said, 'I'm nearly ten you know, my birthday's next month.' She didn't tell him it was in the last week of October; every week was important to convince him of her maturity.

'Is that so.'

'And lots of girls marry when they're sixteen.'

'Yes, they probably do.' He knew he couldn't smile, but a tremor passed over his face as he turned away. He hadn't expected to find any humour in the morning, when he had received the telephone call from one of the governors first thing, but he had reckoned without the fighting spirit of this tiny little morsel. He extracted some clean dressings from his bag and kept his voice brisk as he said, 'Shall we take a look at that wound on your neck, Sarah?'

She should have asked him if he'd got a sweetheart. The

thought suddenly occurred to her and it was more how she was going to approach that, than the pain of having the blood-dried dressing changed, that kept her quiet for a few minutes until he had finished.

Rodney found the anger that had flared yesterday begin to boil again as he dealt with the bruised and battered little body, although he was relieved to see there appeared to be no signs of infection. That a woman, the supposedly softer and gentler side of the human race, could do this to a child was beyond him, and she must have gone clear off her head to do so much damage before she was stopped. It was as well she was in the prison hospital, he thought grimly. Far from treating her for smoke inhalation and minor burns, he would have felt like strangling the woman if he'd got his hands on her after this latest madness. But that was it, she was mad, she had to be.

'Dr Mallard?'

'Yes, Sarah?'

'Oh, nothing.' She couldn't ask him, not now. She bit on her lip and then spoke the other thought which had been troubling her all morning and was intrinsically linked with the first. 'Do . . . do I have to go back?'

'Go back?'

'To the dormitory, to . . . the others.' Mary Owen would believe what Mother Shawe had said, and if she believed it the others would believe it, she'd make them. The thought was unbearable and Sarah twisted in the bed now as the doctor finished washing his hands and turned to face her. 'I don't want to.'

'I'm sure Mrs McLevy will lend you her bed until you're feeling better.' He had spoken in a jocular tone but there was no response from the little face watching him, and his own countenance straightened as he said, very gently, 'You won't be able to stay in Mrs McLevy's room for ever, now will you?'

'No.'

'And Mrs McLevy will still be here even when you are back with your friends.' He walked over to the bed as Sarah stared fixedly at him, sitting down on the edge of it and taking one small hand in his. 'You know she is very fond of you, don't you, and there is nothing to worry about as far as the Matron is concerned; she won't be coming back to Hatfield, not ever again. In a few days you'll be back with your friends and all this will just be like a bad dream.'

A few days. Not months, not even weeks – days. Sarah wriggled her small bottom as her heart sank. Oh, why couldn't you just grow up in one big rush? But she wouldn't go back, *she wouldn't*, she'd . . . she'd run away. Anything would be better than seeing Mary Owen's satisfied face.

As she pushed the thumbnail of her free hand into her mouth and started chewing it, still without taking her eyes off Rodney's face, Rodney found he was way out of his depth – and not for the first time since coming to this desolate backwater, as he termed Sunderland. Why hadn't he had the sense to apply for a post in Coventry or Oxford, anywhere but the north? What had made him do it? He felt the harsh rasp of truth against his mind and turned his thoughts sharply from Vanessa. That was dead, gone. She was lost to him as completely as if she was six feet under the earth, and he wouldn't take her back now if she crawled every inch of the way from London. And he'd knock these daily telephone calls of hers on the head too. He'd refuse to take them from now on whatever the consequences.

'I don't want to go back.' Sarah brought his attention back to herself after a full minute of silence, and then she surprised both of them when she suddenly flung herself at him, pressing her small body against his chest as she sobbed quietly into his jacket. He was quite still for a moment and then his arms came round her, and he said, 'There now, there now, it can't be as bad as all that.' His words mocked him. It was every bit as bad as that and the child knew it.

When Mrs McLevy had put him fully in the picture earlier that morning as to the sequence of events that had started the ball rolling, he had been doubly dumbfounded at the insensitivity of some of the people in charge of these young minds. That this woman, this Florence Shawe, had taunted the child with the facts of her beginnings in front of her classmates, was quite incredible. He'd said as much to Mrs McLevy, and her reply of, 'I know, lad, I know, I felt the same meself, but Florrie's conscience is givin' her hell over all that's happened if that's any comfort,' had merely brought forth the sharp rejoinder, 'It's no comfort at all, Mrs McLevy.'

The thought of the tough old northerner now prompted him to say, 'Mrs McLevy will look after you, Sarah. You know she loves you, don't you?'

'But it's not like a *mam*.' The moment she said it she felt guilty, horribly guilty, and it was her self-reproach that helped her regain control, and say, in a very small voice, 'I do love Mrs McLevy,' as she kept her head pressed against him.

'I'm sure you do, Sarah.' Rodney screwed up his eyes against the flood of pity he was experiencing for this small morsel.

'But – but she's not mine, is she? She doesn't belong to me like a mam.'

A heavy silence followed, one which Rodney felt at a loss to break. He was aware that his own childhood had been privileged, one of considerable wealth but also with the security of a close-knit, loving family, in which each member was genuinely concerned for the welfare of the others. Public school, tennis and cricket in the summer, and winter holidays in Europe – he had taken it all as normal life until leaving the safe, comfortable confines of his élite circle in Windsor and travelling north.

Since his arrival in Sunderland two months ago, the rawness of life in certain areas of the town where he visited patients had depressed and saddened him many times. He had felt pity, frustration, anger, and a burning sense of helplessness, but never the desire to protect and shield one of the inhabitants, as he did with Sarah. The child had touched something deep inside him, a fount of tenderness, of strong, parent-like compassion, and it had been instantaneous. She had been on his mind constantly since the day before, and when he had received the telephone call first thing, from a governor who was anxious that the matter should not become public knowledge, he had found it difficult to talk to the man civilly.

A quiet knock at the door, followed by Maggie's shambling entrance into the room, brought Rodney to the realization that the child had fallen asleep against him, worn out, no doubt, by the traumatic events of the last twenty-four hours.

'She was upset.' He explained Sarah's tear-stained face as he placed her gently back in the bed and straightened up, Maggie sighing and flopping into a straight-backed chair at its foot.

'Aye, well it's not surprisin', is it?'

'No, I suppose not.' There was silence for a moment and then Rodney said, 'What will happen to her, Mrs McLevy?'

She liked this young doctor. Maggie stared at the tall broad-shouldered figure in front of her. Dr March had always treated the Home's helpers like dirt – while keeping on the good side of Matron and grovelling for his whisky – but this young man was polite, respectful like, without being patronizing. Her thoughts moderated her tone as she said, 'She'll go on as before, lad, what else? There's no other option.'

'She doesn't want to go back with the other children.'

'No, I can understand that.' Maggie paused for a moment. 'She's different you see, an' bairns bein' bairns, they don't like it. I don't mean her looks, although they're out of the ordinary, but she's bright, intelligent too, an' she feels things. She can't shrug things off like the rest of 'em in here an' they know it an' it makes 'em cruel.'

'Can't – can't you do something?'

They looked at each other for a moment, and Maggie raised her eyebrows as she said, her voice scarcely audible, 'An' what would you have me do, lad? Keep her tied to me apron strings all day, have her sleep apart from the others, eat alone? Even if that were possible, which it's not, it wouldn't do the lass no good. She's in here an' she's got to cope with it the best she can. Now I'm not sayin' that lightly.' She raised her hand as he went to speak. 'God knows I hate to see the bairn suffer, an' I've prayed for things to be different for months now, but it'll be worse if anythin', after this last bit of mischief by Florrie. The bairn used to comfort herself with a story she'd made up about her mam an' da, you know. She thought I didn't know but her little pal Rebecca told me about it a while back. I think it got so she believed it herself in the end.'

Rodney swore, very softly, as he glanced down at the small figure in the bed.

'Anyway, don't you worry about it, lad. You've got enough on your plate from what I hear, what with old Dr March laid up an' you doin' the lot.'

Rodney shrugged the comment into insignificance, before saying, 'I hate to think of any child in a place like this, from what I've seen of it, but especially a sensitive, knowing one like Sarah.'

'Well that's life, an' all you can do is make the best of it. It don't do no good to fight against your lot in the long run; what will be, will be.'

The fatalistic attitude – which Rodney met every day among the very people he considered should be fighting back against the unfairness of society, and which grew steadily more irksome – made his voice curt as he said, 'I disagree. How will there ever be change if the people don't make their voice heard?'

'An' you really think anyone's goin' to listen?'

'Yes. Yes I do, Mrs McLevy.'

'Well perhaps to you, lad, aye, I'll give you that. But to me, an' others like me? It's my belief that most of the gentry still think of us as cannon fodder, whatever they might say in their fancy speeches. Me old gran used to say that actions speak louder than words, an' I agree with her an' all. You think this place is bad now? You ought to have seen it twenty years back afore the Matron was brought in. I've heard stories about it that'd make your hair curl.'

'You're not saying you approve of that madwoman?'

'No, I'm not sayin' that.' Maggie sighed, bending forward and rubbing her swollen knees. 'Not in most things, any road, but she did get this place up an' runnin', givin' credit where credit's due.'

'I don't think I could find it within me to give any credit to that woman, not after what she's done,' Rodney said stiffly. 'Leaving aside the matter of the first attack on the child, she tried to commit what amounts to murder last night, and would have succeeded but for your intervention.'

'Aye, thank heaven I didn't take me usual dose of laudanum.' Maggie straightened with another deep sigh. 'I would have, but for the bairn perhaps needin' me, but I made do with a drop.'

'You shouldn't use it the way you do. You know that, don't you?' Maggie said nothing but her face was eloquent enough. 'Anyway, I'd better be going.' Rodney turned to look down at the sleeping Sarah, his voice soft as he said, 'I'll call by tomorrow to see how she is, but she's doing far better than I expected after everything that's happened.'

'She's tougher than she looks, she's had to be.'

'Yes. Well, good day, Mrs McLevy.'

'Good day, Doctor.'

Maggie didn't move from the chair when the doctor left. She wasn't feeling too good from the residual effects of the smoke, added to her ever present rheumatism, but her eyes were thoughtful as the door shut behind him. It was strange the effect this bairn had on people; they either seemed to hate her or love her, there was no middle path.

She glanced at the child in the bed, her small slight frame hardly making a bump under the thin covers, and her fragile blond beauty giving the illusion of frailty.

But Sarah wasn't frail. Maggie's eyes narrowed. Not in her body and certainly not in her mind. Perhaps it was her strength that caught certain folks on the raw? Because the bairn had an intensity of spirit you could view as either a deficit in her character, or an attribute, depending on which side of the fence you were sitting on. And it was nothing to do with her looks. As yet the bairn wasn't aware of how beautiful she was. Whatever, the lass was going to struggle – with her tenacity of purpose and her courage, she was still going to struggle.

Maggie sighed very deeply, her hand reaching for the small bottle of laudanum in the folds of her voluminous skirt, before it stilled halfway. No, no more of that, she told herself resolutely. The young doctor was right – it had become a crutch, a way of escape, and she was using too much of the stuff.

A slight movement from the bed caught Maggie's eye, and she looked up to see Sarah's gaze fixed on her face. 'Hallo, me bairn.' Sarah stared back at her, her small face unsmiling. 'You ready for somethin' to eat yet?'

'No. No thank you.'

'A sup of tea then?'

'No, I don't want anything. Mother McLevy?' Sarah wriggled about a bit and rubbed her nose before she went on, 'The doctor said I've got to go back with the others. Have . . . have I?'

For answer, Maggie merely nodded her head, her face straight. It'd do the lass no good to show sympathy, she was feeling sorry enough for herself as it was, although heaven alone knew she'd got cause.

Sarah's face puckered slightly but she didn't cry, and when she slid back down under the thin cover and turned on her side Maggie uttered a soft sigh of relief. Sarah had to accept it as it was and she'd be all the better for doing so quickly. Once she'd got it straight in her mind it was the only way, she'd make the best of it. Sarah was like that.

By nine o'clock that evening Sarah was quite sure of what she was going to do, several things having happened during the day to make up her mind, starting with the conversations with the doctor and Mother McLevy. Rebecca had come for a visit, shy and over-awed and not at all like herself, and although Mother McLevy had left them alone they hadn't talked much, and when they had, it had been all about a new girl who had just arrived and was now sitting in what had been Sarah's place in class – next to Rebecca.

'You'll like her, Sarah, she's ever so nice.' Rebecca's plain little face had been earnest. 'And she says I'm like her best friend who lives in her street.'

'If she's got a house and a street what's she doing in here then?'

'Her mam's ill in hospital, and her da can't look after her and work an' all, so she's just staying for a bit – that's what she said.'

'And you believed her?' Sarah's tone expressed her own disbelief and now Rebecca drew back slightly as she caught the criticism.

'Yes.' Her voice was defensive. 'You'll like her, honest.'

Sarah gave a jerk of her head. 'I might not.'

'And she's going to let me play with her skipping rope when her da brings it in. If I ask, she'll let you too.'

'She won't be allowed. You're not allowed skipping ropes and things in here, you know that.'

'She will be, she said so.'

'Huh.'

Conversation waned still further after that and when Mother McLevy came a few minutes later, Rebecca – still nervous and bashful, and a little wary of the aggrieved Sarah – didn't ask to come again and Sarah, heartsore and jealous, fought against suggesting it.

By two o'clock Maggie was suffering the effects of the previous night's furore, her weariness increased by her having spent what had remained of the night on a straw pallet at the side of Sarah's bed, and when Jessie insisted she use her bed for a few hours she went without demur, leaving Sarah in the hands of one of the older girls.

Sarah liked Lizzie Carmichael, and she knew Lizzie liked her, so it made what the older girl had to say all the more credible.

'Coo, Sarah, what on earth were you an' Mother McLevy thinkin' of to have a lighted candle by your beds, eh?' Lizzie's pleasant, but slightly gormless face was full of foreboding, her slack mouth stretched wide. 'You won't half get it when Matron comes back.'

'The doctor said she's not coming back.'

'Matron?' Lizzie's voice was high. 'Oh don't be daft, course she will. She's Matron, isn't she?'

'But he said—'

61

'They had to rescue her you know, out of the infirmary. She'd passed out. Margaret says Mother Preston said it was tryin' to save you an' Mother McLevy an' that she's a hero. Everythin' is as black as the ace of spades in there, they reckon none of it is any good, it's goin' to cost a mint to replace it.' Lizzie's tone plainly stated she was glad she wasn't Sarah and responsible for such destruction. 'I bet Mother McLevy is sent packin', you know what Matron's like.'

'But she didn't mean it.'

'Don't make no difference.'

'Well it should, it should make a difference.'

'Aye.' Lizzie's expression was pitying. 'Do you want me to read to you, or play I-spy or somethin'?'

'I don't care.' She didn't, she didn't care about anything any more. If Mother McLevy was going to lose her job, just because she'd been thinking about her, she wouldn't be able to bear it. It wasn't *fair*, and the doctor had said it would all be all right. He'd lied to her. The awfulness of the thought turned her stomach over. She had to *do* something, but what? What could she do?

The thought that had been there earlier resurfaced. She would run away. She sat quiet, lost in the enormity of it. But she could, and she'd leave a note to say *she'd* lit the candle, not Mother McLevy, and that it was all her fault. A little glow of martyrdom warmed her briefly. She could say she was older and get work as a scullery maid or something in a big house. She knew she could do it. A girl had done something similar in the *Sunshine Review*, a twopenny magazine that Cissie Wright had had smuggled into her and which had been passed round the dormitory.

And then Mother McLevy wouldn't get wrong, and she wouldn't have to see the Matron again, or Mary Owen, or any of them. Her innate honesty forced Sarah to acknowledge her motive wasn't totally sacrificial. Would Rebecca miss her now this new girl had come? The pain which had been grinding away since Rebecca's visit intensified, causing her to press one small fist hard against her mouth. She hated skipping anyway, it was stupid. They were all stupid.

At ten o'clock she slid out of bed carefully and crept to the door. Mother McLevy was sharing the slightly larger room of Mother Bryant next door, they had squeezed another bed into the limited space earlier that evening, and Sarah had been listening to continuous snoring for over half an hour now while she thought out her plan of action.

First she'd have to pay a visit to the laundry – she couldn't run away in her shift – and she just hoped there were some boots drying in the boiler room; it'd been raining that day so there might be. Course, they'd likely be boy's boots – her small nose wrinkled fastidiously – it was normally the boys who got theirs soaked, but it couldn't be helped. And then . . . then she'd climb out of the laundry-room window – the main front door and the two side doors would be locked by now – and if she skirted round to the front and kept to the edge of the main drive she should reach the gates within five minutes. Her stomach turned over with a mixture of nervous anticipation and fear.

It was a pity she didn't dare go to the dormitory first; she'd have liked to have taken the blue velvet ribbon Mother McLevy had bought her for her last birthday, and the sampler she had been working on for the last twelve months and recently finished. It didn't occur to her the sampler was the indirect cause of all her present trouble, precipitating, as it had, Mary Owen's fermenting envy and spite. But she didn't dare – she shook her head in agreement with her thoughts – it'd be just like Mary Owen to wake up and start yelling her head off, she'd got a voice like a foghorn as it was.

The corridor outside was ominously dark and empty, and again her stomach jerked and trembled. Mother Shawe had said the bogeyman would get them if they left their beds at night. She paused on the threshold as her eyes darted into the gloomiest corners, but facing Matron in the flesh was more frightening at this moment than spectres unknown, and so she padded out into the blackness on shaking legs.

When she reached the ground floor the chill of concrete on Sarah's bare feet made her increase her pace to the laundry room, situated at the far end of the corridor. She found this part of the building even more scary than the upstairs, it being almost totally devoid of light and having only two narrow windows, one on either side of the front door.

Her heart was beating a tattoo by the time she twisted the knob on the door and slipped inside the large square room – the familiar smell of damp clothes and disinfectant causing her nose to wrinkle briefly – but it was her physical condition, rather than Mother Shawe's bogeyman, that caused her heart to pound. Lying in bed she hadn't realized how weak she was, but now she was feeling dizzy and somewhat sick, and every little bit of her ached.

She sank to the floor with her back to the door for a few minutes, the cold seeping upwards through her bare bottom and causing her teeth to chatter, then found the strength to stand up and walk over to the far end of the room by the window, where the dry clothes and bedding were stored. She found a pair of the regulation red flannel bloomers along with a calico petticoat and pulled them on quickly over her flannel shift, before slipping into one of the institution's blue smocks which was a trifle too big for her. But it didn't matter, nothing mattered, except getting away as soon as she could. She didn't bother with a pinafore, instead she opened the door to the boiler room which led off the first room and peered inside, having to wait for a full minute for her eyes to adjust to the lack of light.

There were no boots. She could have cried with disappointment. What was she going to do? Should she risk going back upstairs and finding the dormitory, and hope no one saw her take a pair from the end of a bed where each child placed their footwear at night? She didn't dare. But she couldn't go without any boots. She shut the door, panic high, and then she saw them – a pair of old, and obviously adult boots, tucked in one corner close to the big airers. Her feet slid into them, lost in the cavernous depths, but she found that if she laced them tightly and moved slowly they would just about stay on her feet. 'Beggars can't be choosers.' One of Mother McLevy's pet sayings came back to her and she nodded to it. They'd do.

The last thing she did was to select one of the thin blankets and tuck it under her arm. She might have to sleep under a hedgerow or in a barn for a night or two. That's what the heroine in *Sunshine Review* had done, and she'd eaten berries and wild mushrooms and things, and a farm boy had shared his lunch with her . . .

Getting through the window proved more difficult than she'd thought, mainly due to the fact that every time she heaved herself up the boots slipped off, so after two tries she took the boots off and dropped them out first, hearing them thud onto the ground below with a sense of inevitability. She had to go now, she couldn't leave them out there, and she knew once she was outside she would never get back in, the window being six foot up from the concrete path. She stabilized herself on the chair she had pulled across to the window again, and pulled herself up with her thin little arms, her legs waving madly for a few seconds as she steadied herself on the flaking window frame. It took some manoeuvring to get through the gap, mainly because she was frightened of shooting out on to her head, but eventually she was hanging by her arms outside and with a little plop she landed on the ground.

She was immediately conscious of the chill of the night, the blackness, the whispering of the tall looming trees surrounding the building and the other two buildings in the distance taking on the appearance of forbidding sentinels with a thousand eyes. She shrank back against the wall for a moment, the dizziness returning more strongly, and then sank down to the floor to pull on the boots, her teeth chattering uncontrollably with a mixture of fear and cold. Everywhere looked so different compared to the daytime.

She sat there for some time. Her arms and legs seemed to have lead weights attached to them and her head was aching badly; the bed she had just left took on the form of heaven. She must have fallen asleep for a few minutes because she suddenly jerked awake with a panic-stricken start as an owl called out into the charcoal-streaked sky, and then she remembered, and rose slowly to her feet.

She had to get out onto the road beyond, that was the first thing, and then . . . then everything would work out.

The gate was locked, the seven-foot wrought-iron fence either side of it equally unscalable with vicious points to deter even the most intrepid climber – which Sarah wasn't.

'*Oh.*' She gazed up at the gate, and then her eyes went higher still as she muttered, 'Please, God, do something, will you? Please?' There was no answer, no sudden creaking of the gate swinging open, but there suddenly popped into her mind a conversation she had overheard when working in the vegetable garden a few weeks before. Two of the older boys had been congratulating themselves on finding a gap in the fence, through which they had been able to squeeze and undertake a raid on a farmer's orchard some way down the lane. They had been tall boys, too; broad-shouldered. If they could get through . . .

It took Sarah some time to find the gap, which was nothing more than a slight bending of two of the iron poles, but she was through in a trice and out onto the grass verge beyond, where she stood for a moment looking from right to left. The sky was patchily moonlit but still overwhelmingly dark, the rain of the afternoon making the ground stick to her feet. She pulled the blanket round her shoulders in the form of a shawl, and began to trudge along the verge, feeling very tiny and very alone.

She didn't have anyone who loved her. There was a cold wind blowing against her face, and it was only when it stung her cheeks that she realized she was crying. Her mam hadn't loved her, there hadn't been a pink pram and a silver rattle, it was a story, just a story. The pain in her chest was making it tight and she pushed her small fists, in which the edges of the blanket were clasped, into her breastbone.

Mary Owen said you didn't have to have a da to be born, just a mam. She didn't know if she believed that, she admitted to herself, but any road everyone was agreed you had to have a mam, and hers hadn't wanted her. Why? She stopped suddenly, the dizziness intensifying. Her mam was some-where, *somewhere*, and she didn't know where. And she wanted her mam. She did, she wanted her. She didn't care what she looked like – she could look like Mary Owen's mam even, she didn't care, she just wanted her mam. But her mam didn't want her. She didn't know where she was, what she was doing; she could have died and her mam wouldn't have known.

It was becoming increasingly difficult to walk; the nausea was strong now but it was her legs that were all wobbly. She set her face and continued to plod on. The boots were rubbing painfully when she'd covered no more than a few hundred yards, and after hobbling along and twice sprawling on the ground when she tripped over her own feet she decided to take them off and carry them round her neck for a while. She sat down on the verge, but once the boots were off and hung round her neck by the laces she found to her amazement she couldn't get up, an exhaustion so severe as to be paralysing weighting her down. The vomiting took her by surprise, but once it was over the dizziness felt slightly better, although the will to move was quite gone. She curled up into a little ball in the damp grass, pulled the blanket around her and over her head, and shut her eyes as it began to rain again.

'I told you I saw something, Edward, I knew it. What is it?' There was a little squeal. 'It's not a dead body, is it?'

'For crying out loud, Josephine, let me get to it.' A pause and then, 'Good grief! It's a child, a little girl.'

'She's not . . . ?'

'No, she's alive, and it looks like she's from the Home back there by her clothes. Josephine, get out of the damn car, will you, there's more at stake here than your new shoes. And bring that rug from the back seat while you're about it.'

Sarah was aware of the disembodied voices floating above her head but they belonged to the twilight world she had slipped into; they weren't real and she didn't want them to be real. She was comfortable, she didn't hurt any more, and it was only the lack of pain that made her realize how much she had been hurting before.

When, in the next moment, a warm hand was placed on her cheek and a voice said, 'Can you hear me? Can you open your eyes?' she kept them tightly shut, but then as she felt herself lifted up her eyes opened of their own volition.

'Hallo there.' The man's voice reminded her of the doctor, but he was older, much older. 'Don't worry, we're going to take you home. You've gone and got yourself lost, haven't you.'

Lost? She wasn't lost. She wanted to tell him so – the panic at being returned to Hatfield jerking her limbs – but the nausea had returned, stronger this time, and all she could do was turn her face as she began to retch.

There were words passing over her head, but on the perimeter of her awareness, as she grappled against unconsciousness and the crippling sickness, but once the vomiting was over she knew she was being carried again, and then she was inside the car and the engine started.

They were taking her back . . .

Part Two

Fighting Back: 1947

Chapter Five

As the train drew into King's Cross station Sarah smoothed down the jacket of her new blue serge suit, and glanced at her reflection in the smut-smeared window. It didn't look homemade, she reassured herself for the hundredth time, her heart thumping against her ribs. It looked smart and practical, but feminine too – Rebecca was a dab hand with her sewing machine. And anyway, the skirt wasn't as full or as long as some she had seen since the hourglass look first came in some months ago. It was all very well for critics to condemn the New Look as frivolous and wasteful, but women were so sick of ration books and clothing coupons. It had certainly been worth the fourteen coupons the material for the suit had taken to feel less provincial for her arrival in London.

The thought of the hours Rebecca had spent in making the suit, and the six coupons her friend had insisted on giving her towards the material, caused Sarah's throat to tighten and her eyes to blink rapidly, the mental picture of Rebecca, Maggie and Florrie as they had waved her goodbye on the Sunderland platform vivid on the screen of her mind. But then the train had stopped and the picture was swept away as she opened the carriage door and hauled her big brown suitcase onto the bustling platform.

Sarah had been down to London once before, when she had attended the interview for the housekeeping position she was now taking up, but that had been on a Sunday when it was much quieter and slower. Nevertheless, then, as now, the pace of the city had excited her, stimulating the need to leave Sunderland's familiar shores and venture further afield.

She had decided to splash out on a taxi for the first time in her life – it was her first day at a new job after all – and when an obliging porter offered his services to the taxi rank Sarah gladly relinquished her tussle with the heavy suitcase and her big cloth bag, and trotted along at his side as he wove in and out of the jostling throng. 'You new to these parts?' he asked mildly.

'Yes, I'm from Sunderland.'

'Sunderland?' There was a note of surprise in the cockney tones. 'I've a brother who moved up that away some twenty years ago now, and he was speaking the lingo within months. You don't sound as if you're from the north.'

'Don't I?' She didn't tell him she had been practising every night for the last few years, once she was alone in her room, to remove even the slightest inflexion from her voice. Not that she was ashamed of her beginnings, she told herself quickly, it wasn't that, but like it or not it mattered how you spoke if you wanted to get on. And she did, she did want to get on. The thought was accompanied by the pounding of her heart. And this was the first step. She was here, here in London, where anything could happen . . .

'You had your fair share in the war from what our Bert tells me? Too near water you see, with the docks and all.' He had raised a hand as he spoke to a taxi driver who was leaning against the side of his cab eating a sandwich. 'Mind you, can't compare with what we took down here. I told our Bert the last time I saw him, it's a miracle any of us survived to tell the tale and that's the truth. Old Hitler had it in for us Londoners, but he didn't know what he was up against.'

She nodded as the sharp eyes turned to her, but didn't say

74

anything. The war had been over nearly two-and-a-half years, but for some people it was still all they could talk about.

He ushered her into the back of the car as the taxi driver opened the door for her, nodding at her as she gave the address to the driver. 'He's a good bloke, Brian Mullett, he'll look after you,' he said in a stage whisper, his head bobbing as he pocketed the tip she gave him. 'Knows his way about and don't take the long route, if you get my meaning.'

'Thank you, you've been very kind.'

'All in a day's work, love. All in a day's work.'

He stood and watched them as they drove off, and she didn't know quite whether to wave or smile so she did both before settling back in the leather seat, her hand clutching at her throat as she stared through the window at the teeming traffic which seemed a law unto itself. They certainly didn't drive like this in Sunderland. But it didn't matter, nothing mattered, because she was here – she'd arrived, she'd done it! She shut her eyes tight for a moment, then forced herself to let out her breath in a long slow sigh.

'You all right, duck?' The taxi driver nearly made her jump out of her skin as he slid back the glass partition separating the driver from the rest of the cab. 'Not feeling bad, are you?'

'Oh no, no, I'm fine, thank you.' She smiled at him before adding, the lilt in her voice telling its own story, 'I've just moved here from the north you see, and everything is so fast and exciting.'

'Well it's fast all right, but I dunno about the other.' He grinned at her. 'You say you're from the north?'

The tone suggested enquiry, and in answer to it Sarah said, 'I'm taking up a position as housekeeper to Lady Harris. Do you know her?'

'Lady Harris? Well, bless me soul, and there was me round there just the other day for a cup of tea and a cream bun.' The teasing was friendly and light. 'If I'd known you was coming I'd have put in a good word for you.'

'Thank you.' She was laughing now, and the eyes in the mirror smiled back.

'So you're a housekeeper are you? You don't look old enough to keep house.'

'I'm twenty.' It was indignant.

'Twenty? Oh, that's ancient, that is. That explains it. Twenty you say, my, my.'

'I've had a lot of experience.'

Years, endless years, of drudgery, and those before she reached the grand age of fifteen and officially became a supervisor, the title of Mother for the Home's helpers having become redundant two years before. It had been Maggie who had persuaded her to stay at the Home as a paid helper when the job was offered to her. 'Get a bit of experience under your belt, lass,' she'd said stoically. 'I know, an' you know, that you've bin doin' the work for years, but you need it on paper. Use 'em, they've used you since you were a bairn.' It had been the right decision.

One year as a supervisor alongside Rebecca, who had then left Hatfield when she had married just after her sixteenth birthday; one as laundry assistant, rising to laundry manageress the following year; then two as housekeeper to one of Hatfield's governors, before her employers, on deciding to emigrate, had recommended her for the post she was about to take up.

She had upset more than a few at Hatfield when she'd gone for the housekeeping job to the governor, Mr Roberts, she reflected quietly. The general opinion had been that she should have stayed in the background and let others who were older, and in their opinion wiser, have their chance. But Mrs Roberts had liked her, and had appreciated having someone near her own age about the place, she having

76

married a man old enough to be her father, so that had been that. And she hadn't been unhappy there, not by a long chalk, with a comfortable room of her own and most evenings free, as well as a half-day a week to herself.

She had been able to visit Maggie and Florrie in the evenings, more often than not with Rebecca, whose husband had been working permanent night shift in those days; but she'd known even then she wanted more. She had always known it, right from when she could remember thinking at all, but the self-knowledge had clarified and sharpened since the incident with Matron Cox when she was ten.

It entered Sarah's mind, and not for the first time, that it was funny how things worked out. Who would have thought the explosion that wrecked her life then and made her grow up overnight would carry the seeds that, growing and flowering, would encourage her to follow her own star? Because she couldn't have left Maggie all alone in Sunderland, she just couldn't have done it. But she hadn't had to, Florrie was with her. And the two women's friendship had begun that day ten years ago . . .

She had still been very ill with the pneumonia that had nearly snuffed out her life – the result of her attempted escape from Hatfield – when Maggie had asked if Florrie could come to see her in the Sunderland infirmary. She hadn't wanted her to but she had said yes anyway, because Maggie had indicated Florrie wanted to apologize for the part she had played in her troubles, and she had been curious to see the Mother Shawe she knew saying sorry to anyone – especially to her. But as Florrie had stood by the side of her bed, she had hardly recognized her old enemy in the white-faced, broken woman looking down at her, and it had seemed natural to hold out her hand when Florrie had falteringly asked her forgiveness. That the moment had been portentous hadn't been clear at the time, but it had begun a steady metamorphosis in Florrie that had transformed not only their relationship, but also Florrie's with Maggie and Rebecca.

As the taxi bumped over a large rut in the road it jerked her back to the present, and to the taxi driver saying, 'This Lady Harris. One of the top nobs, is she?'

'Yes, I suppose so. Her main home is in the country.'

Sarah didn't feel it was quite right to discuss her employer with a stranger, but he didn't seem to notice her reticence as he said, 'How the other half live, eh? Don't know they're born, some of 'em. Mind you, there's some that are all right, I'm not saying they're all the same, but most of the folks round these parts counted themselves lucky if their place was still standing at the end of the war. Old Hitler weren't too particular where he dropped his bombs, I can tell you. I don't know about your Lady Harris, but there were a good few who nipped off to their country mansions and saw the war out behind velvet curtains. They say money can't buy health but I don't know so much.'

'No.' Sarah nodded sympathetically but made no further comment.

'What do your family think about you moving down here then? Bet they weren't too keen?' The eyes in the mirror flashed over the beautiful face and slim body – she was a looker if ever he'd seen one.

'They didn't mind.' Her family. Well, Maggie and Florrie and Rebecca were the nearest she'd got to a family, and they hadn't minded, although she knew Rebecca in particular would miss her badly. But she spent a good deal of each day at Maggie's house now Maggie had given up working. Not that it was Maggie's house; it was Florrie who paid the rent. And it wasn't a house either, just the downstairs of one, but since Florrie had got the job of laundry manageress at the Sunderland infirmary three years before, enabling her and Maggie to move out of

Hatfield, the two women had never been happier.

'Didn't mind, eh? Well, times are changing that's for sure. You can't expect women to do men's jobs while there's a war on, and then be content to sit at home minding the kids and getting the dinner, can you?' He sounded as if that's exactly what he did expect. 'Mind you, I tell you straight, if my old lady decided to hop it every mornin' there'd be fireworks. Not that I don't think women aren't capable . . .'

Sarah let him ramble on, putting in the odd monosyllable when necessary as she gazed out of the window. Her family. Why, after all this time, did it still hurt so much? A few casually spoken words and all her fine clothes and carefully cultivated composure went out of the window, reducing her to a ten-year-old child inside. Her face stared back at her from the glass, her eyes expressing something that caused her to look quickly away. But just because she had taken this step it didn't mean the dream of finding her mother one day was finished with. Sunderland was only a train ride away, and this didn't have to be for ever – it was up to her. It was all up to her.

''Ere we are then, love. Nineteen Emery Place. You make yourself known, an' I'll bring your case. Feels like you've got a baby elephant in there.'

He was trying to be kind and Sarah forced a smile in response, even as a dart of panic sent her blood racing. She must be mad, coming here like this. This wasn't Sunderland, and Lady Harris wasn't Mrs Roberts. She had always felt years older than her former employer – aeons – and it had given her an edge she'd been grateful for at the time, but there was nothing girlish or immature about Lady Harris.

She had learnt as she'd gone along at the Robertses, and no one, least of all her young mistress, had been aware of any shortcomings. But here . . .

'All right, love?' She was aware the taxi driver had opened

her door and was peering at her, his leathery face slightly perplexed, and it was on the tip of her tongue to tell him to drive round the block again to give her some time to find her courage, but the certain something inside, that had drawn her to London in the first place, wouldn't let her. And then the door to the large, imposing, double-fronted terraced house opened, and the trim little maid she had seen on her one and only visit stood framed in the doorway.

Well, in for a penny, in for a pound. It was one of Maggie's pet sayings and perfectly suited to the moment as she climbed out of the big black cab, walking across the pavement and into the small railed front garden, before mounting the eight or so white scrubbed steps to the front door where the maid was waiting. Little did they know this wasn't her, this calm, well-dressed woman in the neat suit and smart shoes; inside she was scared to death she had bitten off more than she could chew. But Lady Harris had chosen her from all the other applicants for the post because she had convinced her prospective employer she was up to the task. *And she was*. She took a deep, silent pull of air. She would make sure she was, even if she had to work twenty-four hours a day. The alternative – staying in Sunderland for another few years at a mundane sort of job, or worse, doing what Rebecca had done and marrying the first man who asked her – held no attraction whatsoever. She wanted to see life, experience new things, *feel* them . . .

'Miss Brown?' The maid was pretty and fresh-faced. 'Lady Harris is expecting you, she's in the morning room.'

'Thank you.'

The taxi driver had followed her up the steps and now placed her case and cloth bag just inside the large square hall – which was as big as the rooms the helpers had been expected to live in at Hatfield – and she turned to him, feeling as though she was saying goodbye to the last normal person in the world. 'Thank you very much, you've been very kind. What do I owe you?'

'Five bob'll cover it, love.' He pocketed the five shillings, and the sixpence tip, and then he was gone.

The morning room was smaller than the ornate drawing room where she had had her interview, but undeniably grand, the long velvet drapes at the wide bay window and thick carpet the same shade of dull pink, and the upholstered couches and two high-backed winged chairs of the finest quality.

Lady Harris was sitting at her writing bureau in a far recess of the room, but rose immediately at Sarah's entrance, her smile of welcome going some way to quieten the legion of butterflies that were fluttering madly in Sarah's stomach. 'Miss Brown, how nice to see you again. I trust you had a pleasant journey?' It was for all the world as though she was greeting a visiting acquaintance, and this impression was strengthened when she added, 'I've asked Peggy to serve us tea in here. Why don't you come and sit by the fire, you must be exhausted.'

The fire, set in a deep high fireplace with an exquisitely carved wooden surround, was piled high with blazing logs, and as Lady Harris led the way to the two chairs, pulled comfortingly close to the warmth, Sarah found herself studying the bright little birdlike creature in front of her, the snow white hair and tiny bent frame belying the perkiness that would have sat well on a woman half her employer's age.

'Do sit down, my dear, and try to relax.' The keen gaze was understanding. 'It must have been quite a wrench to leave all your friends and everything that was familiar, and come down here? I like the sort of spirit that takes life by the horns and wrestles it into shape, and I recognized it in you, you know. My dear husband used to say I was far too independent for my time, but he was a good man, a very good man. Did you know I was a suffragette?' she added with surprising suddenness.

'A suffragette?' Sarah was too startled to hide her amazement.

'Oh, it was quite a scandal at the time.' This was accompanied by a quiet chuckle that told Sarah Lady Harris had loved every minute. 'Of course poor Emmeline had the worst of it. Men can be quite hateful when they're threatened, can't they, my dear? I'm still in touch with Christabel and Sylvia and they are very much their mother's daughters. Yes, I like boldness, when accompanied by a desire to rise above injustice and intolerance on behalf of our fellow man. I feel it is that which takes us above the animal kingdom.'

What a remarkable woman. Sarah stared into the bright brown eyes set in flesh that was parchment thin. She had thought so at their first meeting, though that had been formal, unlike now; even then something of Lady Harris's indomitable spirit had shone through.

She was just trying to think of something to say when the door opened and the maid entered, pushing a tea trolley complete with silver tea service and plates holding an assortment of small wafer-thin sandwiches and a large fruit cake, that must have used up a week's rations all by itself.

'I hope you have a healthy appetite, my dear?' Lady Harris smiled at her before raising her eyes and saying, 'That's all right, Peggy, we'll see to ourselves.'

'Very good, ma'am.'

Sarah had served tea in the Roberts household many times when Mrs Roberts had had her bridge afternoons and 'good works' meetings, as she had termed them, and now, as Lady Harris smiled again and said, 'Won't you be mother, my dear,' she felt on safe ground. After serving Lady Harris her tea with lemon – Mr Roberts had liked his tea that way and the lemon squeezer held no mystery for her – she helped herself to a cup with milk, but found she could manage no more than one salmon sandwich and a small piece of the cake, the nerves that had gripped her making her stomach tight. Nevertheless, something had settled in her spirit and the brief panic was over. There was no one to smooth the way here, it was up to her whether she sank or swam, and by golly, she intended to swim.

'Now.' They had finished tea and Peggy had wheeled the trolley away with a shy smile at Sarah. 'I think I fully explained your duties three weeks ago?' Lady Harris said quietly. 'Is there anything further you wish to ask me?'

'No, I don't think so, Lady Harris.'

'In that case I think it opportune to tell you a little about myself and the family, and the callers you might expect. As you know I normally spend most of the year on the estate' – the estate being a large, fifteen-bedroomed country house in Kent with several hundred acres and a farm – 'but of necessity I need to be in London several months of the year, and I prefer home comforts these days.'

She smiled and Sarah smiled back.

'However, I have to say that as I get increasingly older these visits are endured rather than enjoyed, but no matter, no matter.' She shook her head at herself. 'My son and his wife and family live at Fenwick most of the time; Geoffrey took over some of my husband's affairs on his death, but if they come to town they reside here. My widowed sister visits, but rarely, and my niece will occasionally stay for a week or two. Other than that we are normally a quiet little household of four. You met Hilda, my cook, on your previous visit?'

'Yes, I did, she seems very nice.'

'Oh, Hilda is the guardian of my digestion: where I go, she goes. Peggy is responsible for most of the household chores, but when the house is full I would expect you to take on light duties, perhaps arranging the flowers, things like that? The work is not arduous, but I do like things to run smoothly, I cannot abide fuss.'

'No, Lady Harris.'

She stared back into the bright little face, the crackling fire and the swiftly darkening sky outside adding a cosiness to the beautiful room which had been missing before, and then was more than a little surprised when her employer leant forward and touched her hand lightly as she said, 'Smile, child, smile. I'm not such an ogre when you get to know me. Victoria Roberts said you were discreet, loyal, trustworthy – a tower of strength was her final summing up, I think, and I am a great believer in personal recommendation. I've known George Roberts for a good many years and he is nobody's fool. He too spoke very highly of you when I asked him to endorse his wife's reference. Now, perhaps you would ring for Peggy to show you to your room, and if there is anything you require please don't hesitate to ask her.'

And then, as Sarah rose, she added, 'On the evenings I don't have guests I wonder if you would join me for dinner? It's unconventional, I know, but I do not care to eat alone and I enjoy the sort of spirited conversation the young are so adept at providing. Besides which' – again the round eyes twinkled – 'I rather enjoy flouting convention.'

Sarah looked down at her in stupefied silence before managing to say, 'Thank you, Lady Harris. I'd like that.'

'Good.' Once Peggy appeared in answer to the bell cord at the side of the fireplace, Lady Harris rose briskly to her feet, her thin tiny body in its starched black dress trimmed with white lace seeming to spring upwards with childlike vigour, and she was seated at the bureau again before Sarah had had time to leave the room.

Sarah had seen her accommodation three weeks before, but

with no more than a cursory glance as Peggy had shown her round the enormous town house, which boasted six guest bedrooms, besides the servants' quarters, and now, as she followed the young girl along the hall to the back staircase which led to the top floor and attics, she found herself marvelling at her good fortune. She doubted if there was another employer like Lady Harris in the whole of London, she thought bemusedly, Maggie's last words to her suddenly clear in her mind.

'You're doin' the right thing, lass. Never look a gift horse in the mouth 'cos sure as eggs are eggs you won't get a second chance. Look how that Mrs Roberts went on an' on about how good the old lady was an' all, an' she wouldn't put you wrong – thought the world of you, she did. Have a go, lass, you can't lose by it.'

'Here we are.' They had reached the top landing – the main staircase, with its thick red carpeting and open banisters some fifteen yards away – and now Peggy opened the first door on their right where Sarah saw her suitcase had already been placed in readiness for her arrival. 'Lady Harris said to light the fire this morning so it should be nice and warm.'

'Thank you.' Sarah smiled at the maid, who couldn't have been more than fifteen or sixteen, before saying, 'Did you carry my case up here? I'd have helped you if you'd waited.'

'That's all right, miss, I'm stronger than I look. Wiry, my mum says.'

'Oh, call me Sarah.'

'I can't.' Peggy looked askance at the suggestion. 'Cook says for me to call you miss.'

'Oh.' Her first faux pas, Sarah thought wryly, but no doubt not her last. 'Well thank you anyway, I know it weighs a ton.'

'Cook said to ask if you want to come down to the kitchen when you're ready and she'll run through some things with you before she starts on the dinner.'

'Yes, of course. In about twenty minutes?'

'Right, miss, I'll tell her.'

Left alone, Sarah glanced about her. The room she had had at the Robertses would have fitted into the space several times over, and she knew the door on the far left of this room led to her own private bathroom, and yet for all its largeness it wasn't intimidating. Perhaps it was the fire? Lady Harris had already told her over their tea that the trees on the Fenwick estate provided much of their fuel, and that the rationing which affected most of the country wasn't a problem, but she hadn't expected to have such a splendid fire in her own room.

She glanced at the roaring blaze which was shedding a soft pink glow over the furnishings, the light from the large standard lamp in one corner and the muted glow from the darkening sky outside the window at the other end of the room casting grey shadows here and there.

Her bed, a small double with a brass headboard and a thick, tapestry-like woven bedcover, was at the far end near the window and bathroom, and where she was standing now was almost like a small sitting room, complete with two easy chairs, a small bookcase, a big fitted cupboard which she took to be the wardrobe, and a little occasional table. The furniture wasn't new but it was highly polished, if a little battered, and the large square of carpet in the middle of the room, and the long drapes at the window, made it luxurious by Sarah's standards.

It was like a little house. She sat down suddenly in one of the chairs as her legs gave way and emotion flooded her chest. Her first real home. And she was glad, oh she was, she was glad but . . . she was nervous too, nervous that all this would be snatched away and she would return to being Sarah Brown again, instead of Miss Brown, housekeeper to the illustrious Lady Harris.

She shut her eyes tight, pressing one fist on top of the other into the hollow between her breasts as she swayed back and forth with a mixture of excitement and apprehension before the realization of what she was doing brought her upright, the voice in her mind saying, Stop it, that's enough of that, you're as good as anyone else and don't you forget it.

It was something she had told herself every day of her life since the time she had run away from Hatfield, only to be ignominiously returned the same night, and it had only recently occurred to her to question why she still had to say it ten years on.

Not that things hadn't been better under the new matron for her remaining years at Hatfield; they had, much better, and she had sensed most of the Mothers were secretly relieved that Matron Cox was safely locked away in the lunatic asylum where she could no longer terrorize children and staff alike. Her worry of being supplanted in Rebecca's affections, brought about by her low physical and mental state after Matron's attack, had been groundless too; from the day she had returned to Hatfield Home after her stay in the Sunderland infirmary, she and Rebecca had been as close as ever. So why did she feel so adrift, alone, at times?

She rose now, walking to the end of the room where a tall thin rectangular mirror had been fixed to the wall one side of the bed, and stood quietly gazing at her reflection before moving closer, her eyes searching the delicate features for long moments. There was no vanity in her inspection, and she couldn't have explained to anyone why this scrutiny was a regular practice, but she just felt she needed to *know* each contour, each eyelash.

When she turned away from the mirror and faced the far door again her head was drooping, but within seconds her shoulders were back, her posture straight, and her chin uplifted, as she prepared to face the world outside this little oasis.

Chapter Six

There is always a serpent in Eden, and when Sarah came face to face with Sir Geoffrey Harris, a few weeks after she had taken up the position as housekeeper to his mother, she recognized the tall broad man in front of her as such.

She had acquired the habit of an afternoon sojourn in the small but pleasant wooded park across the street to Emery Place, often taking the opportunity to sit down and read the latest letter from Maggie and Florrie or Rebecca in the peace and quiet of the fresh air. On this particular day she had almost fallen into the hall on her return to the house, a gust of wind from the tempestuous November day helping her through the doorway and whipping the envelope containing the letter she had received that morning from Rebecca out of her hands.

'Dear me, dear me.' Sir Geoffrey had been about to enter the drawing room but swung round at her boisterous entry, and as Sarah quickly smoothed a few tendrils of hair into place which the wind had teased from the confining chignon at the nape of her neck, he bent down and retrieved the envelope. 'Here.' His speckled eyes slid over her flushed face as he handed her the letter. 'You must be the reputable Miss Brown I've been hearing about. You came highly recommended. I am Sir Geoffrey Harris.'

'How do you do, Sir Geoffrey.' She had expected Sir

89

Geoffrey and Lady Margaret to arrive the following day – the family had seats in Westminster Abbey for Princess Elizabeth and the Duke of Edinburgh's wedding three days hence on the twentieth of November – but they had obviously decided to arrive a day early from the country. She was finding it an effort to maintain her polite smile; she hadn't liked the patronizing note in Sir Geoffrey's voice, but it was more the way he was looking at her that bothered her. Not that she wasn't used to men looking at her. Maggie had told her long ago, just after her thirteenth birthday when the changes in her body had come to full fruition, that as long as they just looked she had no cause for worry. But this was different somehow. There was a quality to the heavy-lidded gaze that made her uneasy, something almost . . . reptilian, and the pale, full-lipped face and big heavy figure were faintly repulsive.

'Miss Brown?' As Lady Harris called from the drawing room she walked quickly towards the open door, and she noted Sir Geoffrey turned to allow her to pass him just a fraction too late, his shoulder brushing the side of her bosom under her coat, the contact slight, but – she felt uncomfortably sure – intentional.

When she entered the room she saw Lady Harris was not alone. A plain thin woman, whom Sarah took to be Sir Geoffrey's wife, was seated next to her employer on one of the blue velvet couches which had been drawn close to the blazing fire, and two equally thin and plain children, a boy and a girl, were sitting in one of the deep-cushioned window-seats which overlooked the street. All three glanced at her as she came into the room, the children without interest, the woman with keen regard.

'Miss Brown, my son and his family have arrived a little early.' Lady Harris's voice was expressionless but Sarah felt sure she was put out. 'Perhaps you would be so good as to advise cook that there will be five for dinner? And could you ask Peggy to light a fire in the appropriate bedrooms. She will know which ones.'

'Certainly, Lady Harris.' Sarah was aware Sir Geoffrey had come into the room behind her but he hadn't moved into her vision, and now, as she turned to leave, it was to see him holding the door for her.

It wasn't until she was in the hall again and the sigh left her in a silent whoosh that she realized she had been holding her breath as she passed Sir Geoffrey, and now she sped along the passageway to the kitchen as though she had wings on her heels, and not at all like the sedate, composed Miss Brown the household had seen thus far.

Peggy and Hilda were setting the tea trolley when she entered, the former unusually subdued and the latter tight-lipped, and it was Peggy who said, 'Do they want the fires lighting now, miss?'

Sarah nodded, turning to Hilda and saying, 'It will mean five for dinner, Hilda. I think Lady Harris was annoyed Sir Geoffrey didn't let her know they were coming earlier than planned,' before she added, 'Lady Harris said you would know which rooms the family use, Peggy?'

'Oh yes, I'll see to it, miss.'

Peggy left the room as though she was glad to escape, and Sarah raised her eyebrows at Hilda when the two of them were alone. In the few weeks she had been in Lady Harris's employ the two of them had become friends, in spite of the cook being as old and idiosyncratic as her mistress.

'I've just warned her to behave herself.' Hilda answered the silent enquiry with a frown and a disapproving sniff as she added, 'Bit too free and easy in some quarters, if you get my meaning.'

'I don't think I do.'

'You've met Sir Geoffrey?' Sarah nodded. 'And his wife?' She nodded again. 'And Peggy is young, very young, and impressionable.' Hilda's chin went down into her neck as she eyed Sarah.

'You mean she . . .' Sarah didn't quite know how to continue.

'Let's just say I've known Sir Geoffrey since he was in his cradle and he's always had an eye for the ladies, only lately it's the younger the better. Of course Lady Harris is blind to any goings-on, Sir Geoffrey is her weak spot, always has been, but his father used to keep him in check pretty well. It was he who insisted on the marriage some nine years ago now, a good match to the only daughter of Lord and Lady Havistock of Cheshire, you know?'

Sarah didn't, but she nodded again anyway.

'I think he thought marriage would calm Sir Geoffrey down, and of course the association of the two families wasn't to be sneezed at either, but it took a while to bring Sir Geoffrey up to scratch.' Hilda's voice was reflective. 'I felt a bit sorry for him at the time to be honest, I mean she's no oil painting is she, but I have to say that of the two I think he got the best of the deal. According to the staff at Fenwick there are high jinks at times with his philandering.'

'But doesn't Lady Harris disapprove?' Sarah couldn't imagine her principled, idealistic employer countenancing such behaviour from her own son.

'He pulls the wool over her eyes most of the time,' Hilda said shortly, gesturing with her hand as they heard Peggy's scurrying footsteps in the passage outside. 'Dab hand at it, he is. Had a lot of practice.'

Over the next three days – busy, hectic days as far as Sarah was concerned, as Lady Harris and the family prepared for the royal wedding – Sarah often mused on Hilda's words as she went about her daily business and observed the family whilst doing so.

That Sir Geoffrey fooled his mother was in no doubt; she clearly worshipped the very ground her son walked on. His wife was a different matter, however; Sarah could feel the other woman's eyes on her every minute they were in the same room, and it wasn't pleasant. That Peggy felt the same was of little comfort. The girl was young and silly, and if Hilda was to be believed, had been both flattered and overawed by Sir Geoffrey's attention on his last visit, no doubt attracting Lady Margaret's ever-suspicious gaze in the process. But Sarah couldn't help feeling indignant at being tarred with the same tawdry brush.

She said as much to Hilda on the evening of the royal wedding day, when the two of them were alone in the kitchen enjoying a quiet cup of tea. Peggy had gone to bed early, tired out with the furore of the day, and the family had just retired for the night, equally exhausted. It had been a wonderful day for them all, but Sarah had a sneaking suspicion that she and Peggy and Hilda had had more fun than the family, in spite of their prestige seats in the Abbey.

Lady Harris had given them all permission to go into the heart of London straight after breakfast, where much of the crowd who thronged the Mall and down Whitehall fifty deep had slept out overnight despite the cold and the rain, and they had all cheered wildly and waved little Union Jack cloth flags as the King and his daughter had driven by on their way to Westminster Abbey. The beautiful tasselled and bedecked Irish state coach, escorted by the Household Cavalry resplendent in scarlet tunics on black horses, had been breathtaking, and she and Peggy had even caught a glimpse of the bride's ivory dress embroidered with flowers of beads and pearls, and her tulle veil hung from a circlet of diamonds, as the coach had driven past with Princess Elizabeth waving to the crowds.

A group of pearly kings and queens, salt-of-the-earth cockneys in their full regalia, had made way for them to squeeze to the front of the crowd as the coach had approached, although Hilda, fearing the crush, had stayed at the back. And then, once the happy pair were married and had emerged from the Abbey to half of London cheering and waving, there had been dancing in the streets with roast chestnut stalls and other vendors doing a roaring trade. Sarah had bought a decorated mug each for Maggie, Florrie and Rebecca, along with a little flag and beautifully painted plate with Prince Philip and Princess Elizabeth's heads on, entwined in a heart-shaped ribbon with the date.

Yes, it had been a wonderful day, but once back at Emery Place she had again been conscious of Lady Margaret's watchful gaze, and it had irked her more than ever after the magic of the last few hours.

'It's since that do with little Alice, the kitchen maid at Fenwick, that she's been like this,' Hilda said in answer to Sarah's protest that she hadn't *done* anything to incur Lady Margaret's obvious mistrust. 'Lady Margaret isn't daft, she puts on a brave face most of the time but she knows what's what all right. They sleep separately since the Alice affair anyway.'

'But hasn't that made Lady Harris ask questions, if nothing else?'

'Probably, but mothers tend to believe what they want to believe about their precious offspring, don't they?'

'I wouldn't know.' She smiled as she said it, her voice light, but the familiar pain stabbed swiftly and it was to combat that more than anything else that she said, 'But Peggy is such a child in many ways, far younger than her years, and there is something about him I don't like, Hilda. I'm worried.'

'Tell her then, she'll probably take more notice of you. She clearly considers me an old fuddy-duddy who's out to spoil her fun, and I have to say my patience with the silly girl is wearing thin. If there's one thing I don't need at my time of life, it's all this aggravation, and there'll be hell to pay if Lady Margaret finds out about any carryings-on. Have a word with her, Sarah.' Hilda nodded at her encouragingly. 'The sooner the better.'

Sarah pondered on Hilda's words over the next day or two. She didn't want to put ideas into Peggy's head, give solid form to any notions that might be nothing more than her imagination. It was one thing for the fifteen-year-old maid to be flattered, and quite another for her to do anything concrete about it should the opportunity present itself. For all she and Hilda knew Peggy was merely indulging in a spot of harmless hero-worship or something similar. She was disabused of this idea, and her mind made up for her in the process, on the morning of the sixth day of Sir Geoffrey's visit, when she happened to be on the second floor early in the morning taking fresh towels along to the children's rooms, one of them having been sick in the night.

She was just passing Sir Geoffrey's suite when the door opened and a flushed and dishevelled Peggy exited, her cap askew and her eyes bright; but it was more the look on the girl's face as she saw her that convinced Sarah something would have to be said.

'Oh, hallo, miss.' After swiftly closing the door behind her, Peggy said, 'I was just seeing to Sir Geoffrey's fire. He – he rang down to say it had gone out.'

'Did he?' Sarah's voice was cool and her glance full of meaning as it passed from Peggy's hot face along to the end of the corridor where Lady Margaret's rooms were situated.

'Yes. I'd better scoot, miss, Cook wanted me to start the boiler—'

'I would like to have a word with you later, Peggy.' Her voice was still cool and she didn't smile as she added, 'About lighting Sir Geoffrey's fire.'

'I . . . I had to come if he asked, didn't I?' For the first time a touch of bravado showed through. 'I mean—'

'Of course you have to attend to your duties, Peggy.' Sarah allowed a slight pause before she added, 'And I would still like that word later. Now, hadn't you better see to the boiler?'

After an ensuing few seconds of staring at each other, Peggy's eyes dropped away, her voice tearful as she said, 'Yes, miss.'

Oh, there was trouble brewing here. Sarah's stomach was churning as she hurried along the richly carpeted landing to the children's rooms. What on earth was that silly little thing thinking of? Couldn't she see what sort of a man Sir Geoffrey was? What if it had been Lady Margaret on the landing? What then? Well, she'd lay it on hot and strong when she spoke to her later. It was up to Peggy to nip this in the bud, and if Sir Geoffrey didn't accept defeat gracefully she'd speak to him herself. She had made it very clear over the last few days exactly how she expected to be treated, and although she was aware he didn't like it he seemed to have acknowledged her repudiation of any familiarity without rancour. Oh, Peggy, *Peggy* . . . Her irritation was high as she replaced the used towels with fresh ones and checked on the children, both of whom still seemed unwell.

When Lady Harris and the children's mother both succumbed to nausea later that morning the doctor was called.

'Food poisoning.' The diagnosis was immediate, and as he straightened from examining Lady Harris, the doctor said, with a smile at Sarah, 'Please tell me they ate out somewhere yesterday, or Hilda will have my guts for garters.'

'Yes, they did.'

She smiled back as Lady Harris weakly expostulated from the bed, 'I can still speak for myself, Charles, I'm not dead yet.'

'Not for a long time I hope, Geraldine.' He winked at Sarah, his eyes twinkling, before turning back to his patient.

How was it, Sarah silently asked herself, that one man could smile and wink and you would know immediately there was nothing more behind his friendliness than a desire to make you feel comfortable and included, and another, with just one glance, could make your flesh creep? And Sir Geoffrey made her flesh creep, oh, he did, and it was that more than anything else that made her determined to talk to the young fresh-faced maid who had her whole life in front of her.

Unfortunately, with four invalids in the house – Sir Geoffrey not having partaken of the salmon starter the day before which seemed to have caused all the trouble – the opportunity to talk to Peggy didn't arise, the staff being run off their feet as the patients got worse before they got better. However, by late evening all four were quietly sleeping, exhausted by the unpleasant manifestations of the virulent bug, and as Sarah sat in a state of semi-stupor in the kitchen, having sent Hilda and Peggy, both asleep on their feet, off to bed some minutes before, she found her mind wouldn't let her body – tired as it was – rest quietly.

She would have to talk to Peggy before she went to sleep. She nodded to herself in the quiet of the night. She wouldn't get a wink of sleep otherwise, not with this uneasy feeling gripping her so strongly. It was clear that Peggy had been hopelessly dazzled by a title and the allure of a few affectionate, and no doubt well used trite phrases, because she was sure that's all it was. The little maid was nothing more than a young nubile body to the man who would use her to service him and then discard her without another thought.

Sarah shook her head at the prospect, then rose wearily from the chair. Peggy wouldn't appreciate being told the truth. What fifteen-year-old would? Although how any female could let that man touch her of her own free will . . . Her lips drew back from her teeth at the thought. She'd rather die, she would really.

After leaving the kitchen she checked all the doors and windows on the ground floor, her last job each night, before switching off the lights and slowly ascending the staircase to the upper floor. She wasn't looking forward to the coming confrontation. From Peggy's attitude that morning it was clear the girl was flirting with danger, and just as clearly didn't want to admit it. But apart from concern for Peggy herself, it was part of her job to control the other staff, be there one or twenty-one, and she couldn't shirk her responsibilities.

She passed the second floor on which the family's rooms were situated and on reaching the third floor paused, taking a deep breath before walking past her rooms to Peggy's small bedroom, which was sandwiched between her quarters on one side and Hilda's on the other.

The landing was lit by the weak glow of one low-watt bulb almost directly outside Peggy's room, and as she raised her hand to knock she paused again, her stomach churning, before a small voice inside her mind that was all Maggie said, 'Come on, lass, what are you waitin' for? You don't earn your wage with just the arty-farty side of things, so get on with it,' and brought her clenched knuckles lightly against the wood. When there was no answer she waited for a few moments before knocking again, more sharply this time, only to stand irresolutely for a full minute more.

Was Peggy asleep already? It was possible, she supposed; the day had been a long one. But then again the next one might be just as long with the family still unwell, and she needed to talk to her *now*. The decision made, she knocked once more before turning the handle of the door slowly, stepping into the room quietly only to find it quite empty. The possibility of Peggy having gone to talk to Hilda flashed into her mind, only to be dismissed as quickly, Hilda's muted snores from the adjoining room proving the elderly cook was dead to the world.

Then where was she? Sarah's eyes screwed up as another reason for Peggy's absence dawned, and she leant against the closed door in the darkness of the room, her hand coming across her mouth at the thought. She wouldn't. She *wouldn't*. Not here, in the house, with his wife just down the corridor ... would she? Surely even Sir Geoffrey, licentious as he was, wouldn't take such a risk? The thought held no conviction.

But she was going ahead of herself here, of course she was. Peggy could be in the bathroom just down the landing, this tiny boxroom not having the facilities she and Hilda enjoyed. The possibility brought her sagging with relief before she turned and opened the door, stepping into the corridor again and making her way to the bathroom. It was empty.

What was she going to do? Oh, what was she going to do? She stood on the threshold of the bathroom for long minutes, her arms about her waist as she swayed back and forth, her head buzzing. Part of her – a big part of her – wanted to scurry back to her room and shut the door on it all, put her head under the bedclothes and pretend what she knew was happening wasn't real. But she was responsible for the way Peggy conducted herself whilst in Lady Harris's employ. Her employer had made that very clear at her initial interview, both with regard to Peggy's duties within the house and the young girl's moral conduct without. The fact that corruption might come from within clearly hadn't occurred to Lady

Harris. Well, it hadn't to her either, Sarah thought miserably. But with Lady Harris and his wife and children all around, Sir Geoffrey must be mad, or supremely arrogant, or both. Whatever, she had to do something about it. What if one of the invalids needed assistance and went to his rooms? Little William, or Constance?

That possibility brought Sarah spinning round and down the landing within seconds, and once she was on the second floor, the thick piled carpet silencing any sound, she made her way to Sir Geoffrey's room still without any clear idea of what she was going to do. She could stand guard and grab Peggy when she came out, although how she could explain her presence if one of the family happened along she didn't know; or perhaps knock and ask for Peggy to accompany her back to her room, embarrassing as that would be? There was even the chance, faint admittedly, that Peggy hadn't yet fully committed herself, that she would be in time to stop the maid making such a terrible mistake, if she took the bull by the horns and knocked. Fifteen, *fifteen years old*, and Sir Geoffrey nearly old enough to be her grandfather, let alone her father.

She could never really explain afterwards what made her try the handle of the door. Perhaps it was some sixth sense, a feminine intuition that picked up something from the atmosphere within, despite there being no noise. What she did know was that as she approached the door to Sir Geoffrey's rooms the hairs on the back of her neck rose and her flesh prickled, a sense of urgency overcoming her. Once inside, she walked through the small sitting room to the door beyond without pausing, although it was pitch black except for a faint beam of light from under the door leading to the bedroom and en suite. She turned the handle gently and the door opened the merest crack, but immediately she could hear thick grunting, the sound a pig might make when rooting for food, mingled with gasping sobs and the low twang of bedsprings.

'No, no, please—'

It was Peggy's voice, followed immediately by Sir Geoffrey saying, 'A little tease, a little tease, eh? Well this is what you get for leading a man on, my girl. Little whore, that's all you are, and don't you forget it. You can't tell me you didn't know what was in store—'

Sarah's thrusting open of the door and subsequent spring into the room seemed to occur in one motion, so violent was her entry, and at the sight of Sir Geoffrey's fat white buttocks pounding a spreadeagled Peggy into the mattress her momentum didn't stop. She had grasped his thinning hair, pulling him savagely backwards and off the young girl beneath him, before either of the pair on the bed realized what was happening, and as his face came into view she realized that Peggy had put up quite a fight at the end, whatever had gone on before. The scratches on his face were deep and fierce.

As Sir Geoffrey arched backwards, his head making loud contact with the carved wooden surround at the foot of the bed and his naked body, with its grotesque erection, flailing helplessly, Sarah pulled the stunned and shaking Peggy up into a sitting position, noticing the blood on the bottom sheet from her brutal deflowering with a spurt of white hot anger as she tried to pull some covers around the weeping girl.

Sir Geoffrey was on his feet now, his face livid, and making no effort to hide his nakedness, he spat, 'What the *hell* do you think you're doing, woman, have you gone mad? What gives you the right to come in here—'

'Rape? Reason enough, don't you think?'

'Oh no. No, no, no, you aren't going to try that one on me. She came here of her own free will, I didn't have to drag her screaming and kicking.'

'He said, he said—' Peggy was crying so much she was barely coherent. 'He said that I was special, that he just wanted to talk to me and make me understand what I meant to him. I never wanted—'

'Did you? Did you say that?' Sarah hissed furiously, as Sir Geoffrey, as though becoming aware of his nakedness for the first time, grabbed his dressing gown from a chair. 'Did you trick her here and then force her?'

Sir Geoffrey swore, crudely and with great venom, before narrowing his eyes as he said, 'Keep your voice down or so help me I'll silence you myself.'

'*Did you force her?*'

'She wanted it. Damn it all, they all say no, don't they. But she knew why she was here all right, they grow up early where she comes from—'

'*She is barely fifteen years old.*'

'There's plenty been on their backs for years at that age.'

'What are you?' She didn't care that he was her employer's spoilt and adored only son, or that he was the gentry, the upper class, with wealth and privilege and power behind him. As she glared into the turkey-red face, suffused with colour from frustration and rage, Sarah saw only the man himself, and her contempt and disgust was written on her face for him to read. 'A pervert? A sick excuse for a man, who fights the passing years with a taste for younger and younger flesh?'

It was so near the truth that the man in front of her was silent for a moment, but only a moment.

'What's the matter, girl? Put out because you weren't invited too? Well, I've nothing against three in a bed, enjoyed myself like that more than once.' It was said softly but with great emphasis. 'Now if you're not going to join us, you can get out, and if you know what's good for you you'll keep your mouth shut about this night's business. I can make sure you never get another day's work in your life.'

'Don't threaten me, Sir Geoffrey.' She stood up from her sitting position on the bed where she had been holding the half-swooning Peggy against her chest, and faced him squarely. Her voice was very level as she said, 'I'm going to take Peggy to her room, and if I have anything to do with it the matter won't rest here. I came here tonight with the intention of sparing your mother any concern, but now I realize that was a fruitless endeavour. She needs to know what her precious son is before you use your wealth and connections to attack any more young girls—'

'*How dare you.*' Sir Geoffrey Harris had never had anyone talk to him the way this little chit of a housekeeper was doing, and he couldn't have been more astounded if she had suddenly sprouted horns and a forked tail. 'You cross me and you'll rue the day you were born, I'm warning you.'

She made no answer whatsoever, merely staring at him with a composure that was all the more damning for the scorn at the heart of it.

'Do you hear me?' He took a step towards her now, spittle gathering at the sides of his mouth as he ground out, '*Do you hear me?* If my mother, or my wife, hears anything of what's happened here tonight I shall know who's to blame.' And he had thought she was a prim piece, reserved, knowing her place. It had excited him, the thought of gradually breaking down her resistance over the next few visits until he had her where he wanted her. He'd thought of jewellery, perhaps a nice pair of earrings to start with, to soften her up a bit. She was older than he normally went for – the last couple had been younger than Peggy – but there had been something about this one that made his loins ache. And now? He'd ruin her, if it was the last thing he did, and when she was broken, grovelling in the dust, he'd take her and use her and have her crawling at his feet.

When she still made no reply beyond bending down and

drawing the still weeping Peggy to her feet, wrapping one of the bed covers round the shaking girl as she did so, the rage that gripped him created a red mist before his eyes. As his fist came out to punch her in the face she amazed him for the umpteenth time that night by lifting her knee and hitting him a blow between the legs that felled him to the ground like a log, a shrill scream escaping his lips as he writhed and groaned at her feet, clutching himself as he felt the pain tear him apart.

Sarah wasn't surprised to see Lady Margaret, closely followed by Lady Harris, burst from their rooms as she led Peggy onto the landing, and to Lady Margaret's query of 'What's happening, what is it?' she said nothing beyond glancing down at the young maid who was cradled against her. But when the children emerged from their quarters she shut the door of Sir Geoffrey's suite behind her, gesturing their way before she said, 'I think it might be better if you went in to see Sir Geoffrey alone, ma'am.'

'Sarah?'

'I'm sorry, Lady Harris.' As Lady Margaret sent the children back to their rooms with a sharp admonition, she answered her employer's unvoiced question with a weary shake of her head. 'It was Sir Geoffrey you heard, and I think matters are self-explanatory, don't you? As you can see, Peggy is very distressed.'

'Are you suggesting what I think you are suggesting?'

'I'm not *suggesting* anything, Lady Harris.' The old lady's face was imperious and her voice sharp, but Sarah refused to be intimidated, her tone equally sharp. 'The facts speak for themselves.'

'How *dare* you accuse my son—'

And then Lady Harris's voice was cut off as Lady Margaret muttered angrily, 'Oh, open your eyes, Mother-in-law, for goodness' sake. This is not the first time Geoffrey has behaved in such a fashion, and no doubt it will not be the last.'

'*Margaret.*'

'Yes, Margaret. Poor, plain, left-on-the-shelf Margaret.' The other woman's voice was cutting now, with an edge that suggested deeply held-in fury. 'You think I don't know how others see me, Mother-in-law? How your son saw me when he agreed to marry me?'

Lady Margaret was talking as if she was completely unaware of Sarah and Peggy's presence on the landing, and as a sound from inside the room came to their ears, a thud followed by the tinkle of breaking glass, Margaret's back straightened, as though preparing to do battle. 'You talk about rights for women, don't you – social and political change for all the classes? How can you be so – so *hypocritical*?'

'*Margaret.*'

As Lady Harris's eyes flicked to Sarah and Peggy, Sir Geoffrey's wife seemed to grow another few inches in stature, and her face was calm, composed even, as she said flatly, but with a voice heavy with meaning, 'They know all there is to know, Mother-in-law, so stop fooling yourself. One has been molested, if not raped, by your son, and the other has fought off his advances for the last few days whilst aiming to keep matters civil. And I am tired, *tired* of fighting a fight I can never win.'

'Margaret, you're mistaken—'

'No, I am not mistaken. Would that I was.' There was a softness in the younger woman's voice now that could have been pity as she looked into the face of her husband's mother. 'But more shocking than that, I have realized tonight that I no longer care. Times are changing, it is no longer necessary to suffer degradation and humiliation.' She turned now and looked straight at Sarah. 'You will see to her?' She meant

Peggy but didn't acknowledge the young girl by so much as the flicker of an eyelash.

'Yes, ma'am.'

'Thank you, Miss Brown.' Lady Margaret was the noble lady again, stiff and cold, and this façade did not change as she glanced at Lady Harris. 'If you wish to confer with your son that is your prerogative, of course; as for myself, I have no such wish. If you see him you may inform him I shall be leaving in the morning for Cheshire, and I shall take William and Constance with me. Good night, Mother-in-law.'

She walked back along the corridor, stopping before she reached her own rooms and entering those of the children, whereupon she shut the door gently.

'Do you see what you have done?'

It was to Sarah, and not the weeping Peggy, that this remark was directed, and as Sarah opened her mouth to remonstrate, Lady Harris continued, 'I hope you are satisfied with your night's work?'

'Me?' It was so unfair, so ridiculously unfair, that all Sarah could do was gape at the furious little woman in front of her.

'I feel I have harboured a viper in my bosom—'

'Lady Harris, your son has just raped a fifteen-year-old child whom he lured to his room with sweet words and false promises.'

'*How dare you!*'

'I dare because it is true.' Sarah took a long deep breath and prayed for composure. 'Peggy was foolish, very foolish, to put herself in such a vulnerable position, but the blame for this atrocity rests on Sir Geoffrey's shoulders. He raped her and then he tried to attack me when I intervened. That is the truth, Lady Harris, and it is up to you what you do with it.'

She was aware of Lady Harris's open mouth as she turned, with Peggy in the crook of her arm, and walked towards the back staircase, and also that her worthy employer would not appreciate the scapegoat answering back.

It was one thing to further the cause for women's liberation and social change on a general level, quite another when those same principles were called for in one's own household, Sarah thought grimly. Lady Harris was a product of the old class system – a dyed-in-the-wool aristocrat, despite her connections with Emmeline Pankhurst and her daughters. And what was Peggy after all? Merely a servant, and as such, expendable. That, *that* was reality.

Sarah suddenly felt an acute pang of homesickness for Sunderland in general, and Maggie, Florrie and Rebecca in particular, and the feeling persisted long after she had settled Peggy into bed after giving the girl a drink of hot milk containing a sleeping draught, and gone to her own room.

Her mind continued to dwell in the north as she began her nightly toilet, and she admitted to herself that she never felt entirely happy about Rebecca these days, when she had time to think about her friend. Not that married life was a bed of roses for anyone, of course it wasn't. Even the Robertses, contented with each other as they had been, had had the odd hiccup in their relationship, when she had sensed things were strained. But it was more than that with Rebecca . . .

After washing and brushing her teeth, Sarah slipped into her long linen nightdress and climbed into bed, but her troubled mind was too active for sleep, Peggy and Rebecca both swirling round and round in her head.

Rebecca had changed in the last few months since Willie's mam had died, Sarah acknowledged now, however much her friend tried to pretend otherwise. There was a nervousness about her, something elusive Sarah couldn't quite put her finger on, but which was there nevertheless. And it had begun before the other girl's pregnancy, so it wasn't that.

Oh . . . Sarah turned over in the bed, thumping the top pillow, which seemed to have developed rocks in it, and twisting and turning as she tried to get comfortable. Life could be a complicated affair at times.

Many miles away, if Sarah had but known it, one of the objects of her restless thoughts was also enduring a sleepless night.

Rebecca lay very still in her marital bed, listening to Willie's deep breathing punctuated by the odd raucous snore. She had learnt to lie still over the last months since Willie's mother had died, knowing there was less chance of her husband waking then, and demanding his 'rights' yet again.

His rights. She clenched her hands into fists at her side, but the tensing of her body aggravated the bruises on the tops of her arms and legs and her torso, and she forced herself to breathe deeply and relax again.

Was there another woman in the whole of Sunderland who had been taken in like she had? Rebecca asked herself bitterly. She doubted it, that she did. Oh, she had been a fool, such a blind, *stupid* fool. But Willie had been so affable when they were courting. Not refined, no, even Willie's undoubted ability at acting a part hadn't been able to rise to that, but he had been polite, civil.

She had heard rumours he had something of a reputation for uncouthness, but he had never been like that with her . . . then, and she had taken that as a sign that he cared about her, respected her.

Had his mam known what he was like? She didn't want to believe that. She had liked Willie's mam in a way, and she'd thought the old woman had liked her. Surely, if Mrs Dalton had known, she would have warned her? But the old lady had wanted grandchildren. In fact her mother-in-law's desire for grandchildren had been bordering on the obsessive.

Rebecca tensed as the fat bulk at her side snorted and stirred. It hadn't been love or desire or any of those things that had prompted Willie to start courting her, she knew that now. He had seen a girlfriend as a way of placating his mam, and Rebecca had been malleable enough for his purposes. Oh, why hadn't she seen it then? But she had wondered at times, she had to admit that. Occasionally she had caught a glimpse of something suspect in the dutiful son and ardent suitor, but she had closed her mind to it. She had so wanted to believe he loved her. And the security of a ring on her finger and her own home? Yes, that too. She answered the accusing voice of honesty silently.

She had had the fear she was too plain to get anyone else; that had been at the heart of her going out with Willie in the first place. So when he'd asked her to marry him, she'd nearly bitten his hand off, so quickly had she said yes. But she was paying for her pride, and her cowardice, now.

It was ironic when you thought about it – her mother-in-law had demanded a grandchild but hadn't lived to see her become pregnant, and that same child had trapped her more effectively than anything else could have done. She had believed he'd stop the other stuff when he knew about the bairn, but it had been a vain hope.

As though in confirmation of the thought, the tempo of her husband's breathing changed, and when, in the next moment, a large meaty hand clamped itself tightly over her left breast, Rebecca couldn't stifle a moan of fear.

'Waiting for it then?' Willie's voice was thick, he had sensed her terror and it was like an aphrodisiac, and Rebecca was already crying before he had even begun.

Chapter Seven

'Landsakes . . . And all this was going on when I was snoring my head off? My husband, God rest his soul, always used to say I'd sleep through my own funeral.'

The remark was typical of Hilda and brought the glimmer of a smile to Sarah's face despite the direness of the morning. She hadn't slept at all, and had risen well before five in order to have a word with Hilda before the day began.

'Mind you, I suppose at the bottom of me I'm not surprised, Sarah. I always thought Sir Geoffrey was capable of violence if he didn't get his own way, he could be a nasty little child, although to go as far as forcing the girl . . . ?'

'It was rape, Hilda. Nothing more and nothing less.' Sarah's voice was flat, and she gazed into the elderly cook's quizzical eyes as she said, 'And he would have attacked me if I hadn't stopped him with my knee. One of the boys at Hatfield taught me that little trick.'

'I don't know, the things that go on in this household.' Hilda drew in her lips and rummaged her cheeks before saying, 'There's never a dull moment, I can tell you. When the mistress was younger the house fair hummed with all her goings-on, but this is different . . . nasty. You know what I mean?'

Sarah didn't answer beyond nodding her head slowly. Yes, it was nasty, it was very nasty, and it had all the potential to get still nastier, because she could see Peggy and herself out on their ears before the day was through. She bowed her head deeply, sagging back against the wide, flat footboard of Hilda's bed as the apprehension she had been fighting all night reared its head again.

She didn't want to go back to Sunderland with her tail between her legs – there were some at Hatfield who had resented her appointment with the Robertses, and still more with Lady Harris, and who would crow their heads off with delight if she did – but . . . She paused for a moment in her thoughts, then straightened her back, raising her head to glance at Hilda propped against her pillows and resplendent in a thick Victorian-style nightdress and severe hairnet. If she had her time over again she would do and say exactly the same.

Hilda looked back at her in the silence that had fallen on them, and her voice was tentative now when she said, 'Is she going to report him? To the authorities? It'll kill the mistress.'

'*Hilda*.'

'Oh, I know, I know – it's awful for the girl, don't get me wrong, Sarah, but . . .' Hilda moved her toothless gums some more before she continued, 'I can't help feeling sorry for Lady Harris in all this. I mean for one of your own to do something like that, and the mistress has always been scathing about men abusing their power and all that type of thing. For your own son . . .' Hilda shook her head, and then said, 'It'll hit her hard.'

'Well, all I can say is that she was blaming everyone else but him last night.' Sarah could hear her voice and it sounded ordinary, but she wasn't feeling like that inside. Inside she was angry; angry and nervous and full of something she couldn't put a name to, but which made her want to find Sir Geoffrey Harris and beat him to a pulp. She didn't like how she was feeling but it was there, and she couldn't do anything about it. If she lived to be a hundred she would never forget the sight of him on top of Peggy, or the sound of it either. It was enough to put the little maid off men for life.

'It'd be the shock that made the mistress react like that.'

'What about Peggy's shock? And mine, if it comes to that?'

Hilda didn't reply immediately, her eyes narrowing and her gaze sweeping Sarah's strained face before she said, her voice soft now, 'It must have been awful, Sarah.'

'Yes, it was.' Sarah took a gulp of air and it was some seconds before she said, 'He was like an animal.'

'They're not all like that, thank the Lord. My Arthur was a gentle soul, and there's plenty like him in the world. Now then, I'll get myself dressed and we'll see what's what with Peggy. I'm going to have to do without her help in the kitchen today, I'll be bound.'

It was just after six o'clock when Sarah knocked on Peggy's bedroom door and, after standing for a few moments on the landing where Hilda stared at her uneasily, Sarah opened it and entered the room. The young maid was fast asleep, lying curled under the faded quilted eiderdown in what looked like the foetal position, the impression of childishness heightened by the fact that her thumb was in her mouth. Whether it was that, or the blue-mauve bruise already beginning to stain one cheekbone, Sarah didn't know, but Hilda's attitude seemed to undergo a lightning change as she looked at the pathetic little figure in the bed.

'He shouldn't be allowed to get away with this, the lecherous old so-and-so.' The elderly cook continued to stare at the sleeping girl as she spoke, before they turned together and made for the door. Once on the landing, Hilda poked her head towards Sarah as she asked, her voice still soft but trembling slightly, 'What will you do?'

'Do?' It was the same question she had asked herself all

113

night, but now she said it as if it had just occurred to her. 'That depends on Peggy of course, but if she wants to take it further I'm with her every inch of the way.' Her chin rose slightly as she added, 'Lady Harris or no Lady Harris.'

'You're very like her, you know. I think that's what makes me feel I've known you for a long time instead of just a few weeks.'

Coming from Hilda it was the highest of compliments, and Sarah recognized it as such, the knowledge softening her voice as she said, 'We've got on well, haven't we?'

'Don't say it as though it's all over.'

'No.' Sarah half turned from her, and now her voice was without expression as she said, 'Perhaps Lady Harris will surprise me.'

And to Sarah's eternal amazement, Lady Harris did just that, when, on the old lady's arrival downstairs before breakfast, she asked to speak to Sarah privately in the morning room. There was no roaring log fire in the grate that morning; it was normally Peggy's first job on rising to clean out the old ashes in both the morning room and drawing room and to light fresh fires, and this must have struck Lady Harris because her first words were, 'There are some luxuries we take entirely for granted; the warmth and cheer of a fire for example. I used to tell myself, when I was young and idealistic, that I would never take such things as a matter of course, but age makes one forget. Still, this is not a morning for warmth and cheer, is it, Sarah?'

Sarah didn't know what answer to make, or even if one was required of her, and so she said nothing, her gaze steady on the indomitable old lady standing in front of her.

'Shall we sit down?' Lady Harris waved her hand at the two chairs set before the empty fireplace, and after a moment Sarah sat, still without speaking.

In any other circumstances, *any other*, she would have gone out of her way to try and make things easy for her employer, even if the end result was going to be her dismissal, but today her mind was saying, 'Yes? Go on, then – say what you have to say. Tell me why Peggy and I will be the scapegoats, and why your son will get off scot free.' Because he would. She had taken a cup of tea up to Peggy a few minutes earlier, in order to see how she was and ask what she intended to do about the assault, and also to advise her to stay in bed that morning and that she would make arrangements for the doctor to call.

But Peggy had been fully dressed and packing her suitcase when Sarah had entered her room with the tea, and the young girl had been adamant about her intentions. 'I'm going home to me mum, miss.'

'But aren't you going to do anything about last night?' Sarah had stared at her aghast. 'Peggy, you can't just let him get away with it.'

'With what?' Peggy's chin moved up and down. 'He'll say I wanted to, that it was just a bit of fun, won't he? And he's Sir Geoffrey Harris, and who am I? Who is going to believe me? And . . . and I couldn't bear to have to tell anyone anyway, miss.'

'They *will* believe you, Peggy, listen to me. I was there, I *know*, and I'll tell them. It wasn't your fault.'

'It was. It was, miss, in a way.' Peggy gave a little gasping sound, so desolate it caught at Sarah's heartstrings. 'You tried to tell me, and Cook, but I wouldn't listen. I thought – I thought he liked me, as a person, you know? Not, not just in that way. I didn't think he'd make me . . .' Her voice trailed off and she shut her eyes tightly before opening them very wide. 'It was horrible. *Horrible.*'

'I know, I know.'

'And if I told anyone, made a fuss, me dad'd kill me anyway.'

'Peggy, it's not making a fuss, for goodness' sake. He *raped* you and he ought to be brought to account for it. And your father would want that, don't you see? He wouldn't want the man who had hurt you to get away with it.'

'You don't know me dad, miss.' Peggy shook her head slowly. 'The only thing that matters to him is being respectable.' The last word seemed to stick in her throat and she almost spat it out. 'All me life I've heard him going on at one or other of us. There's ten of us altogether and half of me brothers and sisters aren't talking to him because he's upset them in some way, and when our Mary had to get married last year . . .' She shook her head again. 'He went mad, *barmy*, miss. It nearly drove me poor mum up the wall. And it wasn't as if anyone knew, that was the thing. She was engaged anyway, and they just brought the wedding forward a month or two, but to hear him speak it was the end of the world. I couldn't tell him, miss, I just couldn't.'

'Aren't you going to tell your mother?'

'Oh I shall tell me mum, she'll understand.'

'But won't she feel obliged to inform your father?'

The withering glance Peggy bestowed on her suddenly made Sarah feel years younger than the little maid.

'No, miss, she won't tell me dad. Least said, soonest mended, eh?'

'Oh, Peggy.' As Sarah's hand went out to touch Peggy's face, the young girl shut her eyes again, biting on her lip before she said, 'Don't, don't, miss. I – I can't stand it. I know you mean well but I've got to keep meself together this morning, and I can't do it if you're nice to me.'

'But what will you do? I mean when you get home? What about work and so on?'

'Oh I'll find something. There's always work to be had if you're not too fussy, and I can't be fussy now, can I?'

The words had a double meaning, and Sarah now

scrutinized Peggy's white face with some anxiety. 'Of course you can be fussy, Peggy. Look, drink this tea while it's hot. I've got to go downstairs for a minute or two but I'll be back shortly, and we'll talk some more. Promise me you won't leave until I come back?' she added quietly.

'No, I won't leave, miss.' Peggy sat down very suddenly on the bed as she said, 'I'm feeling a bit funny to tell you the truth.'

'Drink the tea and I'll bring you some breakfast when I come back. You need some food inside you.'

'Oh no, miss, you'll get into trouble. Lady Harris won't like it.'

Sarah looked at the small wan figure in front of her, who seemed much younger than her fifteen years at that moment, and could have cried, and her voice reflected the fruit of this feeling as she said, 'I really don't care what Lady Harris does and doesn't like, Peggy. You are my only priority this morning. Now, I won't be long, and in the meantime' – she paused, drawing back the bedclothes – 'you take off your shoes and get back into bed for a while. It's enough to freeze you in here.'

'Miss?' Peggy's voice stopped her at the door and Sarah turned, her hand on the doorknob as she said, 'Yes? What is it?'

'I . . . I meant it, about you getting into trouble. Oh, I don't mean about breakfast, but the . . . the other thing. There's no need for you to lose your job as well as me, and Lady Harris won't like it if you go against her. What's done is done and nothing—' She gulped and paused before continuing, 'Nothing can alter things now. I'll get by, miss.'

'Yes, I know you will.' Sarah smiled at her reassuringly, even as her mind grappled with the fact that the little maid reminded her very much of Rebecca this morning although she didn't understand why. 'But for now you snuggle down and drink your tea. I'll be back soon.'

'I reacted badly last night, Sarah.' Lady Harris's steady voice brought Sarah back from the conversation with Peggy, and as Sarah raised startled eyes to the old face, she added, 'Oh yes, my dear, I'm quite aware of it. How is the child this morning? I assume you've been to see her?'

Sarah paused for a moment before she answered, 'Yes, I've been to see her, Lady Harris. She is in the state one would expect after being attacked so viciously.'

'You don't mince words, Sarah.'

There was nothing to say to this, but Sarah was thankful Lady Harris couldn't see the pounding of her heart.

Geraldine Harris waited for a moment before she said, her voice soft, 'You are angry and distressed on Peggy's behalf, and rightly so, but I need to make one thing perfectly clear. I am not your enemy, neither am I Peggy's, and I wish you to convey that to her when you ask her to come and see me. But first I would like you to tell me how she views the situation. Does she wish to go home, and is she intending to take the matter to the authorities?'

Sarah stared at her employer as she tried to gauge what was behind her words, and then she quietly related her conversation with Peggy, finishing with, 'Are you going to dismiss her?'

She had no right to ask, but Lady Harris didn't imply she found the question impertinent by voice or expression when she said, 'No, Sarah, I am not. Perhaps you would be so good as to go and fetch her, and I would like you to stay while I speak with the girl if you don't mind. I'm sure Peggy will find your presence comforting.'

Comforting? What did that mean? Sarah's mistrust must have shown in her face, because Lady Harris smiled slightly, relaxing back into the chair where she had been sitting stiffly upright, as she said, 'My grandmama, a singularly noteworthy woman who gave her life to doing good works and being an obedient and prodigious wife, always said that my face would get me into a great deal of trouble. She was quite right.' The bright brown eyes were sharp but not unkind. 'I am afraid I was a trial to Grandmama. I had a mind of my own even then you see, besides which she didn't really care for children, unless they were the seen-and-not-heard variety, which I, sadly, was not. But even when I held my tongue I could not please her. She would say that my face talked for itself.' The birdlike eyes twinkled at Sarah. 'As yours does.'

Sarah wasn't sure if Lady Harris expected her to comment, but she said nothing, deciding to let her face – as Lady Harris said – say it all. This turn-around in attitude was both a surprise and suspect, and she couldn't pretend otherwise.

'You are wondering if this is a ploy to dispose of Peggy quickly and quietly, is that not so?'

'Yes, but I have no wish to appear offensive.'

'No, I am aware of that, Sarah. You were merely using the mind God gave you and that does not displease me – just the reverse, in fact. I also appreciate honesty where I find it; it is a rare commodity these days. Now, I think it would be a good idea to have a word with Peggy, so if you wouldn't mind . . . ?'

Peggy was quite literally shaking in her shoes when Sarah ushered her into the morning room a few minutes later. Sarah could feel the girl trembling through the arm she had round the little maid's shoulders, and when Lady Harris said, 'Peggy, my dear, you have nothing to fear from me. Has Miss Brown told you?' she knew their employer had noticed the small girl's quivering too.

'Yes, ma'am.' Peggy tried to smile but it was beyond her.

'Sit down, please, both of you.' Lady Harris gestured to one of the low upholstered couches, and when they were seated she moved from the fireplace where she had been

119

standing at their entrance, and sat opposite them.

A silence ensued between them for a moment or two, then Lady Harris said, her tone so quiet that Sarah found she was leaning forward slightly in order to hear, 'I am more sorry than I can say that you were subjected to such an experience at my son's hands, Peggy, and also that I was less than discerning of the true facts. Lady – Lady Margaret has acquainted me with certain matters that should have been brought to my attention years ago—' She stopped abruptly before continuing, 'But I am using that as an excuse, and there isn't one. Nevertheless, you do realize that you were very foolish to visit Sir Geoffrey's rooms at such an hour?'

'Yes, ma'am.' Peggy's head was drooping down, and now Lady Harris said, 'Look at me, child,' before continuing. 'I am not blaming you for last night's occurrence, I wish to make that clear. The blame rests with Sir Geoffrey and only Sir Geoffrey.' She took a deep breath before saying, 'Miss Brown informs me you do not wish to take the matter further. You are sure about this?'

Peggy glanced from Lady Harris to Sarah, and then back again to her employer before she said, 'I'm sure, ma'am. It's . . . it's me dad you see. I'll just go home, ma'am, if that's all right with you.'

Lady Harris stared hard at both of them for a full minute without saying a word, during which time Sarah steeled herself to remain seemingly relaxed and perfectly still, and then her expression changed as though she had come to some kind of decision. Her words seemed to bear this out when she said, 'I feel I would like to be frank with you, Peggy, and then if you still feel you wish to leave, I will see to it that you are placed in a good position. I assume you do not particularly wish to return home?'

'Not if it can be avoided, ma'am, but – but I don't feel right about staying here now, after . . . after what's happened.'

'Yes, I can understand that, of course.' Lady Harris rose now, walking across to the mantelpiece again, and standing with her back to the room as she stared down into the dead ashes in the ornate grate. 'Sir Geoffrey has left these premises and I do not expect that he will be staying here again. Neither will he reside at Fenwick in the foreseeable future. If you wish to remain in my employ, Peggy' – she turned and faced them – 'I would very much like to retain you, but if you feel this is not possible in the circumstances then we can arrange something different. Whichever decision you make, I would tell you now that I intend to open a bank account for you with a deposit of five hundred pounds to be used in any way you favour.'

Peggy's mouth fell open in a gape. If Lady Harris had suddenly sprouted wings and flown out of the window she couldn't have been more amazed and bewildered.

'Do you understand what I am saying to you, child?'

'I – I don't – I can't . . .'

'There is no need to make a decision one way or the other until you have had time to reflect. For now I would suggest you go to the kitchen and have something to eat, then go to your room and rest.' Lady Harris's tone had softened, and when Peggy burst into tears she moved forward to stand in front of them, patting Peggy's shoulder as she said, 'Come, come, my dear. Try and look at this as a hurdle to be dealt with and overcome. Miss Brown will take you to the kitchen. And Sarah?' The piercing gaze fastened on Sarah's face. 'Perhaps you would be good enough to return here when you have seen to Peggy?'

'Of course, Lady Harris.' Sarah rose, drawing Peggy up with her. The events of the last few minutes had surprised her not a little and alarmed her considerably. This smacked of Peggy being bought off, and she didn't like the idea of Sir Geoffrey getting away with such brutality, and yet . . . Lady

Harris *had* made the offer to Peggy after the little maid had said she intended to go quietly without any fuss. Oh, she didn't know what to think.

Hilda made no pretence of tact when they entered the kitchen. 'Well?' She eyed the weeping Peggy before transferring her gaze to Sarah and saying, 'What's happened?'

'Peggy will explain, I've got to get back. Could you give her a cup of tea, Hilda? I think she needs one.'

'I think we all need one.' Hilda led the still weeping Peggy to the kitchen table, pushing her down in one of the hard-backed seats as she said, 'How about a nice bacon sandwich then, Peggy? I've still got an ounce or two from our rations and old Perce is sending a meat parcel from the farm this week. How we'd manage without that I don't know, one ounce per person goes nowhere in this house. You can't tell me it's not encouraging the black market, now then . . .'

Sarah left them to it and returned to the morning room to find Lady Harris still standing exactly where they had left her. The old lady spoke without preamble. 'I came face to face with myself last night, Sarah, and I didn't like what I saw. Lady Margaret came to see me after the incident, and by the time she left my eyes had been opened, both with regard to my son, and myself. I had a . . . a difficult night. It is not pleasant to find out the truth about oneself in such circumstances.'

It wasn't at all what Sarah had expected, and when Lady Harris waved for her to be seated in one of the chairs in front of the empty grate, then sat opposite her, Sarah said, 'I'm sorry, Lady Harris. It must have been very distressing for both you and Lady Margaret as well as Peggy.'

Lady Harris didn't comment on that as she continued, 'I asked Sir Geoffrey for an explanation this morning and I'm afraid the conversation escalated into something . . . unpleasant. I don't like being lied to, I have never tolerated it, and neither am I a foolish woman – however present circumstances might appear. Sir Geoffrey's attitude this morning was inexcusable—' For the first time Lady Harris's ironclad composure slipped a little, but she recovered herself almost instantly, saying, 'And suffice to say Sir Geoffrey will be staying at his club indefinitely.'

'And Lady Margaret?' Sarah asked quietly.

'Lady Margaret and my grandchildren will continue to treat both Fenwick and this house as their own.'

She'd chosen her daughter-in-law over her son? Sarah could hardly believe her ears. And not just that, Lady Harris had virtually barred Sir Geoffrey from the family homes by the sound of it. He'd be furious, absolutely furious. She couldn't see him taking this without a fight.

'Now, a rather delicate matter . . .' Lady Harris adjusted the snow-white lace collar at the neck of her black alpaca dress and cleared her throat, then said, 'There may be another complication arising from last night's' – a pause – 'attack. You understand me?'

'I think so.'

'Of course I hope it won't be necessary but if it is, I want the child to understand that she must consult my physician at once. These things are best dealt with immediately.'

These things. A baby could be dismissed as 'these things', and it was clear Lady Harris meant she would expect Peggy to get rid of the baby, Sarah thought grimly. Not that she thought there was much likelihood of a baby; Sir Geoffrey had been interrupted too soon. But if Lady Harris thought her money could buy a life – or a death in this case – she was wrong.

Sarah stared at her employer for a moment, then said, 'If Peggy found she was expecting a child, the decision of whether to continue with the pregnancy would be hers and hers alone, Lady Harris, but I will mention what you've said.'

123

'Thank you.'

It was stiff, but Sarah didn't care. These people! In spite of everything Lady Harris had said that morning, at bottom she would still be more upset at the thought of a bastard grandchild than at the attack on Peggy. She wanted this thing hushed up. Well, Sarah could understand that in a way, it was human nature she supposed, but she couldn't agree with it. The man was an animal and he should get his just deserts. How many other young girls had he seduced or attacked and raped? He thought he was some feudal lord, able to take what he wanted without a thought for anyone else, secure and protected by his wealth and power.

Sarah stood up now, her voice cool as she said, 'Is there anything else, Lady Harris?'

'Not for the moment, Sarah, thank you. Perhaps you would be so good as to keep me informed on what Peggy decides to do when she has had time to think about her future?'

Sarah inclined her head, but said nothing more before leaving the room.

She was still reflecting on the conversation with Lady Harris later that morning as her fingers deftly arranged a bowl of white-flowered madonna lilies in the drawing room, and she nearly jumped out of her skin when a tentative hand touched her shoulder at the same time as Lady Margaret's voice said, 'Oh, I'm sorry, Miss Brown. Did I startle you?'

'It doesn't matter.' Sarah smiled. 'I usually do this before breakfast, but—' She stopped abruptly. She had been about to say, 'with the house in turmoil this morning they got left,' before she realized it wouldn't be tactful. 'But I'm all behind this morning,' she finished instead.

'Yes.' Margaret Harris looked at the younger woman, her clear blue eyes moving over the face which she considered quite classically beautiful. She had always been particularly receptive to beauty wherever she found it; one of her first

124

memories was of hanging precariously over the windowsill in the nursery one evening, and calling for her nanny to come and see the fine sunset, and that appreciation had seemed to grow as she became aware of her own plainness.

But this young housekeeper had more than mere beauty; she had a strong spirit to match, a spirit which hadn't allowed itself to be subjugated by either circumstances or personalities last night. 'May I speak with you, Miss Brown?' Lady Margaret asked softly.

It was a rhetorical question, and Sarah did not answer it, merely following the tall thin figure of Sir Geoffrey's wife as she swept across the room to seat herself on a small chaise longue upholstered in blue velvet, and indicated for Sarah to take the chair opposite.

Sarah sat down and waited for Lady Margaret to speak, her face quiet and composed but her mind racing. She had felt, from the first moment that the older woman had laid eyes on her, that Sir Geoffrey's wife didn't like her, and her reserve had been chilling. So now, when Lady Margaret leant forward and said quickly, even urgently, 'I want to thank you for last night,' she really didn't know how to react, her mouth falling open on a little O of surprise as she drew back slightly.

'That sounds strange, heartless, doesn't it, in view of what that little maid suffered? But I cannot pretend, Miss Brown. Not any more. I . . . I don't often speak to people like this. In fact I can't remember doing so before.'

It was a plea for understanding and Sarah rose to it, in spite of feeling far out of her depth. 'Last night must have been a shock for you too, Lady Margaret.'

'It came more in the nature of a release, to be truthful.'

Sarah stared at her, a straight look. 'You mean because it all came out into the open?' she asked baldly.

'That is exactly what I mean. Oh,' Lady Margaret shook her head, 'I wouldn't have wished such an experience on a child like Peggy, please believe that, but – but other such occurrences have happened in the past to even younger girls.'

'Then why . . . ?'

'Knowing it and proving it are two quite different things, I'm afraid. My husband has a way of taking care of matters – bribery, threats, I'm sure he has used them all, but to date I have been unable to prove so. Last night, due to your courage, he was exposed for what he is, and I am glad.'

Sarah shifted uncomfortably before she said, 'Lady Margaret, I don't think you should be talking to me like this.'

'I am sure I shouldn't. It isn't done – that's what you mean, isn't it? Miss Brown, last night I went to see my mother-in-law, and for the first time in nine years of marriage to her son, I actually *talked* to her, but it took a catastrophe to make it happen.'

Sarah detected a slightly animated note in the hitherto even voice, and after a moment she inclined her head slowly. 'Yes, I can understand why you are feeling relieved this morning,' she said quietly.

'Last night I came to the end of my tether, and that is what I tried to explain to Lady Harris. I have always found the list of dos and don'ts that go hand-in-hand with my class extremely tiresome, and when I married Sir Geoffrey they became even more so. The stiff upper lip is a crippling British tradition, Sarah.'

Lady Margaret now straightened, her hands resting either side of her thighs on the velvet seat as she leant slightly forward and said, 'I am very grateful that you stood up to my husband in the way you did. I know it can't have been easy, and I won't forget it. I – I would like to talk with you again sometime, if I may? I find town life rather dull on the whole.' Then, her voice changing, she said, 'Well, this really won't do. I have promised to take William and Constance for a turn round the little park opposite before lunch. Although their tutor set some lessons for them before we left Fenwick, they do get rather bored at times. They miss their ponies and their friends, no doubt.'

She rose now, nodding and smiling as Sarah followed suit. 'I'll leave you to the flowers, Sarah.'

Two Sarahs in as many minutes! In spite of the emotion of the night and the revelations of the morning, Sarah found it was Lady Margaret's softened attitude towards her that occupied her mind as she finished arranging the bowl of flowers, and then made her way to the kitchen to help Hilda with the lunch, Peggy having been sent back to bed. Pausing in the passageway before opening the kitchen door, she realized that her previous assumption that Lady Margaret disliked her had been unfounded. It wasn't that Lady Margaret had held any animosity towards her, just that she had been – Sarah searched for the right words and found them – locked into herself, into her situation. Poor soul.

She surprised herself on the last thought, but then inclined her head slowly. Lady Margaret *was* a poor soul, and just as much a victim of Sir Geoffrey as Peggy. She must have had a terrible time of it before she broke out last night, and that was the right phrase sure enough. She had the appearance this morning of a person who had been released, set free. It just showed that you never really knew what was going on in other people's lives.

The thought brought Rebecca to the forefront of her mind again and she frowned. For months now she hadn't been able to rid herself of the notion that her friend was hiding something, but every time she had asked her, Rebecca had denied anything was wrong. Something was troubling her, though, and it had to do with her pig of a husband. Her description of Willie Dalton brought Sarah up short. Therein lay the problem: Rebecca knew what she thought of Willie, she'd always known it, as did the man himself, and Rebecca

127

was always careful to say nothing that would inflame her low opinion. Not that it could get any lower.

Sarah thought back to the first time she had met Rebecca's husband, when he and Rebecca had been courting for a few weeks. She had heard plenty about him from her friend before then, Rebecca having met Willie at a barn dance the local vicar had put on, the proceeds of which had gone towards the war effort. Sarah had been ill on the night of the dance, but Rebecca had come back to Hatfield glowing, and full of the young docker who had monopolized her all evening. She had fully expected to like Rebecca's choice of beau when she had met him – Rebecca had been able to talk of little else for weeks – but she hadn't, and he hadn't liked her either. Oh, he'd been charming enough, obsequious even, but he had known she could see right through him, Sarah thought flatly.

'Your busy little friend'; that was how he had always referred to her, his thick lips moving in the semblance of a smile; but he had known, and she had known, that he was being insulting. Why hadn't Rebecca been able to see the type of man he really was? But she hadn't, in spite of Sarah's repeated warnings. And so Rebecca had married him . . .

It hadn't been too bad when old Mrs Dalton was alive. Sarah pictured the formidable virago in her mind. Willie's mother had actively encouraged her to call at the house, and Willie had tempered his attitude accordingly, but with his mother's passing the resentment that had always been lurking under the surface had turned into open hostility. Oh, he was a horrible, *horrible* man.

Sarah shivered suddenly, before pushing open the kitchen door and stepping into the warmth of Hilda's domain.

The elderly cook turned from stirring a pan of soup at her entrance, nodding her head as she said, 'All quiet out there now? What a to-do, eh? Mind you, my Arthur always used to say, the gentry have too much time on their hands for dillydallyings. Half of 'em are skittering from one bed to another, it's a wonder any of them find their way home at night, if you ask me. They ought to talk about this tidal wave of divorce that has hit the country, and I don't agree it's all down to the war. Fifty thousand divorces they reckon this year, you know. Fifty thousand! That's double what it was two years ago, and now they've cut the time between the decree nisi and the decree absolute from six months to six weeks. What sort of an idea is that giving people? And it all comes from the top, I'm telling you, Sarah.'

It was one of Hilda's pet hobby horses, and Sarah had heard it all before, so now she said, 'Well I wouldn't blame Lady Margaret if she wanted a divorce, Hilda.'

'Well no, perhaps in those circumstances. Mind you, she must have known what he was like before she married him.'

'She might not have.' Sarah sat down at the kitchen table and pulled a metal bowl of peapods towards her as she spoke.

'I'd dare take a bet on it. Besides which, looking like she does, I suppose she thought any man was better than no man at all.'

Sarah shut her eyes for a moment before opening them and starting to shell the peas. Hilda didn't mean to be unkind, but that made it worse somehow. People could be cruel, oh, they could. There were times when she could honestly say she hated people.

As though it was yesterday she could hear Mary Owen, and Jane, and the rest of their cronies, chanting out the song Mary had made up about her, the soft chorus bitingly distinct in the dark dormitory.

> Sarah Brown, Sarah Brown,
> Mam's on the streets and da's a navvy,
> Didn't want her, couldn't keep her,
> Left poor Sarah in some old lavvy.

It had started on the first night she had returned to the dormitory from the hospital, and continued every evening for a week, until she had rounded on Mary, who had been a good deal heavier and bigger than herself, dragging her out of bed by her hair and pinning her against the wall, whilst threatening she would bash her face in if she ever uttered the words again. Like all bullies, Mary was something of a coward, and the chanting had stopped, although other, more subtle forms of spitefulness had continued.

The only bright spot in her days had been when the doctor called and she managed to have a word with him. She had always seemed to sense when he was in the building, and had homed in on him like a small and very determined pigeon, something which had often seem to amuse him. And then the war had started, and Dr Mallard had gone away to fight, and that had been that.

She had heard, some time after the war had ended and when she was first working for the Robertses, that Dr Mallard had been a prisoner-of-war of the Japanese. She hadn't liked the thought of that. She had been glad he was alive, but from the news reports, and the way Mr Roberts had spoken about the atrocities committed on their soldiers, she had wondered if he might have been better off if he had been killed outright.

'Has Peggy told you she's thinking of moving out and taking a course in book-keeping and typing?' Hilda's voice penetrated the past. 'Seems she's always fancied the idea but her father wouldn't hear of it, wanted her working and sending her wage home the minute she was able.'

'Moving out?' Sarah finished the last of the peas, and rested her hands on the table, her brow furrowed. 'I don't like the idea of that, Hilda. She's very vulnerable at the moment, and where would she go?'

'Oh, there's lots of families in the East End who take in

130

the odd paying guest to make ends meet, decent folk most of them, she'd be all right,' Hilda said stolidly.

Sarah nodded slowly. She hoped so, but Peggy was a very young fifteen-year-old and, as the incident with Sir Geoffrey had proven, could be both foolish and naive on occasion. But then, the young maid was little more than a bairn.

The northern word, which had sprung so naturally to mind, brought Maggie into the kitchen, and suddenly the longing to see her again, and Florrie and Rebecca, was so strong she could taste it. Those three knew all there was to know about her, and they didn't mind. She didn't have to pretend with them, to talk properly all the time, to act a part. They accepted her for what she was. But then, she didn't know what – or more to the point, who – she was herself, not really. She never would until she confronted the woman who had given birth to her then abandoned her so completely.

The weight in her heart seemed to drop right through her so her feet were tethered to the floor, and she remained quite still, half leaning on the table, as Hilda bustled away to the dining room with the trolley containing the soup tureen and bread basket.

There was a hole at the beginning of her life, a wide gaping hole, instead of a family with grandparents and aunts and uncles and cousins. She could be anyone. Even her name wasn't her own – it hadn't been *chosen* for her by her parents, merely assigned to her by strangers. Had her mother hoped she would die in that freezing toilet? Had she really wanted her own flesh and blood dead? She had to find her one day and ask her that, among other things. She would never feel completely at peace until she did.

'One day . . .' She said the words out loud, but softly. She would do it one day. She brought her lips tightly together and drew them inwards between her teeth. What was it Maggie always said? Oh yes: 'Choose your own road and

then you've only yourself to blame if it comes to a dead end.'
Maggie was full of such aphorisms, born of her northern
roots. Well, she *had* chosen her own road and she was going
to make sure it didn't come to a dead end. It was up to her.

She nodded to herself, narrowing her eyes. And one day
she would find her mother and show her that she had
succeeded in building a life for herself, that she was *worth*
something. She just wanted to see her mother's face once,
talk to her, ask her *why*, that would be enough. It would, it
would be enough.

The emotion in her chest caused her body to sag briefly,
and she consciously turned her mind away from herself and
back to the problem in hand, namely Peggy. She would go
with the girl if Peggy decided to take lodgings somewhere,
make sure she was with a good family and so on, before she
let Peggy move in. Peggy had as much right to choose her
own road as she did, but the fewer byways and culs-de-sac
available to the little maid, the better.

That thought was still with her when, a few days later and
with the confirmation that there would be no 'complication'
arising from Sir Geoffrey's attack on Peggy, Sarah
accompanied the girl to a street in Whitechapel.

'It's number forty-four.' Peggy was clutching a card she
had obtained from the local newsagent's window as they
walked along the street of terraced houses, the murky winter
twilight accentuating the grimness of their surroundings. They
passed a group of raggedy urchins intent on a noisy game of
hopscotch on the greasy pavement, and Sarah was disturbed
to notice that despite the coldness of the evening one or two of
them were without coats or jumpers. Not that shivering
children were a new sight; no, far from it, she told herself
silently. Up north they were ten a penny. But this was London,
where the streets were supposed to be paved with gold . . .

'I hope you're going to like this one, miss.' Peggy's tone was slightly reproachful. They had visited three houses so far, and Sarah hadn't approved of any of them. 'With me course being in St Martin's Street I don't want to live too far away, and the new maid is starting Monday. I need to get somewhere today.'

'It's very important you get the right establishment, Peggy.'

There was a long pause and then Peggy said, 'I don't think any of these will be establishments, miss. They're just ordinary houses, like me mum's.'

'Nevertheless, we'll know the right one for you when we see it.'

Sarah had to admit that forty-four, Ash Street was an improvement on the adjoining houses either side. There were no cracked windows for a start, and the step had been freshly whitened. The front door was painted a dark sedate green, and the brass knocker, a grinning elf's head, was polished and gleaming.

'Let me look at that advertisement again, Peggy.'

Sarah took the card and read, 'Room available with respectable family, very reasonable and evening meal included.' The advertisement was written in large round capital letters with a pencil, and was reminiscent of Maggie's laboured scrawl. It was that, along with the 'respectable family' which had prompted Sarah to pursue it, despite the district.

'I'll knock, shall I, miss?'

'Yes, all right, Peggy.' At the last house Sarah had forbidden Peggy to do even that.

The door was opened by a small, plump, middle-aged woman, and a pair of bright eyes assessed them for a moment before the woman said, her voice rough but not unfriendly, 'Yes, ducks?'

'Good afternoon. I understand you had a room to let? Is it still available?'

The woman hesitated, then said, 'Well, there's someone bin round earlier, but 'e ain't let me know one way or the other yet.'

'Oh. Oh, I see.' They all stood in silence for a moment, and Sarah was just about to say, 'We'll perhaps come back another time,' when the woman seemed to come to a decision, thrusting out her hand in a sweeping motion as she said, 'Come in then, come in.'

Once in the hall, which again was clean but painted in a dingy brown, Sarah and Peggy followed the woman down the passageway, passing two closed doors on the left and the stairs to their right, to find themselves in a small, square, stone-floored kitchen which was spotlessly clean. And immediately, as though Sarah had made some protest, the little woman swung round, looked directly at her and said, 'I don't normally show folks in 'ere, love, but I'm in a bit of a fix. Me old mum's bin taken bad, an' she 'as the front room, an' the doctor's just talkin' with me 'usband now in the livin' room. 'E'll be finished in a tick if you can 'ang on a while?'

'Oh yes, yes of course,' Sarah said quickly, 'you should have said. We can easily come back another time if you'd prefer, or we'll wait here while you have a word with the doctor?'

'No, like I said, 'e'll be finished in a tick. I just wanted to thank 'im afore 'e went, 'e's bin so good with 'er, you know? Some of 'em can be right touchy when the old 'uns play up, an' me mum's no angel, tell you the truth, but 'e's bin as patient as Job.'

The sharp little eyes moved over Sarah in her smart suit, and then Peggy at the side of her, and again the little woman seemed to make up her mind about something as she said, 'Look, love, why don't you go up an' 'ave a look at the room yourselves? I wouldn't 'ave let 'im who was 'ere afore you go up there, bit of a shifty customer me 'usband thought 'e was, but 'e won't mind two young ladies like yourselves goin' up. I'll come up in a minute. You do know the room's for one?' she asked Sarah.

'Oh yes, yes, I do. It's for Peggy here as it happens, but I wanted to make sure . . . well, that she was somewhere . . .' Sarah couldn't think how to put it without sounding offensive.

'I know what you mean, ducks, don't you worry. Can't be too careful in this day an' age. Me old mum still remembers when Jack the Ripper did away with all them women. She couldn't 'ave bin much older than this young 'un 'ere, it was nearly sixty years ago now, but right to this day she won't go out by 'erself after dark. Course, 'e only 'ad them that weren't any better than they should be, but like she says, when it's dark an' there's no one about, who's askin'? Bit late after to find out you've made a mistake, ain't it?'

'Yes, I suppose it is.'

Sarah could feel Peggy shaking at the side of her and she wanted to laugh herself, but she kept her head averted as she turned and followed the woman back down the dark hall.

They had just reached the bottom of the stairs, the woman standing to one side as she said, 'Me name's Mrs Cole, by the way,' when the door to the room they had just passed opened, and a voice could be heard saying, 'I'll call in again next week, Mr Cole, but if you need me before then you know where I am.'

And then everything seemed to take on a crystal bright clearness. Peggy just behind her, Mrs Cole's squat little figure to one side of a large aspidistra in a shiny green tulip-shaped pot, the open door and the tall dark handsome figure emerging from the room.

'Dr Mallard.' She must have spoken the name out loud, although she had no conscious recognition of doing so, because his face turned to her, and then he said, 'I'm sorry, I'm afraid I don't quite . . . ?' and the brightness shattered. He hadn't remembered her.

Chapter Eight

Rodney Mallard had been more than a little irritated when the youngest of the Cole children had banged on the surgery door earlier that afternoon.

The morning surgery had been a full one and the list of home calls endless, and his stalwart housekeeper-cum-receptionist, a big stout lady with a voice like a foghorn but a very warm heart, had had to keep his dinner hot for over an hour. He had just finished his meal and settled down in front of the fire with a cup of tea and the morning paper, when little Bertha Cole had made her presence known.

'It's me gran.' He could hear Bertha's shrill treble although Mrs Price's gruffer tones were unclear. 'Me mum says can the doctor come quick please?' A pause, and then, 'But me mum says *now*.'

Rodney rose, calling as he did so, 'It's all right, Mrs Price, I'll deal with this,' and joined his housekeeper in the hall, there to see Bertha Cole dancing about on the doorstep in an agony of urgency.

'Me mum says *now*, Dr Mallard.' Bertha was only six but formidable in her own small way. 'You've got to come now, me gran's bin took bad.'

'All right, Bertha, all right.'

Rodney knew better than to argue with this small scrap of humanity; besides which, Bertha's mother was not one to panic unnecessarily. The grandmother – his main patient in the household – was also too stoical for her own good, constantly playing down her bad heart to the point where it became dangerous. He could appreciate the old lady's desire to remain as independent as possible, being the same way himself, but in her determination to be autonomous she often pushed her frail body too far.

But he liked her; he liked the dogged old warrior very much, Rodney thought now as he pulled on his overcoat and took his case from Mrs Price, even though she certainly didn't make his life any easier with her stubbornness. But she was a *real* person somehow; she had grappled with life from childhood like so many of her class, raising a family and living a good life in spite of grinding poverty and a severe lack of education. It was people like Lena who reinforced his conviction that he was where he should be, rather than in a nice private practice doling out sugar lumps and a sympathetic ear to patients who were as healthy as he was.

The Coles' house was only three streets and a few minutes walk away from his surgery, and didn't necessitate the use of his car, and as Rodney walked along the dirty pavements and narrow back alleyways with the child skipping at his side, he talked easily with his small companion.

Once in the house, he had a brief word with Bertha's mother before opening the door to his patient's room, and as he stepped into the limited space it struck him – as it always did when he visited this particular family – that love was a powerful medicine. By rights, the frail old woman in the narrow iron bed by the window should have been dead years ago, but such was her love for this family, and theirs for her, that in spite of her grossly enlarged heart she continued to battle on.

''Ad to call you out, did she? I told 'er to leave well alone,' the quavery old voice gasped slowly.

138

Rodney shook his head at the old woman whom he had come to understand very well over the two years in which he had been treating her, and his voice was soft but firm as he said, 'Your daughter was worried about you, and I can understand why. You're not being fair to her, Lena. You know that, don't you? Look at you, your lips are blue and you can barely breathe. Now, be a good girl and keep quiet for a minute or two while I examine you, and we'll go from there.'

He thought he heard her murmur something that sounded very much like, 'young windsnapper', but she submitted to his examination without further protest, which in itself told him the old lady must be feeling pretty ill.

Rodney's brow was creased when he had finished, and when she looked at him and said, 'Well? I ain't dead yet, am I?' it was on the tip of his tongue to bite back, 'But not for the want of trying,' before he restrained himself. She was old and she was desperately ill, and she didn't need him to tell her she had been silly, he thought compassionately.

There was nothing immediately pressing back at the practice, evening surgery still being two hours away, so he sat down and continued to chat with the old lady, knowing it would accomplish more for her general wellbeing than any prescription he could write.

He rose some time later when he heard her son-in-law return from his job as a clicker in one of the local boot and shoe factories, satisfied the old lady was looking better. He was going to have to have a word with Lena's daughter and son-in-law, much as he disliked the idea, but the old lady was beginning to fail fast and it was only fair to prepare them in some small way for her demise.

He had enjoyed the hour sitting quietly by the glowing fire as much as his patient, he thought now, as he walked through to the hall, and of the two of them it had been a toss-up who needed it most. He had to sort himself out, he couldn't go on like this, but what could he do? Richard needed him. Certainly, at the moment, Richard needed him. In fact he thought his brother might go mad if he didn't have him to converse with in the evenings, and as long as they kept off the subject of the war, he could talk as much as Richard wanted him to.

The war . . . He shut his mind from the horror lurking just at the perimeter of his consciousness. The army psychiatrist had told him it would get better in time, that he would be able to let himself remember, bit by bit, and deal with the memories one by one, until the hatred and bitterness were slowly expunged. But then that psychiatrist hadn't been in the Burma prisoner-of-war camp for two years.

But he was getting better. He knew, deep down, he was getting better. It was mind over matter most of the time, controlling his thoughts and emotions.

He tapped on the living-room door before opening it, and had just poked his head round to say, 'I wonder if I could have a word with you both before I go?' when there was a knock at the front door.

'You tell Bert, Doctor, an' I'll be back in a tick.' Meg, Lena's daughter, had ushered him in, and herself out, and shut the living-room door behind her, before he had time to say any more.

By the time Rodney had finished gently explaining the situation to Meg's husband he could tell the little man was upset, so when Mr Cole leant forward and said, 'She'd 'ave bin a goner months ago if it weren't for you, Doctor. Thinks the world of you, she does, Meg an' all,' he was touched.

When he opened the door into the hall again Rodney was still contemplating the effect her mother's impending passing would have on Meg, and as he stepped through the doorway his surprise at hearing his name spoken – and in a voice that was definitely not Meg Cole's – brought his eyes narrowing as he peered into the dim exterior. 'I'm sorry, I'm afraid I don't quite . . . ?'

And then the years dropped away, and he was back in Sunderland again before the war, staring into the delicately beautiful face he remembered so well which was the same and yet strangely different.

The child had grown into a woman . . .

Chapter Nine

'Don't give me that. Now, don't give me that, lass. I might be in me dotage but I'm not that far gone. You walked into a door indeed!'

'I did, Maggie.'

'Never! Never, lass.' In the nine weeks since Sarah had been down south, Maggie had never longed for her more, and the thought of the girl she loved like her own child prompted her to say, 'What do you think Sarah is going to say when she sees you, eh? She never liked him, did she, an' by gum she's been proved right. The swine. It's one thing to make allowances for the way he talks to you, like you're a bit of muck, but if he's started knockin' you about—'

'He hasn't. He . . . he hasn't, Maggie.'

'An' you carryin' his bairn an' all. Me an' Florrie were wonderin' why you haven't been in the last day or two, an' now I know. I dare say if Sarah hadn't been comin' for the weekend you'd have stayed clear until that had gone altogether, eh?' She gestured at the bruise staining one side of Rebecca's face which had also partially closed one eye. 'There's no excuse for a man hittin' a lass, not in my book. What did you do?'

'I didn't—' Rebecca caught Maggie's glare and paused, gulping deep in her throat before she said, 'I was late with his dinner.'

'Late with his — Saints alive, I've heard it all now. By, I have an' all.' And then, as Rebecca's plain little face crumpled, Maggie pulled her towards her bulk saying, 'Aw, lass, lass, don't take on so. You know me, mouth as big as a Sunderland tram.'

'Oh, Maggie.' The tears were streaming down Rebecca's face, and after a minute Maggie led her to the worn leather couch that, together with two upholstered chairs, a small occasional table and a battered sideboard, comprised the room's furniture. There was no linoleum on the floor, not even one clippy mat, but the thick, dark red curtains at the window – Florrie's latest acquisition – and the blazing coal fire in the blackleaded fireplace, made the room cosy.

Maggie wouldn't have cared if it was cosy or not; it was enough for her that for the last three years or so she had had a place of her own again, after all the years of being dependent on Hatfield Home. The fact that she and Florrie were renting the downstairs of the house, with a family of four occupying the upstairs and sharing the kitchen, didn't bother her at all. Thanks to Florrie she was ending her days without being answerable to anyone.

Who'd have thought it? Maggie asked herself now, pressing Rebecca gently down onto the couch and then sitting at the side of her and taking the sobbing girl in her arms again. Who would have thought ten years ago that she and Florrie would have hit it off like they had? But something had broken in Florrie that time when Sarah had nearly died. Maggie nodded in agreement to her thoughts over Rebecca's dark head. Aye, and after Florrie had seen the bairn in the hospital, Sarah had had Florrie in the palm of her hand, right enough. If she had to say who loved the lass more – her or Florrie – she'd have a job.

And this one here was like a daughter too, but a worry. Aye, Rebecca was a worry. She had none of Sarah's fighting spirit, that was the trouble, and if anyone needed a bit of backbone in dealing with their man, Rebecca did.

The thought prompted her to say, 'Lass, you don't have to put up with this, now then.' Rebecca shook her head slowly, and Maggie moved her back a fraction and looked into the tearstained face before she said, 'Was this the first time? That he'd gone so far as to hit you?'

'He . . . he doesn't make a habit of it.'

'So in other words it weren't the first time then?' Maggie shook her head slowly before she said, her voice soft, 'Oh, Rebecca, lass. Why didn't you tell me afore now?'

'What good would it do, Maggie? It won't' – a hiccuping sob checked the words before she continued – 'it won't change anything. He's my husband.'

'Aye, lass, just so, he's your husband, but that don't mean you don't have no rights, now does it? Get it into your head, Rebecca, that you're as good as Willie Dalton any day. A darn sight too good for that scum if the truth be known.'

'Oh, Maggie . . .'

'Now don't "oh, Maggie" me. I'm tellin' you, you're as good as him.' Maggie's voice was deep and guttural. Good as him? She was worth a hundred of that dockside scum. There he was, barely twenty-five, and with a beer belly on him the like of which she hadn't seen in many a long day. A big bag of nowt, that was Willie Dalton. Why the lass had married him she'd never know.

'Maggie, don't tell Sarah, will you?'

'Don't tell Sarah?' In contrast to a moment before Maggie's voice was high. 'You don't think that story of walkin' into a door would fool Sarah, do you? She'll cotton on the minute she sets eyes on you, lass.'

'I'll . . . I'll stay away this weekend then.'

'An' have her round your place? If his lordship should happen to come home she'll likely do for him.'

145

'You could say I was ill or something, couldn't you?'

'Aye, I could. I could, lass, but such is Sarah's feelin' for you that she'd be round all the quicker if I did. No, just let things take their course, that's all you can do.'

Let things take their course. Rebecca stared back at the woman who, along with Sarah and Florrie, constituted the nearest she had ever known to a family. Her own mother had died within weeks of giving birth to her, and ten months later, when her father had married again, she'd been placed at Hatfield. But then she'd had Sarah, and through Sarah, Maggie, and then Florrie. She wished she lived with them now, *here*, oh, she did. These two rooms seemed like paradise to her, but if she said that they'd all think she'd gone barmy. It wasn't many round these parts who had what she did – her own place, and furnished too. Willie's da had been a dockside foreman for a good few years before he was killed in that accident, and he'd got his place round nice. The three-up, three-down was right bonny – that's what she'd thought when she'd first seen it.

'Did he try it on afore his mam died?'

'What?'

'Willie. Did he knock you about afore old Ma Dalton died?'

'No, no he didn't.' And he hadn't, but with his mother's passing, nine or ten months ago now, Willie had changed. No, not changed, she corrected silently. She had already known there was something there under his skin, waiting to break out – like those great boils he had all over his back. But never in her worst nightmare had she guessed at the sickness, the need to hurt, that drove him. With his mam living with them, and her a right old tartar herself, he hadn't dared to let go. But he'd made up for it once she'd gone. Rebecca shut her eyes for a split second as her stomach quivered. How he'd made up for it.

'No, I couldn't see the old lady standin' by an' allowin' that. Used to rule Willie an' his da with a rod of iron, she did. She married beneath herself you see, when she took Bill Dalton, her da bein' high up at the docks. It was her that got Bill set on as foreman, or her da any rate. Aye, everyone knew. But Bill was a good-lookin' bloke in them days an' he had a way with him; hers wasn't the only head that turned when Bill Dalton walked by.'

She knew what Maggie was thinking, knew it as clearly as if the old woman had spoken it out loud. Bill Dalton was one thing, but his son?

How could she even begin to explain how it had been, let alone how it was now? She looked at people like Maggie and Florrie, the neighbours, ordinary people she met in the shops or down in the laundry, and she remembered when she'd been like them. But now she was someone else, someone she didn't like and didn't want to be – consumed by fear and panic most of the time, and guilt. Aye, guilt. He made her feel as though she had failed him in some way.

It was no accident that she hadn't got pregnant before his mam had died; he had left her alone for months at a time before that and taken his pleasure down in the whorehouses at the docks. And she hadn't understood it, she'd wanted him to come to her bed . . . The quivering started again as the nausea rose. But then, when his mother died and he'd stayed home at nights she'd learnt why their marriage had barely been consummated in the years before. He reached sexual satisfaction by inflicting pain, and his years in the brothels had got it down to a fine art. And now there was no one to hear her scream. Oh, oh what was she going to do? She shivered, her hand clutching her mouth, then rose swiftly to her feet and rushed to the scullery at the end of the house where she was shudderingly sick into the deep white sink, the baby, *Willie's baby*, moving inside her as she retched.

147

'Come on, lass, come on.' Maggie's touch was gentle as she wiped Rebecca's clammy face with a piece of old towel, before helping the shivering girl back into the room they had just left and settling her in front of the blazing fire. 'There's plenty took the way you are with the first, but it passes, hinny, it passes.'

It passes. Rebecca turned now and faced Maggie on the couch next to her. She swallowed hard, then brought out in nothing more than a whisper, 'I'm ... I'm frightened, Maggie.'

'Frightened?' Maggie stared at the white-faced girl for a long moment before saying, her tone flat, 'Why, Rebecca? Why, exactly, are you frightened, lass? It's him, isn't it? That no good husband of yours?'

'I – I –' She wanted to get the words out, *needed* to tell someone. Not all of it – there were some degradations too deep and too humiliating to put into words – but just enough for Maggie to understand. She twisted on the seat, her hands damp with sweat and fear, but the words wouldn't come. He would kill her if she talked to anyone. He had said so and she believed him.

'Come on, lass. You can tell old Maggie.'

But she couldn't. Rebecca blinked twice. She knew now she couldn't. As Maggie herself would say, she'd made her bed and she had to lie on it. With ... with him.

'It's just nerves.' She was clasping and unclasping her hands without being aware of it, and now Maggie took her fingers and held them as she answered, 'Aye, lass, I know it's nerves. What I want to know is what you're scared of.'

'The – the baby, the baby coming. Everyone says it's painful, that you can hardly bear it.'

'Oh, you bear it, lass, same as women have borne it from Eve's time.' Maggie continued to gaze at her, and then she said, very softly, 'So you're not going to tell me then?'

'I . . . I did. I'm just a bit jittery, that's all.'

That wasn't all, not by a long chalk was it all, Maggie thought grimly. The lass had been as miserable as sin from the day she married Willie Dalton, but the last few months or so she had been . . . How had she been? She turned her head to one side, biting on her lip as she lumbered to her feet. 'I'll make us a nice sup of tea, lass. You sit by the fire an' take the load off your feet for a bit.'

But even while she made the tea, the analogy that had sprung to her mind wouldn't leave Maggie; a sick kind of anger, mixed with pain and amazement, made her clumsier than usual. There was a look in Rebecca's eyes that reminded her of a dog her da had brought home one night when she was just a bairn. He hadn't told them the full story, just that he had found it tied up in the back yard of the Fiddler's Elbow where he drank most nights. But she knew the landlord of the Fiddler's Elbow, all the bairns did, and steered well clear if they saw him coming down the street. The dog had been half crazy with fear and pain, and it had taken her da nigh on a week before it would let him touch it, and the look in its eyes – *the look in its eyes was a reflection of what was staring out of Rebecca's*. 'Oh, blessed Virgin, Mother of our Lord, let me be wrong.' Maggie rested her elbows on the kitchen cupboard as she prayed in the way she had been taught as a child. But she wasn't wrong, she knew she wasn't wrong.

She straightened slowly, her mind saying, I'm too old for all this. I am, I'm too old, even as she countered with, to hell with your mortal state, what about the lass? But Sarah would be here soon. She seized on the thought, hugging it tightly to her. Aye, her lass would be here the day, and there was no one like Sarah as far as Rebecca was concerned. She had a way with her, did Sarah. There was something in the lass that drew people, especially them with troubles. Sarah would get to the bottom of what ailed Rebecca if anyone could.

Chapter Ten

Sarah, her fingers nervously smoothing imaginary creases out of the skirt of her wool dress, said to the man at her side, 'It's really very good of you to give me a lift all this way.'

'Nonsense.' Rodney didn't look at her as he spoke, keeping his eyes on the road ahead. 'I'm glad of the company on a drive like this, and as I told you, I've people I need to see in these parts and one weekend is as good as any other as far as I'm concerned. It would have been ridiculous for you to travel all the way up to Sunderland one week, and me another, when we live within virtual spitting distance of each other.' He did glance at her then as he smiled, a brief look which said nothing.

She had grown into a stunningly beautiful woman. The thought had been with him since he had seen her at the Coles' house, and he had found it difficult to put her out of his mind for more than a few hours since then. He was aware he felt disturbed in her presence, but he wasn't quite sure why. Perhaps it was the fact that seeing her again had brought a whole host of memories of that time before the war to the fore? A time when he had been young and idealistic and full of nationalistic fervour. He had changed since then. How he had changed . . .

'It's still very kind.' Sarah paused, before adding, 'And to travel in such style, too.'

'You like the car?'

'How could anyone not like it? It's beautiful.'

'It was my father's pride and joy, he thought he had really arrived when he purchased a Rolls-Royce Silver Ghost. My mother used to protest he treated the car better than he did her, and maybe he did at that. I only use it occasionally, I wouldn't trust to parking it outside the surgery every night and my brother has ample room to keep it in his garage, besides which, with the economic crisis as it is, I can't justify the fuel intake. I have a little Morris Minor as my workhorse.'

Sarah's eyes searched the enigmatic profile before she said, 'Is your father . . . ?'

'He was killed in the war.' It was abrupt, and Rodney seemed to be aware of this as he added almost immediately, his voice softer, 'My parents and my brother were travelling home from the surgery one night when there was an air-raid, and the shelter they took refuge in sustained a direct hit. My parents were killed outright, my brother was badly hurt but he survived, although he lost a leg and has severe facial injuries. My mother had only gone into the surgery that afternoon to stand in for my father's receptionist who had gone home sick. Ironic, isn't it?'

'Yes, yes it is.'

'But that's life, or death in this case.' He must have sensed her discomfiture, because in the next breath he said, 'Oh, I'm sorry, Sarah, really. Don't take any notice of me, I have an unfortunate way of putting things sometimes.'

But it wasn't his way of expressing himself that had bothered her. Before she allowed herself to think further she grabbed at the first thing that came into her mind. 'Your brother? Is he older than you?'

'By four years.' His chin jerked and she wondered why, but then he continued, 'It was my father's plan that Richard and I would join him in the practice once we qualified, he

152

always said that family partners were the best partners.'

'But you didn't want to?'

'No, I didn't. You think that strange?'

'Strange?' She stared at him in surprise. 'Why should I think it strange? Everyone should be able to make their own decisions on such matters.'

'One would think so.'

She didn't like to ask anything more, there had been something in his voice that went far beyond the actual words, and it was all part and parcel of this new Dr Mallard who looked the same – exactly the same in spite of the intervening ten years – as she remembered, but that was all. And yet that wasn't quite true. When they had met at the tearooms in Baxter Street a few days ago for a chat about old times, as the doctor had put it when he'd invited her, there had been glimpses of the man she had known ten years ago. He had spoken kindly, he had looked kindly, and he had even laughed once or twice when she had regaled him with stories from her days in Hatfield's laundry and at the Roberts establishment, searching her mind for anything that would amuse him and take away the serious expression from his face.

And he had been genuinely interested to hear all about Maggie and Florrie, and Rebecca, she knew that, and it had been when she had confided how much she was missing them all that the old Dr Mallard of her childhood had said at once, 'I'm going up that way next weekend, perhaps Lady Harris could spare you for a day or two?'

And Lady Harris had spared her – partly, she suspected, because Lady Margaret had paved the way and reminded her mother-in-law that Sarah had put in a lot of extra hours over the last little while without taking any of the days owing to her. Lady Margaret, Sarah was finding, was a much softer character than her forthright mother-in-law, and in spite of Lady Harris's philanthropic declarations about the working class in general, and women in particular, much more inclined to informality – at least with her. The two of them had had some interesting conversations over the last week or so, and she was finding she liked the older woman very much.

After a few minutes, it was Rodney who broke the silence which was becoming increasingly strained, when he said, 'At least the practice gives my brother a reason to get up in the morning, and once our father had gone he took on two juniors to see new patients and a section of the established ones, so he has plenty of back-up. He has to go into hospital for periodic skin grafts to his face, you see, which isn't easy for him, added to which it was suggested to him that patients of a nervous disposition might find his injuries too distressing.'

'Oh surely not.' Sarah's voice was indignant. 'I mean, with the war and all, people aren't so shallow, are they?'

'It would take more than a war to change some people, Sarah.'

'He's not married or anything then?'

It should have been perfectly easy for him to say, 'Yes, he has been married for over ten years now,' but it wasn't, and he could hear the flat sound to the words as he spoke them.

'Oh.' A pause, and then Sarah said, but uncomfortably, 'At least he's got his wife then.'

'Yes, he's got Vanessa.'

Why was that note in his voice? Sarah asked herself as she stared a moment longer at the straight profile before turning to look out of the window at the familiar northern landscape. Was his brother's wife one of those people who was 'distressed' by his changed countenance? Whatever, there was clearly something wrong somewhere, but it wasn't any of her business, and she had better remember that.

She knew Dr Mallard had been surprised at the change in her when he had realized who she was at the Coles' house; and of course he would be, she had only been a child when he had left Sunderland – and the invitation to the tearooms, and this trip, had been generous of him, but there was no likelihood of renewing their acquaintance further once this weekend was over. She knew that. He was very well-to-do, the social circles he moved in were as much out of her reach as the man in the moon.

'You would like Richard.' Rodney's voice was reflective now, his eyes narrowed as he concentrated on the icy road ahead. The December day was raw, with a biting wind that cut across the bleak northern landscape with a ferocity unknown in the gentle south. 'He's an incredibly good-natured soul, philosophical I suppose.'

What did that mean? Sarah asked herself with a touch of Maggie's cynicism. She had seen plenty of the middle and upper classes who were 'philosophical'. They were philosophical about what they had, and others didn't, about hungry little bairns running about with bare backsides and no shoes. Eeh . . . Her thoughts shocked her. She shouldn't be thinking this way about the doctor's brother, he was probably very nice. He had to be if he was Rodney's flesh and blood.

Her use of his Christian name, if only in her mind, made Sarah sit up straighter. He had told her to drop the Dr Mallard at that first meeting in Whitechapel, but as yet she hadn't been able to bring herself to do so, although after his request the more formal address hadn't seemed right either. Consequently, she had avoided any use of his name whatsoever.

Her thoughts troubled her, and more to banish them than anything else, she said, 'I'm sure your brother is very kind, but it must have taken some strong moral fibre on your part to leave a ready-made career in London, and come to Sunderland when you qualified.'

'Strong moral fibre.' He echoed her words in a voice that brought her eyes swinging to his face, the movement of her head bringing a faint whiff of her flowery perfume to his nostrils. 'That sounds almost noble, Sarah, and I'm afraid I'm not noble, far from it. There were several reasons I didn't want to take a job with my father I suppose, most of them selfish.'

As Vanessa had reminded him again only the night before. Why did she do it? If he'd asked himself that question once, he'd asked it a hundred times, but he was still no nearer finding an answer. Why did she put them all through the torture time and time again? And torture wasn't too strong a word.

'Oh, darling, you're so *selfish*.' The light tinkling laugh had rung out, although the sting in the words was quite intentional, and she had fluttered her white, beautifully manicured hands at her husband. 'Say something, Richard, for goodness' sake. It's so silly that Rodney lives in that dreadful old house that just *reeks* of disinfectant and disease when you need him here.'

'It's a doctor's surgery, Vanessa, that's all, and I prefer to live on the premises. It would be false economy to think of renting or buying something else, when most of the house is unoccupied.'

'But it's such an unpleasant district, Rodney, it really is, and there's no *need*. You know your father wanted you and Richard to take over the practice together when he retired.'

'And you know I had no intention of doing that even before the war changed things.' Rodney had kept his voice level and quiet, and his face pleasant, even as his fingers had itched to wring her long graceful neck. She knew all right; if anyone knew, Vanessa did. And yet she had the gall to fling it in his face, not once, but every time the partnership with Richard was brought up.

What would his life have been like if he had never met her? he thought now, drawing the air in between his teeth, his eyes narrowed on the windscreen. Happier, a damn sight happier. The silent groan inside him twisted his bowels. So why couldn't he let go of her, *here*, in his mind, where it really mattered? How many times had he told himself she was a conniving, gold-digging little bitch, that he was well rid of her, that any woman who could get engaged to one brother, and then marry the other when she found out her fiancé's lifestyle wasn't going to be all caviare and champagne, was no good?

She had called him a communist that night eleven years ago, when she had finally realized she wasn't going to be able to sweet-talk him out of what she called his ridiculous affinity towards the working class. He hadn't known that up to that point she had believed she could persuade him to join his father and Richard in his father's practice in Windsor – or at least if he had, he hadn't admitted it to himself. He'd wanted her so badly, that had been the trouble, and even when he'd found out that other men had been there before him it hadn't mattered, not really. What did he mean, he *had* wanted her so badly? he asked himself with bitter cynicism. He still only had to look at her long slim body and cool beautiful face for his loins to ache. And she knew, dammit. She'd always known. But lately, in the last twelve months or so, her subtle overtures had grown more blatant. She couldn't bear Richard the way he was now, that was part of the trouble. The separate bedrooms hadn't been his brother's idea, he dared bet, but although Vanessa didn't want Richard near her that would have caused its own set of problems, because Vanessa had appetites.

He had been amazed, in those months after he had first met her, how uninhibited, how *hungry*, she was in bed. She looked so cool and languid, so ladylike, and yet the things she had wanted him to do to her . . . It had tormented him constantly, in the early days of Richard and Vanessa's marriage, when he had imagined the two of them together.

And then she had let him know, in that mocking, faintly patronizing way of hers, that her marriage didn't have to signal the end of their intimacy.

He had run then. First to the north, and then further afield when the war had started, but it had been a long time before he could admit to himself that he was running more from his own weakness where she was concerned than from Vanessa herself. She had laughed at him when he had protested he loved his brother and that he would never betray Richard by taking his wife. She'd laughed, and then she had looked at him with those great knowing eyes.

Oh, it was his own fault – he should have been honest with Richard when Vanessa had first returned his ring, along with a brief note to say the engagement was over. But he had played the big man, hadn't he, even to his own family. He had told them the parting of the ways had been a mutual decision, that they wanted different things out of life, and it was better to find out before they tied the knot – all the normal rubbish, to save face. And Vanessa had played him at his own game, seeking out Richard at the tennis club within weeks and casting her net.

They had been married with what constituted indecent haste – certainly more than one of his mother's friends had watched Vanessa's flat stomach for months afterwards – but Vanessa had just wanted to make sure of her life of ease as a rich doctor's wife, and one brother would do as well as the other for that, it seemed.

He swallowed hard, then turned his head for a moment as Sarah's voice brought him out of the dark reflections. 'I'm sorry, what did you say?'

'Have your brother and his wife any children?'

'No, no children.' He forced a light note into his voice as he added, 'I've got to wait a little longer to be an uncle.' How had they got on to this anyway? In an effort to change the subject without appearing rude, he said now, 'How on earth did you think you would manage with all that on the train, by the way?' He inclined his head towards the back seat, stacked high with gaily wrapped parcels, without taking his eyes off the road.

'I wouldn't have attempted to bring all this if I had been travelling by myself,' Sarah said quickly, 'but when you offered me a lift . . .'

'You must have been saving your rations all year for that lot.' His smile was warmer now, what Sarah would term a real smile. 'Perhaps I didn't do you such a favour after all in offering you a ride?'

'You certainly did,' Sarah said indignantly, before adding, 'I would have spent the same but some of it would have been monetary gifts, but they aren't so nice, are they? There's no . . . cosiness with them.'

It was a strange choice of words, but he remembered this about her. Even as a child she had expressed herself differently to anyone else, but although initially her phraseology might seem odd, when analysed, it was not. She had been a truly enchanting child. He was surprised by the sudden pull on his heartstrings, and to cover his emotion his voice was brisk when he said, 'Quite right.'

Quite right? He could do better than that, couldn't he? The poor girl hadn't asked to travel with him, he had suggested it, after all, although he wasn't quite sure why, if he thought about it. Maybe it had been the spur he had needed to answer Martin and Ruth's repeated invitations to visit them again? He'd had a guilty conscience about them for months now. Or perhaps the fact that the hour or so in the little tearoom with Sarah, when they had chatted about old times and Sarah had brought him up-to-date with her life, had been like a ray of sunshine on a winter's day. The simile faintly embarrassed him. He didn't consider himself a poetical man, or even aesthetic.

And he *had* been trying to save her an arduous journey. The rational, logical side took over. The trains were bad enough at the best of times, but near Christmas, and with the bad weather, she could have been standing about on cold platforms for hour after miserable hour. Trains, railways, he hated them – they would ever be synonymous with the living hell of the Japanese camps. How many executions and atrocities had he witnessed in those years on the Burma railway? Hundreds, thousands . . .

It did no good to indulge in such reminiscences, and now he wetted his lips and swallowed before he said, 'I'm glad Maggie isn't still at Hatfield, although I'd be lying if I didn't admit to some surprise at Florrie's benevolence. She didn't strike me as a charitable sort.'

There was more than a touch of cynicism in his tone, and Sarah stiffened defensively before she told herself she really couldn't blame him for thinking the worst. Perhaps in his place she would have thought the same. But he didn't know, he didn't understand, what Sarah's nearly dying had done to Florrie.

'Actually, that's exactly what Florrie is.' It was firm, and suggested further comments on the same lines would not be appreciated.

Rodney took the hint. 'And Matron Cox?' he asked quietly. 'She's still locked away where she can do no harm, I hope?'

'As far as I'm aware.' Oh, this was difficult. He wasn't at all like she remembered, but then she had changed too.

'She was quite mad, you know, dangerously so. It was a wonder she hadn't cracked before.'

'It was probably because she was able to do virtually what she wanted at Hatfield. It was only later, when I was a bit older, that I realized how many of the children were confined to the infirmary for weeks at a time after they had been sent

160

to the Matron for punishment. Everyone, children and staff alike, was petrified of her.'

'Except Maggie.'

'And you,' she returned quickly.

She smiled at him, and he glanced at her and smiled back, before saying, 'You are determined to see me in a good light, aren't you?' But it was the first time for a long long while that he had felt good about himself. It was the feeling of helplessness that had eaten into him in the camp. There he'd been, a doctor, someone who was supposed to save lives, and all around him men – walking skeletons of men – had been dying like flies. He'd been beaten almost to the point of death one time in that first month in Burma, when he'd argued with the camp commander for more medicines, the meagre supplies of antiseptic and quinine useless against the disease and malnutrition which had been rife amongst the prisoners.

What was it that young army chaplain had said, when he had visited the ward shortly after they had arrived back in England? Oh yes, 'unforgiveness is a tool of the devil'. There he'd stood, fresh out of college and never having seen a day's action in his life, and he'd dared to say that to the remains of what had been men in that ward. Ill and weak as he'd been, he didn't know how he had kept his hands off the pious young fool.

'Matron Cox's replacement was just the opposite, though. Hatfield changed considerably once she was in charge.'

'Ah yes, the good Matron Blair.' Again Sarah's voice brought him out of the shadows and he nodded slowly before adding, 'I remember her as the original broom that swept clean. She caused quite a stir with some of the old fogeys on Hatfield's committee.'

What Sarah remembered, as she heard him speak the Matron's name, was that she had been burningly jealous of the new Matron's relationship with 'her' Dr Mallard. Matron

161

Blair had been bright and attractive, and worse – in her childish eyes – very grown up. She could recall endless nights when she had lain awake staring into the darkness, Rebecca's steady breathing in the next bed emphasizing she was the only person awake in the whole wide world, and her mind had played out the doctor and the matron's wedding day. What a fiercely impassioned little thing she must have seemed.

She gave a mental shake of her head at the forlorn little ghost from the past, and changed the subject.

It was over two hours later, and in icy darkness, that Rodney's car, looking somewhat incongruous in the maze of back-to-back dilapidated tenements in which Maggie and Florrie's house was buried, drew up in a narrow street in the heart of Sunderland.

In spite of the numbing coldness of the winter night, there were several young children, most without coats, taking it in turns to swing from a rope which one of the more adventurous had tied to the jutting iron arm of a lamp post, and their shrill voices were loud in the clear frosty air.

'Sarah! Hey, it's Sarah.' One of the older boys came running up to the car when he saw Sarah alighting after Rodney had opened the door for her, the other children following a moment later. 'You come back to see old Maggie, Sarah?' he asked cheerily, wiping his runny nose with the back of a grubby hand.

'Less of the "old Maggie", Tim McNeil.' Her voice was severe, but Sarah couldn't stop herself smiling as she looked down at the dirty little face. 'It's Mrs McLevy to you.'

'Maggie don't mind, she's all right, is Maggie.' The sharp eyes, far older than their years, dissected Rodney as he stood at Sarah's side, before the boy said, 'Who's the toff then, Sarah? He your fancy man or somethin'?' as the other children tittered and giggled behind him.

'*Tim*.' It was a distinct warning, and Sarah wasn't smiling any longer.

'You're not gonna leave that motor round 'ere, are you, mister?' Tim turned his attention to Rodney, who was trying hard not to laugh, quite unabashed at Sarah's rebuke. 'They'd 'ave the drips from your nose round these parts.' And with that friendly warning he returned to the lamp post, the other children following hot on his heels.

Sarah smiled weakly at Rodney. 'That was Tim McNeil.'

'So I gathered.' Rodney smiled back. 'The lad will go far.'

'You'll come in for a minute and say hallo to Maggie? I know she'd love to see you again.'

Rodney hesitated for a moment, and then, as Sarah's smile widened and she said, 'I'll set the formidable Tim to guard the car if you're worried,' he laughed out loud before saying, 'That won't be necessary, but I have no wish to impose.'

'Oh, go on with you.' The words, and the flapping of her hand, were very northern, and he found himself thinking, as he locked the car and turned to join her where she was waiting for him on the pavement, that it was at these times, when he caught a glimpse of the child she had been, that he liked her the most. The new Sarah was a little disconcerting at times, and the directness that had been so enchanting in the child was more than a trifle challenging in the adult woman. But that was probably exactly what he needed, he admitted to himself soberly as he stood behind Sarah while she knocked at the door, looking down at her shining blond head that was a halo of gold in the dimly lit street. To be jerked out of the comfortable rut he had settled into the last few months? He hadn't realized it but he had let his work become his security, hiding behind it, letting life pass him by while he had licked his wounds in his little bubble of

163

isolation. He didn't like the analogy but it was true. And it wouldn't do. It wouldn't do at all.

He had no further time to reflect as the door opened and Maggie's bulky shape stood silhouetted in the opening.

'Thank goodness. Thank goodness you're here, lass, I've been worried to death. I expected you hours ago.' Maggie had enfolded Sarah into her arms as she'd spoken, and now, becoming aware for the first time of Rodney's presence, she peered into the shadows as she said, 'You got someone with you, lass?'

'Hallo, Maggie.'

'Saints alive! I don't believe it.'

'Well, I'm alive, but I'm no saint, Maggie.'

'It's Dr Mallard, as I live an' breathe. Oh, lad, lad, come in, come in. You're a sight for sore eyes.'

The warmth of her greeting touched him, and when Sarah was almost thrust into the hall, and Maggie reached out both hands to grasp his, he felt a lump in his throat and a pricking at the back of his eyes that caused him to say, and over-heartily, 'It's been a long time, Maggie. A long time.'

'It has that, lad, an' with a war between an' all. You come through then?'

'Yes, I came through, Maggie.'

He found himself drawn into a long narrow dark hall, and as he heard Sarah's voice speaking to someone, Maggie said, 'You know I live with Florrie now?'

'So Sarah told me. I have to admit I was surprised at first.'

'She's been like an angel of mercy, lad, I tell you. No daughter could've bin better. Me legs aren't too good, an' me rheumatism gives me jip some days, but she never complains if I'm laid up in bed for a while, just gets on doin' everythin' an' her with a manager's job at the laundry too. She's a good lass.'

He raised his eyebrows, nodding slightly, as he said,

'That's good. I'm pleased for you, Maggie.'

'But?'

'I beg your pardon?'

'Oh, come on, lad, this is Maggie you're talkin' to. There was an edge to your voice, an' war or no war, I know you. Say what's on your mind an' be done with it. It'll be better out than in.'

For the first time in months, years, he felt a bubble of something – which he recognized as the beginnings of the good old belly laughs he used to enjoy – welling up inside. She was a comic; without even recognizing the fact, she was a comic all right. Would that there were a few more Maggies in the world.

He checked the impulse to laugh – he didn't want to offend her – and instead tried to make his voice suitably humble as he said, 'I'm sorry, Maggie.' She had let go of his hands as she'd spoken, and now he reached out and took hers, looking down into her fat face criss-crossed with wrinkles, as he said quietly, 'I think I must be getting cynical in my old age.'

'Folks can change, lad. Oh aye, I've seen it, but in Florrie's case it weren't so much a change as gettin' into the skin of the person she was meant to be. She'd been in the workhouse from a bairn an' she'd been treated rough, no doubt about it, an' it had soured the lass. But I tell you' – she paused, and now her face was straight – 'she loves them lasses, Sarah an' Rebecca, like her own.'

He nodded but said nothing more, and she stared at him for a moment longer, her gaze penetrating, before saying, her tone jocular now, 'Come on in an' have a hot bevy, lad, it's enough to freeze you out there.'

He followed her down the hall and into the second of two rooms to see Sarah crouching in front of a blazing coal fire, her hands held out to its warmth, and Florence Shawe, her tall angular body even thinner than he remembered, looking straight at him.

'Good evening, Dr Mallard.' She spoke as if she had seen him just the other day, her voice quiet and even, and he was immediately aware she was on her guard. The ugly face with its big hooked nose was expressionless but her eyes were wary. 'Can I offer you a hot drink?'

'Thank you.' He didn't like to look about him, but he couldn't hold Florrie's eyes for much longer either, so he walked across to join Sarah in front of the fire, saying as he did so, 'I've been too long in the south. I'd forgotten just how cold it can be in these parts.'

'Put a drop of whisky in the doctor's tea, Florrie lass,' Maggie interjected. 'You're not a teetotaller, are you, lad?'

'No.' He smiled at Maggie as he turned to face the room again with his back to the fire. It was a pleasant room, he noted now, with something akin to surprise. Shabby but pleasant. Whether it was the long red drapes at the window, or the blaze of the fire, he didn't know, but there was an atmosphere of peace and warmth, space even, which was unusual in such neighbourhoods as this one, where living space was at a premium.

'I didn't think you was. All the doctors I've ever known have liked a tipple.' She spoke as if she had known hundreds, and again the urge to laugh was upon him, or at least, he thought it was the urge to laugh until the lump in his throat told him otherwise. 'Anyway, sit yourself down, lad, an' I'll find a bit of somethin' to go with that tea. We've been waitin' on this one arrivin' ' – she inclined her head towards Sarah who had walked over and sat down on the leather couch as Maggie had been talking – 'an' me stomach's thinkin' me throat's bin cut.' So saying she bustled out of the room after Florrie, leaving Rodney and Sarah alone.

Sarah sat quietly on the leather couch without speaking;

she had a strange feeling on her that she couldn't have explained to anyone, but it had to do with the unspoken question in Maggie's eyes. Why hadn't she told them it was the doctor who was driving her up? She should have, she knew that, he had been just as much a friend of Maggie's years ago as he had hers, and it would have given Florrie a chance to prepare herself too, but somehow . . . somehow she just hadn't been able to. She knew he had thought it odd too, when he had asked her earlier that day what time she had told Maggie to expect them, and she had answered she had told Maggie she wasn't sure if she was travelling by train or with a friend, and to expect her any time. *Why hadn't she told them?* She bit on her lip and lowered her head as the answer came. Because she had been frightened to voice it in case the verbalizing of it had prevented it from happening. But that was daft. *She* was daft.

'I should have written and told them you were bringing me.'

It was quiet, and there was a pause before Rodney said, 'Oh, I think it was a nice surprise. At least I hope it was a nice surprise?'

The note in his voice made her smile, as it was meant to, and when she said, 'I think Maggie and Florrie thought it peculiar I didn't mention it beforehand,' she was more relaxed.

'Well in my line of work it could easily not have happened. You wouldn't believe how many cancelled engagements I add up in a month. One of the first things they warn you about at medical school is never to assume anything, whether it's about a patient's symptoms or when you might eat your next meal.'

'It's as bad as that?' She smiled at the mocking hangdog expression on his face.

'Worse.'

'Oh dear.'

'They really shouldn't go to any trouble, you know.' He gestured towards the open door through which voices were filtering from the kitchen at the end of the hall. 'I'm sure Martin and Ruth will be able to rustle up a little supper for me.'

'Where do your friends live?'

'Kelton Park. Do you know it?'

She had heard of it. Nob hill, as Maggie described the exclusive area on the outskirts of town. The small estate of new houses was only five years old, and most of the gardens had tennis courts and you could barely see your next door neighbour for the amount of landscaped ground between you. Kelton Park. Nothing could have emphasized the difference between them more.

She shook her head in answer to his question, before saying, 'Not personally, no, but I'm sure it's very nice.'

They continued to talk until Maggie and Florrie bustled in with plates laden with sandwiches and cake, and when Sarah saw the small sandwiches were cut wafer-thin, and that there were fancy doilies under the food, she wanted to kiss the pair of them and tell them not to worry. She loved these two rooms, and she loved them, and if Rodney couldn't accept them all for who and what they were, then that was his misfortune. Almost in the same moment Sarah berated herself for her hypocrisy. She *did* want him to see her as being able to fit into his world, and that was probably what Maggie and Florrie had sensed.

But that wasn't wrong, was it? To want to improve yourself was natural enough, surely, and a healthy ambition, as long as it was done in the right way and for the right reasons?

As though it were yesterday, a passage from the Bible which Matron Cox had drummed into them every evening after dinner when they were obliged to kneel for a Bible reading and prayers before going up to the dormitories and retiring for the night, came into her mind. 'Then I looked on all the works that my hands had wrought, and on the labour that I had laboured to do: and, behold, all was vanity and vexation of spirit, and there was no profit under the sun.' The Matron had insisted it was God's word to humble and admonish them to work diligently and without reward, but it had depressed Sarah more than she could ever express, because she had known then, young as she was, that she wanted to make something of herself.

But perhaps the Matron had been right? No, no of course she hadn't been, she reproached herself immediately. And she didn't believe God thought so either. He wasn't up there waiting to beat you over the head with a big stick and laughing when it all went wrong, whatever interpretation Matron Cox had chosen to put on that particular verse.

She had dreams, and she wasn't ashamed of them. She didn't want to remain in service all her life, and she *did* want her own home and a family with the man she loved and who loved her. And the other dream, the one that had been with her for as long as she could remember, she would make that happen too. She *would* find her mother, however painful the result of her quest might be.

Rodney left shortly after nine o'clock, and the three women watched the beautiful car drive away down the dark deserted street with very different feelings.

Florrie's thoughts were less than charitable, on the whole. She knew Dr Mallard didn't like her. Oh, he'd been polite enough, smiling and saying all the right things, but she could sense how he felt and she just hoped he wasn't going to make a habit of calling in if he was up visiting these friends of his again. He made her feel . . . uncomfortable. She wasn't proud of her part in the events which had led him into Sarah's life; she'd give the world to undo the hurt she'd caused her bonny lass at that time, but Sarah bore her no grudge and that was the main thing.

Florrie's thin lips compressed and her big nose flared as the car turned the corner with a cheerful honk of its horn. It was all right for him; it was all right for most men if it came to that. Oh, it was a man's world all right, there was no getting away from it.

Maggie, on the other hand, gazed down the street after the car with a feeling of excitement mingling with faint apprehension. Fancy her lass and the doctor meeting up like that – it was fate, that's what it was. And he had no side to him, he never had had, unlike most of his class, but . . . Her brow furrowed. He *was* one of the top nobs when all was said and done.

Times were changing mind you, oh aye, she knew that. Look at Katie Taggart taking up with Colonel Smythe's son, and hardly a raised eyebrow, but still . . . The feeling of unease increased. If she wasn't much mistaken, his attitude towards the lass was more paternal than anything. And that wouldn't matter – no, it'd be just fine if Sarah thought of him in the same way. But if she did . . . Maggie sucked in her bottom lip as her eyes narrowed at the disappearing car. If she did, why hadn't Sarah told them he was bringing her home? And why was she . . . skittish?

Oh, she was probably running away with herself here. Florrie always said she had to have something to worry about before she was happy, but she knew her lass, that was the thing, and although Sarah might not be aware of it herself she was definitely skittish. And she hadn't seen her like that before.

Sarah watched the car until it turned the corner, and then she touched Maggie's arm lightly. 'Come on in, you two, you'll catch your deaths out here.'

It had been strange coming home in such style, she

thought to herself as the three of them turned to enter the house. Strange, but very nice. And Rodney was nice, oh, he was. Different to how she remembered, more serious and reserved perhaps, but then that was the war no doubt. You couldn't go through something like that and come out just the same. But she was glad she had been able to travel up with him, and the last hour or so, when he'd sat and chatted with Maggie and she had been able to watch his face as he had talked, had made him more . . . familiar again.

Her mind was teeming with all the impressions of the long day and she wanted nothing more than to be alone and able to digest her thoughts in peace and quiet, but Maggie hadn't got through the door before she said, 'You didn't mention you'd seen the doctor again, lass. How did that come about? Last I heard, a couple of years ago now, he was still a prisoner-of-war, poor devil.'

Sarah continued walking through into the room they had just vacated, resuming her seat in front of the fire before she said, 'I was visiting Peggy's lodgings and he was attending Mrs Cole's mother. She's got a bad heart.'

Maggie wasn't interested in Mrs Cole's mother's bad heart. 'When was that then?'

'Oh, two, perhaps three weeks ago. I don't remember.'

The reserved note Maggie detected in Sarah's voice gave the lie to the casual answer, and the glance that flashed between her and Florrie was knowing. 'An' he offered to bring you back this weekend then?'

'Yes. I . . . I met him for tea one afternoon, and I happened to say I was missing you all. He'd got friends he wanted to visit up here, so he suggested we could travel together.' Sarah knew she would have to bring it out into the open, it was clear they had thought it odd she hadn't mentioned she'd met Rodney, so now she turned, her cheeks slightly pink as she said, 'Of course, with him being a doctor he wasn't sure if

171

he'd be able to get away until the last minute so I didn't mention he might be bringing me in case you were disappointed.' It sounded weak to her own ears, let alone theirs.

'Aye, I can understand that, lass.'

Sarah glanced first at Maggie and then Florrie before she said, her words rushed, 'Perhaps I should have told you but I didn't want you to go to any trouble. Thank you for making him so welcome.'

'He don't have to wait for an invitation, not that man.'

It was noticeable to both Sarah and Maggie that Florrie said nothing, and the silence stretched before Sarah rose and said, 'I'm very tired, we've been travelling since early morning. Would it be all right if I went to bed and we talked tomorrow?'

Maggie nodded at her. 'Aye, lass, you get yourself off to bed an' we'll do our jawin' in the mornin'. Rebecca was here earlier. She had to go when you were late comin', but she'll be back the morrer no doubt. The shakedown's all made up atween our beds in the other room, an' there's a bottle already in it. Take this last sup of tea in with you, lass, an' have it in bed.'

Sarah took the tea after giving both women a quick hug, and the room she entered a moment later via the hall was similar in size to the sitting room, and like that one gave the overall impression of warmth and cheer in the face of adversity.

It was more cluttered than the sitting room, holding two three-quarter-size iron beds with thick flock mattresses and worn brown blankets, a large and battered oak chest, a small wardrobe, two old straight-backed chairs on each of which reposed a towel, flannel and soap, along with a stone bedwarmer, and a small stool in the corner of the room under the window holding a large enamel bowl and jug.

But it was to the bright yellow curtains at the window, their sunshine colour reflected in the worn satin eiderdowns covering both beds, that the eye was drawn, and to the large, thick, gaily coloured clippy mat which stood in front of the open fireplace in which a glowing fire was burning.

It was strange, Sarah thought now as she sat down carefully on the small put-u-up which had been squeezed between the two beds, that Florrie, with her plain looks and thin angular body, possessed the ability to make an otherwise unprepossessing room glow with warmth and colour. A natural homemaker, Maggie had always called her, and she had added privately to Sarah on more than one occasion that Florrie was the sort of woman who, had things been different, and she'd met a man prepared to look beyond the outward appearance to the real person underneath, would have made a wonderful wife and mother.

Sarah shivered suddenly, rising and walking across to the deep-set black grate where she knelt on the mat and stared into the tiny flickering blue and red flames at the base of the fire. She, like Florrie, had lots to give, and she didn't want to wait for ever. Life is what you make it. How often had she heard Maggie say that? And she wanted to do something more at the moment than housekeeping.

A newspaper advertisement she had seen some days before sprang into her mind. It had been a request for voluntary workers at a hospital. There had been some panic or other the moment after she had read it and she'd forgotten about it, but now she sat back on her heels as the thought took form. She would like to do something like that. She nodded to herself. She'd enquire about that as soon as she got back to London.

Decision made, she undressed quickly – if divesting herself of stockings and shoes, and her heavy wool dress, could be called undressing – and sitting on the narrow makeshift bed she pulled the pile of wellworn blankets, topped by a patchwork quilt, about her waist before reaching for the mug of tea. Away from the fire the room was cold but not chilled, and as she sipped at the tea, the mug cupped between her hands and the steam warming her face, her mind was full of Rodney again, and it continued to be so once she had slid down under the covers and shut her eyes in preparation for sleep.

In the other room, once the door had shut behind Sarah, Maggie and Florrie had remained standing for some moments before Maggie had said, her voice low and uncharacteristically soft, 'Well? What do you make of that then?'

'It was very kind of him to bring her home.' Florrie's voice was slightly stiff.

'Aye, it was.' Maggie paused, and then flopped down into a chair as she said, 'I haven't told her about Rebecca yet, an' there's still the other business. Perhaps you were right, an' we should have written her about that when we found out, but I thought it'd be less of a shock face-to-face.'

Florrie shrugged her thin shoulders before she too sat down, and her voice was quiet when she said, 'What the medical profession are thinking of to let someone like Matron Cox loose on society again, I don't know. She should have been locked away for life. All this current talk about rehabilitation and so on; to my mind they just want to make room for all the war casualties that still need help, so anyone with two arms and two legs gets put back into the community. Never mind if they're a penny short of a shilling, out they go. And after what she tried to do to you and Sarah too.'

'Maud says her sister, her that was in the same ward as the Matron, is as right as ninepence since she's been out.'

'Maud's sister didn't try to murder anyone.'

'No, there is that, lass.'

'And while we're on the subject, I for one would feel a lot

174

better if I knew where she was living right now.'

The two women gazed at each other for a few seconds before Maggie gave a huh of a laugh and said, her tone suggesting her words had been said many times before, 'Don't worry, lass, don't worry. I'm not daft, whatever else I am, an' I'll keep me eyes skinned.'

'You say that, but you can't be on your guard twenty-four hours a day, now then. And don't forget Maud's sister also said that all Matron Cox talked about, before she learnt to keep her mouth shut and aim to get out of that place, was getting even with you. She blames you for it all, Maggie, and you've got to face that and be cautious.'

'If by bein' cautious you mean I've got to live lookin' over me shoulder the rest of me life, it's not worth it, I'm tellin' you straight, lass. The unnatural bitch has won then, hasn't she, whatever way you look at it.' And then as Florrie went to protest she added, 'But I'll watch meself, I will, Florrie. I can promise you that.'

'You better had.'

'Although after ten years I doubt she'll risk bein' put back in the loony bin by doin' somethin' silly. No, old Cox don't worry me as much as Rebecca to tell you the truth, lass. There's somethin' I can't get to the bottom of there, an' I just hope Sarah's able to get her to open up.'

'If anyone can, Sarah can.'

'Aye, you're right there, an' all.' Maggie nodded slowly. 'Well, I'll tell Sarah what's what in the mornin', Florrie, put her in the picture about everythin', the matron too, an' we'll go from there.'

Chapter Eleven

At two o'clock the next afternoon, when Rebecca still hadn't put in an appearance at Maggie's house, Sarah decided to go to her, and so it happened she met her friend just as Rebecca was closing the gate to her small front garden behind her.

The afternoon was a dull one, the sky low and heavy and threatening snow, but on her walk through the freezing streets to Rebecca's neat little house in Bentley Lane, Sarah had barely noticed the cold, anger at what Maggie had told her about Rebecca's black eye and disquiet about Matron Cox's release keeping her warm, along with another emotion . . .

Surprisingly, in view of the rickety old put-u-up, Sarah had slept well, but when she had awoken she had been aware that her dreams – or certainly the last one, fragments of which had stayed with her for some time – had been of a nature to make her blush. How could she, she had asked herself during the journey to Rebecca's house, how *could* she imagine her and the doctor doing such intimate things? She had never dreamt anything like that before, or if she had, she hadn't remembered it upon awakening. She was still blushing when she caught sight of Rebecca.

There was a moment, when Rebecca turned round and Sarah saw her poor bruised face, that she realized her friend had been crying, and then their arms were round each other and Rebecca was saying, 'Sarah, oh, Sarah, Sarah . . .' They clung together for some minutes, and it was Rebecca who drew away, wiping her eyes with the back of her hand as she said, 'Come on in, the curtains will be flapping like mad.'

Bentley Lane was a prim tidy street and its equally prim tidy inhabitants liked to think they were a cut above the surrounding neighbourhood. Respectability was the god of its residents and it was worshipped daily, and with great devotion. However, Rebecca was no longer overawed, as she had been when she'd first come to live there. The neatly painted front doors and white-laced windows were a façade, and she had come to hate them nearly as much as she feared the man she had married.

'But what about Willie?' Sarah caught hold of Rebecca's hand as she turned to open her gate again, the sight of her friend's face strengthening her conviction that Rebecca had to think about leaving this brute of a husband. 'We can go to a café if you'd rather?'

Rebecca's face had had a frightened look about it, but then, as Sarah looked deep into the dark brown eyes, there was superimposed a look of resignation, and Rebecca let out a long slow breath before saying, 'No, you come in. We . . . we need to talk, that's what you've come for isn't it? And we can't do that properly in a café.'

She turned fully now, opening the small wooden gate which was set in a three-foot brick wall, and walking through into the flagstoned rectangle that made up the nine feet of front garden.

Sarah had only been in Rebecca's house once since Willie's mother had died, and that had been a few days after the funeral when she had called round with a box of chocolates and a card for Rebecca's birthday the next day. Willie had been at home on that occasion, and he had been crude and offensive as he had all but shown her the door. Out of deference to the pain and embarrassment the incident had caused Rebecca, Sarah hadn't visited Bentley Lane again, meeting Rebecca at Maggie's, or in a café, or, weather permitting, on the beach or at a park.

Sarah knew only too well that there would be more than one 'good' neighbour who would be interested in Willie's wife's visitors, and impelled by that thought she glanced about her as she waited for Rebecca to unlock the front door.

As her eyes moved probingly to the houses either side of number four, she could feel eyes burning into the back of her neck, and on turning she noticed the curtains of the house directly opposite were twitching.

'Mrs Macintyre.' Rebecca had followed her gaze. 'She doesn't miss a thing, the old bat.'

'Rebecca, I've told you, we could go somewhere else.'

'Aye, we could.' Rebecca stared across the road for a moment before she turned to Sarah and added, 'But this is my home and you are my closest friend. What could be more natural than for you to call on me? Come on in, Sarah.'

The door was open now, and Sarah followed Rebecca into the neat, clinically clean house that smelt of disinfectant and furniture polish. She hadn't noticed this odour when Willie's mother was alive, she thought now. The house had always been clean, immaculate even, but now it was . . . sanitary. Yes, sanitary. Not like a home at all.

Her thoughts prompted her to say, as Rebecca waved her through to the sitting room, 'You must spend ages keeping everything so nice.'

The sitting room was as pristine as the hall had been, and not a thing had been changed from her last visit all those months before. The wooden mantelpiece was shining, and two brass candlesticks either end enclosed a host of gleaming brass ornaments below an imposing scriptural text on the wall which read, 'The fear of the Lord prolongeth days: but the years of the wicked shall be shortened.' Two other texts, with similarly encouraging verses, adorned the opposite wall, above two straight-backed chairs placed strategically underneath. There was a square of good carpet in the middle of the room around which a plumply upholstered horsehair suite sat, and everything from the two prancing wooden horses and crystal fruit bowl on the polished sideboard, to the dignified aspidistras either side of the lace-curtained window was positioned just so. It was like a small mausoleum.

'I see you've kept all Willie's mam's brassware,' Sarah said uncomfortably as she waved her hand at the mantelpiece. The room was positively depressing. 'I used to hate cleaning the brass at Mrs Roberts's, but you obviously don't mind.'

'No, I don't mind.' Rebecca's voice was flat after the emotion she had displayed in the street, and now she added, 'I'd better light the fire, it's cold in here.'

'Blow the fire. Rebecca, what's wrong?'

'How long have you got?' Rebecca tried to smile, but it was beyond her, and when Sarah didn't respond to the flippancy, she said, 'Sarah, if I could tell anyone it would be you, but I just can't. If I did . . . well, I don't want any trouble and you don't know what Willie's like.'

She'd got a good idea. 'Where is he?'

'At a football match.'

'Right, so we've got plenty of time to talk and that's exactly what we're going to do, but not in here. Come on.' She took Rebecca's arm and ushered her back into the hall as she said, 'We'll talk in the kitchen, I bet it's nice and warm in there.' She knew Rebecca's habit of lighting the big stove in the kitchen first thing and keeping it going all day. When Willie's mother had been alive, and Sarah had been a frequent visitor to the house, she had often found the two women ensconced in the large stone-floored kitchen that ran across the width of the house, Mrs Dalton gently rocking in her old rocking chair to one side of the fireplace as she watched

Rebecca working at something or other at the long wooden kitchen table.

When they entered the room at the end of the hall, Sarah saw it was as immaculate as the rest of the house but warm, more homely, although it didn't seem quite right without Mrs Dalton in her rocking chair, and Sarah said, 'Do you miss Willie's mam at all?'

'Aye, yes I do, funny that, isn't it?' Rebecca took off her coat, and after taking Sarah's, walked back into the hall to hang them on the carved wooden coatstand as she continued, saying, 'She used to get on my nerves when she was alive. Oh, we got on all right, we liked each other and that, but she was so bossy it was like being back at Hatfield at times. And she thought she was the cat's whiskers because her da had been high up at the docks. She was forever going on at Willie, he could never do anything right.'

As Rebecca reappeared she stood quiet for a moment, watching Sarah putting the kettle on the hob, before she added, 'I used to feel sorry for him at times.'

'But you don't any more?'

Rebecca looked straight at her, and her voice was bitter as she said, 'No, I don't any more.' Within days of his mother's passing she had learnt that you don't extend the hand of compassion to a rabid dog; not unless you wanted it bitten off, that was.

'Rebecca?' Sarah had seen what Maggie had seen, and it appalled her. 'Tell me, please. Talk to me.' She walked across the room and took Rebecca's hands in hers, and then, as Rebecca's head moved from side to side, her fingers tightened and she said, 'Whatever it is, you can tell me. We've no secrets, we never have had.'

'He said . . . he said he'd kill me if I told.'

'Not while I've got breath in my body.'

Rebecca's head was bowed, her short spiky lashes hiding

her expression, as she muttered, 'It's just that . . . Willie . . .'

'Yes? Go on.'

'He's . . . not normal.'

'Not normal?' Sarah let go of her, peering down to try and see Rebecca's face as she repeated, 'Not normal? You mean he's— He likes men?'

'Men?' Rebecca's head lifted now, and her eyes held something akin to surprise before they cleared. 'No, I don't mean that,' she said distractedly. 'He married me, didn't he, and I'm expecting.'

'That doesn't necessarily mean . . .' She couldn't get sidetracked. 'What is it then, if it's not that?'

There was a pause when Rebecca's head again lowered and then the whisper, 'He likes doing things, unnatural things.'

Sarah's eyes narrowed. What did she mean, unnatural? Her friend's previous comment had revealed an innocence which had surprised Sarah, and now she found herself wondering if Rebecca, in spite of having been married for four years, understood all that was involved within the marriage bonds. But she must do. Of course she must.

'Unnatural?'

'He . . . he uses things, whips and ropes, and he's made objects, horrible objects.' Rebecca shook her head, covering her face with her hands as the tears spurted between her fingers. 'He wants to hurt me, all the time, and sometimes he makes me— Oh, I can't, Sarah, I can't say any more.'

'Oh, Rebecca, Rebecca.'

'And all the time I'm frightened, all the time. I never know what he's going to do next.'

They were both crying now, their arms round each other and their heads pressed close together, and it was some minutes before Sarah said, 'You can't stay with him. You know that, don't you? You can't stay with him, Rebecca.'

'But he's my husband.'

'*Rebecca*.' Sarah felt the muscles of her stomach tighten, and then, as the kettle began to sing, she said, 'Look, I'll make the tea and then we'll talk properly, but you can't stay with him. Is he still doing it now, even with you pregnant?' And as Rebecca nodded once with her eyes closed, Sarah repeated, 'You can't stay with him.'

They drank the hot tea in silence, sitting side by side at the table, and it was after Sarah had poured them both another cup that Rebecca said, 'He didn't use to do things when his mother was alive. I think he was frightened she'd hear. Perhaps when the baby's born he'll be like he was then.'

'*Rebecca*.' Sarah stared at her, horrified. 'You don't believe that, now then, and if he's doing things like . . . like that, there's a good chance the baby won't be born. You'll miscarry or something. Think of your child if you won't think of yourself. You have to get out of here. Now, today.'

'But how can I, Sarah? He says I could never survive on my own, and he's right, he is. I'm not like you, I haven't got any looks and I'm not clever—'

'Rebecca, what's he done to you?' Sarah's voice was high with a mixture of anger and disbelief. 'You don't believe all that, you can't, he's been lying to you. *Of course* you could survive without Willie Dalton.'

'And there's the bairn.'

'Now listen.' She had leant forward, her tone urgent, but before she could say anything more a thick northern voice from the doorway brought both their heads swinging round as though connected by a single wire.

'Well, well, well, look what the wind's blown in.'

'Willie.' Rebecca's white face blanched still further. 'I thought you were going to the football match.'

'Did you now? Aye, well I thought I'd be about surprisin' me wife, especially when a little bird told me Lady Muck

183

here was payin' old Maggie a visit. No offence mind.' The mean little eyes in the fat coarse face had been watching Sarah as she rose to her feet, but now they swung to Rebecca who hadn't moved, and something in their depths made her say, 'Sarah just called by. On the off chance.'

'The off chance? Aye, maybe.'

'Rebecca didn't ask me to come if that's what you're thinking.'

'Now how would you know what I'm a thinkin', eh?' Willie smiled at Sarah, revealing a set of surprisingly white, even teeth, but it was merely a stretching of his thick-lipped mouth and didn't touch his eyes. 'You bin commiseratin' with her then?'

'What?'

He had been watching her closely for her reaction, and when she started, her hand going to her throat as hot colour flooded her face, his eyes narrowed and then moved to Rebecca, who had jumped to her feet saying, 'I – I didn't, I didn't, Willie. We were just talking.'

'Commiseratin' with her,' he said again in a flat monotone. 'About feelin' under the weather with the bairn.'

'Oh, oh I see. We didn't get round to talking about that as it happens. I was telling Rebecca about my job and London and everything.'

'Were you now? An' have you finished tellin' her about your job an' London an' everythin'?' He parroted her words with a viciousness that was threatening, but the intimidation had the opposite effect on Sarah to that which he intended, and as her back straightened, her chin rose and her eyes narrowed into blue slits.

'Willie, please. She's only been here half an hour. Tell him, Sarah—'

'Rebecca, this is your home too.' The expression on Rebecca's face stopped Sarah from continuing further, but

184

she glanced again at Willie, her eyes cold as she said, 'I merely called by to see Rebecca for a few minutes. I wasn't aware that was a crime.'

'I say who comes through that door an' who don't, understand?'

The squat thuggish body took a step or two towards Sarah, but she held her ground, even moving forward a pace herself as she said, 'You don't frighten me, Willie Dalton, you never have.'

'No?'

'No.'

Her cool disdainful voice and apparent unconcern seemed to take Willie aback slightly, but he recovered almost immediately, and his voice was loud as he said, 'Think you're above the likes of us, don't you, eh? But you're nothin', *nothin*'. Even she' – he gestured at Rebecca who was standing with her buttocks pressed against the table, her hands either side of her thighs as she gripped the wood – 'even she knew who her mam an' da were; she ain't no bastard.'

Sarah heard Rebecca's sudden intake of breath, but she didn't take her eyes off the man in front of her as she said, in such a quiet tone that it took a moment or two for her words to register in the piggy eyes, 'I might be a bastard by birth, Willie Dalton, but you're one by nature which is far far worse. I wonder how many times your mother wished she'd had the good sense to remain childless?'

'Why, you—'

'Yes, what am I?' As Willie's raised arm hovered, Sarah stared him straight in the face, her eyes holding his and expressing none of the fear that was trembling in her stomach. 'Or more to the point, what are you? But that's easy, I can tell you what you are, what your mother thought you were if it comes to that. You're nowt. A great big nowt. You always have been and you always will be.' The northern word, scathing in its meaning, had come naturally to her lips, and now, as Willie's drooping arm raised sharply again she cried at him, 'You try it! Just you try it, Willie Dalton, and I'll have you up before the bench before you can spit.'

'*Get out.*'

'Aye, I'm going.' She was vaguely aware that in the heightened emotion of the last few minutes the cultivated veneer she had worked at over the last few years had been stripped away as though it had never been, and her northern roots were showing, but she didn't care. 'And Rebecca is coming with me.'

'Sarah, I can't.'

'She's me wife an' she's stayin'.'

'She's leaving with me now, and if you try and stop us you'll regret it.'

'Oh, aye? I'm shiverin' in me boots.'

Sarah ignored him, walking over to Rebecca and putting her arm round the other woman's sagging shoulders as she said quietly, 'Listen to me, Rebecca. It's not going to get better, it's going to go on and on and you know it inside. Now go and pack a bag with everything you need while I wait here. It will be all right, I promise.'

'I'm frightened.'

'Which is more frightening, staying here with him or leaving with me? You've got the rest of your life ahead of you, Rebecca. You are young, you're going to have a child and you owe it to your baby to be strong now.'

Rebecca raised her head, the tears raining down her face as she whispered, her lips barely moving, 'I won't be a minute.'

'If you're gonna go, you can go now with me boot up your backside, you little—'

'*Don't you dare touch her.*' Willie was at least four or five stone heavier and twice as broad as Sarah, but as she pushed

Rebecca towards the door and moved to stand eye to eye with him she noticed she was slightly taller than the enraged man in front of her, and it added to her natural authority when she said, 'She is going to walk out of here with her head held high, which is more than you could ever do.'

The tone of her voice and the content of her words seemed to check him for a moment, but only a moment, because as she brushed past him into the hall and moved to the bottom of the stairs he followed her, his neck straining out of his collarless shirt and his shoulders back. 'I'll see me day with you, girl, you see if I don't.'

And now she stared him fearlessly full in the face, her lip curling as she said, 'You can't frighten me, Willie Dalton, so don't waste your breath.' And as Rebecca came stumbling down the stairs, a bulging cloth bag in her arms, Sarah reached out and took it from her before saying, 'You'll be hearing from her solicitors shortly,' and then she pushed Rebecca out of the front door.

'You'll be hearing from her solicitors.' There was a touch of hysteria in Rebecca's laughter as the two of them hurried through the icy twilight towards Maggie's. 'Oh, Sarah, the look on his face when you said that. It's the only time I've ever known Willie lost for words.'

'He's a bully, Rebecca, that's what he is. He reminded me of Mary Owen back there.'

'Mary Owen?!' Now Rebecca almost collapsed on the ground with her mirth. 'He'd just love that, being compared to a five-foot-nothing little piece like Mary Owen who's no better than she should be. She's at it now you know – the whoring, like her mam. Jane too.'

'No, I didn't know.' She wasn't interested either; all her energy was directed at keeping Rebecca upright on the pavements which were like glass underfoot, and holding on to the big carpet bag with her free arm. 'But he does remind me of Mary, anyway. They both are nasty bits of work and they both try to make victims of people, or at least Mary used to.' She was a victim herself now it would seem, poor thing, Sarah thought briefly. She wouldn't have wished a life on the streets of Sunderland on any girl, even her old enemy. 'But he's not doing it any more, Rebecca, right?' Sarah's voice was heavy with meaning.

'Oh, Sarah.' Rebecca stopped abruptly, looking up into the darkening sky from which the first lazy fat snowflakes were beginning to fall for some moments before she shut her eyes tightly, only to open them again immediately and say, 'I can't believe I'm free of him, I can't tell you what it's been like.'

'You don't have to. Just tell the solicitor.'

Then they were both giggling; nervous, faintly hysterical giggles, but therapeutic none the less.

It was quite dark when they reached Lea Road, and already the snow had begun to settle in a white mantle over the street, turning it into something beautiful, and dusting the rooftops with mother of pearl.

It was Florrie who answered the door, and even before she spoke, Sarah had heard Rodney's voice from within the house, followed by Maggie's deep laugh.

'The doctor's here?' She glanced from Florrie back into the street as she ushered a now silent Rebecca into the hall in front of her. 'Where's his car?'

'At his friends'. He wanted a walk apparently.' Florrie answered Sarah but her eyes were on Rebecca, and in answer to the question in them Sarah said, 'She's left him.'

'*She's left him?*'

The words brought Maggie into the hall like a cork out of a bottle, and now her eyes skimmed over them all, moving to the carpet bag at Sarah's feet, and she said, 'Thanks be to

God, thanks be to God. He's answered me prayers the night.'

'Sarah had a hand in it too.' It was facetious, but Rebecca knew if she didn't diffuse the charged atmosphere she was going to cry again, and she didn't want to do that with Dr Mallard in the sitting room.

'Come on, lass; you too, Sarah, you both look done in.' Maggie was fussing, something she always did to cover emotion, and as they preceded her into the sitting room, Sarah saw Rodney rising from one of the armchairs which had been pulled close to the fire.

She wasn't sure how much he had heard, but he was going to have to know about it within the next few minutes anyway – Maggie was not renowned for her patience or her tact – and so she said, 'Hallo again. I'm sorry, you seem to have caught us in the middle of a domestic crisis. Rebecca is going to stay with Maggie and Florrie for a bit.'

'I can't think of anyone nicer to stay with.' His voice was soft, and he smiled at them both before saying, 'Hallo, Rebecca. It's nice to see you again after all this time.'

'Hallo, Dr Mallard.' Rebecca's voice was strained, but then she smiled back as she said, 'You haven't changed a bit.'

'Really? I'd like to believe that but I think you're being kind. Now, I really must be making tracks—'

'Oh no, please don't go.' It was Rebecca who responded to Rodney's tactful withdrawal. 'I mean it, really. I'm sure you come across this sort of thing all the time in your work.'

'That's very true.' Rodney nodded easily, but he had noticed the massive bruise covering one side of Rebecca's face, and it was an effort to keep his voice in neutral. The swine had been hitting her?

'Florrie's gettin' us all a cup of tea, lad. Stay an' have a sup to keep you warm on the walk back.' Maggie added weight to her words by flopping down on the sofa as she spoke, drawing Rebecca down with her and continuing, 'I couldn't sleep a wink last night, hinny, for worryin' about you.'

Rodney stood uncertainly for a moment more before he said, 'Come and sit here by the fire, Sarah. You look frozen.'

'It's starting to snow.' She smiled at him by way of thanks as she took the seat he offered, and then, to cover what had become an embarrassing situation, made small talk until Florrie reappeared with the tray of tea.

Rodney drank his tea quickly, standing with his back to the fire, and immediately he had finished, he said, 'Well, I really must be off.'

'I'll see you to the door.' Sarah waited until he had made his goodbyes and then followed him into the hall, shutting the sitting-room door behind her.

'I'm sorry about all that.' She waved her hand towards the closed door, her voice soft. 'But there was really nothing else to be done.'

'He's been hitting her?' Rodney asked grimly.

Sarah nodded. 'He's a brute, he always has been – coarse and horrible.'

There was coarse and there was coarse, Rodney thought to himself. He'd known plenty of men in his time who could turn the air blue when they chose to, but were as gentle as lambs with their wives.

'I'm glad you got her out of there. Once they start that business it's downhill all the way. Her husband wasn't around then?'

'Oh yes, Willie was there.' She gave him a bare outline of what had transpired, and his face was dark with anger by the time she had finished.

'But he didn't touch you?'

'No, no. He's a coward at heart, like all bullies.'

She'd got some guts, he'd say that for her. She might look as fragile as Meissen porcelain, but there was pure steel running through that slender backbone. It brought back memories of the child Sarah with such poignancy that it stirred him to say, his voice soft, 'You don't change, do you?'

'Don't I?' She knew it was a compliment and blushed furiously.

'Not inside, where it counts.' He could just imagine her facing that thug of a man like a lioness protecting her young, and then, his voice becoming brisk, he said, 'Any more trouble from the fellow and you get the police involved double quick.'

'Oh, I would, and I shall tell Florrie to take Rebecca along to a solicitor next week, to start the ball rolling. At least she's safe here with Maggie now.'

He nodded, even as his mind asked: But for how long? He didn't want to discourage Sarah by voicing his doubts, but he had seen too many Rebecca and Willie scenarios in his time not to feel uneasy. It was the mental control these men commanded that was the worst thing and the hardest for the women to break away from. He'd built up a sixth sense after a time about who would make it, and who wouldn't – most doctors did, he supposed – and he'd found there were some women who were born to be victims. Rebecca was a classic case with all the right background history for a disaster. But he could be wrong; he hoped he was wrong.

'Oh, I nearly forgot the reason for my coming in the first place.' He paused in the act of opening the front door and turned to look at her again. 'Heavy snow is forecast late tomorrow and over the next few days, so I called by to see if you were agreeable to leaving tomorrow morning instead of Monday. But don't worry now; with all that's happened, we'll keep to the original plan.'

Sarah glanced towards the sitting-room door before she said, 'I think I need to stay and have a good talk with her tomorrow, but I can easily go back on the train. Please, you go tomorrow if you're worried, I understand perfectly.'

'No, we'll go Monday.' It was definite.

The snow was already an inch or two thick when Rodney opened the front door, although the snowflakes had diminished to a desultory flutter, and as Rodney stood on the doorstep he pulled up the collar of his thick black overcoat which emphasized the height and breadth of his tall lean frame. Sarah caught a whiff of the smell of him – a mixture of aftershave and antiseptic and something which was wholly his and very pleasing – and it caused a funny little quiver in her stomach before she could control herself.

He was so handsome. She caught the thought, stuffing it back into her subconscious before she had time to dwell on it, and answering his goodbye with a smile before he turned from her and stepped down onto the white pavement.

She stood on the doorstep watching him as he walked down the street, his footsteps making large indentations in the unspoilt frosted pearl of the new snow, and his big dark figure turning the scene into a monochrome of black and white.

He turned once as he reached the corner, raising his hand and waving, before he disappeared out of sight, but Sarah continued to stand there in the quiet of the deserted night. It was freezing hard. The thought came from nowhere and was a surface comment to the million and one thoughts below. But then it always froze hard in these parts. Raw winds, snow, ice, gales. Perhaps that was why the people who lived here were so tough and resilient? Her people . . .

Sarah found her gaze lifting, swinging out above the white rooftops as it searched the night, and she allowed free rein to the thoughts that had been with her all evening since Willie's attack. Her mother was out there somewhere, living, breathing, possibly even looking at the same northern sky this very minute. Sarah was sure she was still alive, she had

to be, but the war had taken so many lives in these parts . . .
She pushed the thought from her. No, her mother was alive,
she knew it, *felt* it, she wouldn't believe anything else.

'The doctor gone then?'

Sarah nearly jumped out of her skin as Maggie's voice
sounded right behind her, but she turned with a smile as she
said, 'No, he's in my pocket.'

'Less of your cheek.' Maggie grinned at her, her fat face
all wrinkles and lines, but her eyes were thoughtful as they
took in Sarah's flushed cheeks and bright eyes. 'You've took
your time out here,' she said easily, but still with her gaze
tight on Sarah's face. 'Bin talkin', have you?'

'A bit.'

'Oh aye? He told you he come round 'cos he was worried
about the forecast then?'

'Yes, but we've decided to go back Monday as arranged
because of Rebecca. I said I'd go back on the train if he
wanted to go earlier, but he said he could wait.'

There could be trouble brewing here. Maggie's mind was
racing under her bland exterior. At her age she recognized
the signs even if her lass didn't. Sarah liked him, she liked
him a darn sight too much, and the lad wasn't interested, not
from what she'd seen of him with her anyway. Oh, he was
pleasant enough, solicitous about her welfare and all, but he
treated the lass in the same way a dutch uncle would, kindly,
considerately.

As Sarah brushed past her into the house, Maggie said,
'Well, you do as you think best, lass, but he's a busy man,
perhaps he needs to get back, eh? With his own practice an'
all, an' all his social engagements . . .'

She doubted if Sarah even heard her.

Rodney found he was whistling to himself as he walked along
in a world that seemed reborn and transparently beautiful.

The sound surprised him, he couldn't remember whistling for a long long time. Perhaps it was the snow? He stopped, breathing in deep lungfuls of the icy cold air before walking on again. The snow was usually an enemy, ten to one he would be battling through it at the dead of night in answer to some urgent call, but tonight the silent silvery vista was enchanting, transforming the grim northern landscape.

He smiled deprecatingly at himself. This evening made him think of times past, when he and Richard had been young and had prayed earnestly for weeks beforehand for a white Christmas. They had always dressed the tree together as a surprise for their father when he came home from the surgery, although no doubt the box of shiny coloured balls and tinsel, and the packets of white sugar mice that their mother bought a day or so in advance, had provided something of a clue.

He had had a good childhood, he thought now, solid, secure. Richard's four years' seniority had manifested itself in a protective, rather than authoritarian attitude, and he couldn't remember them ever arguing, although of course they must have done. The thought of Richard brought Vanessa into his mind, and the tranquillity of the night was spoilt causing him to click his tongue irritably at himself. But tonight there was no rush of adrenalin or stirring in his loins, rather a vague feeling of dissatisfaction.

What a difference there was between Vanessa and the bright, freshfaced girl he had just left. He filled his lungs again, noticing the sky was clearing fast and there was the odd twinkling star between the snow clouds. One was cool sophistication and brittle elegance, with an edge that was scalpel sharp, and the other? The other was warm and generous and quite breathtakingly lovely . . .

The way his thoughts had gone shocked him and he stopped abruptly, drawing the breath in through his teeth in a low hiss. Enough of that, what the hell was he thinking of anyway? The girl was young enough to be his daughter, and if she thought of him at all it was in that context.

But she was beautiful, and with a spirit to match. He would have loved to have been a fly on the wall when she gave that excuse for a man such a dressing down – that was before he took the opportunity to hit Willie Dalton square on the nose, of course. How had Rebecca ever got mixed up with such a type anyway? And then he shook his head at himself. How could he, of all people, ask that? If anyone knew about the sticky threads of fate, it was him.

He had been walking steadily, the road inclining upwards slightly, and now he stopped, turning and glancing back over the streets and houses wrapped snugly in their blanket of white, the odd uncurtained window here and there providing squares of warmth in the wintery scene.

But it was up to him to untangle those threads and make a clean break. Look at Sarah – she had defied all the odds to make something of herself and follow her own star, so how could he continue to whine and whinge to himself about something that had always been within his power to control? His shoulders went back slightly.

He had never expected to survive that hellhole of a camp, but he had, unlike many of the poor blighters who had been incarcerated with him. He was thirty-eight years old; that meant he still had a good thirty or forty years of useful productive life in front of him.

He turned and continued walking again, his footsteps crunching on the glazed surface of the snow. It was up to him what he did with that time, but by heavens – he breathed deeply, enjoying the feel of the crisp air in a way he hadn't done for years – he was damned if he was going to waste it.

Chapter Twelve

'And you say she's staying with Maggie and Florrie now?'
Hilda was cooking sausages and onions as she listened with
avid interest to Sarah relating the events of the weekend first
thing on Tuesday morning.

Sarah nodded. 'They're going to the solicitor this morning
while the bruise on her face is still visible.' She had been
sparing in what she had told Hilda, merely mentioning that
Willie could be violent on occasion.

'Strike while the iron's hot.' Hilda was in full agreement.
'Talking of which . . .' She put down the heavy copper frying
pan she was holding and moved closer to Sarah, who was
having a cup of tea at the kitchen table, and said, 'His nibs
was here over the weekend while you were gone, bold as
brass and twice as shiny.'

'Sir Geoffrey?'

'The very same. Apparently it had to do with the separation Lady Margaret has asked for. I don't think he thought
she would go so far as to make it official. Anyway, Lady
Harris showed him the door sharpish and he went off with a
flea in his ear. It looks like Lady Margaret is serious about
not having him back.'

Sarah nodded. It wasn't news to her; Lady Margaret had
indicated her intentions during the increasingly frank talks
they had enjoyed over the last few weeks.

'I had to put Eileen in her place about it all, by the way.' Eileen was Peggy's replacement, a pert fifteen-year-old who had an answer for everything but who, nevertheless, did half the amount of work and took twice as long as Peggy had done. 'She's far too nosy by half, that one,' Hilda continued, drawing her chin down into her neck disapprovingly. 'Always asking about this, that and the other.'

'She's not like Peggy,' Sarah agreed quietly, rising from the table and brushing a few crumbs of toast from her dress. She was glad Peggy was settled and happy. The Cole family were all very fond of her and the son of the house, young Michael as Rodney referred to him, seemed to have taken the new lodger under his wing. She had met Michael once, on her last visit to the house the day before she had left for Sunderland, and had found him to be a tall, surprisingly shy and sweet sixteen-year-old, with a gentle face and quiet manner. Perfect for Peggy, she thought now, as she left the kitchen to begin the day's work.

It was later that morning, as Lady Harris was finalizing the arrangements for the Christmas break, the family having decided to spend some weeks at Fenwick, that her employer mentioned Sir Geoffrey's visit.

'In view of recent developments which I'm sure Hilda's already informed you about' – Lady Harris smiled, she knew her cook's indulgence for gossip – 'I've taken the precaution of having the locksmith call yesterday. You and Eileen will be here alone for some weeks and I would prefer to know the house is secure.' The old lady rose, walking quickly across to the bureau and taking a lavender-coloured envelope from one of the drawers, before returning to Sarah and handing it to her. 'This is your new set of keys, my dear. I have one, along with Lady Margaret. Do I make myself clear?'

'Yes, Lady Harris.' What had it cost her to lock her son out of her house and her life? Sarah asked herself as she looked down at the envelope. This same son who had, until a few weeks ago, been everything to her. Her thoughts made her voice soft as she said, 'Is that all?'

'For now. However, once lunch is over I am sure Lady Margaret would like you to supervise the packing of the children's trunks, and possibly her own. I understand Eileen has everything ready.'

Sarah nodded. It was going to be strange to have the house all to herself – or almost all to herself, she corrected silently. Eileen would still be around, but she had nothing in common with the young maid, who had none of Peggy's natural warmth and amiableness.

The family departed for the country on the seventeenth of December, and Sarah went for an interview at the hospital the following day in answer to the advertisement for voluntary workers. She was eagerly snatched up for the current rota. Could she please start that evening as they were *so* short of helpers due to the influenza outbreak? And so she found the next few days leading up to Christmas were full and busy.

She spent the whole day on both the twentieth and twenty-first, the Saturday and Sunday, working on the children's ward, feeding the babies their bottles and the toddlers their food, reading to them, playing endless games and getting the smaller ones to sleep when they were fractious, and by the end of Sunday evening she couldn't remember when she had felt so tired. But content. Content and fulfilled.

She received a letter from Maggie and Florrie on the Monday morning. Both women were averse to using the public telephone situated at the end of the street, being extremely distrustful of what they considered an unfathomable invention, and consequently had communicated only by letter since Sarah had been in London. The letter informed her that Willie had been round to see Rebecca, cap in hand, and Florrie had stopped him coming over the doorstep.

Sarah didn't trust the cap-in-hand approach any more than Maggie and Florrie appeared to, and she nodded in approval as she read that Willie had been given short shrift.

They added that they had heard from Maud, who'd got it from her sister, that Matron Cox had gone to live with relations down Scarborough way, and was out of the picture so to speak. So, Sarah wasn't to worry about anything but enjoy her Christmas, and they'd see her in the new year as soon as she was able to pay them another visit.

The Tuesday post brought a carefully worded letter from Rebecca that said very little beyond that Willie had called but Florrie hadn't let him into the house. Sarah read Rebecca's letter through twice, then sat down immediately and wrote to her friend telling her to be strong and to stick to her guns. Willie was dangerous, very dangerous, and never more so than when he tried the soft-soap approach. That was how he had got Rebecca in the first place.

She spent the rest of that day making trays of sweets for the children at the hospital with the last of the extra Christmas rations in Hilda's cupboard. Rodney hadn't called her. At four o'clock, when the sky outside was a sombre grey and all the sweets were parcelled up with shiny paper, she acknowledged the disappointment she had been keeping at bay for the last few days. *He hadn't called her*. Not that she had expected him to, she told herself fiercely. She hadn't, not really, not at the bottom of her. But it would have been nice, that was all. She'd enjoyed the drive back down to London when they had chatted about this and that, and she thought he had; but, as Maggie had taken great pains to point out several times on that Sunday just over a week ago, he was a busy man, an influential man, and no doubt his social life matched his hectic working life. No doubt.

At six o'clock the telephone rang as Sarah was watering the plants in the drawing room, and when she lifted the receiver and heard Rodney's voice saying, 'Hallo? I would like to speak to Miss Brown please,' she suddenly found she needed to sit down.

'This is me – I mean, it's Sarah.' She took a deep breath. She sounded like a babbling idiot.

'Sarah? It's Rodney, Rodney Mallard. How are you?'

'I'm fine, and you?'

'Overworked and underpaid, this outbreak of influenza is playing havoc with my beauty sleep. Sarah, I was called to the Coles' last night, the old lady isn't too good, and I saw that young girl, Peggy is it? while I was there. She tells me the family are away in the country and it's just you and the new maid there for Christmas lunch, is that right?'

'Not exactly.' She paused, willing her voice to sound natural as she said, 'Eileen is going home for a couple of days, actually. I told her she could as I shall probably be at the hospital for most of the time anyway.'

'Hospital?'

'Oh, just some voluntary work I'm doing,' she said quickly.

'You're doing voluntary work at the hospital?'

She didn't know why he sounded so surprised – hundreds of people did the same sort of thing all the time. She found she didn't like his reaction and her voice reflected this when she said, 'There's nothing unusual about that, is there?'

'No, no.' There was a pause, and then, 'Well yes, actually, I mean for a girl of your age. Don't you want to go to the cinema, to dances, things like that, with any free time you have?'

'I can still do that if I want to.'

'Yes, of course.' Another pause and then he said, 'About Christmas lunch, I wondered if you'd like to spend the day with me, actually. There is a little party on at my brother's, they always have one on Christmas Day, and I've already mentioned you. They would love you to come if you're free.'

She moved the phone away from her ear, staring at it for a moment before she returned it to her face and said, 'Oh, I couldn't. I mean it's very kind of you, but I couldn't impose like that—'

'Impose?' He interrupted her before she had the chance to say any more. 'You won't be imposing, I do assure you. Richard and Vanessa are having fifteen or sixteen to dinner at the last count, the more the merrier as far as they are concerned.'

'But . . . but I couldn't . . .'

'Are you free?'

'Well yes, but—'

'That's settled then.'

'No, really—'

'*Sarah.*' His voice was quiet now, soft and deep. 'It would spoil my Christmas dinner to think of you eating a solitary meal all alone, so look on it as a favour to me. I don't get to enjoy many meals without an interruption of some kind or other, so take pity on a poor starving man. All right?'

There was a silence, and Rodney found he was holding his breath although he had no idea why, and then when her voice came quietly saying, 'If you're sure they won't mind I'd love to come,' he breathed out slowly, shutting his eyes for a brief moment.

'Good, good.' His voice was louder, jolly. 'I've arranged for a locum over Christmas Day so I can definitely say I'll pick you up at eleven. Is that all right?'

'That would be lovely, thank you.'

'Goodbye till then.'

'Goodbye.'

Sarah found she was smiling as she put down the receiver,

the other hand pressed against her chest where her heart was pounding. Christmas Day at his brother's house? Christmas Day with Rodney? But then the smile dimmed. What was she going to wear? A chill of reality caused her to sit up straighter. Oh, why hadn't she thought of that before? If it was going to be a party everyone would be in their best bib and tucker, and she had nothing remotely suitable. And the people who would be there, they were bound to be the bridge club and musical soirée type, the social élite of Windsor.

Not that she wasn't familiar with such as they – Mrs Roberts had chosen her circle of friends carefully from only the most influential of Sunderland's upper class, and she knew the chatter that went on at dos like this one and how to conduct herself – but she had only seen it all from the other side, so to speak. She would have absolutely nothing in common with any of them.

She was sitting on a very lovely reproduction Louis XV chair, and now, as she raised her gaze and glanced from one exquisite piece of furniture to another, her mind was racing. This was their world, not hers – she was a housekeeper, for goodness' sake. She hadn't been born with a bronze, let alone a silver, spoon in her mouth.

But he had wanted her there. The thought crept in, driving away the chill of panic. He needn't have phoned her, after all; he had thought about it and then asked her. But . . . she glanced down at the neat practical dress she had on, which was another of Rebecca's efforts, him wanting her there didn't solve the problem of what she was going to *wear*.

Rodney, too, was sitting quite still in his big leather seat behind his desk at the surgery, ignoring the fact that his evening surgery still hadn't finished, and that Mrs Price would be on the war path if he delayed much longer. When he ran late, it was his long-suffering housekeeper-cum-receptionist who was first in the line of fire from irate patients. But the conversation with Sarah had bothered him more than a bit, he admitted to himself.

He had been amazed that a young girl like her wanted to take on what he knew was the hard job of voluntary work at a hospital. She should be out, having fun. That's what girls of her age did, wasn't it? But then, Sarah wasn't any girl; she was far from being just any girl. He shook his head, his brow furrowing. Damn it all, he didn't know where he was with all this, how he felt, anything. He hadn't felt so perturbed for years. Mind you, all that last night hadn't helped. His mind ran back over the scene with Vanessa and his brother.

'Don't be silly, old man, of course you must bring the girl to lunch.' Richard had turned to Vanessa, who had been standing just within the open doorway of the sitting room, but without waiting for her confirmation had swung back to face him again as he'd said, 'And you say she was a patient of yours many moons ago?'

'In a manner of speaking.' Rodney had been standing with his back to the gas fire, set in an ivory marble-tiled fireplace, as he had spoken. 'Well, more than a manner of speaking I suppose, but she was just a child then.' He had been very conscious of Vanessa's stillness as she had watched him from across the room, but he hadn't glanced her way. 'Sarah moved down to London from Sunderland in October, and I bumped into her when I was visiting a patient.'

'It's a small world.' Vanessa had spoken for the first time, her voice cool.

'Yes, it is.'

'You get on the phone tomorrow and tell her we'd be delighted to see her.' Richard's voice had carried the hearty note which was always present when his wife was around. 'We wouldn't hear of her dining alone on Christmas Day, would we, Vee?'

'Heaven forbid.' The voice was languid, but as Rodney looked at Vanessa for the first time her chin jerked slightly, and the small, virtually undetectable sign of annoyance told him she was angry. 'Although the girl might feel a little uncomfortable not knowing anyone.'

'She'll have Rodney to look after her.'

'Yes.' Ice tinkled in the one short word. 'Do we know her people?'

'Her people?' Rodney had answered Richard's silent gesture at the drinks cabinet and the open bottle of whisky with a nod of his head, before adding, 'I shouldn't think so, Vanessa.'

'No? What's her surname?'

'Brown.'

'Brown . . . Well, there are the Chadford Browns, they're from the north originally I understand. And the Major, doesn't he have family in that area, Richard? We must ask him—'

'I've told you, you wouldn't know Sarah's family.' She was going to play up, but he'd expected that, hadn't he. The doctor in him knew she was as taut as piano wire most of the time, and perhaps he had been naive to suggest bringing another woman onto her territory? Because that was how she would view it.

But he had had no choice. The alternative of leaving Sarah to eat alone was unthinkable, and if he'd suggested that he take her out, or that she dine at his home, Richard would have insisted they come here. He knew his brother.

'I'll ask the Major anyway, he's a positive fount of knowledge.'

'Get this down you, Rod.' He'd caught the glance, heavy with warning, that Richard had thrown at his wife, but Vanessa had just tossed her head, coming fully into the room and saying, 'I'll have a gin and tonic, Richard. So, how old is this little long-lost friend of yours?'

205

There were times when he really did wonder if he'd end up throttling her, Rodney thought now, as he recalled how Vanessa had draped herself over his arm, her bosom pushed against his chest, as she'd asked the question. What was the name of that new Tennessee Williams play that was causing such a furore in New York, and being held up as so controversial? *A Streetcar Named Desire*. That was it. He'd heard two of the more straitlaced members of his club discussing it only the day before, tut-tutting over their brandies. Well, he could have told those two old codgers a thing or two about real life that would have made their hair curl.

'Dr Mallard?' Mrs Price was making no effort to hide her indignation as she knocked and then popped her head round the door. 'Mr Parsons has been waiting fifteen minutes now.'

'Give me a minute, and then show him in, Mrs Price.'

Once the door shut, with something that almost verged on a bang, Rodney's eyes narrowed as he thought again of Vanessa's behaviour the night before.

She'd pushed and pushed about that name business, like a hound scenting the smell of blood, and it had only been when Richard had said, his voice unusually sharp, 'Don't harp on, woman, for crying out loud. He's come here for a meal, not an inquisition,' that she'd left it alone. It might have been just another uncomfortable evening if Richard hadn't been called to the telephone a few minutes later. He had left to take the call in his study, and Vanessa had risen from her seat on the other side of the room with Richard's departure, strolling to the chair her husband had just vacated opposite Rodney, and after seating herself, staring silently into the glow of the gas fire.

He had glanced at her once when she had sat down, a polite look and nothing more, but when she didn't return the gesture and her face remained straight, he'd let his eyes drop to the whisky glass, swirling the amber liquid round and round as the silence had lengthened. This was an old tack, and one which he knew well. Vanessa was quite capable of keeping it up all night, and had done so on more than one occasion when he had annoyed her.

But then she had completely surprised him, causing his heart to thud with the unpleasantness of confrontation, when she'd said, 'Why are you doing this to me, Rodney?'

'What?'

She had turned her head to face him then, letting her blue eyes travel all over his face before she spoke. 'You know what I mean. Why are you bringing this girl home?'

It had been for all the world as though she were the injured wife addressing a husband who was intent on flaunting his mistress, and his voice had reflected his rejection of such a notion when he'd said, 'She is a friend of mine, Vanessa, and as such I thought she would be welcome in my brother's house. Is that really so surprising?'

'Yes, and you know it.'

'I know nothing of the sort.' It had been bound to come into the open one day, but he hadn't expected it then, that minute. What had made yesterday evening any different to the hundreds that had gone before it?

The answer was clear, spearing his conscience as a voice in his head cried, You know what made it different so don't give me that. You'd never suggested bringing a woman along before, and you'd got a pretty good idea how she'd take it, now then. Was he using Sarah; using her because he had reached the end of the road with Vanessa but wasn't man enough to say it as it was? No. The denial was immediate. Whatever else, it wasn't that. He had told Vanessa often enough in the past, both verbally and in a hundred unspoken ways, that he would never bed her again. And he had liked the idea of being with Sarah on Christmas Day.

But Vanessa hadn't liked it. 'I'm warning you, Rodney, I

won't stand for this. You'll regret it.' Her eyes had been blazing, her mouth a thin white line. 'I suppose you're sleeping with her, that's it, isn't it? And you think you can flaunt your little northern strumpet in front of me.'

Something in his face had altered both her countenance and her voice with one of the mercurial changes she did so well, and when her head had lowered and her voice had trembled as she'd said, 'Rodney, Rodney, please. I can't bear it when we fight,' he'd felt his stomach muscles tighten and contract. The raw silk of her hair had swung across her cheeks, hiding her face but exposing the pure line of her neck, and her shoulders had been bowed as though with an inexpressible weight. It was a classic pose of wounded femininity, and one which Vanessa did to perfection, but somehow, over the last few weeks, he had recognized it wasn't real.

He had drawn breath deeply and silently into his nose, breathing out heavily, before saying, 'It won't wash, Vanessa, so save the dramatics for someone who will appreciate them. Sarah is either coming here or I'll take her elsewhere, so make your decision quickly. Richard will be back in a moment.'

'Oh, *Richard*.' The contempt had been scathing. 'Do you think I care about that gargoyle?' And then, as she raised her head, 'Oh I'm sorry, I'm sorry, I didn't mean it. Don't look at me like that.'

She would have flung herself at him but he'd risen quickly, warding her off with an outstretched palm as he'd said, his voice thick, 'I could kill you, Vanessa. Do you know that?'

He had gone to the bathroom, not trusting himself to stay in the room with her a moment longer, and how long he'd stayed in the pink and white surroundings he didn't know. It had been long enough to convince Richard, when he eventually rejoined him and Vanessa, that he was unwell anyway, and he'd left immediately.

Gargoyle. By all that was holy. *Gargoyle*. He couldn't get the word out of his mind. No man deserved that, least of all Richard. When he thought about the countless skin grafts his brother had endured, the pain he still suffered . . .

The knock on the door informed him Mr Parsons was outside, but it was a moment or two before he could compose himself enough to call out, 'Come in.'

Gargoyle . . . It had been bad enough her suggesting, and within days of Richard's return home after that first time in the hospital, that he take on a locum for the 'nervous' patients. He hadn't been able to believe it when Richard had told him, and although it had happened a year or so earlier, when he was still in the camp, he'd tackled her about it as soon as he'd known. She'd denied it, and stood her ground, but he'd known she was lying. But gargoyle . . .

Sarah was still sitting in the drawing room in a state of quiet panic when the telephone rang some minutes later, and she took a deep breath before she picked it up and said, 'Lady Harris's residence, how may I help you?'

'Sarah?' It was Lady Margaret's voice. 'I'm just ringing to make sure everything is all right. Lady Harris would have done so but she's confined to bed with a slight chill.'

'Oh, I'm sorry, Lady Margaret.' Sarah paused. 'Yes, everything is quite all right.'

'Are you sure? You sound a little strange.'

'Yes, of course.'

'You haven't had any visitors?' Sarah realized Lady Margaret was thinking of her husband, and to put her mind at rest she decided to tell her the truth. She had grown close enough to the older woman over the last few weeks to be able to do so without embarrassment.

209

Lady Margaret listened in silence, and then, as Sarah finished speaking, she said, 'Sarah, I know of few young women who could carry themselves in any type of company, but you are one of them. There are some things that are classless, my dear, and natural dignity and propriety is one of them. I'm quite sure Dr Mallard recognizes that, which is why he knows you will not be out of place in the company of his family and friends. As for your outfit, that is not a problem. I have several dresses which would lend themselves to the sort of function you've described. Of course you would need to make a few alterations here and there, but that shouldn't take too long. Now, let me tell you where to find them . . .'

Once Sarah had put down the telephone she flew upstairs and into Lady Margaret's quarters, opening the large oak wardrobe with eager hands. There were four dresses Lady Margaret had suggested might be suitable, each one plain and simple but with an expert cut that spoke of unlimited wealth.

Sarah laid them out one by one on Lady Margaret's four-poster bed, but she knew the one she wanted even before she tried them on. The light dove grey suit, its lapels edged in a darker shade of thin satin, turned her skin to thick cream and darkened the blue of her eyes to midnight, and it came with a wonderful long thin silk scarf in muted shades ranging from gunmetal grey through to the palest ivory. It was gorgeous, *gorgeous*, and she twirled and pirouetted in front of the mirror for half an hour before she could bear to take it all off, trying various hairstyles to see which looked best. The jacket was a little tight over the bust, but she could soon let the seams out, she thought excitedly, and the softly pleated skirt that hung just below her calves would need taking up an inch or so, but again, nothing she couldn't handle. Oh she did look different, she couldn't believe it, and she'd wear her hair up in thick waves and curls on the top of her head, and Lady Margaret had said she might borrow her string of pearls which was in her dressing-table drawer.

It was going to be a lovely Christmas, a lovely, *lovely* Christmas. She hugged herself tightly. It was nearly Christmas Eve, and then the next morning Rodney would call for her and see her all dressed up ... Oh, she couldn't wait!

She danced out of the bedroom, the suit and scarf over her arm, and then became aware she was grinning broadly at nothing. Eileen would think she'd gone mad. She drew her bottom lip into her mouth and pressed down hard with her teeth. She couldn't afford to let Eileen see her as anything other than the controlled Miss Brown she had come to know wouldn't take any nonsense. She had to chivvy the girl along every moment as it was, and last night they hadn't eaten till gone nine because she had left the maid in charge of preparing their dinner. In fact, she'd better check on her this minute else it would be the same story again tonight.

She took the suit up to her room, laying it on the bed with reverential care, then hurried downstairs to the kitchen, her heart still beating a tattoo of excitement. A bubble of laughter escaped her throat again before she gritted her teeth, composed her face, and opened the kitchen door to see Eileen peeling enough spuds for ten.

Chapter Thirteen

'Christmas Eve tomorrow, Florrie.' Rebecca grinned at Florrie as she watched the older woman take their dinner – finny-haddie and baked potatoes, Maggie's favourite – out of the big oven in the old-fashioned black range. The oven was a bone of contention with Florrie. She kept it spotless herself, but the family upstairs, with whom they shared the kitchen, were less particular, and invariably Florrie had to clean it before she felt happy to use it. Personally she didn't care about a bit of grease or mess, Rebecca thought now, as Florrie smiled back at her with an, 'Oh you, you're worse than a bairn the night,' and carried on dishing up the meal.

At home, and she still thought of the house she had lived in with Willie for the last four years as home, she had felt driven to remove even the merest speck of dust before it could settle. She'd felt that if she kept the house and all the furniture spotless, the uncleanness she felt in herself would get better.

It hadn't of course. How could it, when the perpetrator of that uncleanness had had free rein over her body and her mind? But she was free of that now . . . except in her head.

'Pass them plates that are warming on the hob, lass.' Florrie's voice was quiet, her mind preoccupied. Maggie had written Sarah a nice cheerful letter from both of them the day before yesterday, and they'd been feeling cheerful then,

213

but in the space of a few hours today she felt as though she'd had the stuffing knocked out of her. First she'd seen Maud in the grocers when she was getting the taties for dinner, and the other woman had been full of how Matron Cox's brother had contacted her to ask how her sister was doing.

'He's having a terrible time of it with his sister apparently,' Maud had said complacently. Her own sister was doing fine. 'Keeps takin' off, so he tells me, they had to get the law involved the last time. Found her just a few miles away from here, I mean it makes you wonder, don't it' – Maud was right, it did make you wonder, and Florrie hadn't stopped wondering since – 'an' then she played up somethin' rotten when they took her back to him. He's just about had enough from what I can make out, an' his poor wife is at the end of her tether. He said they're gonna get Christmas over an' then have a think again, but it's really upset him, poor fella. I suppose he'll feel responsible if they lock her away again, but I reckon it's the best thing all round, meself.'

The conversation had left Florrie feeling frightened and slightly nauseous; then on her way home from work that night she'd seen Willie hanging about at the corner of the street. He'd scarpered when he set eyes on her, and just as well, Florrie thought now, her mouth grim, but it didn't bode well. No, it didn't bode well at all. Her and Maggie couldn't keep Rebecca hidden away for ever, the lass would be fed up to the teeth in a day or two, but she didn't fancy the idea of her leaving the house either.

It was as they were carrying the plates through from the kitchen to the sitting room that the knock came at the front door, and Florrie knew instinctively who it was. 'You go in there, lass,' she said quietly as she handed Rebecca Maggie's plate and opened the sitting-room door, 'I'll get that. It's likely for them upstairs.'

Rebecca nodded, saying, 'I'll come back for your plate in a minute, Florrie.'

'No, you leave it and get on with your dinner. I'll bring mine through in a minute.' She waited until the door was shut behind Rebecca before she walked to the front door and opened it.

Willie's eyes looked behind her, and when he saw she was alone, he said, 'Took your time, didn't you.'

'What do you want?' Florrie made no pretence at amity.

'What do you think I want, you stupid bitch—' And then, as Florrie went to shut the door, he thrust his beefy shoulder against it as he said, 'Oh no, not this time.'

'You'd better clear off afore I call the police.'

'Go on then, go an' call 'em.' He knew, and she knew, she wouldn't do that when he was on the doorstep.

'I'm going to shut this door—'

'Not afore I see me wife.'

'She doesn't want to see you.'

'Let her tell me that.'

Florrie heard the door to the sitting room open, and she just prayed it wasn't Rebecca, but it was Maggie's voice that said, 'What's up, lass?'

'Shut the door, Maggie.'

Maggie shut it, and quickly, but not before stepping out into the hall herself and joining Florrie on the doorstep, where she glared at Willie and said, 'I thought we'd seen the last of you. The lass wants nothin' to do with you, understand?'

'Says you.'

'Aye, says me, an' her an' all.' Maggie thumbed at Florrie, and now Willie's lip curled as he said, 'An' you think I'd take any notice of two old bent bitches like you? Queer as a nine-bob note, the pair of you.'

'What?' Maggie's face had gone scarlet with outrage and

disbelief, and she glanced at Florrie for a moment, who was looking equally shocked, before turning back to Willie and hissing, 'You dirty-minded little blighter you. You filthy pig. Florrie's bin like a daughter to me.'

'Oh aye, that's what they all say.'

Quite what Maggie would have done next was anybody's guess – she looked ready to explode – but in that moment the door to the sitting room opened again, and Rebecca's voice could be heard saying nervously, 'Maggie, Florrie? What's happening?'

The change in Willie's voice and posture was immediate. 'Hallo, lass.' He gestured at Florrie. 'I was just askin' her if I could have a word with you, that's all. I was worried about you.'

'*Worried about her!*'

Maggie was beside herself, but Rebecca's hand had gone to her throat as she whispered her husband's name, her eyes wide and fearful.

'Please, lass.' Willie's expression had taken on the pathos of a puppy waiting to be kicked. 'Just talk to me a minute, Rebecca, that's all I'm askin'.'

'There's . . . there's nothing to say.' But she was nervous, uncertain. She had never seen this side of Willie.

Maggie and Florrie had never seen it either, but they both considered it the best bit of acting they had seen for many a long day.

Florrie went to shut the door again but Willie was too quick for her. 'Rebecca?' He reached out his hands in a desolate little gesture as his foot stayed firmly over the threshold. 'I don't know what to say, lass, I don't an' that's the truth.'

'Goodbye will do.' Maggie's voice was grim and Willie had a job to keep his expression from changing, but there was too much to lose to do otherwise. But he'd take it out of Rebecca's hide. By, he would that.

'I want to talk to me wife a minute, that's all, Maggie.'

'All? That's a sight too much if you ask me, Willie Dalton, an' I've had enough of your foul mouth the night. She wants nothin' to do with you, so you get your backside home where it belongs an' leave her alone. You're nothin' to her—'

'Maggie, don't.' Rebecca's voice was tearful, and as it interrupted her flow Maggie turned to look straight into Rebecca's face.

'Don't you see what he's about, lass? What he's tryin' to do?'

He'd got her. Willie could see the indecision on his wife's face. If he could just keep this up without strangling the pair of interfering old bitches in front of him, he'd got her. He'd always been able to control her. Always.

'Rebecca, listen to me, lass. I'm nearly goin' mad without you. Please, lass, come home just over Christmas an' let's talk about things. I'm sorry, I'm sorry for how things have been, lass, but it'll be better now, as God is my witness, it'll be better. Rebecca, we're man an' wife, lass . . . an' there's the bairn. Our bairn.'

'Aye, there's the bairn. An' what bairn wants to grow up with a da like you—'

'*Maggie.*' Rebecca and Florrie spoke in unison, the one upset and bewildered, the other afraid that Maggie was playing right into Willie Dalton's hands in making Rebecca feel sorry for him.

Shut up, Maggie. Florrie's eyes willed her to listen but Maggie was having none of it.

'It's the truth, by all that's holy, it's the truth – the dirty unnatural swine. His mother knew what she'd spawned, she could never stand the sight of him—'

'Maggie!'

'His type aren't capable of lovin' anybody, don't you see, lass? He's flawed, sick—'

217

'Stop it, Maggie.' Rebecca took a step forward, glancing at Willie who was standing with his head hanging down, his shoulders slumped, but his foot still firmly in the door. 'I'll . . . I'll talk to him. I want to talk to him. It's all right.'

'Lass, listen to me—'

'Maggie, I'm going to talk to him, he is my husband, don't you see? Please, I have to.'

It was a dismissal, but Florrie had to practically drag Maggie down the hall and into the sitting room, and the minute the door was closed behind the two women, Willie raised his head, his face puckered as though he was going to cry.

'I don't know what to say to you, lass, beyond I'm sorry. I'm heart sorry. I must have been mad.'

'Willie—'

'No, listen to me, lass. It won't happen again. There'll be none of the other business if you come back, I swear it on me mother's grave. I want us to be a family, you, me an' the bairn. Please, Rebecca, you can ask me for anythin' you want, just give me another chance, lass.'

'I . . . I've only ever wanted us to be . . .' She couldn't say the word normal, and substituted, 'happy' instead.

'We will be. Give me a chance an' we will be. Remember when we was courtin'? You was happy then, weren't you? We got on all right then, didn't we, lass? I – I know the other isn't right.' He lowered his head. 'But I'm done with that, I swear it. All this has made me see what's important, lass. Come home.'

And so Rebecca went home. For Christmas. With Willie.

Chapter Fourteen

Christmas Eve dawned bright and bitterly cold, the bare London trees touched with a feathery mantle of frost that melted away once the weak white sunlight took hold.

Sarah had stayed up half the night altering the suit. It hadn't proved as easy as she had expected – she hadn't Rebecca's special knack with a needle and thread – but now it looked just beautiful.

The post brought one last Christmas card for Lady Harris, and a little note from Maggie and Florrie, which she noticed from the postmark had taken three days to arrive. Sarah took it into the kitchen to read, toasting her toes on the boiler as she skimmed through the short letter which simply wished her a happy Christmas and said that they missed her. She suspected they had timed it to arrive that day in case she was feeling a little homesick on her first Christmas away from Sunderland, but what with sewing half the night, and knowing she had a full day at the hospital with the children, she didn't have time to indulge any heart pangs. But it had been nice of them, lovely, she told herself, their thoughtfulness warming her heart as she made herself toast and tea. She had told Eileen she could have an extra hour in bed that morning, and Eileen being Eileen had stretched the hour into two.

Eileen's sister came to collect the maid mid-morning, and proved to be a much more solid type than her flighty sister, nudging Eileen as they were leaving and reminding her to say thank you to 'miss'. Lady Harris had left it to Sarah's discretion as to whether she allowed the new maid any days off, and the allotted four had been more than Eileen had hoped for.

'Yes, thank you ever so much, miss.' Eileen's pretty pert face was full of smiles. 'I'll be back nice and early on the twenty-ninth, me dad's going to drop me off when he visits me aunty in Lewisham. Don't get too lonely all by yourself, and don't do anything I wouldn't do.'

'I'll be perfectly all right, Eileen.' Sarah was smiling but her voice was cool. The new maid was slow in her work about the house but a sight too forward in every other respect.

'Ta-ta, then, miss, and Merry Christmas.'

Sarah stood for a moment more, watching the two of them walking down the street, then stepped back into the house. She had plenty to do and she had to be at the hospital at midday. She was hoping there would be time, when she left the hospital later that evening, to call in at a couple of the good secondhand shops and have a look for a pair of shoes to go with Lady Margaret's outfit, but if she couldn't find anything she would have to make do with the pair she wore on Sundays and for best. They were nice, fashionable, but being brown, not quite right with the outfit. And she wanted to have a bath and wash her hair tonight before she went to bed, and press the suit ready for morning. Excitement gripped her again, and she found herself humming a Christmas carol as she collected her parcels for the children and made ready to leave.

As it happened, she was later leaving the hospital than she would have liked. One of the children who had taken a particular fancy to her was fractious and over-excited, and she didn't feel able to leave until the little tot was soundly asleep. When she emerged into the foggy December night all the shops had long since shut, and the mercurial British weather had transformed the crisp bright cold of the morning into a bone-chilling dampness, curling wreaths of mist floating in the cold air.

The streets were almost deserted as she hurried home, although it was only just eight o'clock, and circles of dull gold from the street lamps cast an eerie glow on the wet pavements. By the time she reached Emery Place her heart was thudding and she was out of breath, and once in the house she leant against the closed door for a moment or two before walking through to the kitchen and warming some milk.

The problem of her footwear was still occupying half her mind as she drank the milk and ate two chocolate biscuits that Hilda had made specially for Christmas, but when a cat screeched somewhere outside, the sound jarring the peace and quiet of the warm kitchen, it reminded her she was all alone in the big house. But she was safe enough. She made a deep obeisance with her head to the thought. Lady Harris had shutters on all the downstairs windows that could be bolted each night, and the front door and the back door, which overlooked a small paved area surrounded by an eight-foot brick wall, had three bolts each, besides heavy mortice locks. Fort Knox couldn't have done better. And then there was the telephone.

She washed her mug and put it away, and was just crossing the hall, intending to begin the procedure of locking up for the night, when the doorbell rang, making her jump. She stopped dead, staring first at the door and then glancing at her watch. A quarter to nine. Who on earth would be calling on Lady Harris at a quarter to nine on Christmas Eve?

When the sound came again she walked across to the door and put the safety chain on, before opening it two or three inches and peering out.

'Well? Open the door, girl.'

'Sir Geoffrey?' In her surprise she almost did what he said, closing the door again and her hand reaching for the chain before it froze on the cold metal. What was she doing? What *was* she doing? Why had Lady Harris had the locks changed if not to keep her son out?

'I'm sorry, Sir Geoffrey.' He had been standing at the bottom of the steps when she had first opened the door, but as she peeped through the opening again she saw he was now on the top step and just inches away from her. 'Lady Harris and Lady Margaret and the children are away.'

'Are they?' There had been the barest pause, but enough to tell Sarah the family's absence was not unexpected. 'No matter. There are some papers I need, and it is a matter of some urgency.' And then, as he pushed against the door, 'Is the chain still on? What are you thinking of, girl. Let me in.'

'I − I can't do that.' She hadn't seen Lady Harris's son since the night he had raped Peggy, but now, as she met the light, speckled eyes, the intervening weeks fell away and she felt sick to her stomach. 'Lady Harris left orders no one was to be admitted to the house in her absence.'

'And you are following her directive to the letter? Very commendable, I'm sure, but I hardly think it applies to me.' He paused, and as his tongue flicked briefly over his full bottom lip Sarah actually shuddered, the licentiousness she could read in his pale, unhealthy-looking face making her flesh creep.

'I'm sorry, Sir Geoffrey.'

'You will be if you don't open this door, girl. I've never heard of such a thing.'

'Lady Harris—'

'Is your employer, and my mother, *my mother*, got it? I hardly need to stress where that places you with regard to

222

who has the authority here. I'm going to tell you one more time. Open the door.'

'I can't do that, Sir Geoffrey. If you want to tell me which papers you need, I will phone Fenwick now and ask Lady Harris if it's all right for me to get them for you, but I can't open the door without her permission.'

'*Open it.*'

'No. If your mother had wanted you to have free admittance she would have given you a key.'

'You conniving little upstart.' It was soft and deadly, and in the same moment that a string of obscenities began to flow Sarah made to shut the door, but Sir Geoffrey was too quick for her, forcing his foot into the opening.

'No, no . . .' How long she struggled with the door Sarah didn't know, but she was aware of an almost paralysing fear that the chain wouldn't hold, her terror so great that it was strangling any cries for help she might have uttered.

'You think you can get the better of me?' There were bubbles of saliva at the corners of the loose-lipped mouth. 'You? A little whore like you? I'll make you rue the day you were born, girl, you see if I don't. You think I don't know what you're after? Why you've been filling their heads with your poison?'

'I haven't.'

'You might fool those two dried-up old sticks, but not me. Oh no, not me, girl. I've seen too many like you on their backs earning their keep when they've got too cocky. I know exactly how to treat a scheming little bitch like you.'

'Get away, you just get away from me.'

'You'll be begging me to take you one day, do you know that?' He had thrust his face close to the crack now, his fingers wrapped round the edge of the door as she moaned in hysterical panic. 'But I shall enjoy myself first, and I'm a man who knows how to enjoy himself. Oh, you'll beg all

right, but it won't be easy and quick. Oh no. Not for you.'
There followed something so lewd that Sarah fell back a
pace, one hand going to her throat as the other pressed into
her breastbone, and as he seized the opportunity to force his
shoulder against the door again she let out a scream of such
piercing intensity that she surprised both herself and Sir
Geoffrey. Following that she flung herself against the
straining door with such force that she actually heard
something crack at the same time as Sir Geoffrey let out a
shrill screech of pain, and then, as the door bounced against
the chain and released him, he fell backwards, landing in a
heap on the pavement below where he lay groaning and
clutching his foot.

Sarah didn't wait to see any more, shutting the door and
fumbling for the bolts, her efforts hindered by the tears
streaming down her face. When the last one was in place she
leant against the door before sliding down onto the floor,
aware that the commotion outside had ceased and all was
quiet. She felt sick, so sick. It had all been so violent and
happened so fast.

Oh, oh, he was a monster, he was. Her ears were ringing
and but for the fact that she was already on the floor, she
knew she would have fainted. As it was she felt her head
swimming, consciousness fast receding, before she forced
herself to draw long gasping breaths into her labouring lungs.
He had been going to attack her, physically attack her – she
had read it in his eyes.

The dizziness was clearing but now shock began to cut in,
making her shake from head to foot. He must have been
planning this. It wasn't coincidence that he had chosen the
first night she was here on her own to try and force his way
in to his mother's house. No, he had known she was all alone
here tonight. He had been watching the house; either that or
he'd got someone else, a neighbour maybe, to tell him the

comings and goings of its inhabitants. Had he really been after some papers from the morning room, or had it all been a ruse to enter the house with a view to attacking her?

She just managed to reach the big deep porcelain sink in the kitchen before the nausea swamped her, but once the retching was over she felt slightly better, splashing cold water from the running tap over her face and neck and then straightening as she heard the telephone ring in the hall.

'Hallo?' It was all she could manage after she had lifted the receiver.

'Is that Lady Harris's residence? It's Colonel Barnett, number twenty-three, don't you know. You got a spot of bother in there, m'dear? My man heard the devil of a commotion in the street a few minutes ago, and knowing the Robinsons and the Mathers are away, either side of you, I thought I'd give you a bell to make sure nothing's amiss.'

'Oh, Colonel Barnett.' She felt limp with relief at the sound of the kind and terribly normal voice. 'It's just ... There was someone here, and Lady Harris had said not to let anyone in. She's gone to her country house.' She wasn't making much sense, but even in her distress she knew Lady Harris would not like her private affairs becoming public. 'I think he's gone now.'

'Would you like Jackson to see what's what? He doesn't stand any nonsense, Jackson. Whoever the blighter is, Jackson will be up to it. Best batman a fellow could have.'

'That's – that's very kind of you.'

'Not at all, m'dear, not at all. Poor affair if we can't look out for each other, what? He'll have a scout around, don't you worry, but I won't disturb you again if there's nothing to report.'

'Thank you, thank you very much.'

She took down Colonel Barnett's telephone number as a precaution in case Sir Geoffrey came back, although she didn't think there was much chance of that, and after thanking the old soldier again, replaced the receiver.

After checking each of the downstairs windows to make sure the shutters were bolted and secure, and also the front and back doors, Sarah walked through to the kitchen and poured herself a hefty measure of brandy from the bottle Hilda kept in her cupboard for flavouring the fruitcakes Lady Harris liked so much. She drank the neat alcohol straight down, grimacing as she did so, but felt better for the fire in her belly.

The things he had said. She shook her head slowly in a downward swaying motion. What a vile man, and to think poor Lady Margaret had been married to him for nine years. No wonder she said she felt as though she had been reborn.

She warmed some more milk in a saucepan, and added another good tot of brandy to it once she had tipped it into a mug, before leaving the kitchen and walking upstairs with the steaming drink. Once in her room all strength seemed to leave her, and she sat for some minutes on the bed before forcing herself to sip the milk and get ready for her bath.

Should she tell Lady Harris what had occurred this evening? She contemplated the matter as she walked through to the bathroom and ran the hot water. It would upset the old lady though, she knew that, and perhaps all things considered Lady Margaret was the one to tell. She could leave it to her whether she told her mother-in-law and how she broached it. Yes, she'd phone Fenwick once Christmas Day was over and ask to speak to Lady Margaret.

She had a long soak in the hot water, revelling in the luxury as she felt the therapeutic effect of the warmth relax tense muscles and ease the strain from her limbs. She washed her hair after half an hour of wallowing, towelling it almost dry before she left the bathroom clad in her nightie and dressing gown.

What a do . . . It was an expression of Maggie's, and she could just hear her saying it, too. In spite of everything it induced a weak smile. Perhaps Sir Geoffrey would think twice in future before he attempted to force his way into someone's house; he'd certainly got more than he had bargained for tonight. She'd bet his foot was broken.

Once in bed, her eyes travelled to her new clothes, laid out in regal splendour over the backs of the two easy chairs on the other side of the room. The dancing shadows from the flicker of the fire picked up the different shades of colour in the scarf and gave it an illusion of life as she watched, and she curled her toes beneath the blankets, the brandy having made her dozy. She would give the outfit its final press tomorrow, she was too comfortable now to do anything more than turn out the bedside lamp, but one thing was for sure – she wasn't going to let that horrible man ruin her Christmas.

Her gaze moved to the small pile of gaily wrapped parcels on top of the little occasional table in front of the two chairs. There were gifts from Maggie, Florrie and Rebecca, and ones from Lady Harris, Lady Margaret, and even little Constance and William. Peggy had remembered her, and there was a tin of something – she felt sure it was homemade toffee – from Hilda.

Life never ran smoothly for long, it was the same for everyone, but there were plenty of good moments too. Tomorrow was Christmas Day, and Rodney was going to see her in her new clothes and she would meet his brother and his wife for the first time. It would be nice if she got on with Vanessa; she could normally hit it off with anyone if she tried, she thought dozily.

She continued to sit half-propped up against the pillows as she stared across the room at the glowing fire. She would light a fire in her bedroom tomorrow, although she wouldn't bother with the other rooms whilst Eileen was away. But it was lovely to be warm and cosy in here, comforting . . . She could leave it well banked and it would be pleasant to come home to in the evening. Yes, she'd do that. She turned off the lamp and snuggled down under the covers, all thoughts of Sir Geoffrey gone, and within moments she was fast asleep.

It was Christmas Day.

It was Sarah's first thought as she opened her eyes in the morning, and immediately her heart gave a little hop, jump and a skip, before she sat up in bed and gave herself a mental talking-to.

She was going to be cool, calm and collected today, she was, whatever she felt like inside. The people she would be mixing with would consider it bad form to show too much excitement about anything, but oh . . . She wrapped her arms round her knees and hugged herself tightly. It was going to be difficult.

She loved all her presents. Maggie and Florrie had bought her a matching set of scarf and gloves in bright cherry-red wool, there was a beautifully made blouse in soft blue flannelette from Rebecca and toiletries from Peggy and Lady Margaret's children. Lady Harris had given her a box of chocolates and a very generous cheque, but it was Lady Margaret's present that caused the 'oh . . .' from her lips and brought a brightness to her eyes. The stylish little gold brooch in its red velvet box was exquisite, and would go perfectly with her new outfit, she thought happily.

She was ready and waiting when Rodney rang the bell just before eleven, and as she opened the door to him, her face bright and glowing under its cascade of high silky golden curls, and her slim, full-breasted figure shown off to perfection by the cleverly cut clothes, he stared at her for a moment without speaking, and then he said, 'You look lovely; quite quite beautiful.'

'Thank you.' She suddenly felt horribly shy, and it was on the tip of her tongue to tell him it was one of Lady Margaret's cast-offs, but she didn't. She didn't know why she didn't, she just didn't, passing the moment off by saying, 'Happy Christmas, and I hope you enjoy the one meal a year you can eat in peace.'

The church bells were ringing out as they drove into Windsor, and Sarah felt as if she was in some sort of dream, the beautiful car, her lovely clothes, Rodney at her side, all casting their own special magic, and the feeling lasted right until the moment she stepped out of the car outside Richard's large imposing house, and Vanessa Mallard's cool ice-blue eyes slowly dissected her bit by bit as her mouth said all the right things. In that moment she realized that the suit, although lovely, was two or three years out of fashion, that her brown shoes were quite wrong, and that Richard's wife was perfect from the top of her head to the tips of her feet.

At thirty-six years of age Vanessa Mallard didn't look a day over twenty-five, something she worked at every day of her life. The pale silky skin was flawless, her shining cap of sleek silver-blond hair cut perfectly to frame a face in which the slanted blue eyes and beautifully shaped mouth made anyone take a second, and then a third look. She was utterly self-absorbed, possessing a cold detachment which had allowed her, through nearly eleven years of marriage, to take and discard a string of lovers without a shred of guilt disturbing her conscience.

Born into a middle-class family where she had been worshipped and adored by over-indulgent parents, she had never done a day's work in her life, and never intended to. She had flitted from one love affair to another from the age of sixteen, always growing bored within weeks with the current lover, until, at the age of twenty-three, she had met Rodney Mallard.

She had never doubted for a moment that she could dissuade him from playing Robin Hood to the working classes. Once he'd qualified – and she knew he would qualify well, his intelligence was formidable – he would step into the ready-made bosom of the family practice which only catered to the most genteel of Windsor society. Lunch at the Ritz, small select dinner parties, bridge afternoons and winter holidays abroad: Vanessa had had it all worked out to the finest detail, and the added bonus had been that she had fallen in love for the first, and the only, time in her life.

But it hadn't happened. Rodney hadn't let it happen. And now he had brought this girl, this *nobody*, into their home for Christmas lunch.

Vanessa took his arm, Sarah being on the other side of him, and drew them into the large, glass-roofed porch which she felt was such a *satisfactory* introduction to the house, and through into the wood-panelled hall beyond.

But he would regret it. She watched him as he greeted, and was greeted by, their friends, introducing Sarah as he went along. Oh yes, he would regret it all right. She would make very sure of that. Whoever this little chit was, wherever she had come from, she wasn't having him. He was hers. He had always been hers. She ground her teeth silently as she watched Rodney raise a hand to Richard, and then make his way over to his brother. Yes, he'd regret this, and before he was too much older . . .

'Sarah, my dear, good to meet you at last. I've been hearing a lot about you.'

In vital contrast to his wife's coldly polite greeting, Richard's was friendly and genuine, and Sarah warmed to him at once. After her first shock at seeing the mutilated face – fortunately when he had been engaged in conversation with someone else and unaware of her – Sarah had felt an overwhelming rush of pity, and this enabled her to smile back quite naturally now, concentrating on the warm brown eyes that were unmarred by the injuries that had seared and burnt most of the skin surrounding them. The left side of the head had received most of the blast, the left ear was almost entirely gone, and there were several angry red patches where the hair was refusing to grow, but the right side of his face had come in for a considerable amount of damage too.

Poor man. Poor, poor man. What he must have suffered, must still be suffering. And then, as Vanessa joined them, Sarah received a slight shock as the other woman said, her face straight and her voice cool, 'Don't let him embarrass you, Miss Brown. As I recall, Rodney has said very little about you.'

'I'm not embarrassed.' She was answering Vanessa, but smiling at Richard as she spoke. 'And I'm very pleased to meet you too, it's really very kind of you to invite me to Christmas lunch like this.'

'Nonsense.' The burns had dragged his lower lip to one side, contorting his smile. 'You've met my wife, I take it? Come along and I'll introduce you to the rest of the crew, they're a motley bunch but we still call them our friends.'

'Thank you.'

She smiled up at Rodney who was saying, his voice loud, 'That's right, that's right, whisk her off as soon as she steps in the door, won't you,' and put her hand through the crook of the arm Richard had extended to her.

'You have a lovely home.' In truth the splendour of the house had staggered her, both on their approach up the long winding drive, and on entering the baronial hall of the huge stone-built building.

'Thank you, my dear.' He looked down at her, and again she concentrated on the gentle brown eyes. 'We haven't been here too long, as it happens. After my parents died and I came out of hospital, Vanessa decided she wanted something to occupy her mind and moving house seemed to fit the bill.'

He smiled, and Sarah smiled back, but she was thinking, What an upheaval after all he'd been through, and then she caught her thoughts as Richard continued, 'It's strange you know, but I don't feel the house is mine yet, more that I've borrowed it for a time. Funny that, eh? No doubt I'll settle in eventually.'

'And your wife?'

'Oh, Vanessa loves it.' His voice was flat. 'Yes, she loves it. It's ideal for entertaining, of course.'

Yes, she supposed it was, but it wasn't much like a home, was it, although the house was beautiful, and his wife more so. But Vanessa Mallard had something more than beauty, Sarah thought as she made all the right responses to the innumerable introductions. She had a kind of exclusiveness about her, and it had the unfortunate effect of bringing the savage disfigurement of her husband into even more painful prominence. They were like Beauty and the Beast. But no, that was cruel, there was nothing of the beast about Richard Mallard.

She glanced up at him at her side, and immediately the deep brown eyes smiled at her, emphasizing the last thought. No, he was lovely, kind and gentle, and she already liked him as much as she disliked his wife.

The next hour, until lunch was served at twelve thirty, went smoothly, and it was mainly due, Sarah acknowledged silently, to Rodney's stoic encouragement.

He was there at her side when Richard finished the round of introductions and he didn't budge again, his manner easy and his stance relaxed, as he kept their little group entertained with one amusing story after another. They were mostly about his work, and the humour was largely self-deprecating, but

232

he was very funny. So why, she asked herself towards the end of the hour, why did she feel he wasn't as equable as he would like to imply from his actions? It was an act, a clever, polished act maybe, but still an act.

And then, and through just a few well-chosen words, she felt she had an inkling of why he was on edge. The maid had called them for lunch, and as they walked through to the elaborately decorated dining room Sarah saw that Vanessa had taken Rodney's free hand, his other holding his half-finished cocktail, and that the other woman was gazing up at him, her words soft but quite distinct as she said, 'Do you remember our first Christmas, Rodney? When your mother had that wonderful fancy dress party? We made quite an impact, didn't we? My Cleopatra to your Antony.'

'I don't remember.' His voice was offhand and matter-of-fact, but there was something in his attitude that made Sarah feel uncomfortable, and then, as Rodney almost thrust his brother's wife from him, he turned fully to her. 'Come and sit down, Sarah.'

The plushly upholstered dark wood dining chairs were grouped round a table ablaze with crystal and silver, and as he said, 'Here, we'll sit here, shall we,' and pulled out a seat for her, she said, 'I think there are name cards.'

'What?'

'On the table, there are name cards where everyone is supposed to sit.'

'I don't believe it.' It was soft but with a wealth of feeling, and for a moment she thought he was going to sit down anyway and ignore the place settings, but then he said, his voice attempting jocularity, 'Well, well, a new version of hunt the thimble. This is the first time we've been so formal on Christmas Day.'

She knew, even before it was confirmed, that she would be seated at the opposite end of the table from Rodney, and she also had a good idea where their hostess was sitting when Vanessa cried in the next instant, her voice shrill and laughing, 'Find your seats, everyone, find your seats. We're all mixed up, I don't want anyone sitting next to their partners, nothing so boring as that, it's Christmas.' And then Vanessa looked at her, and held the look for some moments, her pale pearly-blue eyes with their thick, darkened lashes opaque and cold.

Richard's wife didn't want her here. Sarah felt the prickly feeling that comes with being in the wrong place at the wrong time freeze her face. But why? What had she done? But then Rodney had found her place and pulled out her chair for her, and everyone was being seated. Sarah found she was sandwiched between a large portly man on her right, and an even larger man on her left, both of whom, after a perfunctory word of greeting to her, talked the relative merits of their respective clubs for the whole of lunch.

As the meal progressed, she was conscious that all the merriment was at the far end of the table, and also that the food wasn't up to Hilda's standard; in fact, it was disappointingly bland, although she felt ungrateful and not a little guilty for thinking so.

She was also hot and sticky. The heating was of the hothouse variety and was making her head ache slightly, added to which a strange feeling of deflation was making her want to run away and hide.

She had been so elated that morning, when she had looked at herself in the full-length mirror in her room and hardly recognized the tall elegant woman staring back at her. She had thought . . . Oh, she didn't know what she had thought. She bit down on her lip hard, then raised her gaze from her plate to the end of the table where another burst of laughter had erupted. Even Rodney was smiling, and as she watched, she saw Vanessa turn to him, one hand moving to tap his arm lightly as though in answer to something he had just said.

She didn't belong here, but he did. Suddenly the new clothes and hairdo meant nothing and she felt herself shrink down to child size again. She wished she was at Maggie's at this precise moment, oh, she did. Maggie was real, Florrie was real, but these people . . . She should never have come.

And it was as this thought reverberated in her head that Rodney looked straight at her, as though his eyes had been drawn by her thoughts. All right? It was mouthed, not spoken out loud, but for the life of her she couldn't respond with the requisite smile and nod he would expect, merely moving her head stiffly as she mouthed back, Yes thank you, and then lowered her gaze to her plate, attacking the soggy Brussels sprouts determinedly.

He could sit there and laugh and talk with Vanessa all day for all she cared, it didn't bother her in the least. He was just like the rest of them, he was, and she had thought he was so different. Well, she'd show him, and them. Her head came up and her shoulders straightened. She was as good as this lot any day.

It was this frame of mind that drove her, once the meal had finished, to walk swiftly out of the room ahead of the others, who had all risen at Vanessa's announcement that coffee would be served in the drawing room, and into the downstairs cloakroom. She needed a few minutes to compose herself after that terrible meal and get her thoughts in order, and she couldn't do that whilst making small talk.

She sat in there for a few minutes, willing the cool, calm girl who had so impressed Lady Harris at the interview into play, and then smoothed her hair in the fashionable gilt mirror before splashing a little cold water over her wrists. She looked fine, just fine. Not as bang up-to-date as Vanessa maybe, and her shoes weren't Italian leather by some designer or other as she had heard Vanessa informing another woman

235

guest hers were, but she was dressed well. And now she had to get out there and continue to act the part until she could leave. Oh, Rodney . . . The thought came from nowhere and with it a weakening desire to weep, and she quickly thrust it away. No, no, none of that. He had invited her here today because he felt sorry for her. She had to face that and live with it. He'd always felt sorry for her. Her stomach muscles clenched and she looked into the mirror again, into her deep blue eyes that were trying to tell her something.

She loved him.

It was there in her face and she couldn't deny it. She loved him. Oh no, how could she have been so stupid? How could she, how could she, how could she? She shut her eyes tightly, breathing in and out slowly for some moments before she opened them again and looked at the girl in the glass. 'All right, so you love him,' she whispered quietly. 'And he doesn't love you, he'll never love you, so you get on with it, right? You don't snivel and whine, you get on with it.' And part of getting on with it was getting through the rest of this nightmare day.

She partly opened the cloakroom door, pausing and taking a deep breath in preparation for what lay ahead, and it was as she stood like that, able to see out but without really being visible herself, that she saw Vanessa dart across the hall and push someone, who must have been standing within the open doorway of the dining room, into the room, shutting the door after her.

Sarah couldn't have explained the gut instinct which prompted her to walk across to the dining room, and as she paused outside the door she could hear a man and woman's low tones, before Rodney's voice, sharp now with annoyance, said, 'Open the damn door, Vanessa.' More murmuring and then, 'I'm not discussing this with you now or at any other time, and what was the reason for putting her between Miles and John at lunch, incidentally? I should think she was bored out of her mind.' Vanessa's softer tones again, and then Rodney's voice saying, 'Only because she is too well-mannered to show boredom, that's all.'

They were discussing her. Sarah felt such a burst of indignation she didn't stop to think before she rapped smartly on the door, opening it a moment later to see Rodney and Vanessa standing just within the room.

'There you are.' Rodney stepped forward, speaking as though he had been searching for her all day, and taking her arm said, 'There's coffee in the drawing room.'

Sarah didn't answer him beyond an inclination of her head, but she turned her gaze on Vanessa's watching face and said, 'Thank you for a lovely lunch, Mrs Mallard' without smiling.

'Oh please, call me Vanessa.'

The paleness of the light blue eyes accentuated their piercing quality and made it difficult to hold Vanessa's gaze, but Sarah managed it, and it was the other woman who looked away first, saying, 'Come along then, let's go through, shall we? I know how Rodney loves his coffee after a meal.' She tapped Rodney's arm in much the same way she had at lunch, but now there was no smile on his face.

He totally ignored Vanessa, and it was noticeable that he didn't allow his sister-in-law to precede them from the room as he took Sarah's elbow and ushered her out into the hall. Sarah was very conscious of Vanessa just behind them as they stepped into the buzzing drawing room, and when someone called out, 'Oh, Vee, there you are, are you game for charades?' and she heard Rodney groan, she said as naturally as she could, 'You don't like charades?'

'How can anyone like charades?' And then, as the noise and laughter swelled, he said, 'It's unbearably warm in here. How about if we take our coffee into the garden? It's fine out, and quite mild, and there's a sheltered spot down by the rose arbour which catches any sun that's around.'

She hesitated. 'They won't mind?'

'Good grief, no.'

There was nothing she would like better than to escape Vanessa's hawk-like gaze for a while, and so she said, 'All right, if you're sure it's not rude.'

'Trust me.' He grinned at her, and she forced a smile back, which faded as she watched him cross the room for their coffee. How could she have ever thought for a minute he would be interested in someone like her? He was so handsome, so in command, so . . . so everything. But she hadn't, not really . . . had she? Oh, she didn't know what she'd thought any more. She turned abruptly, walking over to the large wide french windows and staring out over the neatly laid-out grounds, her body tight. What on earth had possessed her to fall in love with someone so completely out of her reach as Rodney Mallard? But then, she hadn't chosen it. Love didn't conform to any neat tidy social pattern, that was the trouble. And in a way, she'd always loved him, but her love had changed, grown up, become adult-to-adult instead of child-to-adult. Her thoughts emphasized their age difference and again she shut her eyes tight for a moment, before opening them and staring blankly ahead. He was an experienced man of the world, he'd done things, seen things she could only dream of. Why, why would a man like that ever look twice at a raw young thing like her? Well, he wouldn't, that was the truth of it.

She was still standing there looking out into the garden when Rodney started to make his way back with their coffee, and he found himself caught by the picture she made as she stood framed against the shining glass, the light gold velvet curtains either side of the windows the same colour as her hair. She was stunning. He glanced briefly round the room before his gaze returned to Sarah. Absolutely stunning, and she'd got something none of these other women had – poise, natural dignity, call it what you will; it was there.

His gaze travelled down the back of her head, lingering on a wayward curl that had escaped the elaborately upswept waves as he came within a foot of her, and then past the slender shoulders and tiny waist to the long long legs encased in fine stockings. He felt something quicken inside him, and immediately the brake came on.

'Thank you.' She turned as he reached her side, taking her coffee with a smile.

'I think we'll drink the coffee in here and then go for a stroll once we've finished,' Rodney said with a wry grimace at the coffee already half filling the saucers. 'I'm not very good at walking and carrying.'

'It's a good job you're a doctor and not a waiter.'

He laughed out loud. 'I don't know if some of my patients would agree with that statement.'

'Oh, I'm sure they would.' She was finding it physically painful to look into his face and keep her own from expressing how she felt, and she drank the coffee quickly, leaving Rodney only halfway through his when she left the room to fetch her coat from an upstairs bedroom which had been designated for the lady guests' use.

The wife of one of the men she had been sitting next to at lunch was fixing her hair in the dressing-table mirror when Sarah entered the bedroom, and she turned on the little stool and smiled as Sarah walked across to the bed where the coats were all lying. 'Hallo, I'm Elizabeth Redfern, Miles's wife. We were introduced but I expect you've forgotten everyone's names. You're a friend of Rodney's, aren't you?'

'Yes.' Sarah smiled back. The middle-aged face was curious but not unkind.

'It's so nice to see Rodney enjoying himself. He really doesn't socialize much, you know. Of course he's *devoted* to his work, but then you'd know that.' The heavily made-up eyes were magpie bright. 'Absolutely dedicated.'

The conversation continued along the same lines for some moments before the other woman said, 'Did I hear you say before lunch that you are a volunteer at St Anne's? Such a worthwhile use of your time, my dear.' She nodded approvingly. 'There are a group of us from the Women's Institute that do the same sort of thing. I can see why Rodney was drawn to you; one needs to have the same motivation as one's partner, don't you think?'

'Oh, but it's not like that—'

But the stout matron was in full flow. 'Miles and I always felt Vanessa and Rodney were wise to call it off, it really wouldn't have worked, you know. And of course dear Richard is devoted to her, quite devoted.'

Call it off? She wanted to ask more, but the words wouldn't come.

'And there's never been any animosity between the three of them, Miles and I have always admired them for that. Of course, when Richard married Vanessa, Rodney was his best man. That speaks for itself, doesn't it?'

'Yes, it does.' Sarah took a deep breath. 'Did . . . did they see each other for long?' She hoped the fairly ambiguous question would draw out more facts without her having to be too specific.

'Rodney and Vanessa, you mean?' At Sarah's nod, Elizabeth wrinkled her brow before she realized what she was doing, and quickly smoothed the lines again. 'I'm not sure, some months I think, before they got engaged, but it's Richard whom Miles has always been friendly with, so I don't know too much about Rodney. The engagement only lasted two months, I do know that, and then by the end of the same year Richard was walking down the aisle with her.' She leant forward conspiratorially. 'It caused quite a stir at the time, you know, but Miles thought it was a great hoot.'

A great hoot.

'And of course it's all worked out wonderfully well, although poor dear Richard has had his share of tragedy, hasn't he? That awful war . . .'

Another guest walked in at that moment, and after a bright nod and smile, Elizabeth turned her attention to the newcomer, who, it appeared, was one of her bridge partners.

They had been engaged? Rodney and Vanessa had been engaged? Sarah's head was spinning as she found her coat and walked down the stairs in a daze. Who had ended it, and why? Well, it must have been Vanessa of course – she had married Richard within months, it seemed. Had the lovely blonde been engaged to Rodney, met his brother, and then realized she'd made a mistake? Or had they had a quarrel, or . . . She continued blindly down the stairs, her head teeming with a hundred variations on a theme. Did Rodney still have some feeling for her? She stopped dead in the hall, the rise and fall of conversation from the drawing room sounding like a swarm of bees. Vanessa was beautiful, cultured, elegant . . . and she was part of his world.

She stared at the closed door and then reached for the curving brass handle. The day wasn't turning out quite as she had expected, all things considered.

The gardens surrounding the house were extensive, and laid out in a formal pattern of flowerbeds and rectangles of lawn, interspersed with neat circles of bushes and strategically placed young trees. The air was indeed mild, unlike the day before, and it was more reminiscent of an early spring day than late December as Rodney and Sarah strolled down to the little rose arbour at the perimeter of the grounds.

Sarah was finding conversation difficult – her newly acknowledged feelings made her tongue-tied and uncomfortable – and it was after Rodney had enquired as to the security procedures at the house that she blurted out the events of the night before. Rodney's response had shattered the calm of the December day, and sent a host of twittering sparrows zooming into the sky, as he'd bellowed, '*He did what?*'

She hadn't expected such a dramatic reaction, but as the full story had come out, she became aware he was genuinely very upset.

'*And you just went to bed?*' He was staring at her as though she had come from another planet. 'You didn't phone anyone? Maggie, Lady Harris, the police – me?'

'Well, nothing actually happened.'

'Nothing actually happened.' He repeated her words slowly. 'I don't believe you just said that. At the very least you should have reported the incident to someone in authority at the local police station. What if he had come back?'

'He didn't.'

Rodney continued staring at her a moment longer before he said, 'Sarah—' And then stopped abruptly, taking a deep breath.

'It's all right, really.'

'It's far from all right.' He shook his head slowly. 'First Peggy and now this. The man wants locking away. Now, there is no way you are staying there alone tonight, and Lady Harris needs to be informed without delay. Are you going to do that, or do you want me to?'

They had reached the little rose arbour, which had been cut into a semi-circle in the lawn the path was bordering, and as they sat by unspoken mutual consent on the small slatted wooden seat enclosed on three sides by trellis, Sarah found she was staring at him. She wasn't quite sure if she should be feeling so thrilled at his concern, and to hide her emotion she lowered her head as she said, 'I had intended to call Fenwick over the next day or two.'

'Tonight.'

'All right, tonight.'

'And we'd better see about sorting out some accommodation for you—'

'There's no need for that,' she said quickly. 'I'd feel awkward about leaving the house unattended at night, but I could always ask Peggy to come and stay for a couple of days. I know she wouldn't mind.'

'She hasn't gone home for Christmas?'

'You don't know what her home's like! No, she's with the Coles, and as she knows all there is to know about Sir Geoffrey I won't be betraying any confidences if I explain things to her. I can just say to the Coles that I'm nervous about being alone until Eileen is back.'

'Right, we'll do that then. We'll leave here early and go there on our way back to Emery Place.'

Silence reigned for a few minutes, and it was clear to Sarah that Rodney wanted to say something and didn't know quite how to put it, so when he leant forward, his elbows on his knees and his hands loosely clasped, she wondered what she was going to hear.

'Sarah, you're a young woman, a very young woman, just starting out on life, and I don't want you to think all men are like Sir Geoffrey or Rebecca's husband,' Rodney said slowly. 'There are good men, decent men, out there, and in the fulness of time you will meet one who is right for you. I've known couples who have something which takes them all through the trials of life together, the Coles are one such pair, and my parents were another.'

She stared at the bowed profile without speaking, her vantage point making her aware of the way his hair grew into little curls at the base of his head, and the broad line of his shoulders, and she really didn't know if she wanted to kiss him or hit him. He was talking as if she was five years old and he was a hundred, for goodness' sake!

'You had a tough time of it at Hatfield, and that's putting it mildly, and one of the consequences of such segregation of the sexes at an early age is that you didn't come into contact with many members of the opposite sex during your formative years. Certainly you didn't experience a father's influence.'

If he was going to suggest he could be a father to her she definitely *would* hit him.

'Look, what I'm trying to say is this.' He straightened, leaning back against the slatted wood and turning to look at her. 'You must not let the men I've mentioned spoil things for you, do you understand me? It would be easy to assume the whole male race is a mixture of philanderers and bullies and worse, but you mustn't disregard the millions who devote themselves to their wives and families, and who live very contented and happy lives with just one woman.'

'I know.' She did, she did.

'Good.' He smiled. 'There is a young man out there for you, Sarah, that you've yet to meet, but you'll know him when you see him and he'll know you.'

Right, enough was enough. She stood up abruptly, and her voice was tight when she said, 'Perhaps we ought to get back now? The others will be wondering where we've got to.'

He'd upset her, talking so familiarly. She must look on him as a member of another generation, it wasn't like a friend of her own age chatting to her. Damn it, he'd embarrassed her, made her feel uncomfortable with him, he should have left well alone.

Rodney remained sitting for a moment more before rising slowly, suddenly feeling every one of his thirty-eight years as her youthfulness swamped him. Well, that was his answer to the question whether she might ever see him as something more than a friend. He checked his thinking immediately. He hadn't wondered that, had he? *Had he?* Perhaps he had at that. Damn it all, he was a fool. He'd been a fool where Vanessa was concerned, and it seemed he wasn't getting any brighter with age.

'What's the matter?'

They were walking back to the house, and he hadn't been aware her eyes were on him until she spoke.

'Nothing, nothing.' He forced a smile. 'Well, on to the charades I suppose. That was one good thing about the war, they didn't expect you to play charades in the camp.' It was the first time he had been able to talk naturally about the war that he could remember, and it surprised him.

'No, I don't suppose they did,' she said softly. 'We heard things, awful things, back in England. It must have been hard for you, and I suppose all this, the social side of life, must seem very unimportant now.'

'Unimportant?' He considered the word as he breathed in the sweet scent of her that he had noticed before, a mixture of magnolia and musk, he thought. Vanessa had always used Chanel No. 5 from the day he had met her, and only now did he acknowledge that he had never liked the perfume on her, although his mother had worn it and it had smelt quite different. 'No, not unimportant,' he said quietly. 'Surreal at times, maybe, but it's comforting in a way to know that life goes on even when we think the world's coming to an end. And I did think the world was coming to an end at times, even when I was back home in England. But the rain continues to fall, the sun shines, babies are born . . . and Vanessa plays charades,' he added with a wry smile.

Vanessa. Yes. Quite.

She spoke quickly now to hide the sudden jealousy which she wasn't proud of but couldn't do a thing about. 'Talking of babies, we had a new arrival in the children's ward yesterday, on Christmas Eve of all days, bless him. He's only six months old and he'd managed to fall out of his cot. His poor mother was frantic.'

'Oh yes, how's that work going? I meant to ask you about it earlier.' And so they walked back into the house chatting away, as though the undercurrents which were beginning to bubble beneath the surface hadn't touched either of them.

Rodney and Sarah left the party early, much to Vanessa's chagrin, and drove straight to the Coles' house, where Peggy seemed to understand the situation at once, despite the fact that Sarah could only explain fully to her once the young girl was seated with them in the car on the way back to Emery Place. However, mainly due to the fact that Meg pressed them to have a mince pie and a cup of tea, and it had seemed churlish to refuse the little woman, it had turned ten before Sarah opened the front door of 19 Emery Place, and first Peggy, then Rodney, followed her into the hall just as the telephone began to ring.

She picked it up quickly, fully expecting it to be Lady Margaret, or even her employer if she was feeling better, but after stating the number there was no response, and she repeated it, adding, 'How may I help you?'

'How may you help me?' A pause, and then, 'You think a vicious unbalanced little slut like you could help *me*?'

She dropped the receiver as though it had bitten her, and as it clattered on to the little table, Rodney sprang forward saying, 'Leave it, leave it, I'll deal with it.' He picked up the instrument quickly, barking into the receiver as he said, 'Who is that? Who's there?' And then, 'Answer me, damn it.'

'Are you all right, miss? Sit down.'

She didn't answer Peggy, leaning against the wall with her eyes on Rodney as he slowly replaced the receiver. 'He's gone. It *was* him, wasn't it?'

Sarah nodded, her stomach churning, before sheer rage replaced the sick shock of the call. 'How dare he, how *dare* he do that?' she said to the other two. 'He's got no right to call me names.'

'Oh, miss.' Peggy's indignant voice lightened the atmosphere somewhat when she said, 'An' you're so good an' all. He's a swine, that's what Michael called him when I told him about – well, you know. An' he was right, wasn't he, Dr Mallard? He's nothin' but a swine, an' to call the miss names . . .'

Rodney nodded at the young girl as he said, 'Michael was spot on, Peggy. Look, why don't you go and make Sarah and yourself a bit of supper while we phone Lady Harris, and perhaps you'd bring her a cup of hot sweet tea as soon as you can?'

'Yes, I'll do that.' Peggy shot a look of concern at Sarah's white face. 'An' I'll put somethin' in it.'

'No, no thanks, Peggy,' Sarah said with a weak smile. 'The tea would be lovely but I drank half the brandy bottle last night after Sir Geoffrey's visit. The man will turn me into an alcoholic if I'm not careful. Just plenty of sugar.'

'All right, miss.'

Sarah asked for Lady Margaret when she got through to Fenwick. She didn't feel up to talking to Lady Harris about her son but Lady Margaret had become more of a friend than anything else the last few weeks, and the phone call wasn't as difficult as she had expected it to be. It seemed nothing surprised Lady Margaret with regard to her husband. However, the older woman was angry and upset, and she insisted on returning to Emery Place within the next day or two, although Sarah assured her repeatedly it wasn't necessary, and promised Sarah she would put Lady Harris fully in the picture the next day. Her mother-in-law had ways, Lady Margaret said meaningfully, of bringing Sir Geoffrey to heel

– the handsome allowance Sir Geoffrey was designated sprang to Sarah's mind – and the matter would be addressed immediately. Sarah needn't worry about it any more.

It was as Rodney was leaving that he reached inside his jacket and surprised her by bringing out a small gold-wrapped parcel, handing it to her with a smile as he said, 'I was going to give this to you earlier, but there didn't seem a right moment.'

'Oh, thank you.' She felt awful. She hadn't got him anything but she hadn't expected to see him over Christmas, and by the time she had known she would, she'd been committed to working at the hospital for most of Christmas Eve.

She said as much, but he stopped her with a raised hand before opening the front door and saying, 'It's not anything I've bought, so don't worry, just something I was rather fond of at your age.'

'It's yours?'

'Was.' He smiled, and then he was gone, and for a moment she felt quite bereft as she stood on the doorstep watching him walk to the car.

She unwrapped the little package once she was in bed and alone, and it revealed a much-thumbed first copy of Rupert Brooke's *1914 and Other Poems*. The hot milk she had taken up with her grew cold by the side of the bed as she devoured poem after poem, the only sound in the room being the rustling of pages and the odd spark and splutter from the fire, which Peggy had replenished before she had retired to her own quarters.

Sir Geoffrey's phone call, Vanessa's antagonism, the feeling that there was something still left between Rodney and his sister-in-law from the past, it all had faded into insignificance by the time she put the small book down on the coverlet, and sat staring ahead across the room.

248

The idealistic patriotism of the wartime poetry had touched her, but more than that, she could see Rodney had been moved by it . . . once.

Why had he given her the book now? Was it simply something he thought she would enjoy reading, or – and she felt this was more likely – was it another way of showing her a glimpse of the great divide between them, accentuating the difference in age, outlook, experience, and highlighting the change between what he had been then, at twenty, and what he was now? He couldn't have guessed how she felt about him, could he? The thought brought her bolt upright in the bed before she relaxed back against the pillows, telling herself not to be so silly. Just because he had given her a book of poems he used to enjoy once, it didn't mean there was a covert message in his actions. She was reading too much into things here.

She finished the last of the now cold milk and settled down for sleep. It was her new knowledge of her love for him that was making her take two and two and reach five, she told herself firmly. She hadn't thrown herself at him, or flirted, there had been none of that. The events of the day flashed into her mind, Vanessa's tall slim body draped languidly across him at lunch as she had repeatedly leant over his chair on the pretext of talking to the woman on the other side of him, and her eyes narrowed. Not by her, anyway.

She felt emotionally and physically exhausted, and suddenly trying to think at all was too much. She would go to sleep and consider everything in the morning, not that all the thinking in the world would alter anything. He didn't love her. She loved him, and he didn't love her.

It only took a minute or two for her to fall asleep, but her face was wet with tears none the less.

Chapter Fifteen

Lady Margaret returned to Emery Place on Monday 29th December, and on the Wednesday, the eve of the year nineteen forty-eight, when the hit song 'They Say It's Wonderful' was still reverberating the air waves, Sarah received her first telephone call from Maggie. It was to say that Rebecca was fighting for her life in the Sunderland infirmary, having been beaten to a state of unconsciousness by her husband, who had then apparently either walked into the sea on Hendon beach in an acute state of intoxication, or passed out on the sands. Either way, the result was the same – Willie Dalton was dead, drowned.

'Willie's dead?' Sarah couldn't believe her ears.

'Aye, lass, an' it looks as though Rebecca might be goin' the same way,' Maggie said loudly, so loudly that Sarah had to hold the telephone away from her ear, only to hear Maggie trumpet in the next moment, 'I'm not shoutin', Florrie, but it's no use me whisperin', the lass won't be able to hear anythin'.'

'He's hurt Rebecca?' Her stomach had come up into her throat. 'But how did he get past you and Florrie?'

'She went back to him, lass, the night afore Christmas Eve. We tried to stop her, the good Lord knows we tried, but he played her like a gypsy with a fiddle.'

'Maggie' – she had to get the facts, and fast, but at a pitch

251

that didn't make her head ring – 'tell me exactly what happened, but speak a little more quietly, would you?'

There was a pause, and then Maggie's voice came saying, 'Oh, lass, I shouldn't have broken it to you like that, but it's this infernal machine.'

'I know, I know.' She could just picture poor Maggie standing in the telephone box at the top of the street, yelling her head off, and her heart went out to the old woman. She took a deep breath, her voice as soothing as she could make it through the burning anxiety for Rebecca, and said, 'Maggie, just speak in your normal voice and tell me how bad she is.'

'Bad.'

'And they are sure it was Willie?'

'Oh aye. Seems the neighbours were disturbed yesterday evenin' with a bit of carry on, but then it all went quiet. That must've bin when he started the drinkin'. Anyway, old Emily, you know the midwife from North Shields, well, she was attendin' a birth up Rebecca's way, an' she noticed the front door was open when she passed, but didn't think anythin' of it at the time. Then when she was on her way home, at gone one, it was still open, an' knowin' Rebecca from a bairn, she went to see what was what. An' like she said this mornin', she near passed out. There was the lass in one of the bedrooms upstairs all trussed up' – Sarah heard Florrie's voice cut in in the background, and Maggie saying, 'I wasn't goin' to tell her all of it, Florrie, give me some credit' – before Maggie continued, 'Anyway, the room was freezin', lass, an' she wouldn't have lasted till mornin', not the state she was in.'

Sarah was vaguely aware that Lady Margaret and Eileen were both in the hall, but she didn't look up, concentrating on Maggie's voice at the end of the line. 'And Willie? Where was he?' She was feeling sick at the picture in her mind but spoke quietly, forcing herself to form the words through the rushing in her head.

'Well they didn't know at the time, no one did, an' they was more concerned with gettin' the lass sorted than findin' out where he was, but then one of the fishermen found him at first light washed up on the beach. Appears he was already three parts to the wind when he started drinkin' in Oldfellows, you know that rough pub on the seafront that's his local, an' he was mouthin' then he'd given his wife a good hidin'. That old biddy across the road, Mrs Macintyre, she's bin at her sister's for Christmas but come back this mornin', and she's bin tellin' the constable a right tale about the carryin' on there was afore she went on Christmas Day mornin'. Willie's bin drunk more than he's bin sober from what I can make out, but the rest of 'em, even the ones next door to the lass, are keepin' their mouths shut. Sanctimonious so-an'-sos, the lot of 'em. Rebecca could've died an' they wouldn't have lifted a finger as long as it was done quietly. If that's respectability, give me the other thing, lass.'

Sarah's mind was spinning, it was all too much to take in, but then as a thought suddenly occurred to her, she said urgently, 'The baby? Has she lost the baby, Maggie?'

'Not as I know of, not yet any road, but I can't see a bairn survivin' what he put her through, lass, an' she's got nigh on three months to go yet.'

'I'm getting the next train up.' She raised her eyes to Lady Margaret at this point who nodded energetic approval.

'Now, lass, think of your job. They've been right good to you, but if you start takin' liberties—'

'I'm coming up, Maggie. If . . . if she comes round, tell her I'm on my way.'

'Lass, are you sure?'

'Quite sure.'

'Oh, lass, I won't pretend I won't be glad to see you.'

There came the sound of muffled weeping, and then Florrie's voice came gently saying, 'Sarah? You're coming up then? Be – be quick.'

'Oh, Florrie.'

Sarah was quick, but it was still approaching eleven that night by the time she was shown into a small side room by a starched, prim nurse, who told her she would have to wait for the sister – she couldn't possibly authorize Sarah seeing Mrs Dalton at this time of night, and did she realize Mrs Dalton was very very ill indeed? Sarah stared at her for a moment before she said flatly that yes, she did know, it was the reason she had rushed up from London that day.

'I see.' The nurse was small and plump and pretty, with a round face and wisps of fluffy blond hair showing from beneath her cap – the sort of person Sarah had always thought jolly – but her officious manner didn't soften in the slightest when she said, 'And you did say you are just a friend? You aren't family, related in any way?'

'Mrs Dalton and I were brought up together as children, and neither of us have family of our own, so it's not a case of "just friends",' Sarah said as calmly as she could. 'We're like sisters.'

'But you aren't actually related?'

'No.'

'Ah.'

When the door closed behind the important little figure, Sarah sat down very suddenly on one of the four polished wooden chairs that, together with a low table holding one or two dog-eared magazines, made up the sum total of furniture in the green-painted room. She felt better now she was here. The journey had been a nightmare of anxiety and the train had seemed to crawl along. She was determined she was going to see Rebecca, she had to see how bad her friend's injuries were for herself, and more than that, try and let

Rebecca know she was here. She would will her to live, that's what she'd do. She couldn't die, she was too young to die . . .

The sister was very tall, with the sort of severe face and tightly scraped-back hair that was intimidating in itself, but as she took Sarah's hand, she smiled, and her voice was sympathetic when she said, 'I understand you have come all the way from London to see your friend?'

'She's more than a friend, she's . . .' How could she explain to a stranger what Rebecca meant to her? 'We were brought up in a children's home together.' She couldn't go on, but the sister seemed to understand anyway.

'Come this way, Miss . . . ?'

'Brown, Sarah Brown.'

'Ah yes, Mrs McLevy spoke of you this afternoon. We sent her and the other lady home earlier, they were both exhausted.' Once in the corridor outside the room, the sister put her hand on Sarah's shoulder, bringing her to a halt as she said, 'You might find your friend's appearance a little distressing, Miss Brown, although most of her injuries are on the bottom half of her body. You understand she has been badly beaten and abused?'

Sarah nodded, her heart thudding.

'She hasn't regained consciousness since she was brought in earlier this morning, but that is quite to be expected in the circumstances.'

'Maggie, Mrs McLevy, said – she indicated there's no hope . . . ?'

'There is always hope, Miss Brown, even in the direst of cases, and sometimes the patients who are the most ill on admittance make the best recoveries. However . . .' The brisk voice softened. 'Your friend is very poorly, and it would be as well for you and the other ladies to be prepared.'

'And the baby?'

'Mrs Dalton was having mild contractions when she was

admitted, but that seems to have subsided for the moment.'

'If . . . if Rebecca did recover, and she didn't miscarry, would the baby be all right? When it was born, I mean?'

'Let's cope with this one day at a time, shall we, Miss Brown? There had been an – implement used, which might suggest some complications internally, so speculation as to the consequences for the baby would be just that. Speculation. Now, if you're ready . . .'

The sister drew her forward towards a room just a few feet away down the left of the corridor, and as she opened the door, Sarah's gaze moved past her to the waxwork figure in the bed. 'Rebecca, oh, Rebecca.' She wasn't aware she had spoken out loud, but as the sister touched her arm and she turned dazedly to look at her, the woman said, 'You understand she could be unconscious for some time yet, but it may help if you talk to her. There is a new school of thought that suggests the subconscious mind can respond even when in a coma.'

Coma. The word hit Sarah full in the chest. She walked over to the bed slowly and as she looked down at the alabaster face on the pillow, she wondered for a moment if Rebecca had already gone. The skin was a sickly white colour, except round one eye and her mouth where it was a livid red, and black stitches stood out in the swollen flesh under the eyebrow like grotesque black maggots. Only Rebecca's head and neck were visible, her body, in spite of her pregnancy, making only the slightest mound beneath the thin hospital blankets.

Oh, Rebecca, my darling, darling Rebecca . . . What's he done to you?

She was aware of the sister's hand on her shoulder again, and of her voice saying, 'There, there, my dear. Let it out, let it out, you'll feel better then.'

She did let it out, but she didn't feel a lot better. She knew the constriction in her chest and overwhelming weight pressing down on her heart wouldn't lift until she was sure Rebecca was going to pull through. However, she dried her eyes and took control of herself because it was the only thing she could do to help her friend. If talking might help, she'd talk and talk until she was blue in the face.

'It was the shock.' She explained her tears with a wave of her hand at the bed.

'I know, my dear, I know. After a time one gets conditioned to accept the accidents and illnesses, part of life's rich pattern as they say, but something like this . . .'

'Man's inhumanity to man.' Rodney had used that phrase at some time, she couldn't remember when, but it suited this situation more than any other words could have done.

'Yes, exactly.'

'Can I stay and talk to her now?' Sarah knew it was against hospital procedure for her to be here at all at this time of night, but the sister merely smiled and nodded, pulling a chair close to the bed before she left the room.

The plump little nurse arrived a couple of minutes later with a cup of tea for her, again strictly at variance to the rules, Sarah imagined, and actually patted her hand and smiled before she left.

Once she had finished the tea and composed herself, she began to talk to Rebecca quietly, first about her job and London, then Rodney, before she went back over their childhood, reminiscing about the good times and the bad, the laughter and the tears, their hopes and their fears. It was only when a tentative dawn crept across the grey northern sky outside the window that it occurred to her a new year had begun while she had sat in the clinical surroundings. She just wanted Rebecca to live to see it. That was her one, her only, wish, she thought fiercely. Everything else, *everything*, paled into insignificance besides that.

The day sister was as kind as the night one, but when it got to midday, and Sarah still hadn't left Rebecca's side except for a hasty visit to the bathroom next door once or twice, the sister gently informed her that she should go home and rest, they really didn't want two patients instead of one. There was nothing she could do, the sister said quietly, and she could come back once she had eaten and rested.

Sarah did go home to Maggie and Florrie's and rest, but only for an hour or so. By half past four she was back at Rebecca's bedside, and at just gone seven that evening, Rebecca opened her eyes in the middle of a monologue about Hilda's different cake-making methods, but there was no recognition in the glassy stare.

'It's quite normal, don't worry.' The day shift were preparing to hand over to their counterparts, but the sister came and sat down with Sarah, taking her hand as she continued, 'She's fighting back, she's not giving in, which is vital in cases like this one. She'll sleep almost all the time, for days yet probably, but there will come a moment when she'll become aware of her surroundings, and then we'll know we're really winning. But this is hopeful, very hopeful.' She rose to her feet, and her voice was soft as she said, 'Now you stay a little while longer if you feel you need to, but you really can't sit here twenty-four hours a day, you'll make yourself ill. Go home and get a good night's sleep, and we'll see you again in the morning.'

It was bitterly cold outside the antiseptic warmth of the hospital, and as Sarah trudged the dark streets to Maggie's house the wind cut through her clothing like a knife. It had snowed all over Christmas, and now, due to a partial thaw a day or so ago which had then frozen over again, the ground was a sheet of ice between the great banks of snow piled against the pavements and walls.

Sarah was concentrating so hard on just staying on her

feet that she didn't raise her head until she was halfway along Lea Road, and then she came to an abrupt halt in the middle of the pavement, her eyes taking in the noble lines of the Rolls-Royce as her mouth gaped open. Rodney? Rodney was here?

She practically skated the last few yards, and had just reached the step of number nineteen when the door opened and Rodney himself stood above her. There was a moment's silence when they both just looked at each other, and then his voice came softly saying, 'How is she?'

'She – she's opened her eyes, but she doesn't seem to know anyone.'

'That isn't uncommon in cases like this at first.'

'That's what the sister said.'

He reached down and drew her up the steps as he said, as though she hadn't just walked the couple of miles from the hospital, 'Careful, careful, the ground is treacherous.'

'How did you know?' Sarah was vaguely aware of Maggie halfway down the passage, but she couldn't take her eyes off Rodney as she asked again, 'How did you know about Rebecca?'

She didn't ask, 'Why are you here?' or acknowledge the fierce emotion she had felt at the sight of his car; she didn't dare. It was enough he was here at this precise moment, and she was too bone-tired to think further.

'I telephoned the house yesterday, and Lady Margaret explained what had happened. I only got to Maggie's a minute or two ago.'

'You telephoned?'

Yes, he had telephoned. He knew he was being ridiculous, and he had told himself he had wanted to see her simply because time spent with Sarah was never banal or boring, but just how much he had wanted to see her he hadn't realized until this moment when she was standing in front of him.

But they were both free agents, there was nothing wrong in pursuing a friendship, was there?

Friendship? The word mocked him. And was it friendship that had brought him all the way up here? He was attracted to her, admit it and be done with it, the little voice in his head challenged.

He continued to gaze down into the lovely young face as he said, 'I telephoned the house to ask you to a dance, a dinner dance, for New Year's Eve, you know?' And when she stared blankly at him, 'A friend of mine had tickets but his wife was taken ill at the last minute, so he offered them to me.' Now why add that? Why not come out into the open and simply say he had wanted to take her out for the night and see the new year in with her? But the memory of her reaction to him on Christmas Day, when he had tried to talk to her in the garden, was still vivid, and nothing had changed since then.

No doubt, if he asked her directly, she would say she felt he was too old for her. And he could understand that, of course he could, it was perfectly natural.

'Oh, I see.' Sarah didn't know whether she should feel peeved that the invitation had come about through the circumstances he had described, or elated, regardless of that, because it had been *her* he had thought of asking. Not that that meant anything, she told herself firmly in the next breath. He had probably assumed that everyone else he knew had already made plans.

And as though to confirm this last thought, he said, 'I usually see the new year in at Richard's place. Vanessa packs the house with everyone we all know.'

'Does she.' Her tone suggested she wasn't interested in what Vanessa did.

'Any change, lass?' Maggie entered the conversation for the first time, and Sarah looked at her as she said, 'She

260

opened her eyes, Maggie, but she didn't know I was there. She's still in a world of her own.'

'I could have a word with her doctor if you like and see what I can find out?'

Sarah and Maggie answered in unison as they said, 'Could you do that?', and then, as Maggie added, 'Oh, lad, would you? It'd put me my mind at rest to get it from the horse's mouth?' Rodney nodded.

'Of course, that's one of the reasons I came. I still know a few people there from my time up here, and one in particular whom I've had quite a bit to do with recently over this national health service Aneurin Bevan wants to push through. Donald is a good chap so it won't be a problem. Have the police been to see you?' He was speaking directly to Maggie now, and she inclined her head towards the sitting-room door before looking upwards with a meaningful gesture.

'Let's talk inside, lad. Some folks have lugholes like elephants' an' flap 'em nearly as much.'

Once in the sitting room they all sat down – Sarah, at Maggie's bidding, close to the blazing fire, once she had divested herself of her coat and hat – and as Rodney said, 'Well?', Sarah asked, 'Where's Florrie?'

'Gone to see Maud about somethin'.'

Maggie didn't elaborate further, before turning to Rodney and saying, 'The constable come about half past four this afternoon, lad, just after Sarah'd gone back to the hospital. Wanted to know the ins an' outs of an old mare's backside, same as they always do. I told him what I knew, which isn't much.'

'Did he say how they thought Willie had come to be on the beach and get himself drowned?'

It was Sarah who had spoken, and Maggie nodded as she turned to her. 'Aye, they've got a good idea, lass, now they've checked around. Seems even them sorts that get down

261

Oldfellows have had their fill of him recently, the constable heard some right tales from what he said to me. By, that Willie was a nasty bit of work all right. Anyway, he could barely stand when he left the pub, or when he was thrown out, I should say. He started to get rough with one of the regulars when this fella told him what he thought of him, an' the landlord had had enough an' threw him out. The last anyone saw of him he was wanderin' down on to the sands singin' his head off.'

Singing his head off. Sarah's mouth tightened. He could sing his head off after the things he had done to Rebecca.

'And no one went after him?' Rodney asked quietly. 'It must have been apparent he was pretty much incapable of looking after himself, the state he was in.'

Maggie glanced at him, shaking her head as she answered, 'Lad, from some of the bits the constable said, I reckon there wasn't one person in that pub that gave a monkey's. Even the worst of 'em have standards of some sort. Anyway, like I've always said, justice will out in the end an' God won't be mocked. He got his come-uppance all right, an' not afore time.'

A silence followed, and then Rodney rose, clearing his throat before saying, 'I'll pop along to the infirmary now and see what I can find out there before I call in on Donald.'

'Where are you staying?'

He turned to Sarah as he replied, 'With Martin, like before. I telephoned him before I left London so it's all arranged.' And when she didn't comment further, 'I won't come back this evening, I'm sure you must all be exhausted, and it might take some time to find out anything worth knowing. I'll call by tomorrow morning, if I may?'

Maggie's voice was hearty as she said, 'Course, lad, course, an' thank you, thank you from the bottom of me heart. To come all this way like that. Well, thank you, lad.'

262

That's what *she* should have said. Sarah watched Maggie ushering Rodney out after they had said their goodbyes, and she was mentally kicking herself for not behaving more naturally.

That Maggie had noticed her reticence, and thought she understood the reason for it, became apparent when the old woman came back into the room and, staring hard at Sarah, said, 'It can never be, lass. You do know that, don't you?'

'What do you mean?'

'You an' the doctor.'

'Me and— Maggie, I don't know what you mean.'

'I'm too old in the tooth for beatin' about the bush, lass. I don't blame you for havin' some feelin' for him, hinny, there's many that would in your place, but it wouldn't work. He's from a different world, lass, an' although he's a good 'un, better than most of his sort, they don't wed out of their class. They might have a bit of fun on the side, but they don't wed, an' it's no use you hopin' for the moon.'

'I'm fully aware that there can never be anything of that nature between Dr Mallard and me,' Sarah said stiffly as her face flamed.

'I know you're thinkin' I'm speakin' out of turn, an' maybe I am at that, but bein' up in London an' mixing with the nobs in your job an' all, you can get to forgettin' how things really are. I don't want you hurt, lass—'

'Maggie, I said I know we can never be anything more than friends, and it's not an issue, really.'

'I'm only sayin' it for your own good—'

'*Maggie.*' Sarah pushed her lips tightly together, turning her head on her shoulder before she said, 'Leave it, Maggie, please. I know you mean well, but leave it.' There was a tone to her voice that conveyed her feeling better than any bellow could have done.

'Aye, all right, lass.' Even Maggie knew when she had said enough.

The three women were sitting waiting for Rodney when his knock sounded at the front door at just after ten the following morning, and when Maggie lumbered into the hall Sarah got to her feet, walking across to the blackleaded fireplace and staring down into the fire, her hands resting on the frilled mantelpiece.

How could she be worried to death about Rebecca on the one hand, whilst longing to see Rodney's face so much it hurt? Her mind kept seesawing from one to the other of them, and it didn't help that Maggie suspected how she felt either. She couldn't talk to her about it, she just couldn't, beyond assuring Maggie that she knew exactly how she stood with regard to any possible romantic attachment between Rodney and herself. And she did. She hadn't needed Maggie to point out that he wouldn't look at her twice.

As she heard his deep male voice, and then footsteps coming along the hall, she turned, forcing a smile to her face as Maggie, then Rodney, came into the room.

'Good morning.' His eyes were warm as he nodded first at her, then Florrie. 'I'm sorry I'm a bit late, but I couldn't get hold of Donald last night, he was at some function or other.'

'That's all right, you aren't late,' she said quickly.

'Sit down, lad, sit down.'

'No, I won't if you don't mind, Maggie, I've things to do, but I wanted to let you know how things stood as soon as I could. It appears she's already making progress, and they're as sure as they can be at this stage that she's going to be all right. Of course they don't want to get your hopes up only to have them dashed if she has a relapse, but from what Donald was able to tell me, I don't think there is much chance of that. However . . .' He paused, and his voice was a little gruffer as he said, 'They aren't too hopeful about the baby, so be prepared for that. Rebecca was damaged quite badly internally.'

'Oh.' Sarah stared at him as her hand fluttered to her throat, and her senses registered what he was saying. 'They said they didn't know if she would miscarry.'

'They still don't, but perhaps . . . Perhaps it would be kinder all round if she did,' Rodney said flatly. 'Anyway, regardless of that, Rebecca herself will need to stay in hospital for weeks yet, certainly until the child – if she goes full term – is born.'

'But she's out of danger?'

'Yes, I think so, although she is still very ill, Sarah.'

'Oh, thank you, thank you for finding out and everything.' She said what she should have said the night before, and it was easy. He was good, he was so good, and it wasn't his fault she loved him.

'That's all right, I was glad I could help in some small way. If you need me, you only have to shout.'

Now what did that mean? Maggie asked herself grimly as she stared at this tall handsome doctor she had always felt a warmth for, the essence of which had its core in the way he had stood up to Matron Cox that night in Hatfield's infirmary. What was he really thinking; or more to the point, what did he think about her lass? He wouldn't dally with her feelings would he, or worse, use them to his own advantage? Even the nicest of men – and the lad was nice, she'd give him that – could be right so-and-sos when they felt the urge, and Sarah was enough to stir any bloke from sixteen to sixty, and aye, above. He had the sort of face that gave nothing away, and if he did like the lass, he wasn't letting on, but to come charging up here like that . . .

Her thoughts made her voice abrupt as she said, 'Aye,

thanks, lad, from me an' Florrie an' all. I suppose you've got to be gettin' back to London pretty quick, eh? You bein' a busy man, an' all.'

'In a day or two. I've got one of the locums I use standing in for me at the moment, so there's no rush.' His glance went to Sarah. 'If you are ready to leave on Sunday, you're very welcome to ride back with me, of course.'

'Thank you.' Sarah smiled, but it was strained. 'I'll see how Rebecca is first if that is all right?'

'Yes, of course.' Perhaps he shouldn't have come? Maybe he had made himself look ridiculous chasing up after her, but once he had heard the news from Lady Margaret he had just wanted to see how Sarah was taking it, knowing how she felt about Rebecca. He had wanted to be near her, helping in any way he could. 'Well, I must be off. I hope you find Rebecca much improved when you visit her today.' His voice was brisk, professional.

Maggie saw him out, and when she returned a few moments later her voice was unusually subdued as she said, 'That was nice of him, offerin' you a lift back, lass.'

Sarah nodded quietly but said nothing. She would travel back by train. She had lain awake for some hours last night, Florrie and Maggie keeping up a medley of snores and grunts either side of her, and she had done some serious thinking. Rodney was a kind man and a generous one, but she couldn't let herself be persuaded that that kindness and generosity, when extended to her, meant anything more than they did when extended to anyone else.

It had disturbed her greatly that Maggie had suspected how she felt about him, she acknowledged silently. She couldn't abide people who wore their hearts on their sleeves, and she would die – she would just die – if Rodney guessed how she felt. So, it was safer not to be alone with him; besides which Rebecca needed her for a while yet, and Lady Margaret had indicated that she expected her to be in Sunderland for at least a few days until the situation clarified.

No, she would go home by train, and she would treat it as the first step in dealing with this thing that had come upon her. She had her job, she had her work at the hospital, and that was more than enough to keep her busy at the moment and stop her from thinking too much. It would have to be.

And later that day, when she was sitting by the side of Rebecca's bed and the dark brown eyes fastened on hers with recognition this time, she remembered her new year's wish.

'Rebecca?' She hardly dared hope that what she was seeing was true. 'Rebecca, it's Sarah. You're safe, darling, you're perfectly safe. Everything is going to be all right.'

'Sarah.' It was the faintest whisper from the colourless lips, and then Rebecca's brown eyes filled with tears that spilled out over the poor battered face as Sarah bent close and took the hurt little body gently in her arms.

Chapter Sixteen

It was a full week later before Sarah felt able to leave Sunderland, but it was with the knowledge that Rebecca had indeed turned the corner and was going to make a full recovery . . . in time. The 'in time' was something the doctors had emphasized over and over again.

The doctor dealing with Rebecca's case had asked to see Sarah the afternoon before she left – she suspected the sister had told him of her intended departure the next day – and she had known immediately she entered his office that it was bad news.

'Miss Brown, do sit down, my dear.' The doctor had reminded her of Rodney in a way, although he was much older and heavier, but his manner when he had greeted her, the gentleness and consideration with which he had spoken, had linked him in her mind with Rodney.

'Is anything wrong?' This was slightly ridiculous in the circumstances, and she had qualified it quickly by adding, 'Something unforeseen I mean?'

'Unforeseen, yes, but not in the sense of Rebecca's physical condition, so please don't be alarmed. Nevertheless, I do have some rather disturbing news which I feel might come best from someone who is close to her.'

Sarah had spent some ten minutes with the doctor, and had emerged shaken and worried at what he had revealed.

She had walked along to Rebecca's ward wondering how on earth she was going to broach the matter to her friend, and how Rebecca would take it.

Rebecca had been lying in bed, her eyes on the door, when she'd got there. Her face brightened at the sight of Sarah, and it was some minutes later, once the initial greetings were over and Sarah had asked her how she felt, that Sarah had said, 'Rebecca, this might sound like a daft question, but did you ever see a copy of Mrs Dalton's will?'

'Her will?' The stitches under her eyebrow were out, and the swelling had gone down considerably, but Rebecca's face was still a mixture of colours from the bruising it had endured, and now she winced slightly on frowning as she said, 'Willie's mam's will? No, I don't think so. Why?'

'There's a problem with the house.' Sarah paused, running her fingers over her mouth, but there was no easy way to say it. 'I've just been talking to Dr Sanders; Willie's solicitor had contacted him with some bad news, and he thought it might be better for me to tell you.'

'Go on.' Rebecca's eyes were tight on Sarah's troubled face.

'It appears that the house wasn't actually Willie's,' Sarah said gently.

'What?' Rebecca stared at her before she gave a little huh of a laugh. 'Of course it was Willie's, someone's having you on, Sarah. Who else would it belong to if not Willie? We were living in it, weren't we, and his mam had had it from when she first got married.'

'I know, but it wasn't as simple as that.' Sarah took Rebecca's hand and held it tightly in hers. 'Apparently Willie's grandfather, his mam's father, did buy it for his daughter when she got married, but he only arranged that Willie's mam lived in it, rent free, for her lifetime. On her death, this benefit was to pass to any children still living on

270

the premises until such time as they married and moved away, or left for some other reason. Apparently this didn't include any in-laws that might outlive Mrs Dalton's natural children and wish to continue living on the premises.'

'But that's not right, it can't be right.' Rebecca's face had gone lint-white between the bruising. 'They can't turn me out of my own home, can they?'

'It wasn't Willie's, that's the problem,' Sarah repeated softly, 'so it isn't yours either. The solicitor told the doctor that Willie's grandfather considered his daughter married below her station, and was displeased with the union. Whilst he wasn't prepared to let his daughter or her children suffer, he wanted no financial gain to pass to her husband if he should happen to outlive Willie's mam.'

'But who . . . who does own the house if I don't?' Rebecca asked weakly.

'It belongs to a nephew of Willie's mam.'

'But it can't, it can't.' Rebecca's eyes had filled with tears, her face crumpling. 'After all I went through, everything that happened, they can't take away my home.'

'Rebecca, listen to me, it will be all right,' Sarah said, her voice urgent. 'I promise you we will sort something out when you are ready to come out of hospital, I promise you.'

'But can't I stay there and pay rent or something?' Rebecca asked pathetically. 'I don't mind, I'll manage somehow. There's all my things – Willie's mam's things,' she added as she burst into a storm of weeping, falling against Sarah's chest as Sarah's arms went round her.

Sarah waited until the worst of the weeping was over, making little comforting noises deep in her throat and holding Rebecca tight, before she said, 'Rebecca, the house and everything in it, apart from your personal things like clothes and so on, belong to this nephew, and he wants to sell it as soon as possible. It seems he's got money problems of his own, and wants the money the house will bring. He's not prepared to rent it.'

'Oh, Sarah.'

'But you are not to worry, I mean it. I'll sort everything, I promise you, and you trust me, don't you? Don't you?'

'You know I do.'

'The main thing is that you are going to get better, and there is the baby to think of too. If you get upset and depressed now, it won't help. All your energies, everything has got to be put into getting better, and maybe it has all happened for the best anyway. Every time you were in that house things would remind you of Willie and what it used to be like. You want a clean start, Rebecca.'

Brave words. Sarah stared out of the window as the train sped south through a windy, snow-swept landscape, her mind gnawing at the conversation of the day before. The truth of the matter was, if anyone deserved something good from Willie Dalton, it was his poor widow. Rebecca had endured years of a loveless marriage, the last ten months or so degenerating into hell on earth, and for what? She hadn't even been left with a roof over her head. And then there was the baby. The doctor had told her straight that a stillbirth was likely, and she knew they expected it to be an idiot, or disabled or something, if it was born alive.

Oh . . . Sarah took off her felt hat and smoothed back a wisp of hair from her forehead, sagging back against the hard seat and shutting her eyes. She had promised to take care of Rebecca, and take care of her she would, whatever that entailed. It was a poor sort of love that compromised when the going got tough, and Rebecca needed to know the burden wasn't hers alone. They would get through somehow, whatever happened with regard to the baby. And on that thought, with the train wheels droning a soothingly monotonous refrain, Sarah fell immediately into a deep sleep which lasted the remainder of the journey to King's Cross.

Sarah kept nothing back when she related the outcome of her trip to Lady Margaret. She hadn't had time to go into detail about Rebecca's circumstances before she had left so hurriedly for Sunderland the previous week, but on her return she told Lady Harris's daughter-in-law the full facts.

'The poor girl. The poor *poor* girl.' Sarah and Lady Margaret were in the morning room, and now the older woman leant back in her chair as she shook her head slowly. 'Man can be the noblest or the very basest of creatures, Sarah.'

'I know which kind Willie Dalton was, Lady Margaret.'

'Quite. And having lived with Sir Geoffrey for some years I feel I know a little of what your friend has suffered, although of course her situation is a hundred times worse than mine has ever been. He called Lady Harris twice last week, incidentally, and she refused to take the second call; the first one was not pleasant.'

'I'm sorry.'

'Not for me, I hope,' Lady Margaret said bluntly. 'For his mother perhaps. I confess I would be heartbroken if William were to behave in such a fashion when he is grown.'

'I don't think there is any chance of that, Lady Margaret.' Sarah thought of the serious little boy who already, like his sister, seemed a lot more outgoing since his father had not been in residence in the house. Lady Margaret had confided that her husband had been a harsh father, and an erratic and unfair disciplinarian, often frightening and confusing the children.

'No, neither do I.' Lady Margaret smiled before she added, 'I shall certainly try to temper discipline with love, too much of one without the other ruins a child. Geoffrey had little of the former and I had none of the latter. Perhaps if I had

273

valued myself more at the beginning of our marriage things would have been on a different footing.'

She was talking to Sarah as she would to an equal, now a regular practice when they were alone, and Sarah responded in like fashion as she said, her eyes twinkling, 'Or perhaps you wouldn't have married him in the first place.'

'True, true.' Now they were both laughing, but in spite of Lady Margaret's smiling face, Sarah recognized an emotion lying deep in the blue eyes that she identified with. It was loneliness. Lady Margaret had been born with the proverbial silver spoon, and she in the worst of Sunderland's slums, but loneliness was no respecter of persons.

It was Sarah who leant forward now and said, 'You only wanted what most women want, a husband and family. I want that myself, the more so for not having known family life as a child.'

'Is that so? I understood you spent some time in a children's home, Sarah, but I didn't know any details.'

For a moment Sarah didn't know whether to turn the conversation into other channels. She had mentioned Hatfield briefly at her interview with Lady Harris, but Lady Harris had asked no questions and she hadn't volunteered anything further, and now she was conscious of thinking that she didn't want Lady Margaret to look at her any differently if she told her of how she had been placed at Hatfield and the circumstances of her birth and childhood. The shame and sadness which always accompanied thoughts of her beginnings were as keen as ever, but that aloneness that stared out of Lady Margaret's face pulled at her. She took a deep breath and began talking.

Lady Margaret swallowed deeply when Sarah finished speaking, and her voice was soft when she asked, 'And you still don't know who your mother is?'

'No.' Sarah shook her head slowly. 'I have no idea who

she is or where my natural family are; even if they are alive or dead. The war hit Sunderland very hard, there were whole communities wiped out.' It was something which had haunted her for the last few years, and this was evident in her voice when she said, 'But I still want to try and find the people I came from, even . . . even if they don't want me. I'd just like to know my real surname, something, anything. I feel like there's no foundation somehow, I can't explain it. I look in the mirror and my face stares back at me, but it's just me. I'm not *like* anyone.'

'Oh, my dear.' Lady Margaret swallowed again. 'I understand, I do understand. Undoubtedly the circumstances are different, but I used to wonder how I could possibly have come from my parents. I still do in fact. But . . .' She paused, and now her voice had a bright positive note to it as she said, 'But thanks to your bravery in confronting my husband I am actually learning to like myself a little. It's a good feeling, Sarah.' She smiled suddenly, adding, 'And I like to think we have become friends?'

It was in the form of a question, and Sarah returned the smile, her voice warm when she said, 'Of course, Lady Margaret. You know I'll always serve the family to the best of my ability—'

'No, no.' It was sharp but not offensive, and immediately followed with, 'I don't mean that, Sarah, not at all.' Lady Margaret rose, walking across the room to stand by the fireplace, and she turned, saying, 'No, I haven't explained myself very well. I would like you to think of me in the same way you do Maggie and Rebecca and . . . ?'

'Florrie.'

'Ah yes, Florrie. Yes, that is what I would like. Do you think you could do that?'

Sarah didn't hesitate when she said, 'Yes, I could do that.'

'Good.' Lady Margaret smiled again. 'I think there are

very few people who go through life and meet even one good friend, you know.'

'You're probably right.'

'And one thing is for sure, Sarah.'

'Yes?'

'Whoever your mother is, be it fishwife or duchess, she could not fail to be proud of the person her daughter has become.'

Chapter Seventeen

'I'm sorry, but I still cannot understand why you felt it necessary to go running up there after this girl as though she were a bitch on heat.'

'*Vanessa.*'

Rodney's tone of voice brought Vanessa Mallard's head higher, and then she raised her eyebrows coolly, her perfectly modulated voice cold and clear as she said, 'If the simile offends it's just too bad, Rodney, because that is exactly how it looks to me. The least she could have done was to make contact with you before she left, instead of making such a drama of it all.'

Why, oh why, hadn't he rung first to make sure Richard was already home, before he had arrived at their house for dinner? He always did, or almost always, but he'd had other things on his mind tonight – the main component of which was featuring in this present conversation.

He had seen Sarah twice since her return from Sunderland, and then only when he had called round at the house on his way home from the surgery. His more formal invitations to a meal out and the cinema had been politely, but firmly, refused. Always with a cast-iron excuse, he reminded himself now with a trace of frustrated irritation, but refused nevertheless. But he just couldn't seem to let go. It would be the sensible thing to do, the logical, and he was a man who had always prided himself on being logical, but such was this feeling that had grown and grown – perversely, it seemed, the less he saw of her – that sense and logic had flown out of the window. And now Sarah was thinking she might leave London altogether and move back up north in the summer over this affair with Rebecca. He could accept that a young mother and child might find it difficult to live in the two rooms Maggie and Florrie occupied, and no doubt it would prove something of a strain for the two older women as well, but the thought of Sarah taking on the responsibility for Rebecca and the baby made it difficult for him to sleep at night. It would be too much for her, damn it. And now Vanessa had the bit between her teeth again . . .

'It wasn't a case of making a drama out of anything, Vanessa, as well you know. Sarah had just been informed that her dearest friend was seriously ill after being beaten to a state of unconsciousness by her husband. Why should she spend valuable time trying to track me down? Talk sense, woman.'

'Don't "woman" me, Rodney. He does that and you know I hate it.'

'Then don't be ridiculous.' He ignored the reference to Richard, he had already had as much as he could take tonight, and he'd only been in the house five minutes. 'And anyway, what Sarah does or does not do is of no consequence to you.' He had been about to say, no business of yours, but knowing Vanessa as he did – and with Richard expected home any minute – it wouldn't have been wise to push her that far.

'Yes it is, when it affects an event I had been looking forward to for weeks.' She eyed him coldly, her mouth tight, as she added, 'As well you know.'

'Vanessa, I had already told you and Richard that I wouldn't be seeing the new year in with you; Sarah being called up to Sunderland was incidental. Besides which, this happened all of six weeks ago now. Can't you let it drop?'

Vanessa shrugged elegant shoulders. 'I don't appreciate being let down, so give me one good reason why I should make things easy for you.'

'*Give me strength.*'

'I could give you a lot of things, Rodney, but you seem determined to hang on to some outdated concept of right and wrong. You want me, you have always wanted me, you just haven't the guts to follow through, have you?' Her head tilted slightly, her silky hair swinging across one pale cheek as she said, 'You have committed mental adultery with me from the very first night I married Richard. You know it and I know it.'

He looked at the exquisitely beautiful face, which was as perfect and as cold as a sculpture in fine marble, and found it the very antithesis of Sarah's warm, vibrant loveliness. How could he ever have thought himself to be in love with her? He must have been mad. And it was in that moment, when he acknowledged the end of his obsession with this woman who had haunted him, in one way or another, for years, that his brother's voice just behind him said, 'Is that true, Rod?'

It was his worst nightmare come true, but as Rodney swung to look at Richard standing in the open doorway, Vanessa laughed, a tight brittle sound that had no humour in it at all.

'Eavesdroppers never hear anything good, Richard, you should know that.'

'This is my home, Vanessa, and I'm entitled to go where I please in it.' Richard's face was white but his voice was steady as he looked at his wife.

'Your home.' She curled her lip as she glared at the man she loathed, but before Vanessa could say anything more, Richard spoke to Rodney.

'Well, Rod? Do you want her?'

This macabre little tableau had been played out in his darkest moments from the first time Richard had announced his intention to marry Vanessa, and now a grim sense of *déjà vu* filled Rodney's mind. He didn't want to lose Richard. Oh, God, if you are up there, listen to me. I don't want to lose him.

'Tell him, Rodney.' Vanessa's voice was of a quality that could have cut through steel. 'Tell him the truth.'

Rodney took a breath, looking Richard full in the face as he said, 'No, I don't want her, Richard,' and then, as Vanessa spoke his name, he turned to her. 'That's the truth, Vanessa, and at the bottom of you you know it, don't you? You've known it for some time.'

She stared at him, standing very still before saying, 'I don't believe you, you have loved me for years – we've loved each other for years.'

'You don't know the meaning of the word.'

'Oh, and you do? Since you met your little slut of a housekeeper, I suppose?'

'That's enough, Vanessa.'

'Enough? I haven't even begun!'

'Vanessa, admit defeat.' Richard's voice was amazingly steady. 'He doesn't want you, but I am sure it won't take you long to find someone who does. You've had enough practice over the years, haven't you?'

'What does that mean?'

'I don't want to have to spell it out but I will if you make me.'

'Oh I see, I see it all now.' Her furious gaze swung from one to the other of them as she spat, 'I'm to be the sacrificial lamb, is that it? How cosy, how very cosy and convenient. Rodney is whiter than white, and I'm to clothe myself in sackcloth and ashes. Well, no thanks. The pair of you are cowardly hypocrites, that's the truth of it. He knows and I know that he has lusted after me for years, and while we're on the subject, it didn't worry you too much that Rodney and I had been lovers before we got together, did it? In fact, you couldn't get me up the altar quick enough, and don't tell me it was because you appreciated my mind. Your thinking was motivated by what's between your legs, and it still is. That's the problem now, isn't it?'

She had risen and walked across the room as she had been speaking, and now she paused in the doorway, turning to face them both as she delivered her parting shot. 'Now I can't stand you touching me, now you *disgust* me, it's all suddenly coming out into the open, isn't it?'

'I want a divorce, Vanessa.' Richard's face was like lint, the scarred flesh standing out in angry contrast to the surrounding skin. 'Any terms you like, but I want it settled and done with.'

She didn't answer him, beyond a slight shrug of her shoulders that spoke of utter indifference, then she swung round and disappeared from their view.

They stood quite still, neither of them saying a word, but Richard was breathing heavily through his nostrils, his hands clenched at his side. It was a full minute before he said, without glancing Rodney's way, 'I'm going to ask you this once, and then that's the end of it. Did you ever try to touch her after we were married?'

'Not once, I swear it.'

'You knew about her lovers? You knew you could have been one of them, that the offer was always there?'

'Richard, for crying out loud, you're my brother. I wouldn't do that to you.'

'No, I know you wouldn't, but I had to ask.'

When Richard walked across to the sofa and sat down, his back bent and his brow almost touching his knees, Rodney joined him, his arms going instinctively round his brother in much the same way as Richard's had used to do when he was small and had hurt himself. How long they sat there, Rodney didn't know, it could have been minutes or hours, time seemed immaterial; but when they both rose it was still without another word being uttered. And even when they collapsed in the two winged armchairs in front of the gas fire, Richard having fetched a full bottle of whisky and two glasses from the cocktail cabinet en route, silence continued to reign.

It was Sarah's full day off, and she had spent it working at the hospital which was fairly buzzing with the news that in a British Medical Association poll, eighty-six per cent of doctors had voted against joining the proposed national health service due to be introduced later in the year. Although the doctors and nurses had been full of it, it hadn't interested Sarah that much. One of the children she had got to know really well over the last eight weeks had had a relapse, and she had spent virtually the whole day at his side, trying to jolly him along. Besides which, Rodney had already indicated that he considered the proposed changes to be long overdue and essential for the working classes of Britain, so as far as she was concerned they couldn't be bad.

It was gone eight o'clock by the time she left the big square red-brick building, and the evening was dark and cold, but she didn't take the short cut that would have taken ten minutes off her walk home. Since Sir Geoffrey's threats at Christmas she always kept to the main roads and thorough-fares, walking briskly and keeping alert. Not that she really thought he would try to attack her again, she told herself reassuringly as Emery Place came into view. Lady Margaret had told her that Lady Harris had made it quite clear to her son that the continuation of his generous allowance, along with all the privileges he enjoyed, such as membership of his club and so on, was entirely dependent on his behaving himself. Sir Geoffrey hadn't liked it, Lady Margaret had reported with understandable satisfaction, but he had known better than to push this new matriarch, who had materialized in his mother's tiny frame, too far.

The London air was chilled and misty, the pavements wet and shiny, and as Sarah walked the last few steps she found herself comparing it with the clean, sharp, biting cold of the north. She shook her head at herself, a little smile playing at the corner of her mouth. Fancy her feeling homesick for the raw freezing conditions she had moaned about all her life. But she did. She couldn't help it – Sunderland was home. Not that there was anything wrong with London, and she was glad she had come and experienced the difference of life in the capital in spite of Sir Geoffrey and everything, but ... Sunderland was Sunderland. It was where Maggie and Florrie and Rebecca were, and that other shadowy figure she intended to search out one day.

She stopped, glancing up into the grey sky as droplets of mist attached themselves to her hair and eyelashes like minute diamonds.

She would never be truly at peace with herself until she had done everything within her power to find her mother, she knew that now, had always known it deep inside. And being down here ... it was too far away, somehow. Not just in road miles, but in a way she found it difficult to explain even to herself. In Sunderland, when she was under the same northern sky, looking at the same stars, breathing the same air, her mother seemed closer. It was a link. Tenuous maybe, imagined possibly, but it was how she felt.

She reached the steps of Emery Place, mounting them quickly and opening the front door, then walking through to the kitchen. Its warmth was full of the scents and smells of one of Hilda's baking days, and her mouth watered even as her brow wrinkled at finding the elderly cook and Eileen in the middle of a tiff.

'I did clean it out.' Eileen was at her most sullen, a trait which seemed to have developed more and more over the last two months or so. 'I scrubbed till me hands were raw.'

'Never mind your hands.' Hilda pushed the offending articles away as Eileen thrust them under her nose. 'What about my pan, eh? Cleanliness is next to godliness, my girl, and don't you forget it. Now you have another go at it with a bit more elbow grease before you get yourself off to bed, and I want it clean this time mind. None of your slapdash antics.'

'Huh.' As always, Eileen liked to have the last word, another thing which Hilda found exasperating, but tonight the cook just gave her junior a scathing glance before turning to Sarah as Eileen flung herself down at the kitchen table and attacked one of the big copper saucepans.

'You're back late today, and you look all done in. Sit yourself down and I'll put the kettle on. There's some fresh fruit buns in that tin by the way, help yourself.'

'Thanks, Hilda.'

Eileen's puffing and blowing increased to gale force over the next few minutes as she laboured over the heavy pan, and when Hilda couldn't stand it a moment more, she said, 'All right then, off to bed with you, Eileen,' and the young maid was out of the door like a shot.

'That's the first time I've seen her move her rear end all day. I don't know what's wrong with that girl, straight I don't.' Hilda's voice was tart as she served up their cocoa and gestured for Sarah to have another of the delicious moist buns that were packed with fruit and candied peel, and thumbed their noses at even the concept of rationing. 'She's too big for her boots if you ask me, and lazy isn't the word. And I'm not at all sure she's telling the truth about where she

284

goes on her time off either. Last week, when she said she went to that musical, *Annie Get Your Gun*, with her cousins from Lewisham, and was so late back because her cousin Harold's car broke down? Well, I asked her a bit about it the next day, just out of interest, you know, and she couldn't remember hardly any of the songs.'

'You think she was lying?' Sarah asked through a mouthful of bun.

'I don't know, but she's a bit too secretive for my liking. Say what you like about Peggy, but she was as straight as a die, that girl.'

Sarah had to hide a smile. When Peggy had worked for her, Hilda had done nothing but criticize and complain, but as soon as she had left and been replaced by Eileen, Peggy had achieved sainthood.

'I'll have a word with her again tomorrow' – it would be the latest in many 'words' – 'but her time off is her time off, Hilda, and if she tells us one thing and does another, it's almost impossible to prove. And that was the first time she has been late back, to be fair.' Sarah was aiming to pour oil on troubled waters, and so she didn't add that she agreed one hundred per cent with Hilda. But she didn't trust Eileen either.

It wasn't the young flighty maid she was thinking of later that night, however, as she lay in bed watching the flickering shadows from the fire. It was Rodney. It was always Rodney.

Had she done the right thing in refusing his invitations to the cinema and a meal out? she asked herself for the hundredth time. She knew he had made them out of kindness. She hadn't been able to hide her concern for Rebecca and how everything was going to turn out with the baby and all, her anxiety was too fierce, and it was his way of comforting her, providing a release, she supposed. But she didn't want him to be kind to her when the underlying motive was pity, in fact she couldn't stand the thought of it. And she had no intention of turning into one of those sad sort of human beings that pined and wasted away with unrequited love either, or worse, tried to manipulate themselves into the other person's life. She loved him. She couldn't imagine ever loving anyone else. But, if she couldn't have him – and she couldn't – then she would have to make another sort of life for herself than the one she would have chosen. Perhaps nursing?

She flexed her toes under the covers as she considered the idea that had grown over the last few weeks. It would mean years of training, and it would have to be put on hold until she knew what was what with Rebecca and how soon she could make definite plans for herself, but eventually, that was what she would like to do. It satisfied something inside her when she was dealing with, and looking after, people.

And if Rodney asked her out again? The thought intruded, as it had done on and off since she had refused the last invitation. Perhaps she could say yes just once and spend an evening with him? She wanted to, oh, how she wanted to; and surely, if she was fully aware of how everything was, it could do no harm . . . could it?

And Vanessa? The name popped up like an evil genie. Well, she didn't *know* anything for sure, did she? She didn't. Not for sure. It might just be her putting two and two together and coming up with ten, never mind five. '*Oh* . . .' She sighed out loud, irritable with herself and the situation. She couldn't keep rehashing everything over and over again. If Rodney asked her again, she'd say yes. She knew it could lead nowhere, but she deserved a treat, and she could think of no better one than an evening with Rodney. It might not be wise, it probably wasn't at all clever, but she didn't want to be wise or clever. The decision made, she snuggled down under the covers, shut her eyes, and was asleep within minutes.

* * *

'Miss Brown, please.'

The voice at the other end of the telephone was cool and crisp, and Sarah wrinkled her brow at it as she said, 'Speaking.'

'Oh, Sarah? This is Vanessa Mallard, Richard's wife. You probably know what I am ringing about.'

Did she? She didn't think she did.

'I presume Rodney has told you that Richard and I had a heart-to-heart last night, and that we have decided to separate?'

Separate? Sarah just stopped herself saying the word out loud, and instead, forcing her voice to match Vanessa's tone, said, 'No, he hasn't, but I haven't seen him in the last twenty-four hours, and I wouldn't expect him to discuss your personal affairs anyway.'

'Hardly just Richard's and mine, in the circumstances.' When this little loaded statement got no reaction from Sarah, Vanessa continued, her voice sharper, 'We need to talk, Sarah. Would it be convenient for me to call on you this morning?'

'No, I'm sorry, it wouldn't.' There was no way she was allowing the other woman to engineer what Sarah was sure would be an unpleasant meeting in Lady Harris's house. If they had to meet, and she had observed enough of Vanessa to know the other woman would manage it by hook or by crook once she had set her mind to it, then it would be on neutral territory. 'I can see you this afternoon after three if you like.'

Sarah suggested a tearoom just a few minutes' walk from Emery Place, and after agreeing the time, Vanessa put the telephone down with an abrupt little click that didn't bode well.

Sarah made sure she was already seated and waiting in the superior little tearoom, with a pot of fresh tea and a plate of scones with cream and jam for two, by the time Vanessa arrived. She knew the meeting was going to be an ordeal, and she wanted to set the pace from the word go.

'How lovely, darling, scones and tea.' Vanessa managed to make it sound as quaint as some rustic country tradition that hadn't hit London's modern shores.

'Do sit down.' Sarah smiled politely as she indicated the seat at the side of her, and Vanessa, accepting the initial round was one-nil to Sarah, complied with languid grace.

It took Richard's wife no time at all to get round to the purpose of their meeting. She had left Richard for good, she told Sarah crisply, and had seen her solicitor that morning to file for divorce. She was at present staying with a very dear friend, and had no intention of returning to the marital home.

Sarah hid her thudding heart under a calm exterior that gave nothing away and irritated Vanessa Mallard not a little.

'So . . .' Vanessa forced her tones into less abrasive mode, and even managed a quick smile, before she finished with, 'You can see it's all very delicate, but I'm sure Rodney and I can count on your support? I know he's always looked on you as someone akin to a daughter.'

'Rodney?' It was the first time his name had been mentioned, and now Sarah strove to keep her voice from showing any discernible emotion as she said, 'Have I missed something here?'

'You mean he hasn't told you how things have been between us?' Vanessa couldn't quite manage a blush – even her acting prowess had its limits – and so she fluttered her hands instead as she said, 'Oh, how embarrassing, what must you have thought of me when I asked to see you? I was quite sure he would have confided in you how things are, and I just wanted to make sure you didn't think ill of him. Please, don't let him know that I've spoken to you, I'm sure he will speak to you about everything when he feels the time is right.'

Richard had played right into her hands when he had agreed to let her divorce him – honourable fool that he was. It made all this so much easier.

'What are you insinuating, Vanessa?' Sarah's heart was thumping so hard she could feel it in her throat.

'Well, darling, perhaps I shouldn't say if Rodney hasn't told you, but he and I have always been . . . close, you know? And really, that isn't so bad as it might sound when you consider that I *was* engaged to Rodney before Richard whisked me away from him, and Rodney and I had always enjoyed a very . . . intimate relationship.'

She made Richard sound like some sort of Arabian sheik who had stolen into the bedroom in the middle of the night and stolen her from Rodney's bed, Sarah thought bitterly, her disgust evident on her face as she stared back into Vanessa's watching eyes.

'I think poor Richard always felt he had been a little unfair to Rodney, but that's old history now. Suffice to say love triumphed in the end, and Rodney holds no grudge. He's such a *dear* man, but then, of course, I freely admit I'm prejudiced. Oh Sarah, perhaps it is as well after all that we've had this little talk, I'm sure you'll try and understand that even those we respect and look up to as father figures can still be human? Now,' Vanessa straightened her shoulders and smiled bravely, 'I hope you will give us your blessing?'

Sarah felt sick, and she was thankful she was sitting down and that the trembling which had begun in her legs wasn't visible to those pearly cold eyes. She stared at the other woman without speaking, and after a long moment of looking at her face Vanessa rose, trying to keep her satisfaction from showing. 'Goodbye for now, Sarah, and please, don't hold any of this against us, will you? I know Rodney would want you to visit us when everything is sorted, he *so* admires you for the effort you have made to better yourself.'

Vanessa left without saying anything more, and as Sarah stared after her through the window of the tearoom, the resolution she had made only the night before came back to haunt her. How could he? How *could* he? Oh, she hated him. She did, she hated him. Well, at least she knew exactly where she stood now. He had been carrying on with his brother's wife for years, and now they were going to be together. She didn't know which emotion was foremost, pain or anger. She had known there was something between them, she had sensed it from the first moment she had seen them together, but she hadn't imagined he would actually—

A shaft of weak sunlight came glancing through the glass, and she lifted her face to it as she watched Vanessa get into her car further down the street. She wouldn't make him happy. She doubted if Vanessa Mallard was capable of making any man happy for long, but right as this moment she felt Rodney deserved her. One thing was for certain – she straightened her shoulders against the unbearable ache in her heart – he didn't deserve *her*. She took a sip of hot tea quickly, knowing her lips were quivering but determined not to cry. 'He admires the effort you have made to better yourself.' Vanessa's words, spoken so patronizingly, burnt in her mind. Oh, she really, really hated him . . .

Vanessa was smiling to herself as she started the car engine, settling back in the seat with a gratified little sigh. Her hurt pride had been wonderfully soothed by turning the knife so satisfactorily in her rival's heart. She would teach Rodney; she'd teach them both. His name hurt her, before she thrust the emotion aside and gritted her teeth as she swung out into the traffic.

It had been amusing to see the chit's face when she had realized her knight in shining armour had fallen from grace, and however much Rodney tried to explain, some little grain from her words would remain with the girl. She had seen Sarah looking at them on Christmas Day and wondering. Yes, she would teach Rodney Mallard a lesson he would never forget. How dare he think he could put her to one side like a pair of old gloves?

But she'd show him, and his precious brother, that she didn't need them, that she had far bigger fish to fry than those two non-starters. She glanced down at her jacket, fingering the beautiful little ruby and diamond brooch that nestled on one lapel, as her mouth twisted in a bitter smile. Lord Simmons was a very generous lover, she really couldn't fault him in that direction, and he did have a title after all. Since they had started their little amour a few months ago he had positively showered her with gifts, half of which she had had to keep hidden but could now wear with impunity, and he adored her, he'd do anything for her. It was a pity he wasn't much fun in bed – Rodney, young and virile and passionate flashed into her mind for a second – but he *was* ridiculously rich with all the right connections. Lord Simmons. Lady Simmons. Her pale eyes narrowed reflectively. Could she put up with being married to him? He was a widower, she'd soon be free, and she knew he would propose with very little prompting. And it would show Rodney Mallard she didn't care a fig about him if she made it happen fast, very fast.

The sudden awareness that if she took this course she would probably never see Rodney again caused her to sag briefly in the seat, before her back straightened almost immediately. She wouldn't allow it to be known that it was Richard who had finished the marriage, she wouldn't, and this way any rumours that might arise would be scotched immediately. Lady Simmons . . . It was growing on her.

She made an instant decision, turning the car round with a disdain for other road users that made horns honk and vehicles swerve, and set the car on course for Lord Simmons's grand town house in Richmond.

Chapter Eighteen

The morning after Sarah's talk with Vanessa, she awoke early after a night of tossing and turning and tears, but a busy day in the house, and an evening spent working until gone ten o'clock at the hospital, restored her equilibrium somewhat.

She couldn't alter anything, she told herself as she lay soaking in a hot bath at gone midnight; and to be fair to Rodney he had never indicated, by word or deed, that his intentions were anything other than friendship. She didn't hate him – it was a relief to admit it after the anger and pain of the day before – she loved him, she would always love him, and that wouldn't alter whatever he did. She didn't like the thought of him with Vanessa. The pain hit hard and she squirmed in the bath before reaching for the big towel on the floor. But then she wouldn't like the thought of him with anyone.

She fell asleep immediately, worn out by the sleepless night the night before and the hard work of the day, and when she awoke the next morning the positive mood continued as she determined to count her blessings.

Nineteen Emery Place had become a happy household since Sir Geoffrey's departure, the only fly in the ointment – and it was a very small fly, Sarah conceded – being Eileen, who continued to drive poor Hilda mad, with her lack of diligence and brazenness. The young maid seemed to think it was her mission in life to flirt and carry on with every man who came near the house, be it the milkman or the young lad who delivered their meat ration from the butchers, or Bill Mason from Fenwick who brought the vegetables and dairy produce from the farm once a week, and was married with six children.

But Rebecca was progressing very well according to her letters, which arrived nearly every other day. She had little to do in the hospital other than read and write, and her letters to Sarah were almost in diary form. 'Perhaps you were right about it being better I can't go back to Willie's mam's house,' she had written in her last missive, 'with all that's happened. At least this way I've got to make a new start when I leave here, and there'll be less of the past to remind me about the bad times.' She had gone on in the same vein, and Sarah had been relieved to see Rebecca was thinking so confidently, and also that her unhappy experience of married life had not coloured her attitude regarding her unborn child, whom she wanted very much.

Maggie and Florrie were clucking about like two mother hens with the same poorly chick, but the daily visits Maggie made to the hospital were good for the old woman, who had got lonely at times with Florrie being out at work all day.

And as for herself – Sarah gritted her teeth and refused to let images of Vanessa in Rodney's arms into her mind any more – she had her work here in the house to keep her busy, added to which the time spent at the hospital was becoming more and more challenging and rewarding. There were big decisions looming in the future, not the least of which being how and when she was going to set about the job of finding out about her roots; but all in all, life was good. It was, she told the pain in her heart that protested at her thoughts, it was good.

The statement was put to the test that same evening when,

Sarah having heard nothing from him for a full week, Rodney phoned the house.

'Sarah? It's Rodney.' He sounded unforgivably *normal*, and she had the unreasonable urge to put the phone down before she restrained herself just in time. 'How are you?'

'Very well, thank you.'

'Good, good.' There was a pause and then, 'I was wondering when you next had some free time? We seem to have been like two ships passing in the night lately, and I hear there's a very good film on at the Plaza this week.'

'Is there?' She didn't enquire what it was, and her voice was very steady when she said, 'I've got Friday afternoon and evening off, but I've arranged to work at the hospital. I'm sorry.'

'What time do you finish?'

'What?' He had thrown her. She had expected him to offer a few polite words of regret and put the telephone down, satisfied his duty had been done to this little waif he looked on as a daughter (Vanessa's words had rankled more than she had known until she'd heard his voice), and feeling free to get back to Vanessa.

'I asked you what time you finish?' he repeated patiently.

'Oh.' She thought for a moment. 'About nine o'clock, I think.' That was too late for the cinema.

'Right. I'll pick you up outside, and we can go for a meal instead. All right?'

No, it was not all right, but she couldn't very well say so. He certainly owed her no explanation regarding his private life, nor did he have to answer to her or anyone else for the way he lived, so how could she legitimately object because he had chosen to cast his lot with Vanessa? But his poor brother. And poor her, the little voice of honesty jibed.

'Sarah? All right?' There was an edge to his voice now, and it enabled her to say, and quite coolly, 'You really don't have to worry about me, Rodney, I'm sure you're terribly busy.'

'I'm not worried, I am busy, but I'm asking you out to dinner.'

Oh yes, a definite edge, but it helped somewhat that she had got under his skin.

'Thank you, if you're sure.'

'Quite sure. Nine at the hospital then.'

Sarah stood looking at the phone in her hand for a few moments more after the call ended. He had snapped at her. Those last words had had a definite bite to them, and it was she who had reason to be upset, if anyone. Anger brought her chin up sharply. He'd got a cheek . . .

When the phone rang the moment she replaced the receiver it made her jump, and as she snatched up the receiver she wondered if it was Rodney ringing her back to say he had changed his mind about the meal in view of her lack of enthusiasm.

It wasn't.

'Sarah?' Maggie's bellow was unmistakable. Sarah immediately suspected the worst, knowing Maggie's dislike of William Bell's invention, and Maggie must have read her mind because her first words were, 'There's nothin' wrong this end, lass, Rebecca's doin' nicely so don't worry. I'm just ringin' to make sure you're all right?'

'Me?' Hell could freeze over before Maggie made a social call, there had to be something wrong. 'Of course I am. Why have you phoned, Maggie?'

'Well . . .' Maggie hesitated before she said, 'I don't rightly know, hinny, an' that's the truth, but I've a feelin' on me I can't explain. The only thing I could think of was that there might be somethin' wrong with you I was sensin', but you say you're all right?'

'I'm fine.' Sarah frowned, Maggie wasn't the sort of

person who imagined things. 'And you say you feel something is wrong?'

'Aye, I've felt it for a day or two now, an' when it first come I thought it might be Rebecca an' the bairn, you know, but she's not started, so it's not that. Tonight it got so strong I couldn't rest till I phoned you. Oh, it's old age, lass. I'm goin' barmy.'

'You're not barmy, Maggie, not you.' She could tell Maggie was really perturbed and she added, 'I expect it's probably all the worry about Rebecca and the baby. These things prey on the mind even when you aren't aware of them, and she's getting nearer her date now.'

'No, I don't think it's that, lass, me mind's at rest about Rebecca; well, as far as it can be, that is. I know she's in the right place for the moment an' they'll look after her. This . . . it's somethin' else, but I'm blowed if I can put me finger on it. Still, you're all right, lass, an' that's the main thing.'

'You go home and try to get a good night's sleep, Maggie, you're probably tired. Is Florrie with you?'

'Aye, an' she wants a word an' all. Hang on a minute.'

Once Florrie came on the line, Sarah was able to move the receiver closer to her ear, and Florrie's voice was apologetic when she said, 'I'm sorry about this, lass, but I've got to get off to work in a minute, and she's been whittling all day about this funny feeling of hers. I didn't want her walking to the phone box when I'd gone, the ground's a sheet of ice up here and all we need is for her to fall and break her neck.' Florrie sounded all bunged up, and this was emphasized when she sneezed loudly three times in quick succession and gasped, 'I feel more like me bed than work if the truth be known, I've got a stinking cold, but there's already three off and they're desperate. Here, Maggie wants a last word, and then I'll see her home. Good night, lass.'

Once Maggie was back on the line Sarah injected as much

brightness in her voice as she could, and just after they had made their goodbyes, she found herself saying, 'Maggie, I love you.'

'Me an' all, lass. Me an' all.'

Now why had she felt it necessary to say that? Sarah stood in the hall feeling slightly uneasy after she had replaced the receiver. She and Maggie weren't ones for vocalizing their feelings for each other. They never had been. Maggie was wont to say that actions spoke louder than words, and Sarah agreed with her.

Oh, this was ridiculous. She shook her head at herself. Maggie was making her jumpy now. Perhaps Maggie had had too much of the medical cocktail she imbibed daily for her rheumatism and her swollen legs and numerous other complaints? She did that occasionally if she got muddled, and the last time she had had Florrie running around swiping imaginary spiders off the walls. She smiled indulgently. Yes, it could well be that. Her and her feelings.

A couple of hundred miles away, Maggie was feeling better now she had made the telephone call and checked on Sarah. She could go to sleep with an easy mind now she knew her lass wasn't ailing, she told herself firmly, and she needed her sleep, oh aye, she did that. The last couple of nights she'd tossed and turned like a dog with fleas, and she knew she'd disturbed Florrie once or twice, and her with a cold on her like she hadn't seen in many a long day.

Maggie had been shambling slowly down the dimly lit street; she had insisted Florrie stay where she was rather than come all the way back with her only to have to retrace her footsteps in the next minute, and now, on reaching her front door, she turned and waved to the dark figure outside the telephone box, who in turn raised an arm before disappearing from sight round the corner.

Bless her. Maggie smiled to herself. Florrie had insisted she watch her back, for all the world like a mother anxious about its bairn, and just because there was a bit of ice about. Florrie was a good lass and no mistake, and to think that filthy swine Willie Dalton had tried to suggest they were – like that. Florrie was more like a sister than a friend, but then scum like him wouldn't understand honest friendship, would they, not if it rose up and bit 'em in the backside. Still, he'd got his just deserts. And she was a lucky woman, aye, she was. She hadn't thought that at her age she'd be living in comfort, and have a good friend, her two lasses, and – God willing – perhaps even Rebecca's bairn to brighten her last days.

She turned creakily, opening the front door and stepping into the dark hall that wasn't much warmer than the raw night outside. She walked straight through to the sitting room and took off her coat and hat, shivering in spite of the warmth in the room. Florrie had banked down the fire with plenty of slack just before they had left the house to telephone Sarah, and she had added some damp tealeaves for good measure, and now the fire was smoking profusely, tiny flames licking at its base, but it was without real warmth.

She walked across to the fire and held out her hands to the weak heat, the sense of impending doom that had been with her all day increasing as she shivered again. She'd make herself a hot bevy, that's what she'd do, and take it to bed with her, but first she'd see about getting the warmer in her bed. The kitchen was free now, them upstairs were all in bed, and she might have a bit of that lardy cake Florrie had made to go with her drink.

She turned, and in the split second it took for Maggie to become aware of the silent figure behind her, she also saw the upraised hand with the heavy cudgel bearing down, and then she felt the impact of the violent blow, a pain that was indescribable exploding the light into white fire, and then – nothing.

The red mist was buzzing, and she felt sick, so so sick – there was something pressing her mouth. Maggie forced her eyes open slowly as she attempted to reach to her lips, only to find she couldn't move either her arms or her legs. She couldn't see anything for a moment, the room was merely a mass of nauseous dancing lights, and then, as her senses slowly returned, her eyes focused on the face in front of her, and she knew what it was to lose control of her bladder, so great was her fear.

'Hallo, Maggie.' The mouth talked, and more terrifying still, the voice was soft and sing-songy, whilst being strangely devoid of expression.

She must have made some noise, although she wasn't aware of doing so, because Matron Cox straightened from her squatting position and shook her unkempt grey head slowly as she said, 'Shush, shush, shush. Quiet, Maggie. It's no use trying to call anyone, there is just the two of us. Now isn't that nice? I think it's nice, I do, really, Maggie. In fact you could say that it's this moment that has kept me going for ten years.'

The gag was digging into Maggie's flesh, her upper lip drawn down so tightly she felt the skin was splitting, but it was the feeling of nausea that was overwhelming, even as she told herself she couldn't be sick. She would choke, she'd choke and die, suffocated by her own vomit whilst secured to this chair as though she were the mad one. And that the Matron was mad she had no doubt; stark staring mad . . .

'They tried to stop me coming, you know, my brother and his wife. Said they'd put me back, back in *there*—' The voice had risen angrily before it suddenly stopped, and the Matron took several deep breaths with her eyes shut, before they sprang open again. Then, as the mouth moved in a parody of a smile and the voice came softly saying, 'They understand now, I had to make them understand, didn't I. It wasn't my fault,' Maggie realized what the dark brown stains on the jumper beneath Matron Cox's open coat were.

Oh, dear God. God, help me, help me. Maggie was looking at the smiling face in front of her and pleading with the Almighty. Help me, help me, help me . . .

'They tried to say I was sick, Maggie, in that place. Me, sick.' A cackle of a laugh, and then, 'But I knew, I knew you see, only they wouldn't listen. I knew you wanted my place, and that you'd turned them all against me. You told lies, Maggie, wicked lies, and you have to be punished when you tell lies. You understand that, I know you do. Yes, you have to be punished, but there was no one to punish you, Maggie, except me. That's what they didn't understand. And so I knew I had to be strong, and clever. They were stupid anyway, they made it easy, and I said yes, doctor and no, doctor in all the right places.'

The head nodded, the eyes bright and seeking approval. 'And you want to be punished, deep inside, don't you? They all want to be punished deep inside.' And under Maggie's fascinated gaze the hunched figure drew out of its voluminous clothes the bludgeon it had used earlier.

'This will purify you, Maggie.' The voice began to tremble with excitement and anticipation. 'My father used to purify me, and when he had finished he would make me thank him. I didn't want to thank him at first, but then, after a time, I understood. You'll understand, Maggie.'

Maggie began to struggle wildly against the bonds that secured her, shaking her head as she tried to speak, and now the voice was sharp, sounding exactly like the old Matron Cox for the first time since it had spoken: 'That is enough, do you hear me? There is no one going to come to your aid,

I made sure of that. I told you I am clever, and I am, I am. I have been planning this very carefully, I always plan carefully – expediency, efficiency and enlightenment, remember? You used to laugh behind your hand, back then, didn't you? Oh, I knew, I knew. I knew everything then and I know everything now.'

The Matron circled once round the chair, in the manner of a hungry predator relishing the foretaste of what was to come, before coming to a halt in front of Maggie again, whereupon the head tilted slightly and the voice, still cold and controlled, said, 'You need to be punished, and punished you will be. You are sinful and contaminated, tainted and foul, but pain is the purification that cleanses and I am the instrument of your exoneration.'

When the first blow hit Maggie she arched upwards with the gag biting into the soft flesh of her face, the paroxysm of pain taking her and the chair sideways to land with a crash against the wall. 'Oh, you bad girl. You bad, *bad* girl.' This was accompanied by more frenzied blows, but evidently finding that Maggie's twisted body, with the chair still fastened to it and providing some protection, was not accessible enough, Matron Cox bent over her, heaving and pushing as she struggled to right the chair.

And then, as the chair tottered half upright, Matron Cox gasping and straining as she pitted her thin angular frame against Maggie's considerable bulk and the weight of the chair, she suddenly let go of it so Maggie fell heavily to the floor again, her brow making harsh contact with the floorboards.

'Ahhh . . .' The sound was long and drawn out, almost one of surprise, and when the Matron slumped down by the side of Maggie's unconscious form, her back against the wall and her arms and legs stretched out in the floppy manner of a rag doll, she made the sound again until it gurgled away to strained, laboured breathing. And then she continued to sit, staring across the room without moving her head or her body, as the ticking of the mantelpiece clock and the odd hiss and splutter from the damp tealeaves on the fire sounded loud in the silence that had fallen.

When Florrie walked into the house an hour later – having been sent home from the laundry due to her cold which was becoming worse by the minute, and was portentous of influenza – she continued straight through the hall to the kitchen first, to see about heating her bedwarmer. She was feeling hot and sweaty, and chilled and cold, by turns, and the thought of her bed had never been more enticing.

She frowned at the sight of Maggie's bedwarmer next to her own on the side of the table. It was unusual, on a raw night like this, for Maggie not to warm her bed through before getting under the covers, but then she shrugged wearily, the thudding in her head becoming a tattoo that was knocking her brain to jelly.

She sat down at the kitchen table while the kettle boiled, her aching head in her hands and her throat feeling as though it were on fire, and once the warmer was ready went straight through to the bedroom, thinking only of bed.

She noticed the fire first; Maggie had been going to bank it down before she turned in, but the coal had blazed away to almost nothing and it was in danger of going out altogether. Florrie made a sound of deep annoyance low in her throat, glancing towards Maggie's bed – furthest from the fire and in deep shadows – as she did so, and finding it empty.

'Oh, Maggie . . .' For a moment, just a moment, the temptation to forget everything but the call of her bed was overwhelming, but she pushed it aside guiltily. She knew what Maggie had done, the reason for the bedwarmer in the kitchen and the unbanked fire becoming clear. She'd fallen asleep in the chair again. Twice, in the last two night shifts she had done at the laundry, she had found Maggie cramped and stiff in the chair when she had got home in the morning, and then the old woman's rheumatism would give her jip and it'd mean a day or two in bed. And she had to take her turn on the shifts, she couldn't keep to days only, much as she would like to.

She had told Maggie and *told* her not to settle herself down in front of the fire in the sitting room once she'd gone to work, but would she listen? Would she heck. Oh, it was worse than looking after a bairn at times, at least you could smack their backsides when they played up.

Still grumbling to herself, Florrie walked through to the other room, her head lowered and her nose streaming, and pushed open the door with an irritable, 'Maggie McLevy', before coming to a stunned stop, her mouth falling open into a gape and her brain refusing to accept what her eyes were seeing.

And then she was screaming, leaping across the room towards Maggie, who was lying very still with the chair attached to her like a grotesque outer shell, in an effort to protect her from the woman sitting so quietly at the side of her, but who, Florrie was sure, would spring to her feet and renew the attack on Maggie any moment.

It seemed as if Mr Connor from upstairs was there in a second to assist her in lifting the chair, with Maggie still tied to it, into an upright position, and when his wife rushed into the room a moment later, it was Mr Connor who said, his voice low and shaking, 'Send our Tommy to get a doctor, an' quick mind. An' – an' then he'd better scoot along to the police station.'

'Is . . . is she . . . ?' Mrs Connor's terrified gaze was riveted on Maggie's slumped body and white face, and her husband shook his head, saying, 'She's still breathin' but only just, an' this one seems to be in a trance or somethin'.' He gestured with his head towards the strangely still figure on the floor, and as he did so, the eyes – but only the eyes – flickered at his words.

'Maggie, oh, Maggie . . . I told you. I told you to be careful.' Florrie was crying and moaning as she cradled Maggie's head against her chest, while Joe Connor struggled to untie the corroding thin rope that had bitten deep into Maggie's flesh, and when he said, 'I can't get her free, lass, I need a knife or somethin',' she was quite unable to move away from Maggie's side, and it was Joe who left them, returning a few moments later with a small sharp knife from the kitchen.

The two stalwart constables arrived a minute or two before the doctor, who had been out attending the departure of one of his elderly patients into the next world when Tommy had called, and they, like him, were brought up short at their first sight of the extraordinary scene in the otherwise ordinary-looking room.

The bonds which had held Maggie were gone, but she remained slumped in the chair, unconscious and barely breathing, because Florrie and Joe Connor hadn't dared to move her, but it was the inert figure of Matron Cox who dominated the room. She was quite motionless, but strangely there was nothing quiet or benign in the lack of movement as one would have expected, and the sight of her was unnerving.

'What – what's happened here?' It took the doctor two attempts to get the words out, and as he said afterwards to his wife, 'It was just as if something unspeakable was in that room with us, my dear, and you know I'm not one for exaggerating. I haven't been to church for some time, but I shall be going this Sunday.'

'We don't rightly know, sir.' It was the younger of the two

constables who answered, and he, like the doctor, could feel the hairs on the back of his neck standing up as he gestured towards the silent figure at his feet. 'It seems as though this one here broke into the house and attacked the other lady. Her friend says there was an incident some ten years ago which is at the bottom of it all.'

'How long has she been like this?' The doctor was less interested in the whys and wherefores than he was in Maggie herself.

'An hour and a half maybe, two at the most. Miss Shawe'– he indicated Florrie with a wave of his hand – 'left two hours ago.'

The doctor's prognosis on Maggie was brief and to the point. 'She shouldn't really be moved, but it's imperative we get her to hospital immediately.'

And of the Matron, after a cursory examination which nevertheless called on all his professional detachment, 'Massive stroke. I'm afraid it's hospital, not the cells, gentlemen.'

Maggie lay, slipping in and out of unconsciousness, for just over twenty-four hours, and during that time the doctors were unable to ascertain to what degree the shock of her encounter with Matron Cox would affect her recovery.

Sarah responded immediately Florrie called her with news of the attack, but on reaching her destination, her loyalties were split by Rebecca going into premature labour some three weeks early, on hearing the circumstances of Maggie's sudden admittance into the hospital.

Florrie was waiting for her when she reached the Sunderland infirmary, and after a few brief moments at Maggie's bedside, she left Florrie there and went along to Rebecca's ward, where she found her friend lying curled up on her side with her back to the room and her head under the pillow, which she had pulled tight across her face.

'Rebecca?'

'Sarah?' The pillow was tossed aside, and Sarah was amazed when Rebecca pulled herself into a kneeling position on the bed, and, flinging her arms round Sarah's neck, burst into a torrent of weeping.

'Rebecca, don't, don't. Come on now, you mustn't cry like this, it isn't good for you or the baby.'

'She's dead, isn't she? Maggie's dead.'

'Of course Maggie isn't dead, whoever told you such a thing?'

'We have been telling her that Mrs McLevy is as well as can be expected, Miss Brown, but she won't believe us.' The nurse who had been sitting by the side of Rebecca's bed had clearly had more than enough of this latest development. 'She feels we are merely jollying her along, don't you, Mrs Dalton? You tell her, Miss Brown. Perhaps she'll listen to you.'

'You swear Maggie's all right, Sarah?' Rebecca leaned back and shook Sarah slightly as she said again, 'You swear it?'

'I do, I swear it. I've just left there and she's very poorly but not as bad as you were when you were brought in, Rebecca.'

'I thought . . . I thought she . . . Oh!' The last was a soft grunt as another contraction took hold, cutting off Rebecca's voice as the pain intensified, and now both Sarah and the nurse, one on each side, pushed her back down into the bed, bringing the coverlet up over her straining body once she was propped against the pillows.

'I couldn't bear it if Maggie died.' Rebecca was gasping now, relaxing back as the contraction diminished. 'She only said to me yesterday that she was looking forward to the baby being born like it was her own grandchild.'

'She's not going to die, Rebecca, get that into your head.' She hoped she wasn't, pray God she wouldn't.

'You'll stay with me, Sarah?' Rebecca's grip on her hand was making Sarah's fingers white. 'You won't go?'

'Of course I'll stay, and listen to me. Matron Cox tried to finish Maggie and she failed, right? Maggie's going to get better and you are going to present her with that grandchild. We're going to get through this, Rebecca, and you concentrate for now on all the people who love you. Me, Maggie, Florrie . . .'

'All right.' It was a tiny whisper. 'And you won't let them send you out? They'll try, I know they will, but I want you here. Oh, Sarah.' Rebecca's grip tightened, her voice shaking as she said, 'I'm scared, petrified. Not so much about the birth itself but about what . . . what the baby might be like. I know they think it might have been damaged. No one's said, but I know all right. They do, don't they?'

Sarah didn't answer this directly, but said instead, her voice soft, 'Rebecca, you're strong inside, where it counts, you had to be to get over that awful night when you nearly died. I'll always remember the sister saying, when you began to come out of the coma, that you were fighting back. And this baby will be like you. I've never thought of Willie as having any part of this child; strange that, isn't it, but it's true. It's yours, all yours, and we're all going to love it – boy or girl, pretty or ugly, we'll love it, and that's all that counts. I promised you I would take care of things and I will.'

'But your job and everything . . .'

'I've an idea about that, so just trust me. It'll all work out. All you've got to do is think about this baby being born and do the necessary work.' She grinned encouragingly. 'And I'm afraid that's one area where, apart from holding your hand, it's all down to you.'

'Oh, Sarah.' Rebecca smiled weakly back, but already her

voice was calmer, and when the next contraction took hold she concentrated on her breathing, holding on to Sarah's hand as Sarah willed her on.

The baby was born at seven o'clock the next morning after a tiring but not unduly difficult labour, and it was a perfectly formed little girl, with strong limbs and a loud lusty voice that told her exhausted mother all was well.

Against all hospital etiquette, and mainly due to the fact that Rebecca and Sarah were both adamant Sarah wasn't going to leave, Sarah was present at the birth. When the midwife cut the cord and, after wrapping the child in a thin blanket, handed her to Sarah while they continued to attend to Rebecca, Sarah stared down at the tiny screwed-up face with wonder. So small, so *perfect*. Oh thank you, God, thank you.

She continued to look at Rebecca's daughter as she wondered how her own mother had reacted to the miracle of new life. Had she searched her baby's features like this, or, knowing what she intended to do, had she barely glanced at her so she didn't have to remember what she looked like? How could her mother have gone through what Rebecca had just gone through, and not felt *something* for her?

There were tears on Sarah's eyelashes as she looked at her friend and said, 'She's beautiful, she's so so beautiful, Rebecca,' and then, as the midwife finished her ministrations, she placed the tiny bundle in Rebecca's limp arms, keeping hold of the baby in fear that Rebecca, in her exhausted state, might let her roll off the bed. And so it was that the three of them were joined in a moment that would be unforgettable: the child blinking milky blue eyes in the bright lights as it mewed softly and grasped the air with tiny delicate fingers, the two women smiling down at new precious life through their tears.

'Look at her hair, and her eyelashes.' They continued to gaze entranced as Sarah noted each tiny feature. 'It's amazing, just amazing, that only an hour ago she was still inside you. What are you going to call her?'

'Lucy-Ann.' Rebecca smiled shakily before adding, 'It was my mam's name.'

Sarah willed her face not to change, she didn't want anything to spoil these moments for Rebecca, and her voice was soft as she said, 'Was it? You've never said. That's a lovely name.'

'Lucy-Ann Sarah Dalton,' Rebecca grimaced as she laughed, 'Bit of a mouthful but she won't mind when I tell her why.'

'I wouldn't be too sure about that.'

It was the evening of that same day when Sarah made a telephone call to Rodney to let him know she couldn't make their dinner engagement. She had spent the afternoon sitting at Maggie's side, Florrie having gone home to rest. The old warrior was in a lot of pain, and the painkillers were making her lightheaded and drowsy, but the doctors had satisfied themselves her injuries, although severe for a woman of Maggie's age, were not life-threatening. It had been the concussion Maggie had sustained when her head had hit the wooden floor that had worried them the most, but now that was clearing and all the signs were positive.

When Sarah had told her about little Lucy-Ann she wasn't sure if the news had permeated the fog, but then Maggie had smiled, her face lighting up, and her hands going out either side of the bed to Sarah and Florrie, as Florrie had said, 'A little lassie, Maggie, a little lassie, isn't that grand? Oh, there's good days ahead, lass. You just think on about them, eh?'

Once Florrie had gone home, Sarah had sat quietly

without speaking and let Maggie sleep, as she herself had dozed on and off for most of the afternoon.

Before calling Rodney that evening, Sarah spoke to Lady Harris and informed her employer of Maggie's condition, and the birth of Rebecca's child, her voice mirroring her emotions, which were mixed.

'Be resolute, child, be resolute.' It was the sort of thing Lady Harris liked to say, and Sarah could picture the old suffragette as she had been in her heyday. 'What will Rebecca do now her child is born?'

'That's something I need to talk to you about, Lady Harris.' Sarah took a deep breath as she continued. 'Until the baby was born we weren't sure how much circumstances would need to change, but now she is here, and she's healthy and well, Rebecca can't go back immediately to the sort of work she did before she got married, but of course she needs a roof over her head and employment nevertheless.'

'Yes?' It wasn't particularly encouraging.

'Lady Margaret is getting more and more involved with the business of the estate at Fenwick, and your other properties' – another deep breath – 'which means Constance, and William to a certain extent even though he's now started boarding school as there'll be the holidays, will need extra supervision from a third party; a nanny, in fact. Rebecca is more than qualified to fill such a role.'

There was a long pause. 'You are suggesting that I employ your friend as a nanny for my grandchildren?'

'Yes, I am.' The butterflies in her stomach were rife. 'I've been thinking about it for some time, and I think it would benefit everyone, Lady Harris.' Well, she *had* told her to be resolute.

'Do you now.' Another pause and then, 'I would need to discuss this in some depth with Lady Margaret, and if she feels the suggestion has some merit, we can perhaps consider it further. That is all I can say for now.'

It was as much as she'd dared to hope for. Sarah tried to stop her elation from sounding in her voice as she said, 'Thank you, Lady Harris.' She felt sure Lady Margaret would be prepared to give her idea a try, it had been Lady Harris she hadn't been sure about.

'And you will be returning on Saturday?'

'Yes, Lady Harris.'

'I will discuss this with Lady Margaret before then, and we can speak again. Please give my good wishes, and those of Lady Margaret, to both Rebecca and Maggie.'

'Yes, I will, and thank you again, Lady Harris.'

The telephone call to Rodney proved less satisfactory. It was Richard's voice that answered her call, his professional tone mellowing when he realized who it was. 'Sarah, I'm sorry, you've just missed him I'm afraid, he's been called out.'

'Oh, I see.' What on earth was Richard doing visiting Rodney's house? she asked herself silently. She would have thought that in the circumstances Rodney was the last person his brother would want to be with. Or had Richard gone there to sort out some of the more unpleasant legal connotations arising from the divorce, maybe even to pick a fight?

Her thoughts made her voice flustered when she said, 'Do you know when Rodney will be back?'

'Not really.' There was an awkward pause, and then Richard said, 'I can get him to phone you when he comes in if you like. I'm staying with him at the moment.'

'Are you?'

She was too surprised to be tactful, and her voice must have expressed her bewilderment, because Richard answered, 'Yes, well it isn't general knowledge at the moment, so I would appreciate you keeping it under your hat, but Vanessa and I have parted. I've put the house on the market, I never liked living there from day one, and when Rod suggested I move in with him while I look for something smaller, a flat maybe, I took him up on the offer.'

She didn't believe this. Was it one of those modern arrangements she had read about in the papers where everyone was terribly civilized, and adulteress, lover and wronged spouse were the best of friends? No wonder the divorce rate was rocketing.

In view of the fact that Richard had intimated his marriage breakdown was still something of a secret, she didn't like to say his wife had been round to see her with all the discretion of a charging bull elephant, but neither could she pretend she hadn't known either, so her voice was stilted as she said, 'I'm very sorry, Richard.'

'These things happen.'

Yes, but the other point of the triangle isn't usually your own brother. Even if their marriage had been floundering for some time, surely present circumstances made it doubly hard for Richard? 'You needn't get Rodney to call me, but I'd be grateful if you could give him a message?' She gave Richard the bare bones of what had happened, hearing his astonished 'Good grief!' as she thought wryly that his own life was only slightly less surprising, and concluding with the promise that she would call Rodney after the weekend when she was sure she would be back in London.

'And you say this woman who attacked your friend can do no more harm?' Richard asked somewhat bemusedly.

'No, she's had a major stroke and is completely paralysed. She's in the same hospital as Maggie and Rebecca, actually.'

Richard said again, 'Good grief,' but there was no disbelief in his tone, just sheer unadulterated amazement.

Sarah stood for some moments by the pay phone in the hospital as she tried to make head or tail of the conversation with Rodney's brother, but after a while she shook her head

313

slowly. It was nothing to do with her if they all wanted to behave like that, but she found the whole thing . . . astonishing. It was a weak word for what she was feeling, but she didn't want to examine the way she felt at the moment, not when she needed to be strong.

The last sentence or two of her conversation with Richard had clarified something in her head. She was going to see Matron Cox. She didn't want to, in fact she would have given the world to avoid looking at the monster from her childhood, but somehow, especially after this last outrage, she felt she would never be free of her fear of this woman until she did.

It took her three attempts before she could force herself to knock on the door of the little room off one of the main wards where Matron Cox had been taken. She had checked with the sister on that ward first, explaining who she was and that she needed to see for herself that this woman could do Maggie no more harm, and after checking with the nurse who was detailed to Matron Cox, the sister had indicated for her to go along to the room.

Sarah entered slowly, nodding at the nurse who was sitting by the bed, before walking round to the far side and gazing down at the sleeping figure who seemed skeletal under the hospital blankets. 'How is she?' She barely recognized the frail, pathetic old woman in front of her as the formidable ogre of former years, but the fact that right up to twenty-four hours ago or so Matron Cox had still had the power and determination to corner Maggie in her own home and attack her in a mad frenzy couldn't be ignored.

'Very poorly.' The nurse was uneasy. She had been told most of the facts about the patient under her care, and the police had been in and out of the room all day like yo-yos, but she still found it difficult to reconcile the fiend they were talking about with the helpless old woman who had been like a lamb under her ministrations, and who had lost control of all her bodily functions as well as her speech and movement. 'It's only a matter of hours.'

A matter of hours.

Sarah looked at what frustrated hate and rage had done to a human spirit and felt a moment's sadness and regret that a life had been so wasted. Maggie was alive, and she and Florrie would go on being happy in this, the autumn of their years. Rebecca had her child now, a healthy bonny daughter who would be a comfort to her after the misery of her years with Willie, and a blessing to Maggie and Florrie to boot. And she . . . she would continue to forge her own destiny and one day root out her beginnings, follow that dream to its conclusion along with others. And she would go into nursing. It was what she wanted to do, and she *would* do it.

She turned from the bed, nodding her thanks to the nurse and leaving the room with unhurried, measured steps. The Matron couldn't hurt them any more, she had lost and they had won, but oh . . . She gazed ahead down the long straight hospital corridor as the sense of sadness gripped her again; the waste of it.

And then her steps quickened as she made her way to Rebecca's ward to say good night before she left the hospital for the night, and there was already a smile on her lips as she entered the room and saw Rebecca, her face bright, cradling her baby daughter in her arms.

Chapter Nineteen

Sarah came back from Sunderland on the afternoon of Saturday, the twentieth of March, on the day when Mr J. Proctor's Sheila's Cottage won the Grand National at Aintree amid cheers and shouts from the crowd, and the Soviet delegation walked out of a meeting of the Allied Control Council, the body officially charged with governing Germany, claiming the Western powers had snubbed them by holding a secret meeting in London to discuss Germany's future. The first event was on the lips of most Londoners, the second – which had a part in precipitating the start of the Cold War with Russia – passed unnoticed by everyone, including Sarah, who was more concerned with the coming meeting with Lady Harris. The sun was shining and the sky was blue as she walked down Emery Place, and there was a scent of spring in the mild London air.

She had left Maggie feeling a lot better, although the old woman was going to be in hospital for a few weeks. Apart from severe bruising and cuts and grazes, her right leg was broken in two places, which, when added to her fluid retention problems and general poor health, constituted something of a problem, and one the doctors wanted to monitor carefully.

Rebecca, on the other hand, would be able to leave fourteen days after her confinement – if she had somewhere to go to, that was, and Sarah intended that she should have.

On entering the house, she made first for the kitchen, where she found Hilda and Eileen in the middle of one of their little skirmishes, which immediately emphasized she was back, and then to the morning room where Lady Margaret was sitting at Lady Harris's desk sorting through some official-looking documents.

'Sarah.' Lady Margaret's face expressed her delight. 'How is everyone?'

Sarah filled her in quickly on the latest developments, enthusing first over little Lucy-Ann, before going on to say how Maggie was and finishing with the news that Matron Cox had died, as expected, the night she had phoned Emery Place. 'Apparently the police went to her brother's home, once they'd established who the Matron was, and the . . . the bodies of her brother and his wife were in the bedroom. She had obviously attacked them while they slept. The police think she used the same implement on them as she did on Maggie.'

'How awful.' Lady Margaret stared at her aghast for a moment before shaking her head and saying, 'What a dreadful woman.' And then, 'Well, on to brighter things. I think your suggestion of Rebecca for the children's nanny is a sound one. Of course, Lady Harris is insisting on some sort of probationary period, perhaps a month, something like that? But I have been thinking for some weeks that Constance needs more attention than I can comfortably give her. There are two free rooms on the staff landing, and one in particular is quite large, with room for a crib and so on. Have a look and see which you think is suitable anyway, and get Eileen to air it and make up the bed. The cot I used to use for Constance and William when we visited here is up in the attics, perhaps Eileen could see to that too, and there is plenty of bedding for the child.'

'That's so kind of you.' Sarah was in no doubt that it was Lady Margaret's influence with her mother-in-law that had sealed Rebecca's appointment, and the older woman confirmed the thought as she smiled, saying, 'What else are friends for?'

Rodney didn't wait for Sarah to call him. He phoned her on the Monday evening and wouldn't take no for an answer when she hesitated in accepting his invitation to the cinema on her first evening off that week, which happened to be on Thursday.

She argued with herself on and off over the next few days, going round and round in circles until she was sick of her own thoughts, and finally determined that seeing him occasionally as a friend, although probably not the most sensible option, was the less painful answer to her dilemma. Certainly every time she refused to see him she threw herself into a right tizzwazz, she admitted to herself, and it wasn't as though she didn't know the score. No, seeing him periodically was the best thing – she couldn't bear the thought of losing contact altogether – and as long as she didn't have to endure Vanessa's company too, she would get by.

It didn't seem quite so simple when Rodney arrived to pick her up on Thursday evening looking so good she wanted to eat him, but Vanessa's words still echoed fairly frequently in her mind and were enough to take the edge off her hunger.

Sarah found the film, *The Lady from Shanghai* with Orson Welles and Rita Hayworth, wonderful but slightly shocking, something Rodney seemed to find very amusing as he teased her with the punchline, 'I told you . . . you know nothing about wickedness', once they were on their way home. She laughed, she forced herself to laugh, but suddenly she didn't find it funny at all; it was too indicative of how he saw her. And Vanessa? Definitely a sultry blonde Rita Hayworth in

319

her slinky black dress that fitted like a glove, with no back and hardly any sides. But Vanessa couldn't have filled that dress like the voluptuous Rita Hayworth had. Silly though the thought was, it was comforting.

Rodney hadn't mentioned his brother or Vanessa once beyond a brief, 'I understand Richard has told you he's living with me at the moment, and why?' when she had first got into the car, and it was the very last thing she wanted to discuss, so when he dropped her off at 19 Emery Place at the end of the evening with the promise that he would call round and say hallo to Rebecca once she was in residence the next week, it was with some surprise she heard him say, 'Unless the two of you would care to bring Lucy-Ann round to meet Richard that is? I am sure we could rustle up some sort of dinner if I speak nicely to Mrs Price.'

A nice cosy evening with Rodney and Richard, and perhaps Vanessa popping by to make the party complete? 'I don't think so. It's going to take Rebecca a little while to settle in, and no doubt she's still very tired after having the baby.' Her voice was slightly cool but she couldn't help it. He'd got a cheek, he had, whatever way you looked at it.

'It was just a thought.'

She looked into his handsome face, into the grey eyes that were so kind, and wondered if the evening out had been such a good idea after all, and her thoughts made her voice even cooler as she said, 'Good night, Rodney.'

And he had thought they'd been getting on so well there for a moment . . . Rodney straightened from leaning against the side of the car, where he had positioned himself after opening Sarah's passenger door, and his voice was abrupt as he said, 'Good night.'

He watched her as she walked up the steps and opened the front door, wondering if she would turn and acknowledge him again before she went into the house. She did, but there was no smile on her face as she raised her hand briefly before shutting the door behind her. Well, what did he expect? She'd made it clear enough in the past that their friendship was only of the most platonic kind. He walked round the bonnet and slid into his seat, resting his forearms on the steering wheel for a moment before straightening and starting the engine, his mouth grim.

She didn't want to visit his home or get to know Richard any further, and why should she? He frowned into the distance as he drove along, feeling absurdly bereft even as he told himself he had no just cause for it. But it was no good, it shouldn't matter so much but it did, and he was suddenly tired of trying to fool himself. He wanted her. No, not just want – want would have been easy to deal with, there were any number of females who could accommodate want – this feeling was more than just carnal desire. Why couldn't he say the words, even in his mind? *He loved her*, damn it.

He revved the engine violently and a passing cat that was sauntering slowly across the road, got the fright of one of its nine lives.

He thought about some of the things she had said in the interval when they had sat and chatted over their icecreams. She'd looked beautiful, beautiful and fresh and virginal . . . He pulled his mind back from that avenue and concentrated on the conversation they had shared. Sarah had made it quite clear then how she saw her life developing, but he just hadn't wanted to take it on board. A year or two more in London, now Rebecca was safe under Lady Harris's protection, and then, once the time was right, nurse's training – possibly in Sunderland, she had thought. Her face had come alive when she'd talked about that. She'd make a damn fine nurse, and there were still plenty of poor devils left from the war who would appreciate a smiling face and a genuine heart. He'd been fortunate to emerge with two arms and legs; yes, he had, he ought to remind himself of that more.

He drove steadily to his house, parking the little Morris Minor outside, the Rolls having found a new home in a lock-up some miles away. But before going in, he glanced up into the dark velvet sky that was alive with stars, and then stood, mesmerized, as he kept looking. He had to put the past behind him, go forward and not look back. He couldn't forgive, not yet, he had lost too many good friends and seen too much to forgive just yet, but it was time to make peace with himself.

It was cold but not damp, the pavements were dry and the street was shadowed and deserted, and as he stood quietly looking upwards suddenly some of the old determination from his youth was there.

Why shouldn't she come to see him in a different light? The thought gripped him, making his heart thud. Why shouldn't he keep trying? For weeks, months now, he had been fighting this feeling that had steadily grown from that first encounter in Meg Cole's little hall, and why? Age didn't matter, not really, and Sarah wasn't young in the giggly, flighty sense some girls of her age were anyway. And his life was more straightforward now than it had been for years.

He breathed in deeply, drawing the crisp frost-tinted air deep into his lungs. No, this thing wasn't done with yet.

Chapter Twenty

It was the last week of May, and the old adage that Maggie was fond of – 'Don't cast a clout until May is out' – was proving true, the weather having been wet and blustery and unusually cold, unlike April which had been warm and dry. But Sarah hadn't had time to notice the weather as she had juggled all the different facets of her life with ever-increasing speed.

The task of helping Rebecca to settle in to the routine and demands of her new job had been time-consuming, often necessitating a comforting pair of arms for little Lucy-Ann, and a shoulder for her mother to cry on after a tiring day when Rebecca was battling with baby blues on top of everything else. But the last week or so things had been going really smoothly, and Sarah felt they were winning at last.

Rebecca had said much the same thing the night before as the two of them had sat in the kitchen enjoying a last cup of cocoa together, the rest of the household having gone to bed and Lucy-Ann fast asleep and curled froglike on her mother's lap, with her nappy-clad bottom sticking up in the air and her face resting against Rebecca's bosom.

'It was worth going through everything with Willie to have her, you know.' Rebecca's hand was lightly stroking the baby's downy head as she spoke. 'I can't imagine my life without her, or you.'

'No, you're stuck with the pair of us,' Sarah agreed softly, smiling into Rebecca's contented face.

'I was petrified at the thought of coming to London at first but I needn't have been, everyone's been so kind. And I think, in a funny sort of way, that it's been the best beginning I could have had with Lucy-Ann. Everything is so different down here, there's been nothing to remind me about the bad times and it almost seems as though it's always been just me and Lucy-Ann.'

Sarah nodded understandingly before she said, 'You've done really well, I'm so proud of you.'

'I don't know what I would have done without you, especially that first week after Willie . . .' Rebecca's voice trailed away for a moment, and then she said, her tone changing, 'But that's in the past and Lucy-Ann is the future.'

'Absolutely.'

And the two of them had risen, yawning widely, and made their way to their respective rooms.

Sarah's workload had not been helped by the fact that Lady Harris had been unwell and confined to bed for most of the last two months. The old lady had never had a day's illness in her life before the attack of influenza at Christmas, and was proving a querulous and demanding patient, her frustration at the enforced idleness making the sickroom a place where the whole household trod on eggshells.

The extra duties hadn't worried Sarah so much as Sir Geoffrey's weekly visits to his mother, which, so Sarah understood from Lady Margaret, Lady Harris endured rather than enjoyed. However, the estrangement from her only child had worried the old lady a good deal in the early days of the separation, so seeing Sir Geoffrey every Tuesday afternoon was the lesser of two evils as far as his mother was concerned. Sarah tried to be elsewhere when he called, but on the two or three occasions when she had been unfortunate enough to come across him, the way he had looked at her had made her flesh creep, and the feel of his light, speckled eyes running across her skin had stayed with her a long time after he had gone.

So what with Rebecca and Lady Harris, and Lady Margaret asking Sarah to take on some extra administration duties besides the housekeeping accounts she had always been responsible for, every minute, it seemed, was catered for, and any time she could drag out of the air was spent at the hospital. But Sarah didn't mind; in fact she welcomed the hectic pace – it stopped her from thinking too much. And one thing she knew she would have thought about, had she the time, was the little announcement which had appeared in the paper stating the separation of Dr and Mrs Richard Mallard of Greyfriars, Windsor. After her conversation with Richard, when he had appeared to want to keep his private affairs just that – private – she could only assume Vanessa had made the announcement for reasons of her own, possibly so she could be seen about with Rodney in the knowledge that it was all above board?

Whatever, since seeing the announcement she had been doubly glad she didn't have a minute to spare, and her subsequent refusal of Rodney's invitations to the theatre, or the cinema, or to dinner, had been made with that in mind.

Rodney had called at the house several times since Rebecca's arrival, and usually Sarah coped quite well, but the once or twice Lucy-Ann had been awake, and she had seen him tenderly cradling the tiny mite, had been difficult. On one of those occasions he had mentioned how much he was looking forward to being a father one day, and she had found herself staring at him with something like disbelief on her face. Did he *really* think, even besotted as he so obviously was, that Vanessa would consider for one moment allowing her body to be stretched and pummelled by a baby? He'd get a rude awakening if he did. She recalled Vanessa's comments on Christmas Day about a couple who had been unable to attend her lunch due to the unexpected arrival of their first child. Richard's wife had been scathing, and no one who had heard her had been left in any doubt as to how she viewed motherhood and children. Still, perhaps Vanessa would make the supreme sacrifice? But she doubted it, she really did.

But it wasn't Vanessa Sarah was thinking about on the rainy May morning as, her hands clasped round the warmth of her coffee mug, she stood gazing out of the long narrow kitchen window at a patch of grey stormy sky above. It was Maggie who filled her thoughts as her mind replayed their conversation of the night before. Maggie was well on the way to recovery and had been home for the last week, and it had been another milestone when she had managed to hobble down the street on her crutches and phone Sarah.

'Sarah? You all right, lass?' The old woman's voice had been probing after the initial greetings were over. 'Rebecca writes me you're doin' too much.'

'Me?'

'Aye, you. From what she tells me you're one step off havin' a broom stuck up your backside an' whistlin' Dixie as you go.'

'Oh, Maggie.' It was the first really good laugh Sarah had had in weeks. 'You're awful.'

'Oh aye, I know it, hinny. You're not the first to point it out.'

'But how are you? That's the main thing.'

'Grand, lass, grand. Florrie's booked me in for dancin' lessons startin' the morrer. Got me eye on one of them dresses that glitters like a Christmas tree an' shows off all you've got up top.'

There was only one in all the world like Maggie, but how would the intrepid old woman take it if she mentioned her desire to search out her natural mother? And she would have to, sooner or later. She would hate Maggie, or Florrie for that matter, to think it in any way lessened the love she had for them, nothing could do that, but . . . She took another sip of coffee. Someone, somewhere, knew something, and since she had faced the fact that Rodney could only ever be a friend, and that she seemed destined to put all her dreams of a home and family into a career, the urge to find her blood kin had become even more urgent. She would have to mention it to Maggie, and soon – bring it out into the open and see how Maggie reacted.

As Hilda came bustling in from the small coldstore at the back of the house, where she kept most of the extra provisions donated from the farm at Fenwick, Sarah finished the coffee in one gulp. She had a million things to do this morning, the first being a quick inspection of Eileen's progress in dusting and cleaning the morning room before Lady Margaret was down, and she couldn't stand dreaming a moment longer.

She had left the kitchen and was passing through the hall on her way to the morning room, when Lady Margaret's voice sounded from upstairs, calling, 'Sarah? Oh, Sarah, come quickly. Please . . .'

She thought, at first, that Lady Harris was merely sleeping. The aristocratic old face was settled in lines of quiet repose, and there was a slight smile on her lips as she lay, her hands folded on the white linen counterpane and her small head barely making a dent in the copious pillows behind her.

'Lady Harris?' She approached the bed, going so far as to lift one frail hand before the truth hit her, and then she turned to where Lady Margaret was standing at the end of the bed, her palm across her mouth and her eyes wide and staring.

'She's . . . she's . . .'

'Lady Margaret, come and sit down.'

'Sarah, she's . . .'

'I know, I know. Please, Lady Margaret, you can do nothing here. Come and sit down and I'll telephone the doctor, while Hilda makes you a cup of tea.'

'But I can't believe it, Sarah. She was talking about getting up today for a few hours only last night. We played cards for a while, and she was laughing and joking. She was the best she's been in weeks. She can't be . . .' The faltering voice stopped abruptly as the hand came across her mouth again, but more tightly this time, as though it would stifle the truth that was nevertheless terribly real in the motionless figure beneath the bedclothes.

'If she could have chosen, this is the way she would have preferred it.' Sarah crossed the room swiftly, taking the tall stiff figure in her arms as she continued, 'You know how independent she was, Lady Margaret. She would have hated to have to endure an illness that robbed her of her liberty; look how irritable she's been the last weeks at being confined to bed. This way is so much better for her, to die with dignity, but I know it's an awful shock for you.'

'Yes, yes . . .' It was a moan, and followed by a sound deep in her throat that was distressing to hear. 'Oh, Sarah, we had such a short time of getting to know each other.' She had drawn away from Sarah as she spoke, and now Lady Margaret clutched at an upholstered bedroom chair behind her, sinking down on to the velvet-cushioned seat as she said, 'But you are quite right of course, she would have preferred it this way and that is the main thing, isn't it?'

It was said in the manner of a child, and now Sarah answered as a mother might as she said, 'Of course it is, and I know she would expect you to be strong.'

Lady Margaret nodded, her eyes limpid with moisture. 'She always admired *your* strength, Sarah, what she called your Boadicea spirit. I . . . I haven't got that, I know I haven't, it wouldn't have allowed me to marry Sir Geoffrey if I had.'

'You're too hard on yourself.'

'No, no I'm not.' Sarah watched her close her eyes for a moment before she opened them wide and said, 'But I have the courage to face my mistakes and learn from them, so that is a start, is it not? I had told my mother-in-law that I did not intend to take Sir Geoffrey back, and she understood, and I shall keep to that. Lady Harris was against a divorce – the scandal, you know – but I am content to let the separation continue indefinitely. It is what she would have wanted.'

Sarah stared at her before her eyes moved back to the bed, and her thoughts were tinged with bitterness. Lady Harris might have been a champion of the underdog, a campaigner for women's rights and all the rest of it, but she was prepared to sacrifice any chance of Lady Margaret meeting someone else and being happy, for the sake of the family name. Which was worse, when all was said and done: letting a new life ebb away in a nameless tomb in Sunderland's slums, or asking someone, in the name of love, to commit themselves to a loveless state for the rest of their life? Both done in the name of respectability, no doubt, and both heartless.

Sarah turned from the bed, and her voice reflected none of her previous thoughts as she said softly, 'Society is changing all the time, Lady Margaret, and I think the war has blown away a lot of the old concepts of what is acceptable and what is not. On some matters, like the one you have just spoken of, I think it is only you who can make the decision as to what is right and wrong.' And then her voice became brisker as she added, 'Come out of here now, and we'll call the doctor together.'

'Sarah?' They had reached the door when the hand at her elbow drew her round, and then she saw Lady Margaret's face was awash with tears as the older woman said, 'I don't know how Lady Harris's passing will affect my financial position, but I want to make it clear at the outset, before all the arrangements take us over, that I would like you and Rebecca to stay with the children and myself. I should imagine Geoffrey will take possession of both this property and Fenwick once he is able to do so, and I cannot live under the same roof as him again. It will mean my circumstances are considerably reduced,' Lady Margaret swallowed hard, 'but I have a little money of my own, a legacy from my grandmother, so I am not entirely destitute. I just wanted you to know . . .'

'Lady Margaret, of course I'll stay for a while if you want me to.' Sarah pressed the hand on her arm as she added, 'I can't speak for Rebecca, but I should imagine she will say the same.'

'Thank you.' Lady Margaret was obviously struggling for composure, her bottom lip trembling as she turned to look one last time at the little figure in the vast bed, and then she took a deep breath, turning as she said, 'And now we had better call Dr Lake. Poor Charles, this will be a shock for him too, he was very fond of her, you know.'

Once on the landing, Sarah said, 'Shall I call Hilda and Eileen into the morning room before you telephone Dr Lake? I suppose Hilda will take this hard.'

'Oh yes, yes, of course. And bring in a tray of tea with you, Sarah, I think we could all do with it. I . . . I suppose I shall need to inform Geoffrey too?' Lady Margaret turned to look at her, and their faces reflected the same thought. There were changes ahead, and knowing Sir Geoffrey, he would not make them easy or pleasant for any of the occupants of Emery Place.

Chapter Twenty-one

'I don't believe it, lass, I don't believe it.' Maggie's face was a picture of incredulity. 'Twenty thousand pounds, you say? I don't believe it.'

'She doesn't believe it.' Sarah was laughing as she looked to Florrie, but there was no answering smile on the old northerner's face as she too stared dazedly at her, her mouth agape and her eyes wide with surprise.

'It's true, Maggie.' Sarah turned back to Maggie, and now her voice was quiet when she said, 'It was in Lady Harris's will, in black and white, and that's not all. She's left Fenwick in trust for William, with Lady Margaret and her solicitors as trustees, and Lady Margaret is to get this London home with a great deal of money besides. Constance was left some property in Devon along with a sum of money, which again is in trust for her until she is twenty-one.'

'And him? The son?'

'Sir Geoffrey received an allowance for life. A very handsome one, but of course in comparison to what he expected . . .'

'By, lass.' Maggie let herself sprawl in the seat at the kitchen table, and then her voice came in a penetrating whisper as she asked, 'An' the old one, the cook? Did she get anythin'?'

'Hilda? Oh yes, of course, Lady Harris thought the world

of Hilda. You'll meet her later. She hasn't been feeling too well, what with the shock of Lady Harris and the funeral and so on, and as Lady Margaret and the children are staying on at Fenwick for a while, she rests in the afternoons.'

'An' you're sure Lady Margaret don't mind us comin' here? We expected to stay in a boardin' house, didn't we, Florrie, but I was of a mind to see the bairn before she's much older. They change so quick at this age.'

Maggie grinned as Florrie cut in with, 'She was of a mind? That's an understatement if ever I heard one. She's been on about nothing else but the bairn since coming out of the infirmary, I can tell you.'

'She's a bonny little lass.' Maggie inclined her head as she repeated, her voice softer now, 'Aye, she's bonny, an' – thank the good Lord – I can see nothin' of her da in her.'

Sarah nodded her agreement, glancing at the door through which Rebecca had disappeared some minutes earlier, Lucy-Ann having become fractious at missing her afternoon nap. 'Rebecca dotes on her, and Lucy-Ann is so good. It's funny how things work out, isn't it? We all thought Rebecca being pregnant was such a problem, but it's been the thing that has aided her recovery more than anything. She's getting so confident in herself since Lucy-Ann has been born, and it's more than Willie not being around. Of course she was a bit weepy in the early days, but lately if she's not singing out loud, she's humming. It's lovely to hear her.'

'Aye, there's nothin' like a bairn for bringin' joy, it'll be the makin' of the lass, you mark my words.' And then Maggie returned to her original question as she asked again, 'An' you say Lady Margaret was of a mind to have us here?'

'It was her suggestion, along with clearing out the room Sir Geoffrey used to use as his study when he was here and making it into a bed-sitting-room for the pair of you, so you wouldn't find the stairs a problem, Maggie. She wouldn't have proposed that if she had minded, now would she?'

'She suggested that? Aw . . .' The last syllable was directed at Florrie, and carried both relief and pleasure, which Florrie replied to as she said, 'There you are, I told you, didn't I? All that whittling about her being one of the nobs and all.'

'You weren't worried about staying here?' Sarah looked from Maggie to Florrie, and then back to Maggie again. 'But why?'

'I . . . I didn't want to let you down, lass.' Maggie's voice was low, her head bowed, as she fiddled with the remains of a piece of cake on the plate in front of her. 'I know me faults, none better, an' you're doin' all right here. I didn't want Lady Margaret to think . . . Well, you're not like me, you're a cut above—'

'*Maggie*.' Sarah stared at her unbelieving. 'You were worried I'd be *ashamed* of you?' Her voice had risen on the last three words, and now, as Maggie said, 'No, no, not that, not really,' Sarah came back with, 'It'd better not be, Maggie McLevy, because I would never forgive you if you thought that. You and Florrie' – she stretched out her arms wide towards them both to emphasize the point – 'you are part of me, a big part of me, the best part. Don't you understand that? You do, don't you?'

'Aye, lass, course we do.' It was Florrie who had spoken, and as Sarah glanced at her and then at the bowed head of the big fat woman sitting next to her, she said again, 'Maggie? You do, don't you?'

'Aw, hinny.' Maggie's eyes lifted to hers, and Sarah saw they were wet. 'I'm a daft old biddy, that's the truth of it. But aye, I know how you feel, lass, I do. It's just that that last do, with Matron Cox, knocked the stuffin' out of me a bit, an' there's still the odd day where I don't feel quite like meself.' And then, as Sarah's arms came round her and she pressed the old woman close, Maggie cried, 'Mind me hair, lass, mind me hair. The blighter cost me a fortune in that posh shop in Brixton Street afore I come.'

'Well, lass, you deserve everything that's come to you, I'll say that.' It was Florrie who spoke now, and her voice was thick with suppressed emotion. 'Aye, there's none deserves good fortune more than you.'

Sarah hugged Florrie too, before she smiled and said, 'It wasn't so much the money in a way, but what Lady Harris said about me in the will. She called me a woman after her own heart – that was nice, wasn't it – and she said I had touched each of their lives in a special way.'

It was Sarah's voice that was thick now as she recalled her employer's tribute, and Maggie cleared her throat loudly, before she said, 'Right, let's hear all about it, proper like. Who told you you'd become an heiress an' joined the nobs?'

Sarah rubbed her nose, and smiled at the pair of them as she reseated herself at the table, before saying, 'The family's solicitor, after the funeral the week before last, but I didn't want to tell you by phone or letter. I wanted to see your faces.'

'Well you've seen 'em, hinny, you've seen 'em.' Maggie shook her head as she eased herself forward in the chair and rubbed at her leg, which although out of plaster was still heavily bandaged. 'By, I've never heard the like, eh, Florrie?' And as Florrie smiled her agreement, 'It must've bin a weight off your Lady Margaret's mind an' all, I should imagine? She's fair set up now.'

'It's wonderful for her. She had made up her mind she wasn't going to take Sir Geoffrey back, but this has made things so much easier.'

'Aye, I don't doubt it.' Maggie's voice held a dry note. 'Money isn't everythin' so they tell me, but it goes a long way to oilin' the wheels. An' how did himself take the news? Fair jumped for joy did he?'

'Not exactly.' Sarah smiled, but in truth Sir Geoffrey's reaction to his mother's last will and testament had unnerved her more than a little.

Sir Geoffrey had been every inch the heir apparent at the funeral, charming with the older contingent of elderly ladies who had been his mother's circle of friends, grave and dignified with the men and somewhat dour minister, and earnest and unsmiling with Lady Margaret and his children.

'A man for all seasons . . .' It had been Lady Margaret herself who had whispered the aside to Sarah, as the two of them had stood just within the perimeter of the tiny churchyard at Fenwick, watching Sir Geoffrey as he had conversed with his in-laws.

Sarah hadn't expected to like Lord and Lady Havistock after Lady Margaret's confidences regarding her parents, but she had been unprepared for the flash of burning resentment she had felt on their daughter's behalf when the floridly handsome man and his pretty doll-like wife had swept past Lady Margaret with the briefest of nods.

'He will be professing to be the noble but misunderstood husband, Sarah, you can be sure of it,' Lady Margaret continued quietly, her voice tinged with bitterness. 'I have already been taken to task by my mother on the subject of a wife's duty to her husband. One turns a blind eye, apparently, to any little indiscretions. In fact it was hinted at that such lapses would not be necessary at all if the wife in question was all she should be.'

There had been a break in her voice as she had finished, and Sarah, deeply indignant on her friend's behalf, had said, 'What utter rubbish.'

'Quite.' The thin chest under its black linen coat had expanded, before Lady Margaret said again, 'Quite, that was my reply exactly, and I'm afraid it was not well received.'

The funeral luncheon in Fenwick's stately dining room had been a lavish affair, but Sarah had been glad to be eating with the housekeeper and the butler in the housekeeper's private sitting room just off the servants' quarters. She had been uncomfortably aware of Sir Geoffrey's presence all through the long morning but she had only met his eyes once, and then she had held the cold gaze without flinching, determined not to be intimidated by a man she loathed and held in deep contempt. But it had been difficult.

All through lunch Sarah reminded herself that there was only the reading of the will to get through in the afternoon, which had been designated to be read in the late Lord Harris's massive book-lined study with family, close friends and staff present, and then, after that necessary formality, they could leave for London. And it couldn't be soon enough.

Fenwick was imposing, the house and grounds were beautifully maintained, but Sarah was aware the staff regarded her with some suspicion. They weren't sure of her standing with Lady Margaret and exactly of how she fitted into the scheme of things, and it showed. No doubt Hilda had been fairly eloquent below stairs regarding the lurid happenings at Emery Place, and the subsequent departure of Sir Geoffrey, under protest, from his mother's home, but it hadn't endeared Sarah to the staff at Fenwick. They were curious about the stranger in their midst, but Sarah detected a certain resentment directed at what they perceived as her quick rise to power. It didn't make for comfortable eating.

And then had come the reading of the will.

The silence had been heavy and absolute as the family solicitor, an august personage with small steel-framed spectacles balanced on the end of his long thin nose, had read from the document in his hand. The immediate family, consisting of Sir Geoffrey and Lady Margaret, Lady Harris's sister and niece and Lord and Lady Havistock, had been joined by several other relations and friends at the solicitor's request, and were seated on upholstered gold-framed chairs in front of the heavy antique writing desk at which the solicitor sat.

Behind them stood the senior members of the household staff at Fenwick, with two grooms and the head gardener making up the rear. And at the back of them all was Sarah, whose initial feeling of awe had changed to stunned disbelief by the time the faintly pompous voice had finished speaking.

The silence had stretched and lengthened with every pair of eyes fixed on the back of Sir Geoffrey's head, but still no one had moved or spoken, and it had come as a relief to everyone present when Sir Geoffrey had at last risen from his chair and turned to face the room. But the relief had been shortlived.

'*You – you*—' He had advanced on Sarah slowly, his eyes almost popping out of his head with the rage he was trying to contain and his sallow face tinged with purple. '*You –*' He had seemed incapable of uttering anything different through his clenched teeth, spittle having gathered either side of his mouth in white blobs, and he went on repeating the word until he was standing in front of her, when he said, 'So you managed it, did you?'

'I don't know what you mean, Sir Geoffrey.' Sarah's heart was thudding so hard it was in danger of leaping out of her chest.

'*Don't give me that.*' He glared at her, rubbing his lips with the back of his hand before saying again, 'Don't give me that. I knew what you were up to from the first minute I laid eyes on you.'

337

'If you are suggesting that Sarah had anything to do with your mother changing her will, then you are quite wrong, Geoffrey.' Lady Margaret spoke for the first time, her face red with embarrassment at the unpleasant scene her husband was making and her voice still dazed from the wonder of her good fortune. 'You know exactly what led her to act in such a manner.'

'I know *who* did.' He was grinding the words out, beside himself with fury, and one of the grooms, a big muscular fellow with a huge barrel chest and arms like a wrestler, moved closer to Sarah's side, obviously fearing Sir Geoffrey meant her physical harm. 'Oh yes, I know who did. You think you've been very clever, don't you, my girl?'

Sarah's face was white but her voice didn't quiver as she said, 'My conscience is clear, Sir Geoffrey. Can you say the same?'

She heard the intake of breath from the Fenwick staff, and Lady Havistock's exclamation of, 'Well, really!', but the man himself continued to stare at her, his teeth gnashing together and his eyes unblinking, and then he said, his voice low but deadly, 'This isn't the end of it, you know that, don't you?'

The solicitor had coughed at this point, before saying, 'Sir Geoffrey, please, please, compose yourself. You are at liberty to contest Lady Harris's will, if you should feel so inclined.'

'Thank you, Mr Bryant.' The sarcasm was vicious, but again he didn't take his eyes off Sarah's face, even when Lady Margaret at the side of them said, 'Please, Geoffrey, come and sit down, and let's discuss this rationally.'

'No, this is not the end of it, my girl, not by a long chalk.' It was as though there was no one else in the room, and she could feel the dark force of his enmity even though his voice had become very quiet as he continued, 'There are ways and

338

means. Oh yes, there are ways and means. All good things come to those that wait.'

He hadn't been talking of his intention to contest the will through the courts. Sarah forced her mind back from the harrowing threat she had sensed in Sir Geoffrey's voice that day two weeks ago, looking quickly at Maggie who had just said, 'It looks like you're set up for life, lass. Any ideas what you'll do with the money?'

'A few, but mainly I'll just carry on as normal for the time being until the dust settles.'

'With twenty thousand sittin' beggin'?'

'I haven't got it yet.'

'As good as, hinny, as good as.'

When Sarah merely smiled, but made no reply beyond saying, as she rose, 'I'll make some fresh tea,' Maggie's eyes narrowed at Florrie, and the two exchanged a long look before Maggie said to Sarah's back as she stood at the stove, 'What did the doctor think to your windfall then? You've told him, I'll be bound?'

'Yes, I've told him.'

'An' what did he say?'

'He . . . he was surprised.'

'Aye, well it wouldn't take the Brain of Britain to work that one out, lass.'

'And pleased. He was pleased, of course.'

Had Rodney been pleased? Sarah asked herself for the umpteenth time since she had dropped her little bombshell during his first visit after the funeral. He had been effusive, after the first blank moment of surprise, but she hadn't felt he was really pleased, not if she was truthful, at least not wholeheartedly . . . There had been something tempering his gladness for her, and she didn't understand what. He had been enthusiastic about what the money could do for her, joking that they soon wouldn't see her for dust, but he had left overly quickly and had seemed preoccupied on his one other visit since then. No, overall she wouldn't say he was really pleased.

'Well, there's never a dull moment, lass, I'll say that. An' you say the doctor'll be callin' in sometime, eh? Calls fairly regular, does he?'

Sarah now turned from the stove, slanting her gaze at the old woman whom she loved dearly, but who had the disturbing ability to read her mind at times, and her face was expressionless when she said, 'Now and again, but he wants to see you two, so no doubt he'll pop in tonight once his surgery is finished. His brother is staying with him at the moment. He's just sold his house but his flat isn't quite ready yet, it's being decorated, so Rodney is putting him up for a while.'

'Aye, well blood's thicker than water, lass.'

'So they say, Maggie.' So they say.

When Rodney did call later that evening Maggie and Florrie were already comfortably established in the room at the far end of the hall, almost opposite the kitchen. It was a large room, which easily accommodated the two single beds, thick oak wardrobe and small dressing table which had been moved in there, along with two comfortable easy chairs and an occasional table which stood in front of the electric fire.

Maggie was sitting in one of the chairs, her leg resting on a small upholstered stool Sarah had borrowed from the drawing room, when Rodney popped his head round the door, and immediately she saw him her lined old face creased in a wide smile. 'Eeh, lad, you're a sight for sore eyes.'

'That's nice to hear, Maggie.' He came fully into the room, with Sarah just behind him, as he added, 'This looks very comfortable. They've done you proud, haven't they?'

'Aye, don't I know it. Me brain thinks me body's died an' landed in heaven.' And then, as Rodney glanced round, 'Florrie's gabbin' with Hilda in the kitchen, she's bin in there half the evenin'.' She wished that slight reserve that still existed between Florrie and the lad could be done away with, but then, folk were as God made them.

Rodney nodded but made no comment, and when Sarah said, 'Sit down a minute, won't you?' he half turned to include her in the shake of his head as he said, 'Thanks all the same but I haven't got time to stop tonight, this is just a fleeting visit to say hallo to this one here.' And then, turning fully to Maggie again, 'Sarah's told you her good news? We have a woman of substance among us.'

'Aye.'

Rodney was smiling, and Maggie smiled back, but her mind was on a different plane altogether. He didn't like it, he didn't like her lass coming into money, she could read it in his eyes. Now why was that then? She wouldn't put him down as a mean-minded man, just the opposite in fact, but her gut instinct was never wrong and it was telling her the doctor was miffed. More than miffed.

'I've told her she needs to invest.'

'Invest?'

'Yes, in property – bonds – something which is a surefire bet.'

'Oh, aye.' Maggie was out of her depth now, and she hesitated a moment before saying, 'It's a lot of money, lad.'

'Invested wisely it could double in ten years, less even, and Sarah could still have enough to do exactly what she likes.'

'I'm not interested in doubling it.'

Sarah's voice was low, and Maggie's eyes were keen as they rested on her face before returning to the man standing just in front of her. There was more here than met the eye.

She'd caught the brief hesitation in Rodney's voice, and it spoke volumes to the old woman. The lad wasn't happy, that was for sure, and she'd bet her life her lass weren't none too bright either, in spite of all that money coming her way. And why did a man like the doctor, a busy man, and good-looking too, why did he keep bothering to come round all the time? Her heart began to thump a bit. Perhaps she'd got it wrong before, she thought slowly. Maybe his feelings for her lass weren't so far removed from Sarah's for him after all?

Maggie nodded now at Sarah as she said, 'Aye, well, it's no bad thing to think on for a bit, lass. You can always make up your mind gradual like. You could put a bit away, travel maybe, meet new folks an' enjoy yourself a while, eh?'

Maggie's voice was casual but her eyes were hard on Rodney, and what she read in his face caused her to give a mental nod to the voice in her head which said, Aye, he liked her all right, the daft blighter, so why was he messin' about? If he didn't open his mouth it was for sure her lass wouldn't. There was plenty who'd be forward enough mind, oh aye, the war had changed a lot of things, and not all of them for the better, but she knew her lass. It couldn't be the money that was holding him back, he'd got more than enough of his own, besides which they'd only known about Sarah's windfall in the last couple of weeks, so what was it? Had Sarah given him the wrong impression, acted as if she weren't interested? He wasn't the type to force himself on a lass, a gentleman through and through, he was, but her lass was beautiful and bright, and wealthy now in her own right. She couldn't remain single for long . . .

Rodney was thinking just the same thing as he continued the conversation with Maggie for a few minutes more. He had thought of nothing else since Sarah had told him about her inheritance. Sarah, Sarah, Sarah. Her name was a constant refrain in his mind whatever he was doing and whoever he was with. He had thought he'd got time on his side, time to woo her and persuade her to see him as something more than a friend, but fate had had other ideas. Not that he begrudged her the money, not a penny of it. If anyone deserved life to smile on them it was Sarah. But it had the potential to move her out of his orbit before he could reach her. Time. Suddenly it had turned from friend to enemy, and overnight it seemed. He felt hot panic grip his bowels, and then he realized Maggie had been speaking and he hadn't heard a word she'd said. 'I'm sorry, Maggie?'

'I said, little Lucy-Ann is the image of her mam.'

'Yes. Yes, she is.'

'An' it'll do the lass good to take care of her own bairn. Therapy like.'

'I'm sure you're right.'

'At least Willie come through with somethin' for her.' Rodney raised his eyebrows at this, his expression indicating surprise at Maggie's choice of words, and she stared back at him for a long moment before saying, 'Every lass ought to get married an' have her own family, lad. There's somethin' in most women that can only be satisfied when they hold their first bairn in their arms, especially ones who've had the sort of beginnin' Rebecca has.'

What was she really saying? Rodney found himself holding Maggie's straight gaze as his mind sought for something to say, and failed. He'd got the impression that suddenly they weren't talking about Rebecca any more, and as he heard Sarah shift uneasily behind him, he felt she had sensed the same thing.

Was Maggie warning him off? he asked himself grimly. She was quite capable of it, that was for sure. Or did she suspect his feelings for Sarah went deeper than friendship, but was testing the water to be sure? Could it even be that she was giving him tacit encouragement? How the hell was he to know? But one thing was for sure, this latest business with the inheritance had taken the softly-softly approach from him, and he was damned if he was going to stand by and see Sarah move on without at least opening his mouth.

With that in mind, he said, 'There's a few women's rights enthusiasts who would disagree with that statement, Maggie, but not me.' He turned to look at Sarah now. 'What about you, Sarah?' he asked quietly, his voice soft but expressing something that went far beyond the actual words.

'Me?' He was asking her approval in making Vanessa an honest woman and mother of his children? Well, she could hardly concur, whether he liked it or not. 'I think some women would make awful mothers actually, just as some men are never meant to be fathers.' Sarah raised her chin slightly. 'But everyone to their own, of course.'

'Oh, of course.' He knew his tone was a touch too hearty, but the heat spiralling up from the depths of him would be reflected in his face in a moment if he didn't get out, and he made his goodbyes and left the house at once.

Rodney drove steadily and without undue haste to a quiet tree-lined street not far from Emery Place, where, after parking between two family saloons, he remained sitting in the car without moving for a long time. She had known what he was asking, he had seen something register in her eyes as he had spoken. And it was fair enough, she had made it quite clear over the last weeks that she didn't want him to embarrass her by putting her in the position where she would be forced to spell it out.

He hit the steering wheel with a clenched first with enough force for it to hurt. It was over, *finished*, not that it had ever begun. He couldn't hound her, coerce or use force to make her love him, and neither did he want it to get so she dreaded the sound of his name or the sight of him.

He stretched in his seat for a moment, pain gnawing at his

vitals. Well, he hadn't let those devils in the camp beat him and he wouldn't let this either, but of the two . . . He straightened, his face grim. Of the two, he knew which was going to be the harder fight to win.

Chapter Twenty-two

'Here, lass, I've just bin sayin' to Florrie, you don't think that's the doctor's sister-in-law, do you?'

'What?'

It was the evening of the next day, and Maggie and Florrie were sitting in front of the fire in their room, Maggie reading the paper and Florrie knitting a little matinee jacket for Lucy-Ann – when Maggie hailed Sarah as she put her head round the door to ask if they would like a cup of tea.

'This bit in the paper, here.' Maggie thrust the paper at Sarah as she came fully into the room. 'You read it, lass.'

It was a small piece extolling the personages who had attended a charity gala, and in the listed names there was a Lord Simmons and a Mrs Vanessa Mallard.

'I know you said she's broke up with him, separated like, but that looks a bit final, don't it, if she's taken up with some Lord or other?'

'But—' Sarah stared at the black print as the letters danced. 'Aye?'

'Oh nothing, nothing. Perhaps . . . perhaps he's just a friend.'

'Aye, an' perhaps pigs fly, but I like me bacon where I can see it. If this Lord Simmons is escortin' her to fancy dos, knowin' how some folk talk, I'd say he means business meself.'

So would she. Sarah stared at Maggie for a moment as her mind raced. Yes, so would she, and that meant – what? That Vanessa and Rodney had parted? Fallen out perhaps? Or . . . or could it be that their affair had never been fact in the first place? But if that was so, why had Vanessa taken the trouble to seek her out and tell her a pack of lies? It must have been true. Oh, she had to go somewhere quiet and think, but there was no hope of that until she was in bed. There *had* been something between Vanessa Mallard and Rodney, she'd sensed it at Christmas, but could it have been just that they'd been engaged once and it had finished? No, it was no good, she couldn't think of this now, she had too much to do. She would think of it later when she was alone.

Once in the hall again she tidied her hair in the large gilt-framed mirror, drawing a few soft golden strands that had escaped the french pleat at the back of her head into place with shaking hands, and noticing the brightness in her eyes with a little sigh of despair at her own foolishness. This probably meant nothing, *nothing*, she told the shining blue eyes staring back at her. He could be a friend of Vanessa's, even a friend of Richard's, there could be a hundred valid explanations. But she could ask Rodney about the article, couldn't she, casually, as though it didn't mean anything one way or the other? There was nothing wrong in that.

Inspection completed she walked back down the hall and into the kitchen, enchanging a few words with Hilda as she busied herself with a tea tray for Maggie and Florrie, and chivvying Eileen along as the girl cleaned the stove for morning with snail-like slowness, before hurrying along to the morning room and spending a few minutes glancing through the housekeeping accounts. But she couldn't concentrate . . .

When Hilda and Eileen popped their heads round the door to say good night she decided to call it a day, checking first on Maggie and Florrie, who were both now tucked up in their beds, before doing her rounds and making sure the house was secure for the night. Once in her room she got ready for bed quickly, her mind continuing to chew at various possibilities for the article in the paper, and after some twenty minutes, when she had given herself a thudding headache, she climbed out of bed again and took a couple of aspirins with a drink of water. She had to go to sleep, she had a million things to do in the morning, and the only way she could get to the bottom of all this was to speak to Rodney anyway. And she would. In the morning she would take the bull by the horns and ring him, even if it did look incredibly nosy. Her mind made up she climbed back into bed and was asleep within minutes.

Sir Geoffrey Harris saw the lights go off in 19 Emery Place one by one from his vantage point in the small park opposite the house.

He had been waiting in the dark mauve shadows of the mild June dusk from before nine o'clock and it was now nearly eleven, but he wasn't tired. His expectations of the night ahead had him on tenterhooks and sleep was the last thing on his mind. She was in there – turning off the lights, doing the housekeeping act she was so good at – secure in the knowledge she now had money of her own and could thumb her nose at all of them when she had a mind to. *His* money. Twenty thousand damn pounds' worth.

He breathed in deeply through his nose for a few moments, his mind cautioning him as it said, Steady, steady, your time will come, the plans have been made.

A fierce surge of excitement and power rose in him, and helped control the frustrated rage which had been burning to a greater or lesser degree for months, but which had reached its climax two weeks before in his father's study at Fenwick.

An allowance. An allowance, blast her. He still found it hard to believe his mother had done that to him, especially as he'd begun to talk her round that last couple of months when he'd visited so regularly . . . or he thought he'd talked her round. But she'd been worked on, oh yes, and by an expert. And that same expert had got Margaret digging her heels in and talking about visiting rights.

. Visiting rights. His eyes narrowed and his lip curled. He'd give her visiting rights, he'd make her regret the day she was born, once he was back in and she was under his control. But that wouldn't happen until the other one was out of the way, he knew that. And then, what with the fancy lawyers pleading his case and him sweet-talking that frigid bitch of a wife of his round, he'd come into what was rightfully his. He could handle Margaret. He had always been able to handle Margaret.

He glanced at his watch, a quiver of excitement making his fat buttocks clench. Another few minutes and then Eileen could do her bit.

Eileen . . . The name warmed him, causing him to move a stealthy hand to his crotch and rub gently at the swelling there. The girl was a natural whore if ever he'd met one. At fifteen he had half expected her to be a virgin, but there had been others there before him – several others judging by what she knew between the sheets. She'd go far, that girl, and he'd follow through on his agreement to set her up in a little flat somewhere once all this was settled. He'd never gone to those lengths before, but for Eileen . . . Yes, he could see himself visiting her for a good few years yet.

He'd enjoyed the illicit meetings on her time off over the last few months, since he'd first approached her after she'd been working for his mother for a few days. He'd thought he would have to work at it, but he couldn't have been more wrong. A couple of nice presents, a bit of sweet-talking, and

350

she'd been putty in his hands. Course, she'd enjoyed knowing she was sleeping with the master, that was part of it. He smiled to himself. She was a cheeky little piece, but he'd had to warn her a sight too often lately not to get cocky – he hadn't wanted any of them at the house catching on. That was always the trouble when you picked them from the gutter. They got ideas.

Although the night was a warm one there were no people about as he rose slowly from the wooden bench on the perimeter of the park at exactly a quarter past eleven, and glanced casually about him. Any activity was always in the centre where the smooth stretches of grassland were dotted with flowerbeds and bushes and trees; there were plenty of courting couples making use of that area until the early hours.

But he wanted comfort for what he was about to do, and the timing was perfect with Margaret and the children out of the way at Fenwick. He'd see to Eileen first and keep her happy, it'd get him in the mood for what he'd got in mind afterwards anyway – not that Eileen knew anything about that. He felt a little quiver in his loins, his manhood surging, but it wasn't the thought of Eileen that was making him sweat. He was going to have that little stuck-up tart of a housekeeper tonight, he'd waited long enough, and if she was foolish enough to say anything afterwards, it would only be his word against hers that he'd ever been in the house. Eileen would keep quiet, she was no fool and she'd got too much to lose to cross him, and he'd already got his alibi nicely set up. Old Charlie Menton would swear black was white for a few bob. Money could buy anything.

His fingers caressed the small bottle of chloroform wrapped in cloth in his pocket. Mind you, by the time he had finished with her tonight she wouldn't say a word about what had transpired. The things he intended to do to her she'd never be able to repeat to a living soul, and she was a proud piece if ever he'd seen one. She would rather die than let on. But he would let her come fully round before he started; once the gag was in place and she was secured, she'd be docile enough. It wasn't as if this was the first time he'd taken one that was unwilling.

He walked quickly across the road, and right on cue Eileen opened the door for him, her pretty face dimpling up at him. 'Good evening, sir.' It was a laughing whisper, but he frowned, shaking his head as he stepped inside the hall. 'It's all right, they've all been abed since half ten,' she added softly as she reached up and kissed him on the lips.

They mounted the stairs quickly, and he didn't pause outside Sarah's room, pushing Eileen into hers and shutting the door behind them.

Neither of them had noticed the tall thin shadow that had followed them up the stairs, and now stood hesitating on the dark landing. Florrie was finding it difficult to sleep in a strange bed, and when she had heard a noise in the hall, the sound penetrating the monotonous drone of Maggie's snores, she had slipped quietly from under the covers and padded over to the door, opening it a crack just in time to see Eileen reach up and kiss Sir Geoffrey. Florrie had recognized him instantly from the family portrait hanging in the drawing room, and her heart had pounded with mingled fear and shock when, in the next instant, the big portly man and little maid had disappeared up the back staircase.

She had followed them without even thinking about it, unsure of what the pair of them were about, and now she looked down at the heavy brass ornament she had grabbed from the hall table, and saw her hands were shaking. But she would have used it on him, oh aye, she would, if he'd gone to their lass's door. By, this was a rum do . . .

She stood for some minutes more outside Eileen's room but there wasn't a sound from within. Not that she needed a diagram to work out what they were up to, she thought grimly. What should she do? It was clear the little maid had been expecting him, and from the welcome she'd given him, Lady Harris's son was no stranger to her. Hilda had told her on the quiet the girl was a trollop and she was right, aye she was. But to let him in the house, and after all that had gone on? The girl wasn't all there, she couldn't be, to act so foolishly.

She glanced at Sarah's door, and then down the corridor to Rebecca's but almost immediately dismissed the idea of waking the two girls. Sir Geoffrey was a big man, and from what Sarah had said he could be violent, but knowing Sarah she'd be straight in there demanding he leave, without a thought for her own safety. And if he turned nasty, who knew what could happen – for all she knew he had a weapon on him. These gentry sort were always out shooting and the like on their estates, weren't they? And Rebecca had the bairn with her.

But was Eileen his sole reason for being in the house? He'd got a grudge against their lass, and Sir Geoffrey wasn't the sort of man who would care tuppence about doing a bunch of servants some harm. But, as Florrie was to admit afterwards, she didn't really think Sir Geoffrey intended anything more than a bit of slap and tickle with Eileen in the luxury of his mother's house, so cocking a snook at his wife and Sarah whom he saw as the ones who had denied him access.

After another few minutes on the chilly landing clad only in her nightie, Florrie's teeth were beginning to chatter, and she came to a decision, nipping quickly back down the stairs and, after consulting the telephone directory next to the phone, gingerly lifting the receiver. She dialled Rodney's number with shaking hands, praying all the time he wouldn't be out on a call. She didn't like this and she needed to ask him what to do.

It was a good thirty seconds or so before she heard his sleepy voice, and then she dare only speak in a whisper. There was a moment's silence the other end, before Rodney's voice, alert and sharp now, said, 'Who is this?'

'Florrie, it's Florrie.'

'Florrie?' The high note of amazement would have made her smile on any other occasion; as it was, she spoke rapidly and softly into the receiver as she detailed what she had seen. Again there was a moment's silence when she finished before Rodney's voice said, 'I'll be straight over. Can you let me in?'

'Aye, aye, I'll be waiting.'

'Don't wake Sarah or Maggie unless you have to, right? And keep your eyes and ears open.'

'I will, Doctor, I will.'

'And, Florrie?'

'Aye?'

'Bless you.'

Florrie tip-toed through to her room, where Maggie was still vibrating the air with her snores, and, after finding her dressing gown and thrusting her feet into her old felt slippers, climbed the stairs once more to keep a watch on the landing, positioning herself outside Eileen's door until she heard Rodney's knock at the front door. But Sir Geoffrey wasn't in Eileen's room . . .

In spite of Eileen's bravado she had been scared to death once Sir Geoffrey was in the house, and that, added to his impatience to get to the real meaning of his visit, meant their copulation was over almost before it had started.

After cleaning himself up he smiled at her, his voice faintly teasing as he said, 'I'll let myself out, girl, I know the way.'

'But I thought you were going to stay a while and talk about the flat. You said—'

'I know what I said.' He smiled again, but this time let his face become straight as he added, 'But you're on edge, aren't you? Don't worry, I'll soon have you in your own place; I promised, didn't I? Now you go to sleep, and here' – he passed a jeweller's box to her – 'a little trinket for you.'

'But I'll have to come and bolt the door behind you, else they'll know someone's been in.'

No, that wouldn't do, that wouldn't do at all. He thought quickly and said, 'No, don't worry for now. There's a few papers I want to have a look at in the morning room, on the quiet, you know, so I'm going to spend an hour or two in there before I go. You just make sure you come down first thing in the morning, before the others are awake, and slip the bolts then, that's a good girl.'

'You aren't going to take anything that might be missed?'

'No, no, girl. What do you take me for?' He gestured at the little box in her hands. 'Have a look at what I got for you, then, and just make sure you're down first thing, and everything will be fine.'

He left her oohing and ahhing over the pendant, and stepped out on to the landing, shutting the door quietly behind him before creeping stealthily along to Sarah's room. The door opened silently at his touch, and he was in the room and leaning against the closed door in a trice as he fetched the chloroform and cloth out of his pocket.

Sarah was in such a deep sleep she barely struggled as he held the soaked wad over her face, and when he was sure she was unconscious he stood for a moment just staring down at her, anticipation making him rock-hard. His hands were trembling as he stripped back the bedclothes, but he made no attempt to remove her white lawn nightie. He wanted her conscious when he peeled that off – oh yes, he wanted her conscious for it all.

He used a thick linen handkerchief to gag her, before

reaching into his pocket again and fetching out a long piece of thin cord, with which he tied her hands together over her head, fastening the rope securely to the bedhead. He left her legs free, he wanted those to be able to flail and writhe.

And then, once he was sure she would be unable to make a sound, he settled himself down on the edge of the bed to wait for her to come round. Funny, he thought to himself, but he was going to enjoy that moment more than any other that followed. He wanted to see the look in her eyes when she realized what had happened, and that she was helpless, vulnerable and exposed . . .

Rodney's gentle tap on the front door was so quiet as to be almost soundless, but Florrie heard it. Once she was down the stairs and Rodney was in the hall, he said, 'Is anyone else awake? Sarah? Maggie?'

'No one.'

'Right. Show me Eileen's room, would you, Florrie. He's probably going to put up some sort of a show, but if we can get him out of there and downstairs before the rest of the house wakes up, all to the good. It's going to give Sarah one hell of a fright as it is.'

Rodney didn't knock on Eileen's door, and she didn't make a sound beyond whispering, 'Geoffrey? You're back?' as Rodney loomed through the darkness.

He reached the bed, and putting his hand over her mouth, said, 'No, not even nearly right, Eileen. Where is he? And answer me in a whisper if you know what's good for you.'

As he removed his fingers the little maid shot up in bed, but her voice was barely audible as she said, 'He – he's gone. He's left.' She was too terrified by the sudden turn of events to prevaricate.

'He didn't get past me, lad.' Florrie had followed him into the room and now her stage whisper brought him upright. It was the first time she had ever addressed him so familiarly but neither of them were aware of it.

'If he didn't get past you, he must have left the room when you phoned me . . .' His voice dwindled away, and then bit out with the force of a bullet as he said, *'Sarah's room, where is it?'* He had swung round to Florrie before he finished speaking, and as her eyes widened in horrified recognition of what he was saying, she pointed to the lefthand wall and he was out of the room before she could move.

If he lived to be a hundred Rodney would never forget the picture that confronted him when he burst into Sarah's room. She was just beginning to stir, and Sir Geoffrey was crouched over her on the bed, his two hands on the front of her nightie which he was clearly going to tear from her body.

The cry Rodney gave as he leapt across the room was blood-curdling, and his sudden entrance took Sir Geoffrey by surprise, but the older man recovered almost instantly, swinging round and landing a punch on Rodney's jaw as their two bodies connected. Rodney didn't even feel it. The momentum of his lunge took them both to the floor by the far side of the bed, and now Rodney was hammering the twisting figure beneath him, who, in his turn, was fighting back with hands and feet and teeth.

Rodney was aware of noise – someone, he thought Eileen, was screaming, and Florrie was in the room, he could hear her shouting – but the red mist in front of his eyes was concentrated on one thing and one thing only, and that was stopping Sir Geoffrey Harris from ever laying hands on Sarah again. The doctor in him, the healer and compassionate restorer of minds and bodies, had vanished. He was merely a man who had seen his beloved trapped and attacked by something foul.

It was Maggie, having bumped herself upstairs on her bottom step by step on hearing the shouts and screams, and gathering enough from the scene in front of her to fear that Rodney was going to kill Sir Geoffrey, who – together with Florrie and the others – hauled Rodney sideways momentarily, and the brief respite was all the other man needed to leap up and make for the stairs.

Rodney flung the women off him as he struggled to his feet, reeling forward, his head spinning from the effect of Sir Geoffrey's blows, and giving chase. He could never quite remember afterwards whether he had grabbed Sir Geoffrey before he started to fall, or whether it was his dive at the other man that started the impetus that took them both flying down the stairs in a tangle of limbs, accompanied by screams from the women above. He was aware of Sir Geoffrey's flailing body along with his own panic as he tried to save himself from serious injury, but then he hit the floor, every bone jarring with the impact, and everything went black.

He could only have lost consciousness for a few seconds at the most, because the women – first Eileen, quite hysterical, then Florrie and Rebecca with their arms round a half-fainting Sarah, followed by Maggie hotching down on her well padded bottom, with Hilda making the rear, were still coming down the stairs in formation when he raised his head.

Sir Geoffrey was lying partly beneath him, and he knew at once the other man was dead from the impossible angle of his neck. He levered himself upright with the help of the banisters, shaking his head to clear the muzziness, and then moving to one side to try and shield Sarah from the sight of Sir Geoffrey's grotesquely twisted body.

'Here, let me have her.' He took her from Florrie and Rebecca, lifting her off her feet into his arms as he looked down into her wan, bleached face rigid with shock, and then turning to the others said, 'Someone call the police,' before stumbling through to the drawing room, his own legs far from steady.

He placed her gently on one of the small sofas which dotted the room, and would have straightened, but Sarah clung to him, and so he knelt down at her side. And then, as her face lifted to his, it seemed the most natural thing in the world to kiss her, and Sarah, all her defences down, kissed him back.

Rodney hadn't expected it; the impulse which had led him to press his lips to hers had been as compelling as drawing his next breath and just as impossible to resist. But as he felt her soft moist lips, salty from her tears, strain against his, he crushed her to him. Then it was her very defencelessness that enabled him to lift his head and say shakily, 'He . . . he didn't hurt you?'

Sarah knew what he meant, and although still unable to speak shook her head quickly as she began to shudder and shake with reaction.

No, he hadn't hurt her, but he would have done, she thought with sick horror. She had seen the lascivious intent in his eyes as he had bent over her, his hands gripping the front of her nightdress and his breath foul on her face. And she had been helpless, so helpless . . .

'Brandy.'

Rodney looked about him as though a brandy glass was going to materialize out of thin air, and Florrie and Maggie, who had followed him into the room while Rebecca phoned the police and Hilda took the weeping Eileen into the kitchen, moved forward from where they had frozen near the door when he had kissed Sarah.

'It'll be over here I should think, lad. Look, what's this?' Florrie lifted up the sloping top of what looked like a bureau to reveal a vast collection of glasses and bottles, and quickly poured hefty measures of brandy into two glasses, passing them both to Rodney as she said, 'You get one down you an' all, you look like you need it as much as her.'

He placed his own on the floor before lifting the other to Sarah's lips, but she took it from him, managing a weak smile as she said, 'It's all right, I can do it. It was just – just the shock of seeing him leaning over me like that.'

They were all, each one of them, talking to hide their embarrassment, but with the kiss in mind it was Maggie, ever tactful, who said to Florrie, 'Come on then, lass, we'll make a cup of tea an' leave these two alone for a bit,' her voice heavy with meaning. Florrie shut her eyes for a brief second before opening them and nodding, and then she almost pushed Maggie out of the room before she could say anything more.

'Better?' Rodney took the empty brandy glass from Sarah as the door shut behind the two women, his voice tender, and she nodded without speaking, her eyes tight on his face.

'Sarah –' He paused, his face working, before he said, 'When I saw him – I can't tell you . . .'

She had never seen him like this, Sarah thought with a separate part of her brain which was still wondering if this was all a dream. His shirt had almost been torn off his back in the fight with Sir Geoffrey and it was hanging open either side of his chest, his dark body hair damp with sweat. He was as unlike the calm, controlled Dr Mallard of daylight hours as it was possible to imagine, and a hundred times more attractive.

His thumbs had begun a slow stroking motion over the palms of her hands, and he was still crouched down at the side of her, his brandy untouched. Rodney didn't know if he was being unfair, but he did know he would never have another opportunity like this again, and the way she had clung to him, her response to his kiss, gave him the courage to go on. And there was only one way to say it.

'I love you, Sarah, I think I've always loved you. In the beginning, even as a child, you were special, but since we've met again you've become my sun, moon and stars – everything. I eat you, breathe you, sleep you.'

She stared at him, her eyelids blinking rapidly. She had dreamt this moment a hundred, a thousand times, but it was far far sweeter than she could ever have envisaged.

'I don't know if you can ever see me as anything more than a friend, but if you need time, I can wait—'

His voice stopped as she lifted her hand and placed it on his lips. 'Don't you know? Don't you know how much I love you?' she asked softly.

He was absolutely still for one moment, and then he rose, lifting her again so that he could sit down with her on his lap and kiss her in the way he had wanted to do for weeks and weeks. She was soft and warm and yielding, intoxicating, as he had always known she would be for the man she loved, and it was him . . . *it was him*.

'I've been waiting all my life for you, do you know that?' He raised his head, seeing her closed eyes and her hair streaming over his arm, before she stirred and looked at him. 'You'll marry me? You'll be my wife?'

'Yes, yes.'

There would have to be explanations, she knew that, but they had all the time in the world to talk and clear up any misunderstandings. He loved her. He did, he did – he loved her. What else was important compared to that? He was hers, and she would never be alone again. *He loved her.*

Chapter Twenty-three

'You look bonny, lass, right bonny.'

Maggie's voice was thick with emotion as her wrinkled hands adjusted Sarah's veil, and Florrie nodded at the side of her as she echoed, 'Right bonny.'

And Sarah, staring mistily back at her reflection in the tall ornate mirror in Lady Margaret's own bedroom, which her friend had insisted she use for her wedding day, could hardly believe the fairy-tale girl in the glass was really her.

She had chosen the wedding dress of her dreams, an off-the-shoulder white satin gown that was sewn with tiny seed pearls and rosebuds of gold lace. Her glossy curls, caught high on the top of her head, were scattered with the same pearls and rosebuds as the dress, and her veil was a froth of several layers of chiffon, edged with gold. She wore no jewellery except Rodney's engagement ring – a delicate star of glittering diamonds that had been on her hand for only three months.

It was Rebecca, seated on Lady Margaret's bed with a wide-eyed Lucy-Ann in her arms, who remarked on this very fact as she said, 'I can understand why he was so impatient, Sarah. I've never seen such a beautiful bride.'

'Go on with you.' Sarah flapped her hand at Rebecca as she turned, her eyes bright, and then said, 'You look pretty good yourself if it comes to that.'

As matron of honour and Sarah's only bridesmaid, Rebecca was dressed in a dark gold satin that went well with her brown hair and eyes, and the two women had had great fun in designing a matching dress and bonnet for little Lucy-Ann.

But Sarah knew, as she turned back to the mirror and again gazed wonderingly at the ethereal vision looking back at her, that she would have looked beautiful to Rodney whatever she wore. He never tired of telling her, over and over again, that she was the most beautiful woman in the world and how much he loved her, and any doubts she may have had with regard to his relationship with Vanessa had long since gone.

He had been so furious, the day after Sir Geoffrey's attack, when she had told him about the incident in the tearooms with Richard's wife, and what Vanessa had said. In fact she was sure, but for the fact that Richard had told them Vanessa was away on the continent somewhere with Lord Simmons and a party of his friends, that Rodney wouldn't have been able to keep his hands off his beautiful sister-in-law's throat!

But she hadn't cared about Vanessa's lies and manipulative mischief-making, not since that first kiss when she had been lying in his arms on the sofa in Lady Harris's drawing room. It had told her all she ever wanted to know . . .

'We'll wait downstairs with Lady Margaret and Rodney's uncle now you're nearly ready, lass. Rebecca can fiddle some more with this veil.'

As Maggie spoke, Florrie took Lucy-Ann, who immediately smiled up into Florrie's long ugly face with a toothless grin to which Florrie responded with a tender smile that was lovely to see.

'She's very good with Lucy-Ann.' Rebecca smiled at Sarah as she slid off the bed and walked over to her, as the door closed behind the two old women. 'Who would have thought the Mother Shawe of our childhood would be so besotted with one small bairn?' she added, as she fluffed out the clouds of white chiffon with deft hands.

'Who indeed.' Sarah smiled back at her in the mirror, her eyes soft as she gazed at this friend of hers who had endured so much, and who had at last come into a safe tranquil harbour. 'But who wouldn't be; she has to be the most gorgeous baby in all the world, Rebecca.'

'You won't get any argument from me.' And then, as the bell rang downstairs, and Lady Margaret's voice could be heard calling, 'Sarah, Sarah,' Rebecca said, 'Looks like the cars are here. This is it then.'

The two girls looked at each other for a moment, the one, small and brown-haired and dressed in gold, the other a vision in clouds of white, and suddenly the years fell away and they were two children again, the love they had felt for each other when it was the two of them against the world clear in their eyes. Careless of her finery Sarah pulled Rebecca to her, and the two exchanged a long hug before Rebecca said, her voice choked, 'Come on, come on you, you'll have us both blubbing and there's you all done up like a dog's dinner.'

'We've had some good times, haven't we, Rebecca?'

'Aye, we have, and we'll have some more an' all.'

'I do love you, you know.'

'Aye, and I love you, you daft thing.'

Rodney's uncle, who was giving Sarah away, was waiting in the hall with Lady Margaret as Sarah descended the stairs with Rebecca behind her holding the train of her dress, and as she reached the hall he moved forward, taking her hand as he said, 'He won't be able to take his eyes off you, my dear. You look quite exquisite. Doesn't she, Margaret?'

'Wonderful.' Lady Margaret's eyes were moist as she repeated, 'Wonderful,' before she turned to Rebecca and said, 'Come on then, the others are already in the car so we'd better join them. You are supposed to get to the church before the bride.'

Once they were alone in the hall, as they waited for the first car to drive off, Henry Mallard looked down at her again as he said, 'I've never seen Rodney so happy as he has been these last three months, Sarah. He adores you; you know that, don't you?'

Sarah nodded, too full at that moment to speak. She was lucky, she was so so lucky.

'Mind you, we all do. I can't believe we've only known you a few months, it seems as though you have always been a part of the family.'

She had grown to like and respect this man and his wife who had taken her to their hearts since she had first been introduced to them, and now she found her voice, dimpling up at him as she smiled and said, 'Thanks – Dad,' in teasing recognition of the duty he was about to perform.

'It would be an honour if I were, my dear, an honour.'

Oh, people could be so *nice*.

The small medieval church in Windsor was packed full with Rodney's relations and friends, as well as a small contingent of her friends and old work colleagues from Sunderland, and the perfume from the cascade upon cascade of flowers lining the walls from floor to ceiling was rich and heavy in the beautiful old building.

Sarah was vitally aware of the tall dark man standing so straight and still at the end of the aisle as she began to walk towards her new life, and of Richard, as best man, at the side of him, but the rest of the smiling figures lining the pews either side were a blur. She kept her eyes on the back of Rodney's head, and then, when she reached him and he turned to look at her, his eyes moving wonderingly over her face, she found she was grinning like a Cheshire cat.

They emerged from the church in a peal of bells and confetti, the warm sunshine of the bright September day turning everything golden. Everyone had cried – Maggie, Florrie, little Peggy who was there with her Michael, even Lady Margaret, and it was the latter who now dabbed away at her eyes under the enormous navy hat she was wearing as she declared, 'I never cry normally. Really, I don't.'

'I think you are allowed to today.'

It had been the first time Richard had spoken, beyond the requisite words in the ceremony. Sarah knew an occasion like this would be an enormous trial for Rodney's brother, and he had only recently endured yet another painful skin graft which was still red and angry, but Lady Margaret laughed back at him, as though he was the most handsome man in the world, as she said, 'Well, if I have your permission, that will do.'

It was the first time they had met, and normally Lady Margaret was very reticent with strangers, but of course it was a wedding . . .

'Happy, my darling?'

Rodney's arm tightened round her waist as he looked down at her, the photographer calling for yet another photograph, and she smiled up at him as she whispered, 'More than you could ever imagine.'

And she was, *she was*, so very happy, but . . . There was just one person missing from the day. Still, she would have photographs. She smiled into the camera, her face betraying none of her thoughts. Yes, she would have photographs, and one day she would show them to her mother . . . if she wanted to see them.

Part Three

Coming Home: 1952

Chapter Twenty-four

It was Sarah's fourth wedding anniversary, and as she sat at the heavy oak kitchen table sipping a mid-morning cup of coffee, her thoughts were not on the pile of cards the post had brought, but the two letters she had read and re-read several times since eight that morning, and which had affected her quite differently.

Her eyes roamed over the wide expanse of landscaped garden leading down to a border of trees and a stream, but she wasn't really seeing the grounds at the back of the large detached house, much as she loved them. The first letter, from Lady Margaret, or Margaret as she now addressed this dear friend of hers, had brought news that she had been hoping for for months, if not years. She and Richard were to be married, Margaret had written in her beautiful flowing script, and they were thinking of a Christmas wedding. Would Sarah and Rodney like to spend the holiday with them as they did so want them to share this happy time. The children were overjoyed, William was to be Richard's best man, and Constance her bridesmaid. That letter was one of pure joy.

The second . . . The second had brought apprehension, mixed with mild panic and reluctant hope. Her heart began to thud again, and she stroked the swollen mound of her stomach wherein her first child lay, the voice in her head stern as it said, Steady, lass, steady, much as Maggie might have done.

This could be something or nothing, as well she knew, having been down the same road several times in the last three years since she and Rodney had returned to Sunderland to live.

Rodney had said much the same thing that morning before he had left for the surgery, after kissing her in the manner that still had the power to take her breath away. 'I don't want you getting your hopes up again only to be disappointed, Sarah, so we'll think some more tonight before we commit ourselves to anything, all right? By all means give Margaret a ring, tell them we'll have a bridesmaid or a page boy available in a year or two if they want to delay a bit, but otherwise we'll be down for Christmas.'

'Oh you . . .' She had pushed at him with the palm of her hand, laughing up into his face as she had said, 'You're a fine one to talk about delaying things. Three months was your limit before you galloped me up the aisle.'

'I couldn't help it if I was so madly in love with my fiancée that I couldn't wait.' He had grinned at her, patting the compact little protrusion as he'd added, 'I'd have married you the week after you'd said yes if I could.'

'Maggie and Florrie would have killed you if you'd done them out of a big white wedding for their "lass".'

'I don't doubt it. It was only that which restrained my hand but it was hard going. Talking of which, I miss you like hell at the surgery. Rodney junior has a lot to answer for.'

'It might be a girl.'

'Ah, that's different. I couldn't blame a little Sarah for anything.'

As Sarah replayed the scene in her mind she found herself smiling, and she stretched like a plump little cat in the warmth of the September sunshine streaming in through the kitchen window. She was lucky, she was so so lucky, and if this latest lead didn't come to anything, that was what she had to remember.

When they had decided to move back to Sunderland over three years ago, she had known she wanted to be part of the practice Rodney had had the chance of partnering. It was a large practice, right in the very middle of the worst part of town, and always desperately busy. The partner Rodney was to replace had not been in favour of the national health service which had come into being the previous July just before they had got married, and the other two doctors, whose vision for the future had exactly matched Rodney's, had been very keen for him to join them.

Within weeks of their arrival, Sarah had recognized the need for an informal baby clinic, somewhere where young, and not so young, mothers could come regularly for an afternoon's escape from their home and often dire circumstances, and shortly after she had set that up, and as a natural progression, had come an emergency call line for families with problems and new mothers at the end of their tether.

All three doctors had been enthusiastic about her ideas, the more so when Sarah had qualified from her nurse's training, begun a few weeks before her marriage, and had been able to take on some of the minor medical complications rising from the clinic and the practice in general. There were many women in the Sunderland area who, despite the earthy poverty in which they lived, still found it unacceptable to talk openly to a man – albeit a doctor – about their more intimate problems, and Sarah had found herself often being used as a sounding board for problems which could have been life-threatening if left unattended.

She missed her job, she thought now, but Rodney was right. She couldn't have worked up until the day she gave birth, and the new nurse was a solid, brisk northerner who had already got the trust of most of 'her' women. She had handpicked her herself, warming to her instantly when the woman had waxed eloquent about the Commons vote in May for equal pay for women doing the same jobs as men. Since returning to Sunderland from London, one of the things she had first noticed was that a lot of the women, and a bigger proportion of the men, still considered a woman to be worth less in the wages realm – never mind if they were doing exactly the same work as their male counterparts. But Jenny was all right. Sarah nodded to herself as she pictured the big-framed young woman who was as strong as an ox and took no nonsense from anyone. She would stand up to some of the male bullies who occasionally came their way, complaining about the practice getting involved in cases of domestic violence and so on. Things were changing – and not before time.

Sarah rose from the table, walking across to the square-paned window and opening it wide as she breathed in the fragrant scents from the little herb garden below. She loved her house in its acre of ground on the outskirts of Roker, with the sea and sands just a ten-minute walk away. It was a good place to bring up children . . .

The telephone rang, interrupting her thoughts, and making her realize she still had a hundred things to do before Rebecca, Florrie and Maggie arrived for lunch. Maggie and Florrie were still in their rented house in the middle of town, and had firmly resisted all her requests to let her buy them a little bungalow of their own, insisting they were more than happy where they were. However, she had managed to persuade them to let her pay their rent, which meant the part-time work Florrie now engaged in at an old people's home in Grangetown was as much for interest and pleasure as to provide for their small wants.

Rebecca had returned to Sunderland at the same time she and Rodney had moved back, taking up work as a house-keeper to one of Willie's old workmates from the docks, whose wife had died in childbirth leaving him with newborn

374

twin sons. She had wanted Rebecca to live with them for a while, but she had to admit the arrangement seemed to have been heaven sent. The man proved to be the very antithesis of Willie, and within eighteen months Rebecca had married him, providing Lucy-Ann with two young ready-made brothers to boss about, something the little girl – who had more than a touch of her paternal grandmother about her – relished.

The call was from Rebecca. The twins had come down with chicken pox that morning and she was unable to make it to lunch. Sarah expressed her condolences, thinking wryly that Lucy-Ann would come into her element with two young patients to tend to, and after telling Rebecca about the forthcoming wedding at Christmas, hung up.

She had a pile of paperwork from the practice to deal with, having taken on the job as secretary along with nurse, teaching herself to type two-fingered on the old portable the surgery had boasted, but the second letter was still nagging at the back of her mind and she knew she wouldn't be able to concentrate.

A small blue butterfly alighted on the open kitchen window only to fly off again as Mrs Freeman, Sarah's stalwart daily, opened the front door and came bustling through to the kitchen, nodding enthusiastically as Sarah offered her a cup of coffee. 'Wouldn't say no, Mrs Mallard.' Mrs Freeman's round face was red and sweating. 'It's like high summer out there, you'd not believe it was the middle of September. Here' – she thrust a large square envelope at Sarah – 'happy anniversary, Mrs Mallard.'

After a brief chat Mrs Freeman disappeared upstairs with the vacuum cleaner and Sarah wandered out into the garden, where she sat down heavily on the long, cushioned swing seat she and Rodney had bought at the beginning of the summer with her pregnancy in mind.

Mrs Freeman was right, it was every bit as hot as a July day, she thought now, letting the breath escape her body in a long sigh. It had been hard work carrying through the summer and she was glad she only had a few weeks more to go. And the thought of her child brought her mind back to the letter sitting on the kitchen table.

Should they follow through on it, with the baby's birth so close? She knew Rodney didn't want her distraught over another false lead, but she didn't think she could bear the thought that it just *might* be genuine and she could miss it.

'Dear Madam' – she knew each word by heart now, the letters written in an untidy scrawl that suggested the penman had no love of writing – 'I am replying to your advertisement in the *Sunderland Echo* of March 1952, with regard to any information about an abandoned baby girl who was left in the public conveniences in Sheep Street on October 26th, 1927. I may know something of interest, but due to family difficulties' – what did that mean? Sarah asked herself for the umpteenth time that morning – 'I would need to speak with you privately first. If you want to meet me, I shall be in the Fox and Hounds in Hansley Road on 19 September at eight o'clock. Ask at the bar for Jack.' It had ended formally, 'Faithfully yours'.

Jack. She hugged the name to her. Jack who? And why hadn't this Jack given her his surname, a telephone number, anything? Could it be he thought he might be related to her? The pounding in her ribcage started again. Or was it a cruel hoax, or just another dead end? Rodney had warned her, when they had placed the very first advertisement some months after arriving back in Sunderland, that such things might happen. Up to now, three advertisements later, she had several letters from people who had been adopted or fostered themselves, and who wanted to write to someone who had been in a similar situation; two replies that had seemed very hopeful at first, but had fizzled out on investigation; and one other that had been someone's idea of a sick joke, and had resulted in Rodney threatening police action. There had been nothing for the last six months since the March advertisement.

Which led her on to her next thought. Why had this person, this Jack, written now, after all these months? Could it be he had only just seen the advertisement? But that didn't seem likely. Or perhaps he had been considering whether to write at all in the intervening time? The pounding intensified. Maybe he had had to weigh possible family objections in the balance?

Oh, all these perhaps and maybes and what ifs! 'Don't get your hopes up.' She spoke out loud into the quiet garden, before shaking her head and sighing softly. Talking to herself now; first sign, that was. Perhaps it would have been better to follow Maggie's advice and leave well alone? Her old friend had not been happy about any of this, she knew that, but she had *needed* to try. She had prepared herself to uncover anything, good or bad, in exchange for some respite to the constant ache at the back of her mind. Genetically, she might belong to someone out there, someone who was still alive. She was only twenty-four – even if her natural mother had had her late in life, she could still be alive. *Her mother* . . . She took a deep breath and willed the agitation to settle. She had to calm down, she'd been through this so many times now it should be old hat, and she'd be having the baby weeks early at this rate.

There were still several days to go to the proposed meeting on the nineteenth, and she wasn't going to spend them whittling and worrying. She had to come to terms with this search for her beginnings. It was a vain hope, at best. She continued to tell herself more of the same, not wanting to admit that yet again her hopes were high, along with the

underlying feeling of aloneness that thoughts of her abandonment always produced. She had expected it to get better when
she had married Rodney, and it had, to a large extent it had,
but since she had known she was expecting a child of her
own all the old feelings had surfaced.

Rodney had sat her down at the beginning of all this and
talked to her like a dutch uncle, emphasizing that even if her
mother was still alive, and they found her, she might not
want to see the daughter she had abandoned twenty-four
years ago. And she knew that . . . in a way. But how – Sarah
screwed up her eyes against the thought – how could her
mother have felt her move inside her, like this baby inside
her was moving now, carried her for nine months, given birth
to her, seen her face, and then followed through on the plan
to get rid of her? How could she not have *loved* her? She
loved this baby now, without ever having seen it and without
knowing if it was a boy or girl, perfect or imperfect. She
loved it, *she did*, and even if all heaven and hell itself were
united against her, she wouldn't let go of her baby.

'Mrs Mallard?' Sarah came to with a start as she heard
Mrs Freeman call from the back door, and, rising slowly, she
answered, 'Yes, what is it?'

'Phone call from London. Lady Margaret.'

Right. Back into everyday, live-in-the-real-world mode.
Margaret would be expecting effusive congratulations and
she would certainly get them. She deserved nothing less,
bless her. The nineteenth was the nineteenth, and would go
on the back burner until the calendar said otherwise, and
then just she and Rodney would share the experience . . .
whatever it held.

'All right?'

'I think so.' She tried to smile but it was beyond her.

'I'm here with you, I'm here every step of the way.'

'I know, I know.' This time she could smile as his love and support reached out to warm her.

'If nothing comes of this, we will try again and we'll keep trying. It follows that only a certain selection of the Sunderland population sees each advertisement, some probably don't read the local paper at all, so we'll think about other ways. Don't be discouraged.'

'I won't, no, I won't.' They both knew she was lying.

The Fox and Hounds public house was on the corner of Hansley Road and Carmichael Street, and having arrived almost half an hour early, Rodney parked some thirty yards down the street outside Fulwell's sweet shop. There was a little café just a few yards into Carmichael Street, and that was where Rodney was insisting Sarah wait, while he ventured inside the pub to – hopefully – keep the appointment with the said Jack.

They had planned to sit in the car until the last moment; from their vantage point in the vehicle they could see who went inside the Fox and Hounds whilst remaining inconspicuous themselves, but Sarah found that as the minutes ticked by her nerves increased, until, at ten minutes to eight, she had had enough.

However, once they had left the car and passed Dunn's toy shop and Wearings' motor stores, and the first large arched window of the Fox and Hounds, Sarah stood stock still, clutching at Rodney's arm as she said, 'You *will* stay for a while if he's not there straight off? You won't leave immediately?'

'I've told you.' Rodney gestured towards the corner of the street as he eased her fingers loose and tucked her hand through his arm. 'Now come on, I'll take you to the café and get you a cup of tea first, then go to the pub and ask for Jack.'

'I wish you'd let me come in the pub with you.'

'*Sarah.*' It was a tone he rarely used, which made it all the more effective. If she'd said she wanted to come with him once, she'd said it a hundred times since they received the letter, and now she said no more, nodding and pressing her lips together as she breathed deeply through her nose. What if, after all this, this Jack had changed his mind and didn't come? Or if it had been a ruse of some kind? Or –

Rodney pushing open the door of the café stopped the brief moments of panic, and after he had got her established at a table in the corner with a cup of tea and a sticky bun she had no intention of eating, he patted her shoulder encouragingly, his eyes tender, before disappearing through the door.

Her mind was buzzing as she sat staring at the rather dispirited looking bun. Maggie was right, she shouldn't have started this, no good would come of it. But she couldn't *not* have. The same old argument, that she had battled with many times in the past, still brought some measure of comfort when she reached the likewise same old conclusion. If she found out nothing then she was no worse off than she had been before; but if she got a name, a confirmation of her nationality, anything, it would have been worth all the disappointments. She continued to sit with her head bent, deep in thought, the other occupants of the café – a young courting couple making a cup of tea do all night, and a burly docker who had obviously called in for egg and chips on his way home – as uninterested in her as she was in them.

'Mrs Mallard?'

Her head shot up as the deep, soft, northern voice sounded in front of her, and she found herself looking at a broad, stocky man a few years younger than Rodney. Her eyelids blinked but she was unable to utter a word – it was only in that moment she admitted to herself she hadn't dared to believe anyone would really keep the appointment, and after an ensuing few seconds of silent embarrassment, it was Rodney who said, 'Sarah, this is Jack. Jack, Sarah.'

'Hallo.' She finally managed to get a word through the blockage in her throat, and then it was easier to smile and say, 'So you're the mysterious Jack then?'

'Aye, I'm Jack all right. Jack McHaffie.' And then as Rodney said, 'Sit down, Jack, won't you,' he inclined his head, still without taking his eyes off Sarah as he said, 'Thanks, man.'

Jack sat at the other side of the little table at arm's length from her, and he looked at Sarah, and she at him, and again it was Rodney who broke the silence by saying, 'Let me get you a cup of tea, Jack.'

'Ta.' He half rose again, nodding as he said, 'Aye, ta, thanks.'

'I won't be a minute.' Rodney hesitated for a moment, his eyes meeting Sarah's, before he left them alone.

'So . . .' She didn't know quite how to begin, she was feeling distinctly odd. It was something to do with the man's face, although it wasn't out of the ordinary in any way – just a nice, good-looking, masculine face. 'You think you might know something about the baby who was abandoned twenty-four years ago?'

'It was you, wasn't it?'

He had a pleasant voice, soft, melodious, but it was some moments before Sarah replied, and then her voice was very low when she said, 'Yes, it was me.'

'Aye, I knew it. I thought it was too much of a coincidence when I read that bit in the paper, but the minute I set eyes on you I knew.'

'Knew?'

'Aye, you're the spittin' image of your mam.'

The constriction in her throat was back and it made it impossible for her to utter a word, so as Rodney returned with a tray holding three fresh cups of tea, his voice over-jolly as he said, 'Here we are then, everything all right?' she merely looked up at her husband in mute appeal.

'Sarah?'

Placing the tray quickly on the table, Rodney sat down beside her and then they were holding each other tightly, Sarah's face buried in his chest, as she muttered, 'He knows . . . he thinks he knows who my mother was.'

And then the man's voice separated them as he said quietly, 'Is. Who your mam is. She's still alive.'

Sarah lifted her head and stared into the big square face, and she saw the eyes were soft with understanding, but it was Rodney who said, 'Look, Jack, I'm sure you mean well, and don't take this the wrong way, but how do we know what you're saying is fact? How do *you* know if it comes to that? It's not that I think you'd deliberately mislead us—'

'It's all right, man, I'd be the same in your shoes.' And then, as he looked at Sarah, her hand clutching her throat, he continued, 'But if you knew her mam you couldn't doubt it. Like I said, she's the spittin' image of our Nancy. An' the dates you put in the paper, everythin' ties in. Was anythin' left with you?' he asked Sarah suddenly. 'Was anythin' wrapped round you, somethin' like that?'

Sarah nodded. Maggie had once told her that she had been found in a scrap of brown sacking, but that any marks of identification had long since worn off.

'Was it a sack, a bit of sacking, maybe?'

She nodded again, her throat working.

'Aye, I thought so. Me da used to bring a load of sacking home with him off the boats whenever he could get it by the deck hand. Me mam used it for towels, bedding, whatever we was more short of at the time.'

'You really think you know who I am?' She felt strange, very strange, as though this were all a dream and she was outside looking in, knowing she would have to wake up in a minute. She knew she was staring at him as though she was half sharp, but she couldn't help it. He knew her mother. *He knew her mother.*

'Aye, lass, I'm as sure as I'll ever be about anythin'. Here.' He reached into the pocket of his rough jacket and drew out a slightly dog-eared photograph, sliding it across the table as he said, 'This was our Nancy when she was a year younger than you are now.'

'Good grief.' It was Rodney who spoke, and now his voice was hushed as he said, 'It's uncanny, you could be twins.'

'Aye, you see what I mean now? An' the night you was left, that was the night our Nancy had her bairn.'

'You're . . . you're related to . . .' Sarah had known there was something about his eyes, and now it suddenly dawned on her. All those years of searching her face in the mirror – they were *her* eyes staring back at her out of the blunt male face.

'Aye, lass.' He drew one lip over the other before saying, a little sheepishly, 'I'm your Uncle Jack.'

Sarah stared at him for a moment more, her heart thudding and a rush of overwhelming emotion making her dizzy. She didn't know whether she wanted to laugh or cry but she did neither, merely glancing at Rodney who was very quiet at her side. His eyebrows were raised, his eyes wide and his mouth agape. In any other circumstances the look on her unflappable husband's face would have made her laugh.

'Look, it might be better if I went back to the beginnin', lass. An' some of it, well . . .' He rubbed his nose before continuing, 'Some of it's not too easy to say.' He had included Rodney in his glance, and now Rodney's arm came more tightly round her, but neither of them said a word.

Sarah wanted to ask him so much: did he know if her mother had ever regretted what she'd done, had she ever talked about the baby she had abandoned, did she want to see her? But she was too frightened of the answers she might get. So she clutched the photograph and listened.

'There was just our Nancy an' me at home the years afore you were born, lass. Our mam had had umpteen other bairns, but they'd all died, five in all, I think, or it could've been six. Anyway, it was only Nancy an' me that survived. Our da was away on the boats most of the year, all over he went, months at a time. The sea was in his blood an' it took him in the end, his ship went down off the coast of Sweden the year after you was born . . .'

The blue eyes were reflective for a moment, and then his voice became brisk as he said, 'Me mam was a hard woman. No, more than that, she was a cruel so-an'-so if the truth be told. How our Nancy an' me ever made it beyond bairns I don't know, 'cos from the minute we was born we looked after ourselves. I reckon one or two of the others would have had a chance if me mam had laid off the drink an' the carousin', every night she was at it, 'cept when me da was home. Frightened of me da, she was.'

'And – and my mother?'

'She's a good lass, your mam.' She watched him close his eyes and bow his head slightly as he breathed out heavily through his nose, before looking her straight in the face and saying, 'But she made a mistake, like many afore her, an' a good few after.'

'Me, you mean.' It hurt. Stupid after all this time.

'No, lass, not you, not you as a person. The mistake your mam made was in believin' a lad when he told her he was goin' to look after her, marry her an' the like. She was desperate to get away from me mam you see, an' she loved the lad too, in her own way. She was just on fifteen when you was born, the swine took her down three months after her fourteenth birthday when she was nowt but a bairn still. I knew Mike Rafferty meself, an' I'd always liked him afore that. He was all mouth an' trousers, but a charmer, you know, gift of the gab, an' easygoin' with it. Anyway, he cleared off the day after our Nancy told him she was expectin', an' within six months he was dead. Seems he got done in by a bunch of miners down South Shields way, he'd bin messin' about with one of their women from what I heard. It was always the women with Mike Rafferty.'

So her father was dead, Sarah thought numbly.

'Anyway, me mam kept our Nancy's trouble from me da, she knew she'd get a good hidin' along with Nancy if she presented him with a bastard grandchild. Me da hadn't got much, but he'd got his pride, right enough. As luck would have it   or maybe it was the brew me mam made Nancy drink, she knew people, did me ma – you come a good few weeks early, when me da was still away on the boats, an' me mam . . .' He hesitated now, and it was only when Sarah prompted, 'Yes?', that he continued, 'Me mam took you.'

'Took me?' Sarah didn't understand.

'Aye.' He had been sitting hunched slightly over the table, his voice low, but now as the docker rose, pulling on his cap as he left with a cursory glance in their direction, he straightened his back and said, 'She told Nancy you were dead, that you'd died just after you was born. I . . .' The pause was longer this time, and he swallowed deeply before he continued, 'I always wondered meself, 'cos I'd seen you when she first brought you down wrapped in the sacking, an' you was alive then, a perfect little lassie. But she told Nancy you was dead, an' you didn't argue with our mam; not if you wanted to see the next day, that was.'

He shook his head, his face troubled. 'She did it 'cos it meant she was in the clear with me da, you see, an' our Nancy was too bad at the time to know much. She nearly snuffed it havin' you, an' she was bad for months after, but me mam put it about she'd had the fever an' nearly died. But Nancy remembered holdin' you for a minute after you was born, afore our mam took you away, an' I reckon it was that, more than anythin', that made her bad for so long. She grieved for you, nearly drove herself round the bend 'cos she thought you'd died.'

'She wanted to keep the baby?' Sarah's voice was shaking but she couldn't break down, not in here, she told herself fiercely. And she needed to hear it all.

'Oh aye, lass, she wanted to keep you all right.' And then his voice came soft and sad when he said, 'She's never had any more, although she married a right good man the year after me mam died when she was goin' on twenty. Bill's a lot older than her, he'd already got two lads from his first wife who died, so she mothers them an' their bairns.'

It was her mother he was talking about. Sarah looked down at the photograph clenched tightly in her hands. Her mother. She wanted to see her, oh, how she wanted to see her, but would Nancy want to see her? She hadn't come with her brother today. Did that mean she was ashamed of her? Perhaps she hadn't even told this Bill she had had an illegitimate daughter who had died.

This thought prompted her to say, her voice very low, 'This Bill? Does – does he know she had a child?'

'Oh aye, he knows. Nancy told him when they was first courtin', gave him the chance to sling his hook if he couldn't handle it, but like I said, Bill's a good bloke. He knew me mam, you see; he knew what sort of a life Nancy had had at home.' He paused a moment before adding, 'Bill knows I'm here tonight, he's standin' by to break the news to Nancy if anythin' come of it.'

'Break the news?' Sarah stared at him. 'Are you saying . . . Do you mean my mother still doesn't know I'm alive, that she thinks her baby died when it was born?'

386

She turned to Rodney as he put in, 'You didn't tell her about the advertisement, Jack? She knows nothing of this?'

'Aye, that's about it.' Jack rubbed his nose. 'I didn't want to say owt afore I knew for sure you was the bairn I saw me mam take away that day. By, I got the biggest gliff of me life the day I saw that bit in the paper a couple of weeks ago, an' that was only by chance. I'm not one for readin' – he rubbed his nose again – 'but the wife was round at her mam's one night with the bairns, an' I got meself fish an' chips on the way home. Your bit was in the page they wrapped me food in, an' I saw it was months old. The bairns round these parts earn themselves the odd penny or two by collectin' all the old newspapers an' takin' 'em to the shop, you see. Any road, I was sittin' at the table eatin' out of the newspaper – the wife'd kill me if she knew, mind, always insists on plates, does my Abbie – an' for want of somethin' better me eyes ran over the adverts. By, I near choked meself, lass. I'd always wondered, you see, at the heart of me.'

He looked at her and she looked back at him.

'I wouldn't have put anythin' past me mam, she was a wicked old devil. I remember when she come back that night, the night you was born. Blind drunk she was, fallin' about in the street with it, an' there was our Nancy hangin' on by a thread in the bedroom upstairs. Oh aye, she was a bad 'un all right. I got a pastin' that night for askin' what she'd done with the bairn, I still bear the scars on me back from the buckle of the belt she used.'

'That was my grandmother.' The statement was painful, and the two men glanced at each other.

'Aye.' She watched the muscles of Jack's face tighten. 'Every family has the odd black sheep, lass, an' me mam was ours, but she's gone now.'

'But how could someone do something like that?'

It was Rodney who spoke, and there was a moment's

silence before Jack said, 'I'm not excusin' her – I'm not, mind – but she had had a hard life herself. Her da was a master mariner an' when his ship went down it meant her mam an' her two sisters an' her were thrown on the charity of the maritime almshouse in Crowtree Road. She never spoke much of it, an' we never dared ask her – her rages were somethin' fierce – but it soured her somethin' bad. Aye, she were a bitter woman, me mam. Anyway, by the time Nancy was took down me mam was on the drink night an' day. It was that that killed her in the end.'

Rodney was quite unmoved, and his voice expressed this when he said, 'I'm a doctor, Jack, and I was working in these parts before the war. I saw poverty like I'd never seen it before, mind-deadening, grinding poverty, but to contemplate the murder – or at the very least the abandonment – of one's own grandchild is something else.'

'Please . . .' The syllable trembled. None of this mattered now, Sarah thought dazedly, none of it. Her mother had cried for her, once she had cried and grieved for her so much it had made her ill. He had said so.

'I'm sorry, my dear.' Rodney's arm tightened round her shoulders, and he looked down into her face before saying, his voice tender, 'Where do you want to go from here?' Then, when she couldn't answer for the lump in her throat, he said to Jack, 'How do you think your sister will take the news?'

'Only one way to find out.'

It was said with typical northern bluntness, but the eyes were soft as they looked at Sarah's white face, and now she leant forward, taking one of his big rough hands in her own as she said, 'I've always wanted to find her, Uncle Jack, always. If . . . if she doesn't want to see me, tell her that.'

'Aye, lass, though I don't think there's no fear of that. But it'll be the shock, you see; people react different, don't they, when they're in shock, that's why I thought it'd be best coming from Bill.'

'Yes.'

'But don't you fret, lass.'

'No.'

Jack glanced rather helplessly at Rodney now, but for once in his life Rodney didn't know what to say, and after a brief pause Jack said, 'You've got three little cousins by the way, an' right tearaways they are too. Our Tim is eight, an' the spittin' image of his mam, but the other two, our Michael who's four an' Billy who's two, they take after my side – our side.' It was added with a grin and Sarah smiled back, although the corners of her mouth quivered slightly.

She couldn't have described the emotions that were surging in her breast, but overriding everything was the fierce, the *consuming* desire to see her mother. She had come so far, further than she had ever dared to hope for, she admitted to herself now; surely the woman Jack had described wouldn't turn her away?

'An' you'll get on with my Abbie like a house on fire. She's a real good lass, my Abbie. Look . . .' Jack hesitated briefly before saying, 'Do you feel up to comin' an' meetin' my lot tomorrow? I don't want to push you, with the bairn an' all, but maybe I could get Bill to have a word with Nancy in the meantime an' see how she feels about things?'

'Would you?'

And then, as Rodney said, 'Don't you want to take a little time to get used to the idea first?' she turned to him, her heart in her eyes, and he shook his head slightly as he smiled and said, 'Obviously not.' But he wasn't smiling inside – he was hoping, with every fibre of his being, that this wasn't going to end badly.

Neither of them slept a wink that night. Rodney brought

Sarah a cup of tea and toast in bed before he left for the surgery the next morning, and found her looking at the photograph again, which she had propped against her bedside cabinet all night like a small child with a new pair of shoes.

He stood over her until she had finished the tea and eaten every crumb of the toast, and only left when she promised him she would take it easy that morning and rise late. He was worried about her. This news, coming so soon before the birth of their child, was not how he would have planned it could he have chosen. If it went well, if this Nancy wanted to make contact, then that was one thing, although even that might have complications if the two women found they had nothing in common, he thought agitatedly as he backed the car out of the garage. But what if Sarah's mother didn't want the past raking up? What then? She might have told this Bill about her dark secret, but that wasn't to say she wanted it broadcast to all and sundry in the shape of a twenty-four-year-old woman.

He checked his thoughts sharply as he nearly ran into the three-foot wall surrounding the front garden.

He would face that with Sarah if and when it happened, but his beloved was strong, inside, where it counted; she'd get through this. Of course it didn't help that Maggie and Florrie, and even Rebecca, hadn't been able to hide their apprehension as to the wisdom of Sarah's quest. Margaret and Richard had been encouraging, up to a point, but Richard had told him on the quiet that Margaret had expressed her fears to him privately as to how Sarah would react if the worst happened and her mother, if and when Sarah found her, rejected her daughter for a second time.

But he knew his Sarah. This wasn't a whim, a light undertaking. She had thought it through and he knew it was something she had to do. It was as simple as that. Funnily enough, the thought comforted him, and he drove the rest of the miles to the surgery with his heart more at peace than it had been all through the long sleepless night.

After Rodney left the house, Sarah snuggled back down under the bedclothes, letting her head drop back against the pillows and looking upwards towards the ceiling, and what she thought was – She hadn't known. *Her mother hadn't known.* It was the refrain that had played in her head all night, over and over, in between odd moments of panic and joy and fear and wonder.

How could a few words by a man she had never met before wipe away all the pain and bitterness of twenty-four years? But they had. Her mother would have kept her, Jack had said so, and there was no point in him lying. If it wasn't true, all he had had to do was not contact her in the first place. Her mother hadn't known . . .

Had Jack told his sister about her yet, and if so, what was she thinking right at this moment? Surely Nancy would want to see her? She had to want that.

Sarah suddenly found it impossible to stay in bed, excitement and apprehension propelling her out from under the covers and into the bathroom. She would keep busy this morning – nothing strenuous, she'd promised Rodney – but she could sort out all the bags and boxes holding the baby's things and put them away in the nursery. They had had the chest of drawers, little wardrobe with rabbit motifs and matching cot delivered the day before, and the pretty bright room, which Rodney had painted sunshine yellow, was a happy place to be this morning. She had to do something to keep herself occupied before Jack telephoned; she'd go mad otherwise.

The call came at twelve thirty.

'Sarah?' Jack's disembodied voice caused her heart to race like an express train. 'I've had a word with your mam' – her mam, *her mam* – 'an' she wants to see you tonight, if you're willin'? You could come round our house, Abbie is itchin' to meet you an' Rodney, an' then Nancy'll come along with Bill a bit later, if that suits you?'

If it suited her? 'That – that sounds wonderful.'

'Right, tonight it is then. Six o'clock suit you, lass? You an' Rodney could come afore that if you've a mind, an' have a bite with me an' Abbie an' the bairns, but it's up to you.'

'I think – thank you very much, but I don't think I could eat anything tonight, Uncle Jack.'

'Aye, lass, just so, that's what our Abbie said you'd say. Plenty of time in the future, eh? Look, me money's gone, I've nipped out in me dinner break an' I've got to get back, but you've got the address, lass? I slipped it to Rodney last night.'

'Yes, yes we've got it.' It was standing alongside the treasured photograph.

'Good. Six it is then.' And then the pips went.

Jack's three-up, three-down terraced house was only some two hundred yards away from the café where they had met the night before, and the woman who answered the door with Sarah's uncle stared open-mouthed at Sarah, before she collected herself enough to say, 'Eh, don't stand out there, lass, come in, come in.'

Once in the hall, which although narrow and small was painted a light fresh blue, the woman continued to stare at her, as she said, 'By, by, lass. By . . .' It seemed all she was capable of saying, and as Sarah looked back into the amazed eyes, the wide-lipped mouth and warm tint to the fresh skin combining to give a brightness to the face that was very appealing, it came to her that she would like her uncle's wife.

'An' you say my manners are lackin' at times.' Jack now dug his wife in the ribs. 'Come on through to the sitting room the pair of you,' he said loudly, with a faintly embarrassed air.

'Ee, I'm sorry, lass, but I can see what Jack meant now, right enough, you are your mam's lass, an' no mistake.' As they reached the sitting room Abbie turned and hugged Sarah, adding, 'Peas in a pod couldn't be more alike. Oh, I'm glad to see you, Sarah, I am that. Who would have thought it?'

Sarah wasn't quite sure if her uncle's wife was referring to her likeness to Nancy, or the situation as a whole, so she merely smiled her answer before she turned and said, 'This is my husband, Rodney,' taking Rodney's arm as she did so.

'Aye, I didn't think it was the lodger, lass.'

And then they were laughing, the others wholeheartedly but Sarah a little nervously, something which Abbie must have recognized because she said, her face becoming straight, 'Here, lass, all this must have taken it out of you. Come and have a seat by the fire, an' I'll get a cup of tea while you take the load off.'

The sitting room was small, but again sparkling clean and homely, with the inevitable blackleaded grate in which a small coal fire burnt despite the warmth of the September night. Once seated, Sarah glanced carefully about her, not wishing to offend her uncle or his wife by being too nosy, and she liked what she saw.

The small three-piece suite was a brown tweed with wooden arms, and relatively new, as was the wall-to-wall carpet, also in serviceable brown. The little china cabinet in one corner holding a collection of treasures, along with an ancient radiogram and long rectangular occasional table, made up the sum total of furniture in the room, but the curtains at the window were a deep red – and faintly reminiscent of Florrie's – and gave a warm cosiness to the practical room that was very appealing.

It was a cosy place, a family house, Sarah felt, and she complimented Jack on his home as Abbie bustled off into the kitchen.

'Aye, well you're seein' the best of it, to be truthful, lass,' Jack said stolidly. 'Abbie's old aunty died a while back an' left the wife a bit, an' Abbie'd been longin' to have a clean sweep in here since we got married. We was given a load of stuff then, an' very grateful we was, mind, but Abbie'd got some ideas of how she wanted it to look. There's a lot of folks round here that have their front room as their front room – high days an' holidays, you know? – but Abbie wanted it done so the bairns could still come in here an' spoil nothin'.'

'It's very nice,' Sarah said again.

'Aye, she's got an eye, has my Abbie, an' it was nice not to have to scrape an' pinch for a change. When we first got married, an' our Tim come pretty quick, your mam was the one that put food in our bellies more than once. Round she'd come of an evenin', just to say hallo accordin' to her, but when she'd gone we'd find a bag of groceries somewhere or other to see us through to payday. She's one on her own, your mam.'

The appearance of her three young cousins who had been playing in the yard outside – the older two protesting that they had been playing chucks with Philip and Rory Drew, and they'd been winning, and *why* did they have to come in now? – brought an air of matter-of-factness to the proceedings, especially when the baby of the trio, little Billy, had an accident and wet his pants whilst sitting on his father's lap. But Sarah still felt as though she might blink and the whole thing would have been a dream. A wonderful, fantastic, impossible dream.

She felt so keyed up she hardly knew what she was saying, and when they were all seated with their cups of tea, the children having been sent out to play again, it was a relief when Abbie broached the subject of her mother's visit, saying, 'Well, lass, she'll be here in a minute or two, your mam. She said she'd call round about half six an' it's gettin' on for that now. Is there anythin' you want to ask me an' Jack afore she comes?'

Sarah stared into the kind face and answered truthfully, 'I don't know where to start, Abbie.'

'No, lass, I don't suppose you do.'

'I still can hardly believe it, to be honest. I mean I know it, but I can't take it in. It's real, but it's not, you know?'

'Aye, lass, I felt somethin' similar when the poor King died this year, an' him still only fifty-six. That was a shock to everyone, that was, an' folk hereabouts said for days they couldn't get it into their heads he had really gone. Mind you, with your mam, it's a nice shock, not like that one, but still, I know what you mean.'

'That's not the same at all.' Jack sounded quite indignant that his wife could compare the demise of King George VI with Sarah finding his sister, but his wife flapped her hand at him as she said, 'Oh Sarah knows what I mean, don't you, lass?' She continued, without waiting for an answer, 'Well, all I can say is that your mam is a lovely woman, Sarah. She didn't deserve what her mam did any more than you did.' Abbie bit down on her inner lip before adding, 'Jack says she was never the same after. Broke her heart, it did.'

Sarah drew in a long breath and nodded slowly. What could she say? She just wanted to see her mother now, she didn't want to talk or ask any questions. She just wanted to see her mother's face.

And then, as if in answer to her heart's plea, there was a knock at the front door followed by a man's voice calling, the tone overly robust, 'Hallo there! Anybody home?'

Sarah had leapt to her feet in a manner that belied her

advanced pregnancy, and now Rodney followed suit, catching Jack's arm as the other man made to go towards the door and saying, 'It's them? It's her?'

'Aye, it's Nancy an' Bill.'

It was going to happen. It was going to happen *now*.

The sensation that had spiralled into Sarah's head and round her body fragmented the light and turned her gaze into tunnel vision that was pointed at the door. She was vaguely aware of Abbie and Jack hastily leaving the room, and Rodney holding her shoulder tightly as he pulled her against him, supporting her with his body, but she couldn't have moved or spoken if her life had depended on it.

And then her mother stepped into the room.

The world stopped revolving and time stood still.

'Sarah?' It was soft and trembling, but still Sarah couldn't speak. She was looking into her mother's face, and she knew her, and she saw the same sense of heart recognition in the beautiful tragic blue eyes staring back at her.

And then Nancy's legs began to buckle, and on the perimeter of Sarah's vision she was aware of Rodney leaping forward and shouting, 'Catch her,' to the tall grey-haired man standing just behind her mother.

It was Rodney who took Nancy's weight, and as the older woman's head fell back limply against his arm and he caught the full force of the amazing likeness to Sarah close to, he realized he was looking at his wife's face in twenty years' time and felt the equivalent of an electric shock pass down his spine. But then his professional side took over, his voice soothing and calm as he said, 'Don't worry, she's only fainted, she'll be perfectly all right. Here, let's lay her on the settee for a minute or two, she's already beginning to come round.'

Sarah was half supporting her mother's head as Rodney carried Nancy across the room, and she sank down onto the settee with her, her arms going tightly round the older woman's slender body that was so slight it could be called sylphlike. There was some silver in the golden hair that was pulled into a low thick bun on the nape of Nancy's neck, and as Sarah saw it her throat seized and locked and she cradled her mother closer.

And it was at that moment that Nancy opened her eyes and looked up into the face of the daughter she had been mourning for twenty-four years. 'Sarah . . .' It was a whisper, but the tone was such that it caused both men to glance at each other and quietly leave the room.

Sarah was blinking rapidly, not wanting her tears to mist the sight of this dear face, and then as Nancy, her own face awash now, said, 'I always called you Jane in my heart, but Sarah Jane is a lovely name . . .' she managed, 'You thought of me sometimes?'

'Always.' Nancy raised herself, her hands taking Sarah's as she said, 'How can you ever forgive me? Do – do you hate me?'

'Hate you?' Sarah shook her head, her tears blinding her as she said, 'I love you, you're my mother.'

'Oh my bairn, my precious precious bairn.' And now it was Nancy who took her daughter in her arms, covering her face in kisses and punctuating each kiss with endearments. And as Sarah clung to her mother, as she felt herself enfolded in the warmth and the scented smell of her, she felt something happening to the empty place deep inside that had been with her since she was a child. It was filling, like an underground geyser sending up a hot column of water to the bright sunlight above, and as it rose all the pain and anguish was melting inwards to meet it until all that was left was pure joy.

And the rocking continued, her mother's voice repeating, 'I love you, I love you, my brave brave little lass. There, there, my bairn, I love you . . .'

She had dreamt this moment as a child so many times –

397

tasted it, lived it, only to wake in the morning and have it taken from her. But this was that morning, this was real, and her voice reflected her ecstasy as she whispered, 'I've found you, mam.'

Chapter Twenty-five

'Rodney? She's started, lad.' Nancy listened to the voice at the other end of the telephone as she smiled at her daughter sitting at the kitchen table, and then said, 'Of course I'm sure. I might only have had the one but there are some things that never change.' A pause, and then, 'Aye, her waters went a minute or two ago.'

'Tell him we'll meet him at the hospital.'

'She said for you to meet us at the hospital.' Another pause and then Nancy laughed before saying, 'All right, all right, lad, we'll wait here, don't you fret. An' drive carefully mind, it'll be hours yet. Aye, I'll tell her.'

Nancy put down the receiver. 'He sends his love, bless him. By, you'd never think he was a doctor an' used to all this, the way he's panicking.' Sarah grinned at her, and then, as Nancy added, 'Any pains yet, lass?' shook her head.

'No, not yet. This will be a doddle.'

'Aye, maybe, but don't count your chickens afore they're hatched, now then. There's some hard work ahead, lass. Well, your man's on his way back, so do you want me to call Florrie at the old folks' home an' get her to tell Maggie an' Rebecca? An' I'll need to let Bill know where I am.'

'Maggie and Florrie are away with the old folk at the home on that weekend coach trip, but you could leave a message for them for when they get back, and perhaps

Bill could pop round and tell Rebecca?'

It had amazed Sarah, over the last four weeks since she had found her mother, how easily Nancy had fitted into their lives, and they into Nancy and Bill's. It seemed ridiculous to say that it was as though they had never been parted, but it was true, and each time Sarah thought of it the wonder never ceased to thrill her.

And Rodney, he had been so good. Her heart glowed as she thought of her husband. Not a spark of jealousy, not the slightest bit of impatience or resentment at her and Nancy's absorption in each other. Oh, he was lovely. And her mother adored him. Maggie had been a bit of a problem at first . . .

She shifted in her seat as the first cramp-like pain, slight but definitely there nevertheless, came and went.

But between the three of them they had reassured Maggie that her place within the family was sacrosanct, and now the old woman acted as though Sarah's search to find her beginnings had been all her idea. And she loved Jack's children, they were already treating her like a favourite grandma.

The thought of the three little boys brought Sarah's mind back to what was happening to her, and she reached out a hand to her mother now as she said, 'Don't forget you promised to stay until it's over. I want you there.'

'I'll stay unless you tell me to go, lass, never you fear. Mind you, I think it's that man of yours that will need more encouragement from what I can make out. Now, let's get your case down an' be ready and waiting when he comes.'

Pray God, she was going to be all right. Pray God.

Once in the bedroom upstairs Nancy found herself on her knees by the bed, her fingers reaching for the rosary in her pocket as she began to pray with a fervency that had been missing for years, her heart and soul straining out to the Almighty.

God wouldn't give her her lass back only to take her away again so soon, would He? she asked herself some moments later when she rose slowly to her feet. But her lass's birth had nearly killed her, and the subsequent infection and lack of treatment had meant no more babies. What if she had passed her weakness on to Sarah, like Molly Pearson in Duncan Street? She had died giving birth to her Emily, and Emily had died when little Gladys came . . .

'Stop it, now. What's the matter with you?' She whispered the words out loud with her eyes tightly closed and her heart pounding. She *hadn't* died with her Sarah, that was the point here, and Sarah wasn't going to die either. Her mam had been fond of saying that you make your own luck in this world, and that was about the only true thing Minnie McHaffie had ever said. Her Sarah was a strong woman, strong in mind and body, and she was healthy too. When she'd had Sarah all those years ago she had been in no state to give birth to a bairn, the lack of nourishment and ill treatment she had endured for years at her mam's hands making her weaker than a child herself. Two days and two nights her labour had gone on, and that wouldn't be allowed now either. She had begged her mam to fetch someone, the midwife, a neighbour, anyone . . .

Enough, Nancy pushed the memories aside. That was then and this was now, and the blight Minnie McHaffie had put on all their lives was over. Sarah had finished it, first by fighting back and refusing to die, and then by carving a life for herself and searching out her roots. The mould was broken, Sarah was going to be fine.

Nancy stood up, folding her arms tightly under her breasts and swaying slightly as she breathed in and out deeply for a few moments, before reaching for the case at her feet. She had never thought to see this day, never dreamt she might hold her own grandchild in her arms, but now the years stretching ahead had taken on a glow that made her count her blessings a hundred times a day. She was a fortunate woman. Aye, she was a very fortunate woman to receive her bairn back from the dead. She raised her face heavenwards, her eyes shut as she whispered, 'Thank you, thank you.'

'Is it always like this?'

'Aye, hinny, aye. Ask the doctor here.' Nancy was trying to make light of it as she waved her hand at Rodney who was standing at the other side of the hospital bed.

'You're doing fine.' Rodney nodded to emphasize his words as he said again, 'You're doing fine.'

They had arrived at the hospital at midday and now it was almost midnight, and Sarah was tired. She felt that her stomach was caught in a huge vice that squeezed and squeezed until she couldn't bear it a second longer, at which point the vice eased until the next time it gripped her flesh. She couldn't believe women went through this torture time and time again. But the medical staff didn't seem worried . . .

She glanced at her mother now, knowing the pain would become excruciating again in a few moments, and said, 'Was it like this with me?'

'Aye, aye, but somehow, the minute you see its face, you'll forget the pain, lass. If the good Lord hadn't made it so, the human race would've died out a long time ago.'

'I don't think Rebecca was in as much pain as this. Or no, maybe she was, thinking back. She shouted a bit.'

'Everyone's different, lass, but it's all the same in the end. Out they pop.'

Sarah wished it would pop out. She could understand now why Rebecca had gone hysterical at the thought of her being sent out of the room when she had been giving birth to Lucy-Ann. This might be the most natural thing in the world, according to men, but she wouldn't have believed it could hurt so much.

With the next pain Sarah got the urge to push, and the midwife sent her mother and Rodney out of the room while she examined her patient.

'Good.' She had begun to get worried over the last half an hour or so, but the cervix was nicely dilated and the girl still wasn't too tired to give some good pushes. 'Now you can start doing some work, Mrs Mallard. I always think it's better at this last stage, you don't just have to lie there and take it any more.'

'Can I have my husband and my mother back in please?'

'It's against hospital procedure, Mrs Mallard, and you are going to be too busy to worry about them.'

'*Please?*'

The midwife was a stout, buxom woman with an iron face and a heart of gold, and she had been touched by the story which had unfolded during the long afternoon and evening about this little family, so now she said, after a moment's pause, 'Well, your husband *is* a doctor, isn't he, and it wouldn't be fair to ask your mother to wait outside by herself . . .'

'Thank you, oh, thank you.'

'I'm petrified, Rod.' Outside in the corridor Nancy had sunk down on to a hard-backed chair against the wall and sat there for some moments without speaking, but now she raised her eyes to her son-in-law, and Rodney saw that they were wet. 'She's having a hard time of it.'

'Hey, come on, Nancy.' He sat down by her side, his arm round her shoulders, and Nancy made a little distraught sound in her throat and turned her face into his chest. 'She's going to be fine, I promise you, and this isn't an unusually long labour for a first child.'

'I couldn't bear it if anything happened to her.'

'Nothing is going to happen to her, Nancy. Trust me.'

'But you don't know for sure.'

'Yes I do.'

He had known, within days of the two women being reunited, that although the physical similarity was striking, their personalities were very different. Nancy had none of her daughter's drive and determination to make things happen, and it had further emphasized to Rodney how very special his wife was. Nancy's salvation had been in meeting her Bill. The man adored her, worshipped the very ground she walked on, and that was good, Nancy needed that.

'Oh, I'm sorry. I am, I'm sorry, Rod.' Nancy raised her head, swallowing and shutting her eyes tight for a moment as she scrubbed at them with a handkerchief, before looking straight at him as she said, 'Don't tell Sarah, will you, but I had a terrible time of it when she was born. An' she's so like me, slight, small-hipped. I know things are different these days under this national health system with all the care beforehand—'

'They are, they are.' He was gripping her hands now and shaking them slightly to emphasize his words. 'And no two people are the same internally, Nancy, whatever they look like on the outside. Sarah might be completely different from you, so don't assume she'll have your difficulty.'

'No, all right, lad.' Nancy was embarrassed now, and it showed. In spite of being brought up in the worst of Sunderland's slums, you didn't talk about such things openly – not with a man at any rate. But he was a doctor. She echoed this thought now as she said, 'Well you're a doctor, you should know.'

'Exactly.'

'Oh, Rod.' Her fingers moved in his grasp as she said, 'I love her so much.'

'I know.' He smiled, his eyes tender. 'So do I.'

And then the door opened, and the midwife beckoned them back in.

Benjamin Rodney Mallard came into the world an hour later, and with a loud lusty cry that made his mother raise her head to look at him. He was a big baby, with well rounded limbs and a shock of black hair that was already curling over his brow.

'Oh, he's beautiful.' Sarah let herself fall back on the bed as she smiled at Rodney, who had tears of joy streaming down his face. 'He's absolutely beautiful.'

She caught a glimpse of her mother's face which seemed to shimmer from the emotion radiating from it, and her smile deepened.

'He's the most beautiful sight I've ever seen.' Rodney's voice was reverent as the midwife handed him his son wrapped in a tiny linen sheet, and he examined each minute detail of the little face before placing him in Sarah's arms and saying, 'Our son, Sarah, *our son*. Thank you, my love, thank you.'

'You did have a hand in producing him too,' she said softly, her eyes loving him.

'Only the easy part. I feel guilty about that, after all you've just gone through.'

'You should.' It was said with feeling, and then, 'Here, Grandma.' This was the moment she had longed for over the last weeks, the moment she had treasured in her heart, the moment she hoped would wash away all the years of heartache and tears Nancy had endured. 'Your grandson.'

Nancy bent to kiss Sarah before she took the baby, and as Sarah felt her warm lips, and heard her whisper, 'I love you so much, my darling,' before she reached for her grandson and held him close to her heart, she knew she had been given it all.

This was love, this was the power of it – it was in Rodney's smile, in the look on her mother's face, in her son's wide, unblinking eyes. She was all in all to each one of them, and they were everything to her.

The emotion which filled her was inexpressible, consuming the legacy of the past and taking her up and out of this world as it lifted her on the wings of a hundred thousand eagles. She reached out her hands to her family, her heart bursting with joy.

She was home.

Candles in the Storm

Rita Bradshaw

A fierce storm is raging when Daisy Appleby is born into a fishing family, in a village north of Sunderland, in 1884. When her mother dies from the fever a few years later, it falls to Daisy to run the household and care for her family. Life's hard: the sea barely yields a living, and then there's always the anxious wait for the menfolk to return . . .

In the storm that takes her father and two brothers, Daisy risks her life to save a handsome young stranger from certain death. Although William Fraser is captivated by his spirited, beautiful rescuer, his rich and arrogant family despise Daisy. A tangled web of lies tears the couple apart, and Daisy must overcome tragedy before she can find her destiny . . .

Acclaim for Rita Bradshaw's novels:

'If you like gritty, rags-to-riches Northern sagas, you'll enjoy this' *Family Circle*

'Catherine Cookson fans will enjoy discovering a new author who writes in a similar vein' *Home and Family*

'Rita Bradsaw has perfected the art of pulling at heartstrings, taking the emotions to fresh highs and lows as she weaves her tale' *Sunderland Echo*

0 7472 6709 X

headline

Now you can buy any of these other bestselling books by **Rita Bradshaw** from your bookshop or *direct from her publisher*.

FREE P&P AND UK DELIVERY
(Overseas and Ireland £3.50 per book)

Alone Beneath the Heaven	£5.99
Reach for Tomorrow	£6.99
Ragamuffin Angel	£6.99
The Stony Path	£5.99
The Urchin's Song	£5.99
Candles in the Storm	£6.99

TO ORDER SIMPLY CALL THIS NUMBER

01235 400 414

or visit our website: www.madaboutbooks.com

Prices and availability subject to change without notice.